THE RECOVERY OF FITZWILLIAM DARCY

LUCY MARIN

Quills & Quartos
PUBLISHING

ISBN 978-1-951033-76-7 (ebook) and 978-1-951033-77-4 (paperback)

Edited by Jennifer Altman and Debra Watson

Cover Design by Cloudcat Design

To B & A for always giving me time to work on my writing and never looking at me funny as I silently acted out the facial and hand gestures my characters were using or whispered the words of the story to make sure they sounded right.

TABLE OF CONTENTS

Forgiveness is the final form of love.

— REINHOLD NIEBUHR

Servants Speak About Child's Kidnapping
John Dickson

READERS OF THIS FINE PUBLICATION HAVE BEEN AS SHOCKED AND Horrified as this reporter by the tragic kidnapping and death of the only son and heir of Mr George Darcy of Derbyshire.

Fitzwilliam George Alexander Darcy, grandson of the illustrious Earl of Romsley, was abducted from his bed at Pemberley Estate in the early hours of the morning two months ago this very day. Mr Darcy's own steward, Robert Wickham, was involved in the deadly plot, along with Mrs Wickham and her brother, James Thorpe.

The Child's death was announced in The Morning Post last month. All three villains are also dead, and must now answer to a higher power. Mr Wickham was shot dead by his brother-in-law, who in turn was killed by men hired by Lord Romsley to discover the whereabouts of the Child and Evildoers. Mrs Wickham was captured and claimed her victim had died almost immediately, although she never said how. One can only imagine it was due to neglect or injuries suffered at the hands of his Depraved Kidnappers. Although a search was made for the Child's body using information provided by the Wicked Woman, he has not been found. A gentleman familiar with the Darcys' actions after the kidnapping assured this reporter that they searched for any sign that the little boy remained alive, using what was known of the villains' movements, but found none. Until her death by fever, Mrs Wickham was interviewed almost daily, but the essentials of her story remained the same.

But how did little Fitzwilliam come to be kidnapped, and how is the family bearing the outcome of this Shocking Crime?

What manner of person would take a child, not yet two years of age, from his home, and why?

According to a pretty, young maid at Pemberley, whom I shall name Sally, Lady Anne Darcy despised Mrs Wickham, who was of vile and vicious propensities. She was more often drunk than not, and known to lose most of her husband's wages at cards. Sally overheard the Darcys discussing the Wickhams on more than one occasion, and assured this reporter that Mr Darcy was on the point of dismissing his steward to please his wife. A footman, a strapping young lad, known here as John, told me that, "The only thing Mrs Wickham loved more than drink and gambling was young men, if you know what I mean. Mr Wickham had no control over her. How could you trust a man like that?"

How indeed. It was an error in judgment Mr Darcy will regret for the rest of his life.

Lord Romsley and his son, Viscount Bramwell, have a particularly interesting role in this Tragedy.

"Lady Anne wrote to her father, but the master didn't know," John told me. "They fought about it—not the master and mistress, but Mr Darcy and the earl. So much yelling." With a bit of coaxing, John admitted he had heard the two gentlemen arguing about how to recover The Innocent Child.

It will be no surprise to learn that money was the motive for the crime. Mr Darcy is one of the nation's wealthiest gentlemen, and the Romsley estate is just as prosperous. Between the families, they could afford to pay a substantial ransom for The Child. My sources say Mr Darcy would have, but Lord Romsley refused to consider giving the abductors what they wanted.

"Mr Darcy would have paid anything for Master Fitzwilliam's safe return," said Sally. "There were never a sweeter baby."

Tears in her eyes, Sally recounted the awful day the family heard that young Fitzwilliam was dead.

"Lady Anne fell to the ground and sobbed as I never knew a

person could. The apothecary and doctor were called, but nothing could calm her. She has not left her rooms since."

John recalled overhearing Lord Romsley, Viscount Bramwell, and Mr Darcy speaking after the heartbreaking news arrived.

"Mr Darcy said it was all the earl's fault, and his son's. See, Mr Darcy never wanted to hire them men, but the earl did anyway, and Master Fitzwilliam, such a grand chap he were, died instead of being returned by Mr Wickham, which is what Mr Darcy said would happen. Mr Darcy was so angry that he demanded Lord Romsley and Viscount Bramwell leave Pemberley at once and never return."

Sally added, "The earl wanted Lady Anne to go with him. Said some very nasty—and untrue—things about Mr Darcy. It made me blush to hear him! Lady Anne refused, which is as it should be."

In the weeks since the appalling end to her child's life, servants at the great estate say there have been dozens of letters sent to Lady Anne by her father and sister, Lady Catherine, wife of Sir Lewis de Bourgh. Mr Darcy has issued orders that anything from those quarters is to be burnt upon arrival. All indications are that a rift, perhaps permanent, has been rent between the two prestigious families. Shall it ever be healed? Will Lady Anne recover from her shock and grief? For now, the Darcys remain at their expansive northern estate, refusing all company except that of Mr Darcy's family. With no body to bury, it remains to be seen how they will honour the Lost Little Boy.

CHAPTER 1

October 1811

WILLIAM LUCAS DID NOT KNOW EXACTLY WHEN HE HAD FALLEN in love with Elizabeth Bennet, but by the age of twelve, he knew he would marry her. For him, there could be no future happiness without his dearest friend as his wife.

It had not been love at first sight. They met when the Lucas family moved to Lucas Lodge in 1795. Elizabeth had marched up to him, and in a manner strangely bold for such a small girl, announced 'Jane likes to play with dolls and only do girl things, and Mary is just a baby, but I shall play with you. As long as you like exploration and do not tell me I cannot run, or scold me if I get mud on my dress'.

William remembered being puzzled by her, annoyed even, when he discovered a month later that she would be sharing the lessons Mr Bennet agreed to give him.

'He is doing you a great honour,' his father told him. 'You will be a real gentleman, William, not just the son of a former innkeeper from Shropshire.' Sir William had sold the inn and moved his family to Hertfordshire not long after being granted his title.

William and Elizabeth's friendship grew over the years as they debated the merits of different philosophies, teased each other into working harder to be the first to solve a puzzle given to them by Mr Bennet, or as they shared their delight in a new book. Elizabeth laughed and smiled her way into William's heart. She had endless energy and curiosity, and was as caring and kind and loyal a friend as one could hope to find.

Over the years, that friendship became ardent love. William knew the love they shared was strong and that nothing could separate them. He had never noticed other young women, and she had never looked at other gentlemen, no matter how much they tried to gain her attention.

In three short months, she would turn twenty, and at last they would become engaged. Mr Bennet had told them several years earlier that he would not allow a betrothal until that time. Soon they would begin their lives as Mr and Mrs Lucas, just as they had been dreaming of for the last five years.

Jane's voice recalled William to the present—he was, with his mother and sister, Charlotte, visiting in the Bennets' parlour —and he stopped staring at Elizabeth, who was wearing a yellow dress that was as cheerful as she was.

"Papa should return in time for the assembly."

The muscles in Mrs Bennet's forehead pulled together, creating a shallow cleft down the centre. "I wish he had not gone to town. It is not safe or healthy."

Elizabeth said, "My father felt it was necessary to see to his business affairs. He will be home before you know it, and full of stories about life in London and, I dare say, with a present or two." She glanced at William, a mischievous twinkle in her dark eyes.

"Presents!" cried Lydia, while Kitty squealed in excitement. "Do you really think so, Lizzy?"

"You should not care so much for material things," chided Mary.

"Well, I do! I dare say my feelings are more natural than yours. Tell her, Jane!" Lydia sat on the edge of a deep blue wing chair, and her long hair swayed as she turned from one sister to another. At moments, her looks and liveliness reminded him of Elizabeth, although Elizabeth was more likely to argue about etymology than gifts.

While Jane mediated a peace between her younger sisters, Lady Lucas and Mrs Bennet fell into a conversation about the delights of London's warehouses. This left Charlotte, Elizabeth, and William to themselves.

The corners of William's mouth crept upward as he looked at Elizabeth. "You should have known better than to mention presents in Lydia's or Kitty's hearing."

Elizabeth slowly shook her head and sighed. "Oh dear. Whatever could I have been thinking?"

Charlotte said, "You knew exactly what you were doing! Your mother would soon have succumbed to anxiety unless you managed to change the subject."

Elizabeth laughed. "It is too lovely a day for nerves!"

A walk was then proposed, and Jane, Charlotte, Elizabeth, and William went into the gardens.

ONCE OUTSIDE, Charlotte said, "Come, Jane. Let us wander together. My brother and your sister no doubt have a great deal to say to each other." She turned to Elizabeth and William and, with mock solemnity, shook a finger. "Behave yourselves!"

"Stay in the gardens," Jane reminded them.

"Yes, Mama," Elizabeth teased. "Give a shout at any time, and I shall tell you exactly what we are discussing, where we are, and, if William is so good as to consult his pocket watch, the time." She laughed and slipped her hand around the arm William held out to her. It was kind of their sisters to give them their privacy. She supposed that under other circumstances, she and William should have a chaperone, but they had been friends for so long that none of the Bennets or Lucases thought of such things.

Elizabeth and William walked for a moment in companionable silence. There was nothing she liked better than to be outdoors with the man she loved. Even though she had recognised that her love for him had become romantic some years earlier, her heart still swelled whenever she looked at him.

Elizabeth sighed happily. "It is such a lovely day. I adore this time of year. The weather is fair, at least until the middle of November, then it is your birthday. After that, I start to anticipate the holidays, and the excitement of parties, and my aunt and uncle visiting, and the New Year beginning."

"And soon after, it will be your birthday."

"I shall be twenty at last." They exchanged a smile, and Elizabeth gently squeezed his arm. He laid a hand over hers.

After a moment of silence, Elizabeth again spoke. "I am looking forward to seeing Captain Farnon." The captain was a cousin of their neighbours, Mrs Long. They had met him a few months earlier, and he and Charlotte had become friends. Elizabeth knew that Charlotte hoped their relationship would become something more.

William nodded once. "To hear Mrs Long speak, the captain is as anxious to return to Meryton as my sister is to have him do so. I hope we are not expecting too much."

"You hope, as do I, that Charlotte and Captain Farnon like each other as well as they did upon their last meeting, that Captain Farnon is as good a man as we all believe him to be, and that Charlotte finds the happiness she deserves."

A cool breeze made Elizabeth shiver, and she edged closer to William. His eyebrows were pulled together, and a frown marred his handsome features. He was fretting about his sister, and she would not allow it.

"I suspect we will celebrate two weddings this winter. I must always think ours will be the happiest union, but I shall rejoice to see Charlotte as a bride. I cannot wait to be married to you. It feels as if we have waited a lifetime." Elizabeth smiled to herself as she anticipated the joys of being married to her William. Her cheeks warmed as her thoughts turned in a direction she knew proper young ladies were supposed to ignore.

Elizabeth plucked a brilliant pink chrysanthemum and twirled the stem between her fingers to make it spin. "I anticipate an assembly since, unlike you, I enjoy dancing. It is Mary's first time attending, which I think deserves to be celebrated, although you know she is dreading it. Kitty and Lydia tease her about it; they can hardly wait until they are old enough to be out and do not understand her feelings." She shrugged. "In a few weeks, the new tenants at Netherfield will arrive, unless they are again delayed. That will add to our gaiety. Perhaps they will be here for your birthday. Lady Lucas has already begun to speak of holding a party to commemorate it."

"We shall have one for your birthday, as well."

"After which, we can prepare for another special occasion. I believe a month will be more than enough time."

She looked at him, expecting to have her grin returned, but his countenance was sombre, and there was something in his eyes that spoke of distress. Stepping in front of him, she dropped the flower and took his hands in hers.

"William? What is it?"

He led her to a wooden bench by the side of the stone path, and they sat. For two full minutes, he kicked at the stones with the toe of his shoe; she waited patiently, looking out over the lush, verdant lawn, knowing he would speak once he had ordered his thoughts.

"Do you ever feel as though you do not quite…belong the way you think you should?"

Elizabeth produced a confused laugh. She regarded him and gently brushed a lock of dark hair out of his eyes. "Not belong? Of course you do! Where could you belong more than you do here, surrounded by those who love you best of all, especially me?"

She smiled, but he shook his head. He opened his mouth to speak, shut it, then tried again, but only managed a soft grunt. He kissed her hand, and she linked her fingers with his. When he looked at her, she gave him a reassuring smile.

"Some weeks ago, Charlotte told me that she recalls a time I was not with them. She distinctly remembers me coming into their home as a small child, little more than a baby but not a newborn. She does not remember my birth or my presence before that."

"One's memory can be deceptive, particularly when one is so young."

William met her eye and shook his head.

She said, "I do not understand what you mean."

The indistinct sound of their sisters' voices and the leaves rustling as a breeze went past filled the silence.

"If her memory is correct, we assume that…I am a natural child of Sir William's. Before you and I get married, she thought I ought to know, although to what purpose, I do not understand."

Elizabeth gasped, but before she could speak, William did, the words tumbling out of his mouth.

"I am not like my mother. Charlotte is. No one could take them for other than mother and daughter. I am tall like Sir William, and our colouring is not dissimilar. Perhaps I do not look like my mother because I am not her child. It would explain that feeling I sometimes have of not quite fitting in."

"It cannot be," cried Elizabeth. "Sir William and Lady Lucas are devoted to each other."

William lifted his eyes to hers. "One could hardly believe it of them now, but what about in their younger years? Perhaps there were…indiscretions."

Elizabeth stared at him, her mouth agape. He could not be serious.

"Charlotte said I should not tell you, because it would only distress you, but I cannot agree. It has preyed on my mind, and you need to understand our suspicions. If we are correct, I would still be a Lucas, but not-not *really*, not the same way my sister is.

I hope for all our sakes nothing ever comes of this, that Charlotte is mistaken, but..."

Elizabeth scowled; she wanted to tell him the very notion that he was not Sir William and Lady Lucas's legitimate son was ridiculous, but held her tongue. "You cannot think it would alter my feelings!"

He squeezed her hand.

"In the *very* unlikely event that there is some question about your parentage, it cannot make any difference to me. What do you imagine might happen? Your mother's family, not that I suppose you have a mother apart from Lady Lucas, would seek you out to right a great wrong that was done two decades ago? Although, I cannot imagine what it would be. That is the stuff of novels, not real life, not *our* lives. In four or five months, we shall marry and go on to live perfectly ordinary, happy, quiet lives right here in our little corner of Hertfordshire."

William closed his eyes and bowed his head. After a moment, he kissed her hand.

She stood and pulled him up with her. "I insist we forget about this. Let us continue our walk. We can talk about what books my father is likely to have with him when he returns. I hope he found the treatise on geology I mentioned."

William groaned. "I shall never understand why you find rocks so interesting."

She laughed. "And I shall never understand how you can find fishing so fascinating. I propose we come to an understanding, Mr Lucas. I shall listen to you speak about fishing only for as much time as I may speak about rocks. What do you suppose is a reasonable weekly allotment of time? One hour? Two hours?"

William chuckled. She was glad to see that her silly banter had served its purpose, at least for the moment. She smiled and ignored the way her limbs trembled. Charlotte *must* be wrong. William illegitimate? It was preposterous! *Even if there is some truth to his and Charlotte's speculation, it matters not. I know the person he is, and I love him, regardless of his parentage.*

Nothing will ever separate us; I will not allow it. I could not bear it.

They wandered for a quarter of an hour before joining Charlotte and Jane. Nothing more was said about Charlotte's memory or William's parentage. Elizabeth's agitation ebbed as she saw William's cheer return. Elizabeth turned the conversation to upcoming parties, and by the time the Lucas siblings departed, she had put the matter entirely out of her thoughts.

CHAPTER 2

Gracechurch Street
19 October 1811

My dear Fanny,

Rest assured, I am well, as are the Gardiners. I had a chance encounter with an old friend of mine today, Mr Frederick Darcy, with whom I was at school. Finding that he soon travels to Norfolk to see his family, I invited him to stop at Longbourn for two or three days. He desires to meet you and the girls. No need to fuss. I am sure he would be pleased to meet the Lucases and some other of our neighbours at dinner on Tuesday.

Yours, &c.
RB

"With no more than that, I am told to expect a stranger in just two days' time! How can I arrange a dinner party with two days' notice?" Mrs Bennet cried.

"For certain, it is very hard on you, Fanny. Gentlemen never think of the inconvenience. We shall not mind such a late invitation," said Lady Lucas.

After listening to their mothers' complaints for another twenty minutes, Elizabeth and William escaped to the gardens.

"Do you know who this friend is?" William asked. "Do you think it could be the one he used to tell us about?"

Elizabeth shrugged and hooked her arm into his. She pointed at the pretty picture the vibrant yellow leaves of a rowan tree made against the cloudless sky. They walked in silence for a few moments until they stopped by a favourite oak. Elizabeth leant against its trunk and took a deep breath.

"You are happy today." William thought that the morning light brightened everything about Elizabeth—the golden hue of her skin, her dark hair, her lovely eyes. He placed his bare hand against the side of her face, and her eyes fluttered closed for a moment. She lifted her hand to cover his. Succumbing to temptation, he pressed his lips to hers. He did not indulge this desire very often; it would be easy for a brief kiss to become more.

"I love you," Elizabeth whispered.

William groaned before kissing her again.

Elizabeth cleared her throat. Her voice was as soft as the caress of her fingers on his hand. "I trust, Mr Lucas, that you are preparing well for my birthday."

He knew she was teasing him, but did not understand what she meant and shook his head.

"I expect to receive only one offer of marriage in my life, and I want it to be memorable."

"Only if you promise never to complain about me as much as your mother does your excellent father." Their marriage would be different from either of their parents'. The years of friendship and intimacy, knowing each other as completely as they did, had resulted in true love and forged a bond so deep that it was unbreakable.

"That is an easy promise to make," she said. "Should I ever feel the urge to complain, I will remind myself of moments such as this—when we were in perfect accord, untroubled, in love, basking in the glory of a fine autumn day—"

He could not help himself; he kissed her again, and continued to do so until they heard Jane calling them to come inside. She sounded exasperated, and he and Elizabeth laughed as they realised she must have said their names more than once without them noticing.

WILLIAM DID NOT MEET Mr Bennet's friend until the day after his arrival. He went to Longbourn to join the family for breakfast and arrived when there was still some time before the meal. Mr Bennet and Mr Darcy, he discovered, were out on an early morning ride, so he and Elizabeth once again went to sit outside to have a few minutes alone.

Elizabeth said, "It was an agreeable evening. I like Mr Darcy very much. I believe he *is* the friend Papa told us about. He is intelligent and amiable and interesting. I cannot wait for you to meet him." She regarded him with her head tilted to the side. "He reminded me a little of you. Both of you are so tall and dark, but it must be more than that. See if you agree."

When they reentered the house half an hour later, they encountered Mrs Bennet.

"Oh, Lizzy, there you are. William." She smiled and patted his cheek. "Lizzy, why you insist on dragging him outside when it is very likely to rain, I do not know. William, you are very good. Mr Bennet, Mr Darcy, and Jane are in the morning room. Oh, where is Cook? Hill!"

Once Mrs Bennet was out of their hearing, Elizabeth giggled. "Do I treat you so poorly?"

"You are jealous that your mother likes me more than she does you."

They were laughing as they entered the parlour. William glanced at Mr Bennet's friend, but did not take the time to study his looks before greeting Elizabeth's father.

"Good morning, Mr Bennet, and welcome back to Hertfordshire."

"Thank you, my lad."

A strangled sound drew William's attention to Mr Darcy. The man was very pale, and one of his hands flew to his chest, while the other clutched the chair he had just vacated. Mr Bennet was beside him in an instant.

"Darcy, what is the matter? Lizzy, send for the apothecary."

She grabbed William's hand, and they flew out of the room to find a servant. His heart raced, and he said a silent prayer that help would arrive for Mr Darcy before it was too late. Just as they were speaking to Thomas, Jane found them.

Jane said, "Mr Darcy says he does not need medical attention."

William's brow furrowed. "But he looked terribly ill."

Jane appeared as puzzled as he felt, but said Mr Darcy insisted he was well. "I do not know what else to say. I shall go see if my mother needs me. She is fretting about tonight."

Elizabeth gave her hand a quick squeeze. "You are so patient with her. More than I ever could be. We shall be in the back parlour."

Ten minutes later, they were called into breakfast. The gentlemen did not join them; Mrs Hill announced that Mr Darcy was ill, although it was nothing to worry about, and Mr Bennet attended him. An hour after breakfast, William was surprised and alarmed when he received a note asking him to return to Lucas Lodge immediately.

"I am sure it is nothing," Elizabeth reassured him. "Some little thing Sir William or Lady Lucas needs your help with. You can tell me about it when you return for dinner."

He promised he would, smiled at her, and set out for home.

ENTERING THE PARLOUR, his eyes grew round when he saw Mr Bennet and his friend. He had never seen such a grave expression on Mr Bennet. Mr Darcy looked perfectly healthy, even excited. Turning to his parents, he noticed tears in his mother's eyes, and evidence that she had been crying for some time; his heart began to race.

"Mother? What—" The words caught in his throat. The air in the room was thick, and he felt dizzy. Something was very wrong.

An ashen-faced Sir William ran a cloth over his forehead. "William, sit down, my b—" He cleared his throat. "There is something we must tell you."

William's eyes slid to Mr Bennet, who nodded, and William sat at the edge of the sofa. Sir William opened and closed his mouth three times before he looked at Mr Bennet, who sighed and rubbed his temple. If he were to judge by his parents and Mr Bennet only, he would think something dreadful had happened to Charlotte, but Mr Darcy would not act so eager and pleased if that were the case.

Mr Bennet said, "William, this will come as a shock."

William's throat felt thick and his muscles tensed. *Oh dear God. Charlotte was right! But, no. Why would Mr Darcy be here?*

Mr Bennet continued, "It has been for me, but you need to know. You are adopted."

"Adopted?" William repeated, not certain he understood what Mr Bennet meant.

When his father spoke, William turned to look at him. "Your mother, that is, Georgina and I, we-we found you."

"Found? W-w-what?" William heard his voice, but it was muffled and weak. He fell against the back of the sofa as Sir William told his tale.

"In February 1789, when Charlotte was four, Georgina and I were coming home one evening. She saw something by the side of the road. It was you. You were dirty and sick, and we took you home. We thought you would die. I listened for news of a lost child, but there was never a single word. We thought no one wanted you, so we kept you. Said you were the child of a distant relative. After a year or so, no one in the village ever spoke about you being adopted." Sir William hung his head.

Mr Bennet said, "Since they believed you were abandoned, they saw no reason to explain the truth to you."

A weight pressed on William's chest, which made it difficult to breathe. He could not seem to form a single thought. His distress deepened when Mr Darcy spoke.

"Except you were not abandoned, never unwanted. You were kidnapped, abducted from your home in Derbyshire."

William stared at him. Charlotte was right, but they were both wrong. This was far worse than being Sir William's illegitimate child. He wanted to ask how this man, this *stranger* knew, but could not form words.

Mr Darcy said, "I believe, with all my heart, that you are the son of my cousin, George Darcy. You are the very image of him. That is why I acted as I did when I first saw you. Sir William kept a record of the events from that time, and the dates, the place, your age—all of it matches. I am convinced you are the child who was stolen, and who we were told had died."

William lost any sense of time passing as Mr Darcy told them an extraordinary tale about people named Wickham and Thorpe and ransom.

"George's brother and I did everything we could to verify the story Mrs Wickham told after she was apprehended. She claimed the child had died almost immediately, that they buried your body in a forest in Cheshire. We searched, but could not find it, which is hardly surprising given the vague directions we had. My cousin hired people to determine where the Wickhams and Thorpe had been, but discovered nothing to contradict her story. I can hardly believe it, but I cannot deny the evidence of my own eyes. You lived."

William stared at him and shook his head, hoping to dispel the numbness that trapped him. He *must* be William Lucas of Lucas Lodge. Anything else was impossible. Yet, as he looked at

Sir William and Mr Bennet, even though they were blurry, he saw that they believed Mr Darcy's tale.

Mr Darcy stopped moving and faced him. "We must go to Derbyshire immediately." He sighed and shook his head. "Unfortunately, your mother died long ago, but my cousin yet lives, and will be the judge of whether he agrees with me— No. There is no other possible explanation; there are simply too many coincidences. You *are* Fitzwilliam Darcy of Pemberley."

Sir William, Lady Lucas, Mr Bennet, and Mr Darcy spoke for a while longer. No doubt they spoke English, but William could not make sense of their words over the buzzing in his ears.

I am not William Lucas? I am someone else entirely? He looked across the room, but despite its familiarity, he could not say what he saw, not even to name the colour of the walls or the sofa upon which he sat. Everything looked different, wrong.

The next hours were dream-like. Mr Bennet and Mr Darcy departed, and after making more incoherent noises, Lady Lucas left the room. An unknown amount of time later, Lady Lucas embraced him, and William had the vague sense of being in a carriage with Sir William and Mr Darcy. The jostling motion made him feel sick, and he sank into the squabs and closed his eyes. It helped to see only the blackness rather than the blurred outlines of his companions. He may have slept.

The next days remained the same. Several times, he had the sensation of getting out of the carriage, of inns and firm ground, the sun on his face, wind piercing his coat, cool air being drawn into his lungs, and of food in his mouth, being chewed and swallowed but not tasted. It was only in the middle of the night, as he lay awake in a strange bed at a coaching inn, that his mind seemed to grasp at the edge of what had happened in the parlour at Lucas Lodge.

He was not William Lucas, not even the illegitimate child of Sir William. He was the son of a relative, a cousin perhaps, of Mr Darcy's. If Mr Darcy was correct, William had been presumed dead for many years for reasons he did not recollect. They were travelling north, to meet the man who might be his true father. There was no mother alive to look him over and agree or disagree that he was her child. If it were true, his name was not William but Fitzwilliam, which Mr Darcy said was a family name. It sounded odd to the ear. How would he ever become accustomed to thinking of himself as anyone other than William Lucas, to people calling him Fitzwilliam rather than William?

He wanted Elizabeth more desperately than he ever had in his life. *When will I see her again? Oh, dear God, please let me see her again. Do not let this, whatever it is, separate us. I can bear anything but that.*

CHAPTER 3

WHEN HER FATHER AND MR DARCY JOINED THE LADIES IN THE parlour almost two hours after William's return to Lucas Lodge, Elizabeth was pleased that Mr Darcy seemed to be feeling better. The rest appeared to have done him good. He announced that he was returning to London so that he could consult his physician. It was odd that Mr Darcy appeared excited rather than anxious, but Elizabeth expressed her regrets, wished him well, and thought no more about it.

Once his carriage was away from the house, her father said, "Lizzy, come into my book room." He looked displeased, which she attributed to concern for his friend.

Elizabeth followed him down the hall. Next to her father, she spent the most time in the oak-panelled chamber, with its hundreds of books, messy desk, and worn yet comfortable wing chairs. Mr Bennet sat behind the table.

Elizabeth dropped into one of the chairs. "I hope no one at Lucas Lodge is ill. A note arrived for William an hour—"

"No, no one is ill." Her father shook his head, sighed, and scratched his nose. "Sir William needed him. They, the two of them, are going away."

"Going away?" Elizabeth leant forward and stared at him. "William said nothing about—"

He held up a quelling hand. "It was…a sudden business. Oh, Lizzy, how do I explain when I hardly understand myself?"

His apparent distress made her stomach churn with sudden anxiety. "Understand what, Papa?"

With a heavy sigh, her father wove a complicated and fantastical tale of a kidnapped baby who was presumed dead, discovered and adopted by the Lucases, and who had been recognised by Mr Darcy as the son of his cousin. She had all but forgotten the conversation about him possibly being Sir William's natural child. If she had not believed *that* was a possibility, what sense could she make of *this*?

When his voice fell silent, Elizabeth blinked her eyes rapidly for a few seconds before croaking, "I-I do not understand. You cannot believe this is true, Papa!"

Mr Bennet sighed and pinched the bridge of his nose. "I do not know what to think, Lizzy. If William is this man's son, it means that his mother was sister to the Earl of Romsley."

Elizabeth jerked backwards. Was he suggesting that William, *her* William, might be the nephew of an earl?

"If Darcy is correct, William is also the heir to a large estate and great fortune."

"This cannot be happening." Elizabeth bent at the waist and put her head in her hands. She breathed rapidly and felt herself growing light-headed. In a moment, her father's arm was across her back.

"Calm yourself, my dear. We must discuss it. Shall I ask Mrs Hill for tea?"

Elizabeth shook her head, sat back, and looked into her father's brown eyes, which were so much like hers. He moved to sit beside her.

"No one must know, Lizzy. I shall not tell your mother and sisters, not until I absolutely must. If I ever must."

"Why?"

"Nothing is certain at the moment. Darcy might be mistaken, which would mean we shall soon see Sir William and William returned to Meryton. The fewer people who know, the sooner their unexpected absence will be forgotten. Consider, dear girl, that if it transpires that William is not this long-lost child, he must live with the awful truth of his past always in mind, perhaps never to know who he really is. My friend wished to leave quickly for this very reason. Sir William agreed. I do not know if they were right." He lifted his hands as if to say it mattered not. "I would not have it casually spoken about. I shall think it a miracle if Lady Lucas does not tell your mother, although Sir William vowed to impress upon her the importance of silence."

Tears filled her eyes. "And if he is who Mr Darcy believes? What then?"

Mr Bennet touched her cheek. "I do not know."

Elizabeth blinked as tears fell down her face. "He *will* return, Papa, will he not?"

Mr Bennet closed his eyes for a moment and sighed.

A hand covering her mouth, she murmured. "This cannot be true. It *cannot*. It is too fantastical."

"I am as astonished by this as you. We must be patient and wait for news. You do not need me to tell you how much he loves you. He would not turn his back on you, to say nothing of the Lucases."

Each thinking their own thoughts, they sat together for almost half an hour before Elizabeth asked for permission to go to her room.

"Of course. Remember, Lizzy, not a word to anyone, not even to Jane."

Elizabeth nodded. In truth, it had not occurred to her to tell Jane. At the moment, she could not imagine trying to explain the situation to anyone. If she were to talk to someone about it, it would be Jane, she supposed, but the person she was most likely to confide in, whatever the secret, was William. *Who, at this very moment, is headed northwards, perhaps towards his true home. One that is far, far away from me.*

OVER THE NEXT DAYS, Elizabeth tried to act as though nothing extraordinary had transpired. She received callers with her mother, Jane, and Mary, but could not follow the conversations, which made Mrs Bennet call her stupid.

Mr Bennet visited Lady Lucas and Charlotte the morning after William's departure and spoke to Elizabeth about it.

"For now, we shall say that Lady Lucas has a cold, and Charlotte must attend her. It is a trifling matter. Not serious enough to recall Sir William and William, who are away seeing to a business opportunity. She is very much affected, Lizzy. I..." Mr Bennet lowered his chin and shook his head. "I shall continue to call and ensure they are both well."

Elizabeth wanted to scream that she was very much affected as well. *Why must I pretend nothing is amiss?*

Lady Lucas's purported illness meant the two ladies would not attend the assembly, which Mrs Bennet discussed at breakfast the morning of the much-anticipated event.

"It is such a shame the Lucases will not be there after Captain Farnon came all this way to see Charlotte. If they hope to catch him, they will have to act better than this."

Elizabeth reached for the piece of toast she had prepared with a healthy amount of strawberry preserves, but could not bring herself to eat it. From the first mention of the assembly, all she could think was how insupportable it would be to go under the present circumstances.

"So much fuss over a cold!" Mrs Bennet shook her head and sipped her tea. "I suppose I shall call tomorrow if I am not too fatigued and suffering from a headache after tonight, as I very likely shall be."

"I will go to Lucas Lodge after dinner and spend the evening with them," Elizabeth announced. "I am sure they would be happy for the company, and I do not mind missing the assembly."

Lydia teased, "You do not want to go to because William is not there to follow you around all evening."

Kitty giggled, as Jane and Mary protested.

Mr Bennet said, "Enough. Lizzy, I know your motives are good, but you will go to the assembly. Lady Lucas and Charlotte would not want you to forgo an evening's enjoyment for their sakes."

Enjoyment? Elizabeth did not wish to go and have people ask where William was or when he would be back and was it not a shame that Charlotte could not attend and every other silly little inconsequential thing she was sure they would say to her.

When Mr Bennet left the ladies a few minutes later, Elizabeth followed him.

"Papa—"

"I know you do not want to go tonight," he interjected. "Remember what I said. We must behave as though nothing unusual has happened."

When she opened her mouth to protest, he shook his head.

"It is Mary's first ball. She is anxious and needs you there." Mr Bennet tweaked her chin. "You know I am right. You, of all my girls, are strong enough to do what needs to be done. For William."

Elizabeth nodded and left without speaking again. She would feign good cheer for Mary's and William's sakes, but she most certainly would not enjoy herself. No one who knew the truth would expect it of her.

CHAPTER 4

DURING THE FINAL LEG OF THE JOURNEY, THEY LEFT THEIR HIRED conveyance and changed to the finest carriage William had ever seen. "My cousin's carriage," Mr Darcy explained in an offhand manner. He looked out of the window, seeming to check their location every few minutes.

William continued to repeat to himself everything Frederick Darcy, Sir William, and Lady Lucas had told him. He could hardly credit that Mr Darcy was correct, but there seemed no purpose to saying so, even had he been able to find the words. William watched the passing landscape, which was more rugged than he was used to. The noise of the horses and wheels deadened any sound the stream they drove along would have made or that of the sheep grazing in the fields.

This might have been my home. Impossible! I would remember... But the child who was taken was not even two years old. It cannot have been me. I am William Lucas. I live near Meryton, in Hertfordshire. Before that, I lived in Ironsbridge, Shropshire, at an inn with my parents and sister. From the time I was a small boy, I helped at the inn. I was always polite, always deferential to the wealthy, highborn guests, just as Father and Mother taught me. They would sometimes give me a coin. That is who I am. I do not belong here.

They entered the largest house William had ever seen and

followed a butler upstairs and into a parlour. William trailed behind Frederick Darcy and Sir William, walking when they walked, then stopping when they stopped. Sir William said something; William glanced at him, then returned his eyes forward, lifted his head, and removed his hat, which had not been taken from him downstairs.

He gasped.

In an instant that was even faster than a flash of lightning, he knew with absolute certainty that everything Frederick Darcy had said about a small boy being kidnapped and presumed dead was true, and that it had happened to him. *He* had been forcefully removed from his father's home and care and left to die. He knew because looking up was like looking into a mirror two or three decades hence.

I am not William Lucas. I never was. I am...I am... I have no notion who I am meant to be.

A sudden tight band across William's chest made it impossible to breathe.

The man, who he presumed must be George Darcy, looked at William, seeming as shocked as he himself was. George Darcy kept his eyes focused on William as he implored, in an unsteady voice, "Frederick?"

Frederick said, "I know, George. As soon as I saw him, I *knew*. I thought I would go mad, or that I *had* gone mad, until I discovered his story. It all fits, George; it *all* fits. As improbable, as incredible as it seems, he *is* Fitzwilliam."

George Darcy stepped towards him and stopped when he was within two feet. Slowly, he lifted a trembling hand and grazed William's cheek and shoulder. "My son. We thought you were dead. I thought you were dead."

Air rushed back into his lungs. He *was* this man's son, not Sir William's. *I am not a Lucas, not even illegitimately, but a Darcy. William Lucas never really existed.*

He felt Frederick take his elbow without realising the man was beside him. "Come, lad. Take off your coat. Here, let me help you. Sit. A little conversation, some dinner, and a good night's sleep will do you wonders. Everything will start to make sense soon. Everything will be well."

William, or Fitzwilliam—whatever he was supposed to call himself—followed his direction as his mind screamed, *Will it?*

THEY REMAINED in the parlour above an hour as Sir William told his tale of finding Fitzwilliam, and George Darcy reviewed Sir William's written account. William felt the man's eyes on him but could not look up. He was glad to be sitting, certain he would fall to the ground if he were standing. Although Frederick Darcy had said that he resembled George Darcy, he had not expected such a marked likeness, and it was disconcerting.

George stood. "It is past the dinner hour. You must wish to change out of your travelling clothes." Addressing William, he added, "For now, we shall say nothing to the servants about your true relationship to me."

The butler, Hudson, escorted them upstairs. When they reached the bedchamber assigned to Sir William, George said, "I shall see the young man to his room. See that Sir William has everything he needs, then send Ashford to us."

George entered another bedchamber; William remained by the door. George appeared to be dissatisfied with the room and frowned as he turned his head this way and that. A quick glance revealed nothing offensive, although furnishings were the last thing on his mind. They were soon joined by a man who paled and made a strangled noise before he regained his composure.

"Ashford, I wish you to assist…this young gentleman. We need no special preparations for dinner tonight. Until we find him a valet, you will divide your time between him and me."

They were silent for a moment until George again spoke. "Ashford will show you to the dining room when you are ready."

He seemed reluctant to go but, with a jerk of his head, did.

DINNER WAS A QUIET AFFAIR. William picked at his food and kept his eyes on his plate for the most part. He found seeing George, who so clearly was his father, sitting next to Sir William, whom he had always believed to be his father, confusing, even oppressive. Sir William looked awed by their surroundings, confused, anxious, and distressed in equal measure. William could do nothing for him, as his own state of mind was alarmingly precarious. It was all too much to take in. Once they were finished eating, George sent Hudson out of the room.

William's head shot up when he heard Sir William's voice. "If I might ask, Mr Darcy, what-what happens now?"

George's face grew ashen, and his hands trembled as he gripped his glass. His voice was low and controlled when he said, "What happens now is that my son stays here, where he belongs, and you leave."

"O-of course. I would not think otherwise. He is your son. If we had known, had suspected—" Sir William hung his head.

Frederick opened his mouth to speak, but George demanded, "Tell me again how you found a small child, hardly more than a baby, and did so little to find out from whence he came?"

"I-I," Sir William stammered.

"Did you even truly attempt to discover his people?"

There was a short, dreadful silence before Sir William, with his hands in his lap, head still bowed, admitted, "I did not know what to do. No one spoke of a lost child. We thought...we could give him a home. We wanted to."

William looked between the three men. George and Frederick did not see Sir William as the man who had rescued him, but as the man who failed to discover the lost child's identity. He did not know what to think himself. Sir William often needed someone wiser to assist him, and William could see his regret. He could not like how George spoke to him. Yet, William was too numb to be touched by any of their demeanours.

"I am grateful that you cared for him, but I will never understand how you could have failed to do more to find his people, whether you thought them to be lowborn or not. He was only a year-and-a-half old. You knew someone had been caring for him! The newspapers wrote about it incessantly. Were you not even curious if the child they spoke about was the one you found?"

Sir William did not attempt to defend his actions further. William knew it was unlikely his father, or any of his friends, had followed the news.

At length, George spoke again. "You have played your part. Now it is time for my son to be with his family again, as he ought to have been all this time. I shall ask you to leave my house, Sir William. Tomorrow morning. Hudson will arrange it."

He stood and walked out of the room.

Frederick said, "I apologise for my cousin. He speaks more harshly than he means to. You cannot imagine... Well, it has been a long, exhausting day. I suggest you both retire. Sir William, I shall speak to Hudson and see you on your way in the morning."

His face contorted by conflicting emotions, Sir William nodded. He remained sitting, chin lowered, as Frederick rose and followed his cousin out of the room.

William went to Sir William and rested a hand on his elbow. "Let us go upstairs."

When they were alone in Sir William's bedchamber, he said, "Fath—" He stopped, not knowing how to address him any longer. *How can I ever look at him as I used to, especially having met George Darcy?*

Sir William walked around the fine guest room, decorated with hand-painted wallpaper and shiny mahogany furniture. His voice trembled when he spoke a minute later. "It has been an unsettling few days. There is a great deal for you to take in and a great change in your life. It is a very good thing that Mr Frederick Darcy came to Longbourn. It is a very fine thing that you are reunited with your family, and"—he looked around the richly furnished room—"all of this. I never thought you or anyone needed to know about us finding you. If I thought you belonged to someone…"

"I understand." He was not sure he did, but what else could he say?

"The Darcys are a very good sort of people. Mr George Darcy is a great man. You are now, too. Always were, I suppose."

"I have no apprehension about them. They have welcomed me, and I…I…"

Sir William nodded a little too enthusiastically for William's mood. "You will do well. This is where you were meant to be all along. This is your home." He glanced around the room. "I shall return to Lucas Lodge, where I belong."

William's heart began to race, panicked by the notion of being left alone at Pemberley. *He is saying goodbye. But-but… when shall I see him again?*

Sickening dread filled him as he recognised that he was to stay in Derbyshire, among strangers who thought that he belonged here, with them. *When will I return to Hertfordshire? I will return, will I not?* Everything was happening, changing too quickly, and he could not keep up. The life he knew had been snatched from him, and he had been thrown into a new one. George, Frederick, even Sir William all agreed that this was for the best, treated it as the natural outcome of Frederick's discovery of him. But nothing about it felt right.

"Well," Sir William said, his eyes on his feet. "It is late. It must be nine, ten o'clock, and we set off so early this morning. I suppose I shall be off just as early tomorrow. I am very tired, and you must be as well."

"It has been a long day." His voice was low and without inflection.

Sir William cleared his throat. "I shall say good night. It would be best if you did not see me off."

After a slight pause, William nodded. *All of a sudden, I am unwanted.*

"Remember what your moth—what Lady Lucas and I taught you. He is your father, and I know you will do right by him and he by you."

He again nodded. "Good night, sir. I wish you safe travels. Please tell Lady Lucas and Charlotte that I am well. I...I shall write soon. And Mr Bennet." He could not bring himself to say Elizabeth's name.

A minute later, William bowed and left the room.

SLEEP ELUDED William despite his best efforts to claim its soothing effects. He tried to read that night and again the next morning as he waited for someone to come for him. However, he could not attend to the books which had been left on the side table. He stood at the window, which faced the back of the house. The lawn was broad and divided by a wide stone path. There was a large copse to one side, which looked like a watercolour painting in yellow, orange, green, and brown. Sunlight danced off a lake to the other side. He supposed it was a beautiful place, but at the moment, all he saw was its vast size; it made him feel small and very much alone.

His brain was on fire. So much had happened, and he was incapable of making sense of it. He had to accept that he truly was George Darcy's son and belonged here, in Derbyshire. Sir William had said as much, and William felt a natural desire to know his true family; or he thought he would, once he was not so addled by the revelations of the last days and the lack of sleep. It had been impossible to understand what George was thinking. Aside from the moment of warmth soon after their arrival, George had said little to him, though he did look at him a great deal. William wished he could know what the man was feeling, and what tomorrow, or the day after that, would bring. The size of the manor was intimidating enough, but everything he saw in it spoke of the Darcy family's wealth, from the exquisite art—

even here in a guest chamber!—to the bed linens, furniture, and book bindings.

He thought again about dinner and the manner in which George had treated Sir William. *I ought to be angry on Sir William's behalf, yet who am I to judge anyone's words and actions, especially when confronted with such an inconceivable situation, especially a man such as George Darcy?*

William had been taught to show proper respect and deference to his social betters, and George was doubtless his superior. *As well as my father, my closest connexion. Honour thy father and thy mother.*

Sighing, he sat in a velvet armchair and ran a hand through his hair. He could not help but feel that Sir William had rejected him; he had made it clear that he did not expect William to return to Lucas Lodge.

What about everyone I left behind? What about Lady Lucas and Charlotte? He pressed his eyes closed. *Lizzy?*

He leapt to his feet and returned to the window. "Why did he never tell me I was adopted?" he murmured. "Had I known that much, this would not be such a shock."

After he and Elizabeth had discussed Charlotte's memory and their supposition that he was Sir William's natural son, he had told himself that if it were ever confirmed, he would be disappointed, perhaps even ashamed, but—with Elizabeth by his side—nothing fundamental would change. But this...

Resting his forehead against the cold glass, he groaned. Sir William was long gone by now. It had been comforting having someone familiar nearby, but he accepted that the separation was inevitable.

I have a responsibility to myself, to know who I truly am, and a duty to this family, who never wished my absence. He is *happy to find me alive.* William did not know what to call George. 'Father' was impossible, 'Mr Darcy' too cold—and confusing with Frederick there—and 'George' too disrespectful. At dinner, Frederick had insisted William call him by his Christian name.

There was a knock at the door, and since both Ashford and Hudson had been to see him that morning, he suspected it was either Frederick or his father. It was the latter.

The two men stared at each other for a moment before George spoke. "Good morning. I hope you rested well."

William inclined his head and stood aside to allow him to enter.

"Ashford said that you were reading. I hope the books were to your liking. If not, we have many others. I shall show you the library today."

Knowing a response was needed, he said, "Thank you."

"Do you like to read?"

"Very much. I-I do like to read."

George nodded. "Good. I do, as well. Frederick too."

Neither spoke for a moment.

"I shall tell the household servants something about you after breakfast. It will allow you more freedom around the house."

After another moment of silence, George suggested they go down to breakfast.

WHILE WILLIAM slowly made his way through a caraway-scented muffin, George and Frederick told him that they had sent news of his return to the Darcy family, telling them to come to Pemberley as soon as possible.

"I hope they will arrive in six or seven days," George said. "Naturally, we shall all require time to accustom ourselves to this remarkable occurrence. Your mother ought to be here to see—"

George pushed his chair back, turned his back to them, and went to stare out of the window. Frederick watched him, a look of regret and understanding on his face, then caught William's eyes and gave him a reassuring smile.

William did not know how to react when Frederick spoke, his tone cheerful, if with a slight edge to it that seemed to suggest George's distress worried him.

"There is a great deal for you to learn about us, such as our names. We are not a very large family. My wife and children, Rebecca and Freddie, are presently in Norfolk. Your uncle, Jeffrey, is in London with your cousin John. Jeffrey is a widower."

William tried to commit the names to memory. However, he forgot them almost as soon as they were said.

"That leaves Lady Sophia, who is a distant cousin," Frederick explained. "You will meet her when you go to town."

William nodded and took a sip of coffee so that he would not have to speak. George returned to the table and fixed his eyes on William, which appeared to calm him. Frederick continued to chat about the family, mentioning grandparents and other connexions that were now dead or whom they rarely saw. Neither man mentioned his mother's people, the Fitzwilliams, after whom he was named. Having seen how discomposed George became at her memory, William was not comfortable asking. He supposed she had no family, or at least, none with whom they were in contact. There was something about the name Fitzwilliam he thought he was supposed to know, but he could not recall and dismissed it for the time being so that he could devote his attention to what his companions were saying.

George said, "We shall not be home to callers for now. I shall explain the truth to Hudson, Mrs Reynolds, and Ashford, but the rest of the servants will be told that you are a distant cousin. I hope we can keep speculation at bay. It will give us time to ourselves before we tell the world about your return."

Finding that both men watched him, William again nodded. George then talked about moving him to a new apartment among the family rooms and them taking a tour of the house that morning.

"Is there anything you care to ask?" Frederick said.

Although he spoke kindly, William remained ill-at-ease. "No. I-I have hardly had time to think about...everything."

He felt like he was desperately clinging to the reins of a

runaway horse. Until it slowed down a little, he could not attend to anything else. Every time he opened his mouth, he worried a howl of confusion, fury, and pain might fall out. How did one even begin to make sense of such a fantastic occurrence? His muscles ached, he was perpetually lightheaded, and he wanted nothing more than to be alone—or with Elizabeth. That, he knew, was impossible, and the best he could do was follow whatever direction George and Frederick gave.

Frederick's smile was reassuring, but it made William feel like he was five years old. George's expression was impossible to read, but William thought he saw a flash of pain and disappointment in his eyes. William returned his fork to the table, and wiped his mouth with a napkin, hoping to hide his chagrin and embarrassment.

I shall have to do better by him. After all, he is...he is my father.

CHAPTER 5

AFTER EXPLAINING THE SITUATION TO THE HOUSEKEEPER, BUTLER, and George's valet, the gentlemen took William on a tour of the house. The more he saw of it, the more he was intimidated by it. About an hour into the tour, he was struck by the notion that one day *he* would be responsible for Pemberley, presuming George intended to make him his heir. Mr Bennet had taught him about estate management, but his efforts were directed at making the most of a small estate. The Darcy estate must be ten or more times the significance of Sir William's.

It does not matter how much larger and grander it is. It is my proper home, and I shall become accustomed to it and to thinking of these men as my family, one of them my nearest relation in all the world. Whatever role he wishes me to take here, I must do my best to fulfil it.

"The library," announced George as he opened a door to reveal an oversized room. An enormous collection of books was arranged on oak shelves that ran from the floor to the ceiling along three walls. The other had windows and French doors leading to a terrace. It made the room bright, despite the preponderance of dark wood and furnishings.

"You will never lack for distraction when you are at Pemberley," Frederick said.

George added, "The library is the work of generations."

Although he was encouraged to select any volumes he would like to read, William declined, saying he was content with those he had for now.

Over the course of the tour, William gained a rudimentary understanding of the layout of the manor. He was pleased to discover that Pemberley had galleries, a conservatory, a billiards table, and many other corners in which he could lose himself and, he prayed, find the peace he needed to come to terms with what had happened. They reviewed several apartments in the family wing, and in consultation with Mrs Reynolds, a new set of rooms was chosen for him.

"I like these best. The view is superior and the size good. The décor, however…" George shook his head.

Frederick chuckled. "It might do for someone of our advanced years, but a young man should have something modern. Freddie assures me that the ways of today's youth are very different than they were when we were his age."

George smiled and turned to him. "I hope you and Freddie will become friends."

Frederick added, "I am sure they will, provided Freddie does not talk his ear off!"

William smiled; he could not manage a laugh, even though he knew it would please them to hear it.

George clapped his hands together. "These rooms it will be, then. Mrs Reynolds, please make them ready for Mr Fitzwilliam to occupy immediately. They can be refurbished later."

William started at being called Fitzwilliam; it left him feeling vaguely nauseous.

Once the housekeeper was gone, George turned to William. "You will be more comfortable in here."

He nodded with more enthusiasm than he felt. "I am sure I shall be." He could fit three or four of his bedchambers at Lucas Lodge—which he had always been contented with—in this space, which boasted a dressing room and small sitting area with a settee, armchair, and desk. *Befitting the son of the house, I suppose, but not Mr William Lucas. He would never have cause to stay in such rooms or even to enter a house like Pemberley, unless it was as a tourist.*

He wandered over to the window to see the view. At least with his eyes fixed on the world outside, he could not see the way the two strangers looked at him with hope and expectation; it was painful to witness.

SEVERAL TIMES, William touched a pen and thought about writing to Mr Bennet or Sir William, but each time, he faltered. *What could he say? Sir William should arrive home today and give them my message. That will suffice for now… Once I better understand what has happened and what the next weeks will be like, then I shall write.*

Whenever he thought about Elizabeth, it was with a sense of loneliness. He longed for her company. Soon, he began trying *not* to think about her and the other people he had left behind. It was not right, but it helped him get through the days. Elizabeth, who knew him so well, would understand that his attention was on trying to make sense of his history and his new circumstances.

George and Frederick asked him about his life—a few questions here and there, a longer conversation over dinner. William believed he saw glimpses of vulnerability and sadness in George's eyes as they spoke.

No, it is more than that. Sorrow and grief, but so deep. The first time he had caught sight of it, William felt as though someone had punched him in the stomach. It imposed an obligation on him, one that was emotional and not just the one he naturally owed George as his father.

What does such a man expect from his son? I can only imagine what he would have given me, the expectations and responsibilities he would have instilled in me, had I not been kidnapped. First, I must find a way to think clearly again. If I cannot even remember what I ate for dinner last night, how can I understand how I should act after finding out I am not the person I always believed I was?

William occupied himself by walking around the grand country house of his father's people. It served to both exercise his limbs and clear his mind. He encountered servants, although he did his best to avoid them. They stared at him. Why would they not when he looked so much like their master? William wondered how many supposed he was George's natural son, not a distant cousin as they had been told. He almost laughed when he recalled that he had once thought the worst thing that could happen to him was to learn that he was Sir William's illegitimate child; now, he was offended by the possibility that servants might believe that was his relationship to George. William made sure he looked past them, his head held high, his spine straight and rigid, his countenance showing nothing of what he felt.

Two days after his arrival, William had a destination in mind when he carefully crept out of his rooms before breakfast: the portrait gallery. While William could readily see his resemblance to George, and even to Frederick—Elizabeth had been right about that—he wished to see other faces that looked like his. Most of all, he wanted to see Lady Anne, his mother. He had learnt that she had died two years after his abduction. William had no memory of his mother, could never have any, and it grieved him. In his heart, he knew his kidnapping had led to her death. It made his sorrow even worse to know that she had died mourning a son who was not truly dead.

He found a painting of his father as a boy with his parents, brother, and sister, who had died before her fifth birthday. After gazing at it for several minutes, noting the likeness between him and his grandfather, he moved on until he found a large portrait of Lady Anne which stretched almost to the ceiling. She wore a pink gown and smiled. Her eyes were brown, as were William's, but beyond this, he did not notice a resemblance between them. Before he went down to breakfast, he looked around the gallery one more time.

My family.

As William Lucas, apart from Sir William, Lady Lucas, and Charlotte, he had never met another person he could call a relation. As Fitzwilliam Darcy, he had a family history recorded in these portraits, the library collection, and in so many other ways, as well as in George, Frederick, and the people he would meet in the coming days.

So much, and yet I feel so empty.

THE THREE OF them went into the library after breakfast. William held a book in his hands and turned the page every few minutes to give the appearance of occupation. He sat by the fire; its warmth was comforting, and he felt in great need of succour. George looked at him a great deal. William tried to imagine what it was like for him to discover his son was alive after so many years, but abandoned the pursuit because it made his stomach clench, sending acid into his throat.

They spoke now and again. Frederick asked about his book. Fortunately, William had read it before and could speak about it with reasonable ease. They talked about sport, and when Frederick and George both encouraged him to ask questions, he admitted a desire to know more about the Darcys. In telling him about them, George mentioned their impending arrival.

"Two or three more days. You will see how happy they are to welcome you home. John is almost your age and will make a good friend for you, particularly when we go to town. He spends most of the year there, with his father. You will like your other cousins too."

William said the appropriate words and thought about his friends in Hertfordshire.

That evening, George said, "You ride, I presume."

He nodded. "Yes."

"Good. I usually ride before breakfast, and we can go tomorrow. I see little harm in it. We are unlikely to meet anyone if we are careful. I would like to delay introducing you to our neighbours and tenants, or anyone else, until I can tell them the truth."

"I would like that." Oh, to be outside and feel the fresh air hitting his face as he galloped! Somehow, William always felt freer atop a horse.

"Frederick does not ride more than he absolutely must."

Frederick grinned and laughed. "Very true. I have work to attend to, so you need not feel as though you are abandoning me." He pushed himself out of a wing chair. "I am for bed."

William decided to retire as well, and so did George.

WILLIAM AND GEORGE thus began a habit of riding each morning, and he was glad of it. The fresh air and exercise were welcome and seemed to revive his spirits a little. It also proved disconcerting as he discovered the vastness of the estate. Yet, the area was beautiful, and he had to admit it was a little thrilling to know that something so magnificent was his rightful home. But accepting that he was a Darcy surely meant turning his back on his past as William Lucas.

Sitting in a heavy walnut Restoration-era chair in his bedchamber, William sighed. He missed Elizabeth and wished she were there. She would help him make sense of his feelings about everything that had happened. Alone, all he could do was dwell on the knowledge that his rightful life had been stolen from him; he knew it did him no good but did not know how to move past it.

Even now, with the villains who stole me long dead, people still suffer. I remain their victim.

CHAPTER 6

ELIZABETH FOUND IT MORE DIFFICULT TO ACT AS THOUGH nothing extraordinary had happened with each day that passed after William's departure. The assembly had been a trial, and now even mealtimes with her family were exasperating. At breakfast, she felt her father's eyes on her. As soon as they were finished eating, she followed him into his book room.

Mr Bennet announced, "Sir William has returned. I saw him this morning."

Elizabeth fell into a chair; she felt her face drain of colour and wrapped her arms around her waist.

When she did not speak, her father said, "Mr George Darcy has accepted William as his son, Fitzwilliam."

Elizabeth whispered, "I see."

"Sir William told me that Frederick Darcy and his daughter —I believe her name is Rebecca—return to London in about a week and intend to break their journey here. We shall learn more then. For now, I understand the family—the Darcys, I mean—is going to Pemberley to meet William. Fitzwilliam, I should say."

Elizabeth noticed that his voice was deeper than usual, and he slouched. *He wonders whether William will return. I see it in his eyes. Why did he meet Frederick Darcy again? Everything was so easy, so right, before he did!*

"The Lucases will call this morning. For the present, we must say nothing about what has happened. William is away, staying with a business associate of Sir William's in order to learn more about some new machine he is developing."

Elizabeth nodded. She wanted to speak, but it felt like her lips were sewn closed.

"Do you have any questions, Lizzy?"

She shook her head. When he remained silent, she stood and returned to her bedroom to await the Lucases' arrival.

"Sir William," exclaimed Mrs Bennet, "how suddenly you left us! Mr Darcy went away the same day you did. All my efforts to arrange a dinner party were for naught. But I do not complain. Georgina, you do look pale. Are you sure you are quite well? And Charlotte! Such a shame you missed the assembly. But where is William?"

When Sir William explained, Mrs Bennet cried, "Staying away? For how long?"

Charlotte said, "We are not certain."

Mrs Bennet shot a suspicious glance at Elizabeth, who wanted to scream. It was just like her mother to think she was responsible for William's absence. Her hands clenched into fists and released over and over.

Mr Bennet said, "Good for William. He takes every opportunity to improve his mind. We shall see him when we see him. Shall we have refreshments, my dear?"

Soon, the party divided into groups. Mrs Bennet told Lady Lucas the latest neighbourhood news; Kitty and Lydia sat with them. Charlotte wished to hear what Jane and Mary had to say about the assembly. Elizabeth manoeuvred her way into a conversation with Sir William and her father. They stood in a corner and whispered so that they would not be overheard. When Elizabeth asked what had happened in Derbyshire, Sir William was quick to share his impressions.

"I have never seen such an estate, not unless it belongs to an earl or marquess! William is very grand. Very grand indeed."

His description of his journey and Pemberley would make an acceptable travel guide, but it was of little interest to Elizabeth. She remained polite as the older man prattled on and, after a quarter of an hour, extricated herself from the conversation only to find she was immediately claimed by Charlotte.

"Your father says you know the truth."

Elizabeth nodded.

"It has been difficult. My mother has hardly stopped crying."

"And you?" asked Elizabeth. Charlotte seemed oddly unaffected.

Charlotte shrugged. "I do not know what to feel. Jane and Mary told me how much they enjoyed the assembly. I hope you did as well."

Elizabeth gaped at her, but Charlotte apparently was too intent on what she had to say to notice or care.

"Mary said you spoke to Mrs Long. Did she mention Captain Farnon? Was he offended I did not receive him when he called?"

Elizabeth huffed. "Yes, she did. I would not dare to speculate about Captain Farnon's feelings. I did not even know he called on you. How can you think that I could have enjoyed the assembly?" She began to walk away, but Charlotte took her arm.

"Lizzy, I am sorry. That was thoughtless." Charlotte averted her eyes and sighed. "You cannot know how important it is to me."

"Then I suggest you talk to Mrs Long."

Elizabeth pulled her arm free and sought a few minutes of solitude. Charlotte's insensitivity distressed her, but not half as much as Sir William's failure to deliver a message from William.

ELIZABETH DID her best to avoid her family for the rest of the day. She was certain they would see her anger; she felt sweat under her arms and had to bite her tongue to avoid snapping at them. Lydia and Kitty teased her about missing William, and Mrs Bennet repeatedly asked about his 'sudden desire' to be away from Meryton.

Jane came into her room after they retired for the night.

"You must be unhappy that William remains away," she said.

Elizabeth sat at her dressing table and brushed her hair. "It is hardly the first time we have been separated."

"Still, I am sure you miss him."

"Mm."

"His birthday is in a few weeks. He will surely return before then."

Elizabeth tried to smile but failed.

"Lizzy, are you not well? You and William did not have a disagreement, did you?"

"No." Elizabeth pressed her eyes closed then turned to Jane. "I am rather fatigued. I apologise for not being better company."

Jane encouraged her to get into bed, and after being assured that Elizabeth did not need anything, left her alone.

Elizabeth, extinguishing her candle, rested her head against her soft pillow, and thought about William. He had hardly been out of her mind since his sudden departure, but now she needed to consider what the situation meant for their future. *William is not the person I always thought him to be. How could the Lucases allow us to believe he was their son?* She kicked the bed with her heels several times.

She knew she was not doing the Lucases justice, yet could not help her feelings. William had been taken away from her with no warning.

I must face the fact that he is not my William. He is Fitzwilliam Darcy. Apparently, as Fitzwilliam Darcy, he belonged to a very different, much grander life than the one William Lucas had lived in Meryton.

She climbed out of bed and went to the window. Pushing aside the heavy, rose-striped drapes, she looked at the moon-lit yard.

We dreamt of such a wonderful future, but now, George Darcy will want to give his son everything he always ought to have had. He will keep him in Derbyshire, away from the life he was living and the people in it. Away from me.

"Nonsense." She kept her voice soft to avoid disturbing the household, but she needed to hear the words. "I am the daughter of a gentleman, and if William truly loves me..."

William had sent her no word, no letter. Had William not thought to say to Sir William: 'Tell Elizabeth I shall write as soon as I am able', or 'Tell Elizabeth I shall be in Hertfordshire before Christmas'?

Frustration, anger, and hurt warred within her as tears pooled in her eyes. She returned to the bed and gave them to her pillow.

AT THE END OF OCTOBER, the Bennets were engaged to dine with the Stuarts. Elizabeth liked them well enough but had no wish to go; she knew everyone would ask about William. She asked her father for permission to stay home with Kitty and Lydia, but he refused and claimed it was better for her to be among people.

At dinner, she sat beside Charles Goulding. "It is very good to see you again, Miss Elizabeth," he said. "It seems an age, but it was not so long ago. At the assembly, was it not?"

"Yes."

"I suppose the difference is that I have not heard Lucas talking about you every other day!"

Elizabeth tried to laugh with him, but the most she could manage was a faint smile.

"Does he return soon?"

"I am not certain."

"He is missing some capital sport. I suppose there is sport wherever he is. West, is it not?"

Elizabeth nodded, and was glad when he took a large mouthful of beef, necessitating that he attend to chewing. She pushed a stewed tomato around her plate; they were too sour for her taste. Hearing laughter, she looked across the table at Jane, who was talking animatedly to her neighbour. Even Mary, sitting beside Mr Goulding's brother, was smiling and laughing.

"I wager he will be back within the fortnight," said Mr Goulding. "For his birthday."

Elizabeth nodded and felt the sting of tears in her eyes. She took a sip of wine; it was as sharp as her conviction that he would not.

After dinner, the subject of the new Netherfield tenants, the Linningtons, arose. Soon, the entire company began to express their opinion of the family's intentions on settling in the neighbourhood, their home counties, and more besides.

"Miss Elizabeth, you have been very quiet this evening. I hope you are well?" Mrs Stuart said.

Elizabeth started at the sound of Mrs Stuart's voice and realised her thoughts had drifted far away from her companions. Her hostess was lowering herself to the sofa beside her. "I-I am afraid I have a slight headache."

Mrs Stuart said words of sympathy, which eased the tightness in Elizabeth's heart, even though they were not about what affected her spirits. A fist clamped around the organ, its hold even stronger than it had been before, when Mrs Stuart mentioned William.

"Once Mr Lucas has returned…"

Elizabeth heard nothing more. Mrs Stuart's voice, and those of the other guests, coalesced to a dull roar.

I cannot remain here. How can I continue to see these people, listen to them talk about William and pretend that he will return? It will be no better once the truth is known.

The question was where she could go. Staying with her aunt and uncle Gardiner was a possibility, but she and Mrs Gardiner had few similar interests. *And once she knows the truth about William, she will insist on talking about it again and again. I will think of something. I must.* She would go mad otherwise.

CHAPTER 7

I T IS THE FINAL DAY OF OCTOBER, WILLIAM REFLECTED AS HE accepted his new valet's help preparing for his morning ride with George. *William Lucas could dress himself, but Fitzwilliam Darcy* must *have a valet.*

He had hinted to George that it was unnecessary, but had stopped when it became apparent that it made him unhappy. Each time William saw such a look and knew it was because of him, it felt as if a rock was placed on his shoulders. The burden was already quite heavy.

At times, he resented that he felt obligated to George, who he had not known existed a fortnight earlier. Yet, George was his father in a way Sir William never had been; he owed his allegiance to him.

He left his room and jogged down the stairs to join George for their morning ride. His relations were arriving that day, and he both dreaded and anticipated it. Would they accept him, or look upon him with suspicion? *At least it will be over soon, and we can move on to whatever comes next. An announcement of my being found alive, I suppose, and going to town. By the time they leave, I shall ask about arrangements for the coming weeks, if I have not learnt of them before then. After that, I shall write to Mr Bennet.* Mr Bennet would show Elizabeth his letters; it would have to do.

AT BREAKFAST, George grumbled over a stack of letters and notes. William's immediate thought was that it had something to do with him, and his eyes moved between his companions as he held his breath.

"Anything worrisome?" asked Frederick.

George shook his head. "Several business matters I must attend to, and letters from friends."

William nodded and slowly cut a sausage into small rounds.

As he ate, he felt George staring at him. William wished he knew what his father wanted him to say.

"The vicar sent a message as well, hoping that nothing is amiss since I was not at church on Sunday."

"Good man, Llewellyn," Frederick said.

"I shall have to have him around soon. We have parish business to discuss." He turned to William, "He is not much older than you. It would be good for you to have a friend in the neighbourhood. His father is a baronet and an old school friend of mine."

Although his heart began to beat heavily in his chest, he kept his voice calm as he said, "I would like that. I had many friends—"

George interrupted him. "You will have new ones now. Here, in your rightful home, and in town, among the sphere you always ought to have inhabited."

William nodded his head and picked at his food. He felt reprimanded. It had been several years since he had given Sir William cause to correct his behaviour—not since he and the Gouldings had entered into a ridiculous riding competition that could have seen one of them injured or worse—but George Darcy would have different expectations regarding his son's behaviour and companions.

George said, "I had a reply from my London solicitor. He expects to be here in about a fortnight. After you have gone."

William dropped his fork and knife. *After I have gone?* His heart stopped. What would he do if George banished him from Pemberley? *I could return to Meryton. I could go home!*

But it would not be so simple. *Knowing the truth, I cannot simply return to Meryton as if nothing has happened. How many people know that I was a foundling, left to die? They would never look at me in the same way again. If I am not Fitzwilliam Darcy, then I am someone else. There might even be some other family waiting for me. How could I rest without first discovering the truth of my past?*

When Frederick said, "I would stay longer if I could, but work calls me back to town," William realised George had been talking about Frederick's departure. He put another piece of sausage into his mouth, using the act of chewing to calm his nerves. He *was* George's son. He was where he should be, and George wanted him here. William pressed his eyes closed and surreptitiously shook his head to clear his thoughts.

George said, "Most of the family will remain a week or ten days. We must get you properly settled; I wish to make the necessary legal arrangements as soon as possible."

William understood that George was talking to him. He murmured a response and stared at the piece of potato he had stabbed with his fork. He was incapable of putting it into his mouth and laid the fork back down beside his plate.

BREAKFAST ENDED, and George went to speak to his steward, while William and Frederick went to the library. William sat with a book in his hands and stared at the page until the sound of Frederick's voice startled him out of his reverie.

"I imagine this is a great deal to take in—learning about your past, being here, meeting your family."

William made a noncommittal sound. He did not want to offend his cousin, but he often thought it would have been a much better thing if Frederick had never come to Longbourn.

And yet, when William thought that, he was ashamed. George had a right to the truth. *We all do, I suppose. If I had ever learnt I was adopted, I would have wanted to find out who my real family was.*

"It will make sense in time. I cannot tell you how happy we are that you are here. George especially, of course."

William watched as a dark shadow swept over his face.

"It is not easy for your father to talk about his feelings. He has had to contend with a great deal over the years. His father's death. They were very close, and I know he always wished to have a similar relationship with you. George was only three-and-twenty when he became master and head of the family. His brother, Jeffrey, was not yet of age. Then your…loss, which was very hard for him, especially because your mother… Well, then she died, which was the final blow. Through it all, he has done his duty, but he has never forgotten." Frederick's voice faded, and he stared at a spot behind William.

William watched him. Frederick did not explain further, but William knew that he meant George had never forgotten his grief.

After a moment, Frederick shook his head and took a deep breath. "I truly believe the happiest day of George's life was the day you were born. His son; his heir. Your birth meant he had done his duty as master of a great estate and secured its future, but his joy was in being a father. *Your* father. Then to have you torn away from him." Frederick gave a heavy sigh and shook his head. "But you are here, among your family again. You can reclaim your proper life, the one George dreamt of giving to you as his eldest son. This is a time to settle in, to get to know us. Your friends in Hertfordshire will be waiting for you."

William was struck in a way he had not been before. If remembering the abduction and his supposed death shook Frederick so deeply, how much worse it must be for George, even if he did not show it.

Hiding his face with the book, he pressed his eyes closed and bit his lips together. Frederick was right, he supposed. He *should* take this opportunity to become comfortable with the situation; he could always return to Hertfordshire in a month or two. It would be nothing to visit Meryton when they went to town, which he believed they would do in the winter.

REBECCA AND FREDDIE DARCY arrived shortly before dinner. William was studying the drawing room's decorations—so much better than seeing how George watched him—when Hudson escorted them in.

William stood aside as George and Frederick greeted them. He knew that Freddie had just turned one-and-twenty, and Rebecca was a year younger. There was an openness about their countenances that lightened the weight on William's chest. They embraced Frederick and were visibly happy to see him and George, whom they called uncle.

The room fell silent, and everyone looked at William. No sooner had George made the introductions, then Freddie and Rebecca launched into speech.

Freddie said, "Of course you are. Uncle George's son, I mean. Anyone could see that you were one of us."

Rebecca added, "We have been very excited to make your acquaintance. Well, at least since we knew that you…"

"Were alive." Freddie shrugged and grinned. "I did not even know you existed until a few years ago."

"I found out before he did," said Rebecca. "Well, a little."

Frederick chuckled. "You are both blathering. Sit down. There is ample time to say everything you like."

To William's surprise, George laughed. It was brief and soft, but it was a definite mark of amusement.

"Yes, please, do sit," said George.

"It is very good to meet you." William wished he had not sounded so hesitant.

"Your mother chose not to come?" Frederick asked.

The siblings exchanged a hesitant look, as if hoping the other would reply.

Frederick shrugged. "Oh well. It is her loss; she will have to wait longer to know Fitzwilliam."

George reacted with indifference, and although William was curious about the lady's absence—and that no one seemed to care—felt it would be rude to ask.

For what felt like a quarter of an hour, the party sat in silence. Freddie and Rebecca stared at William, while Frederick and George watched the young people. William felt like laughing at the absurdity of his situation.

Freddie sat with his elbows on his knees and leant towards William. "I am speechless."

"You look so much like Uncle George." Rebecca's voice was soft, almost as if she were afraid of the words.

Their father said, "I was never more surprised in my life than when Fitzwilliam walked into my friend's sitting room."

"What a shock for you, Papa!" Rebecca turned to William. "And for you! Did you have any notion?"

William swallowed heavily. "N-no."

"It is a shocking, yet very happy occurrence," added George.

A slight heat crept up William's spine at hearing George refer to his pleasure. He ought to be happy as well, he thought, to know the truth about who he was. Seeing how eager and pleased his new cousins were helped. They demanded Frederick tell them about finding Fitzwilliam. As he did, the subject of their conversation began to feel that it would be very good to have more people at Pemberley, especially if Rebecca and Freddie were indicative of the friendliness of the rest of the family.

AFTER DINNER, the five of them went into the withdrawing room. Freddie and Rebecca quizzed William about his life and told him about theirs. The siblings spent most of their time in Norfolk with their mother and grandfather, whose estate Freddie was to inherit. From what William heard, he surmised that Frederick and Julia Darcy had been estranged for at least a decade.

The conversation was the easiest one William had had since coming to Pemberley; even George seemed more relaxed than William had seen him previously. The mood changed noticeably when, after an hour, Hudson opened the door and ushered in two gentlemen.

George jumped to his feet. "Jeffrey! We did not look to see you tonight."

Jeffrey Darcy replied, "We did not like to stop for another night at an inn. The moon is high."

Although he spoke to his brother, Jeffrey's eyes were on William, who was uncomfortable with the inspection; his mouth became dry.

His father introduced him to Jeffrey and his son, John.

Jeffrey's gaze slid from William to Frederick. "You were the one who found him."

Frederick nodded.

Jeffrey's attention turned back to William, but he said nothing further. John acknowledged his cousins and uncle but said nothing to him. William did not know what to make of him, of either of them. Their expressions were unreadable, although that might be because he did not know them. Father and son resembled each other as much as he did George, and had William met either of them, he would have been struck by how much they looked like him.

I wonder whether I would have known them for my kin, even if I did not know that I, too, am a Darcy?

After several minutes, John said, "It is late, and it has been a very long day. I shall retire, if you will excuse me."

"Of course," replied George. "I suspect Freddie and Rebecca are also fatigued after their journey. Perhaps we should all go up."

"George," Jeffrey demanded in a low tone.

"Not tonight. It can wait until tomorrow."

William watched as their eyes met. In a moment, Jeffrey's cheeks coloured, and his chin fell into a curt nod. "We can meet before breakfast."

George shook his head. "Fitzwilliam and I ride in the mornings. After breakfast."

With no more discussion, everyone parted ways for the night.

CHAPTER 8

As much as William appreciated the exercise and diversion of riding, he did not know how much he liked these early morning excursions with George. They were part of his education, however, and he had few other opportunities to leave the house.

They stopped near a river which ran through the estate.

"I am glad everyone is here," George said. "Other than Sophia. Although the connexion is not close—my grandmother and hers were sisters—she is a dear friend. I did not expect her to come. The long carriage ride would be difficult for her."

William mumbled a response, although he did not know what to say. His thoughts were on Elizabeth and how much she would love Pemberley. The gardens were interesting and varied, the park lush even at this time of year, and there were woods enough even for her. George would not be pleased to know how often he dreamt about visiting Hertfordshire. *For now, I should keep my attention on what is happening here. I still think I shall soon wake up, go to Longbourn, and laugh with Lizzy about the nonsensical dream I had.*

After a few minutes, George spoke again. "Well, we should turn back, I suppose. It will be breakfast soon, and I am sure you will be anxious to spend time with Jeffrey and your cousins, and they with you."

As they made their way into breakfast, Rebecca said to William, "I suppose it is a great deal to take in, is it not?"

Not knowing she was beside him, William jumped.

"You will get used to us. You have little choice. None of us do." She blushed, looked at him in alarm, then dropped her gaze. "I do not mean our family is so difficult. Except my mother. My parents' marriage is not a happy one, as you might have guessed. I blame her. My father is all goodness, but she is not easy to like. If you ever meet her, and I do not take it as an inevitability, you will see what I mean. It is enough to make me determined never to marry. What I meant is that no one really has a choice about who their family is. They simply *are*. We are no different."

The air in the breakfast parlour was strained and awkward, which was a marked contrast to dinner the night before. William told himself it was because, now that their party was complete, they could discuss the great matter of his return, although they could not do it with servants in the room. Breakfast only delayed the inevitable.

The waiting is awful. It robbed him of his appetite. His plate was full of food he did not remember taking—baked eggs with mushrooms, ham, a muffin, and some sort of green vegetable. It was silly not to eat, however; he would regret it later when his stomach complained. He picked at his food, each small bite turning to paste in his mouth, which made him drink more coffee than he usually would.

Surreptitiously studying his companions, he discovered that Jeffrey was staring at him. Their eyes met for a moment before Frederick spoke to Jeffrey, causing him to look away. William was relieved; the hardness of his uncle's gaze made his thighs tremble and stomach turn. William avoided looking in his direction again.

THE FAMILY SETTLED INTO A SMALL, bright morning room after breakfast. William sat with George and Frederick on a firm, velvet sofa. Scrutinising the faces of his three younger cousins, William saw that John bore the same unreadable expression as his father. Rebecca bit her lip as she studied George, Frederick, and William in turn, her blue eyes never resting on one for long. Freddie was on the edge of his seat, leaning forward.

Jeffrey said, "Tell us how this came about, George, and why you are so certain he is your son. Aside from his resemblance to you."

Rather than answer, George turned to Frederick, who nodded and relayed his story of finding Fitzwilliam in Hertfordshire. Rather than listen, William looked out of the window. From his place on the sofa, he could see hints of the sculpture garden.

"These Lucases, you believe they are innocent?" asked Jeffrey.

William bristled. "They are." Sir William and Lady Lucas were good people who had taken him in and treated him as a son.

Frederick agreed. "There is no reason to suppose they were in any way involved in the abduction."

Jeffrey said, "We looked and found no evidence that he was alive. How do you know they are telling the truth, that the date is correct and—?"

Frederick interjected, "Sir William wrote an account of the events at the time. George now has it. They lived in Shropshire, Jeffrey. We did no more than a cursory search there, because all the information we had—that you and I and the men George had assisting us discovered—placed the Wickhams and Thorpe further north." He looked at his children, then John and William, as he explained, "Thorpe and Wickham were discovered in Liverpool. Thorpe killed Wickham and was himself killed by the agents who found them. Mrs Wickham was apprehended near Liverpool very soon after. The supposition was that she was fleeing south, but we must now conclude that she was travelling north to meet her brother and husband, having left Fitzwilliam behind. We had six, a dozen men—I no longer remember how many—searching for them and tracing their route. There were never many sightings that we were confident were them, except for one, but the people who were seen did not have a child with them; afterwards, it seemed to support the notion that Fitzwilliam had died soon after they took him. When we had Mrs Wickham's story from her—and both Jeffrey and I questioned her more than once, as did others—there was nothing to contradict what little we had learnt. From the beginning, they were well hidden."

Jeffrey muttered, "Thorpe and Mrs Wickham planned it well."

"Which we said at the time," Frederick agreed.

"The Lucases found him and did nothing to discover who he was?" John asked.

"They tried," Frederick said. "They did not see the news, or, if they did, did not connect the child they found with Fitzwilliam. That is the material point."

"Who exactly are these people?" John asked.

Frederick told the assembled party what he knew of the Lucases, softening their connexion to trade. "There is really nothing more to say about them. They played no role in his kidnapping and did as well as they could for him. They might have left him at an orphanage or treated him like a servant. Instead, they cared for him all these years, for which we should all be grateful."

There were murmured words from several people, but nothing coherent enough for William to catch. He was watching George. As he expected, his father was not happy to be reminded of the circumstances of William's childhood. *He thinks less of me because of it, but I am not to blame, and neither are the Lucases.*

Rebecca asked, "Were they good to you?"

William nodded, and his eyes burned.

"Did you go to school? Have a tutor?" Jeffrey demanded.

"A local gentleman tutored—"

"What sort of local gentleman would take the time to tutor a boy?" Jeffrey sneered.

"My old school friend." Frederick glared at Jeffrey as he spoke. "I can testify to his being a gentleman. A very intelligent one at that."

"Fitzwilliam may have had an irregular education, but he had a very good one, under the circumstances," George said.

Under the circumstances, William repeated silently.

"He is not married, is he?" Jeffrey asked George, apparently done with speaking directly to William.

His father shook his head.

"Thank goodness. One can only imagine what sort of woman—"

"As there is no one, we need not discuss it further," George insisted. "Fitzwilliam is just four-and-twenty; there is plenty of time to discuss when and whom he should marry once he has taken his rightful place in society."

Rebecca looked apologetic, but William hardly noticed. He felt like ice flowed through his veins. George had not responded favourably when William had mentioned having friends in Meryton several days earlier. Now, after listening to Jeffrey, William felt certain that neither gentleman, likely none of the Darcys, would welcome Elizabeth, the Lucases, or anyone else from William Lucas's life.

All is not lost, a voice from the deep recesses of his mind assured him. *We are just at the beginning of this. Whatever this is.*

"Let us return to the important issue," said Jeffrey. "These Lucases found a child in Shropshire, and you believe he is Fitzwilliam, despite our being certain at the time that he was dead."

"But he is not!" Only George's flaring nostrils betrayed his vexation. "The *only* thing that matters is that Fitzwilliam did not die. He was found, he lived, and now he is where he belongs. For that, we should all thank God. I certainly do."

"As do I," Rebecca said.

"How do you *really* know this young man is Fitzwilliam?" insisted Jeffrey.

Frederick began to speak, but before he could say more, George did. His face was red, and he spoke through clenched teeth. "He *is* my son. I *know* he is. If you do *not* see it, I would ask why you are so unwilling to accept him."

"Let us calm ourselves." Frederick went to George and rested a hand on his elbow. "Jeffrey forgets that here he is a brother and uncle, not a Member of Parliament facing his political opponents in the House."

Jeffrey and George stared at each other. After a moment, Jeffrey raised his hands in surrender. "If you are satisfied, then so am I. I think only of you, George."

To William, his uncle looked like he would prefer to continue debating the issue, but had decided to accept George's authority. He supposed he understood his uncle's scepticism. There was no way to know for certain, but there were too many coincidences for him to believe this was all a mistake.

George sat. "Let us all rejoice that Fitzwilliam has been found. That is why I asked you to come. I understand how incredible this news is, but there is no doubt in my mind or Frederick's or Fitzwilliam's or, I dare say, in Sir William Lucas's. This is my son, mine and Anne's, sitting beside me."

Jeffrey asked, "Does he have *any* preparation for the life he is now so fortunate to have? I think not. Happy as his situation is, he is not ready for it."

Happy? William supposed he should be pleased to know the truth, but at the moment, he was not.

Frederick made a noise of exasperation. Glancing at his cousins, William saw that Rebecca rolled her eyes and Freddie looked uncomfortable. Only John seemed to accept his father's combative stance.

"Enough, Jeffrey," George barked. "I asked you here to welcome your nephew home; that is all I want from you and his cousins. I shall decide what my son needs and how he will get it."

Rebecca said, "I think that if anyone has questions about Fitzwilliam's life when he was...not here, he could answer them better than anyone else could."

"Rebecca is correct," George said. "Fitzwilliam has told Frederick and me a good deal about his life. Yes, he is unfamiliar with our ways, but he is intelligent, well-read, sensible, and he is my son and fully capable of learning what he needs to know. He *is* a Darcy."

"He did not attend a university," John stated.

"One hardly needs to attend university to learn to dance or play cards or any other such social nicety," Freddie said.

George stood. "Enough. Jeffrey, Frederick, and I shall continue this conversation on our own. Rebecca, my dear, I am sorry you are, once again, the lone female. I am sure your cousins will see you are properly amused."

John muttered, "I am going for a ride." He left the room without asking if anyone would like to join him, although William did not think the others noticed.

Heads bent together, the siblings followed John out of the room. William regarded his father to ensure he truly was no longer needed; when George offered him a small smile and nodded his head, William went to find Freddie and Rebecca.

CHAPTER 9

THE NEXT WEEK PASSED QUICKLY, AND PEMBERLEY WOULD SOON be emptying of its guests. Freddie would return to Norfolk, fulfilling his duty to his grandfather and mother, although he confided to William that he would much rather go to town. Rebecca was joining her father in London for the winter; although Jeffrey and John were also going to town, they were remaining at Pemberley several days beyond Frederick and Rebecca's departure. William was both glad and disappointed that his newfound family was leaving. It was a relief because it meant fewer people who wanted to talk to him and ask about his former life. He could not even regret Freddie and Rebecca, with whom he felt most comfortable. Yet, the sooner everyone left, the sooner he would be alone with George.

William still had not written to anyone in Hertfordshire. He had no idea what to say to them or how to send a letter without George discovering it. He prayed that the mixture of anxiety and grief he saw in George's eyes whenever someone so much as mentioned William's former life would abate with time. When it did, it would be easier to reconcile his father to William's wish to maintain his connexion to the Lucases and Bennets. William told himself daily that not much time had passed since his departure from Meryton; given the extraordinary event, they would understand his present silence.

Rebecca unknowingly gave him important insight into what George and the family had suffered. The morning before she and Frederick left, they were sitting in a corner of the morning room. They had been discussing history—a favourite topic of hers—when she suddenly changed the subject. George, Frederick, and Jeffrey were there as well, but too far away to overhear their conversation.

"I hope it has not been too awful having all of us here. I suppose it is not so many when you consider the hordes you will meet when you are in London. Then there are the Fitzwilliams." She bit her lip and frowned. "I do not know what Uncle George has done about telling them. He has refused to acknowledge them since, well, since *then*."

William looked at the trio sitting across the room to make sure they remained occupied. He lowered his voice and stayed as still as possible, as though that would make it easier to understand her response. "Oh?"

"I refer to your mother's family. You do know that?"

He nodded. "And that my mother died two years after I was taken. I assumed there was no family, or no one close enough to consider."

Rebecca rolled her eyes. "I ought not to be surprised that no one thought to tell you about them. We are all so used to not knowing the Fitzwilliams. Not that Freddie and I would have had the opportunity to meet them. Freddie is too much in Norfolk to know many people in town, and my father hardly ever goes into society, so I do not either when I am with him. John is in the same set, though, and he does not talk to the earl or his sons."

Frederick laughed, and after glancing at him, Rebecca stood and walked to the window. William followed her to it and pretended to admire the view. It was a grey day, and if the draught from the window was any indication, cold.

Just as impatience was itching at his spine, Rebecca spoke. "Lady Anne was the daughter of the old Earl of Romsley. She was just the sort of wife the heir of Pemberley would marry—the daughter of a peer with a great fortune. Thirty thousand pounds. Still, they were very happy. From what I understand, when you were taken, Lady Anne wrote to her father, against Uncle George's wishes. The old earl and Lady Anne's brother came to Pemberley. Your grandfather hired people—I do not know what to call them—to search for you and your abductors. Your father believed that Mr Wickham would keep you safe. It was the men the earl hired who confronted them."

"Which is when Thorpe and Wickham died, then Mrs Wickham was found, said I was dead, and so on." The events had been the subject of conversation several times.

Rebecca squeezed his arm. It was done so quickly that he hardly noticed. "Uncle George blamed the Fitzwilliams. If the earl had not hired those men…"

William nodded to show he understood.

"The families have been estranged ever since. Your grandfather died, oh, I do not know how many years ago, but you have an uncle and aunt and two cousins, both men. And another aunt, Lady Anne's sister; I believe she has a daughter. They will have to be told about you, but I do not know when or by whom. Was I right to tell you?"

WILLIAM HOPED he had thanked her, but now, the day after her departure, he did not know. In some ways, she reminded him of Elizabeth. She was intelligent and, more than any of the others, seemed to worry about how he felt about the drastic change in his life. She was pretty too, although to his eyes no lady would ever be as attractive as Elizabeth, not even Jane, who was considered the most beautiful lady in the neighbourhood.

I wonder if Rebecca is the sort of lady my father expects me to marry. She is not titled, but she might have a respectable dowry—something Lizzy does not have—and she is a Darcy, which must count for something. But if my father married the daughter of an earl, he might want me to make a similar marriage. He ran a hand through his hair and shook off the reflections; he could not think about marriage when his life was in such upheaval. As much as he wanted Elizabeth with him, he could not even truly imagine them starting a life together until he understood what it meant to be a Darcy.

There was a great deal he had to learn about his family. Estrangements and lesser disagreements were part of it. His father was an intimidating figure, forceful and proud, yet vulnerable. The way the Darcys lived, what they wore and ate, all of it marked them as far above the Lucases and Bennets of the world. Frederick and his children did not seem to care that his life had been so different from theirs. He could not say the same for the others. Jeffrey remained aloof and suspicious. John was neither friendly nor unfriendly; William decided the most appropriate word to describe him was cautious. It seemed like they would outwardly accept him but inwardly retain some reservations about his identity.

He learnt from Freddie that John might have had expectations which Fitzwilliam's return destroyed. The two of them were taking a walk on the terrace during a brief interlude in the rain one morning, when Freddie said, "Uncle Jeffrey and John assumed John was my uncle's heir. He is the elder nephew and Uncle George's godson, but I never heard any proof of it. I am not sure who else my uncle would leave the estate to. I have my grandfather's, and there are no other men in our generation. But Uncle George never had John here more than the rest of us, and he encouraged him and Uncle Jeffrey to prepare John for a career."

William and Freddie also spoke about books and life in the country. Freddie longed for more diversion than he found at his grandfather's estate and hoped to spend this winter in town.

Freddie said, "I must convince my mother and grandfather that they can do without me for a few months. Thanks to your return, I have an excellent excuse. My father said Uncle George will want all of us there. I do not know why, but I suppose it is because my uncle does not like town. I do not think he has been there during the Season in years." Freddie grinned and began to speak about a trip he, his sister, father, and George had taken to the Lakes several years earlier.

William discovered that Freddie and John did not seem to like each other very much. When the entire family was together, they were polite; when it was just the three of them, some of their mutual antagonism became evident.

They were in the billiards room one afternoon when Freddie asked John, "What will you do now that you can no longer dream of being Uncle George's heir? Choose a career as you ought to have done years ago?"

John's neck snapped between Freddie and William so abruptly that William worried he would injure himself. John walked around the billiards table, studying the position of the balls as he spoke. "You know very well I assist my father so that I can adopt a career in politics. Do not make it sound as though our cousin's miraculous recovery causes me distress. I am very happy for my uncle. *Very*. And for my cousin to have learnt the truth and be returned to us."

Freddie scoffed. "Admit it, you are disappointed. It is perfectly natural. I am sure Fitzwilliam would agree."

John stopped and faced Freddie. His back was to William, so he did not see John's expression. "What use would it be to dwell on disappointment, if I felt any. It is not as if he will suddenly disappear again. I meant what I said. It is your turn."

William was glad when the awkward moment passed. He decided to forget it. After all, he had no part in Freddie and John's relationship.

Later the same day, George said to him, "I am pleased to see you getting along with your cousins. I do not know how much we shall see of Freddie when we are in town, but John will be there. We must go for the Season, although I shall be honest and say I dread it. I have done my best to avoid the hurly-burly and, when I must go to town to take care of my affairs, do so at other times of the year. Your return changes things. I will see you properly introduced and acknowledged. There will be more dinners and balls and evening parties than I can tolerate, but young people like that sort of thing, and it will be a chance for you to make appropriate friends—as you ought to have done since childhood. John can help you understand the social life of a young man in our circle. Help you find your place."

I have wished for someone to show me what it means to be a Darcy. If he thinks John is the one to do it, then I shall follow his lead.

AFTER FREDDIE, Frederick, and Rebecca departed, William spent most of his time with John. William desperately needed companions he could depend on, and he was determined to like and trust John, just as George did.

They were in a small upstairs parlour one evening discussing the possibility of shooting the following morning.

John asked, "You do shoot, do you not? You lived in the country, and I suppose everyone in the country does."

"I do. You spend most of your time in London?"

John shrugged. He sat sideways on a silk wing chair, his legs slung over one of its arms. "I do; I prefer town. The country is boring, unless one happens to be with a large party of friends."

William's brow furrowed, and he stared at John, who, in a moment, laughed, though William thought it sounded a little forced.

John said, "I like to have my little jokes. You will have to get used to it." He drained his wine glass. "We might as well go shooting tomorrow, I suppose."

It was an agreeable outing. The air was crisp, and the grass made cracking noises with each foot fall.

My mind and body are occupied, and there is little need to talk. John did not say much, which suited William. As they walked back to the house, he reflected, *Perhaps I shall find he is more like me than I first thought. It would be good if we could be friends.*

A breeze hit him, and he shivered. The dogs ran around, still full of energy, and barked. It brought a small smile to William's face, and he bent down to scratch two or three of them behind the ears. *Such simple creatures. No one tells you your life has been a lie and you must give up everyone you loved. How I envy you.*

THE FOLLOWING NIGHT, William again remained with John after their fathers had retired. William tried to say good night but George encouraged him to stay.

John suggested billiards. After an hour's play, he sighed and tossed his stick on the table. "I am bored!" He fell into a brown leather armchair and took a long drink of wine. "I wish we could go into Lambton. We could find diversion there. Not as good as what London has to offer, mind you, but it would be better than always being here. But we cannot. My uncle does not like us to seek our amusement in Lambton. He is very proud of the family's reputation, and takes great care to preserve it. We cannot diminish our respectability by…incautious behaviour."

William experienced a momentary curiosity regarding John's meaning, but his thoughts had drifted to pleasant evenings spent with friends in Meryton.

"London will be better," John stated. "Even outside of the Season, there is always something to do."

John gave a nostalgic-sounding speech about what he and his friends did in London, which hinted at what William considered improper behaviour. He squirmed in his seat but tried to keep his expression neutral, particularly as John spoke of women—not ladies, but women.

"And speaking of, err, romance," said John, "was there no lady for whom you felt a particular *tendre*?"

William opened his mouth to mention Elizabeth, but John did not give him an opportunity to respond.

"I hope not, for your sake. Your father has very particular expectations about our friends and especially marriage partners. My father says George is determined to keep you away from the people you knew. This is your life now, we are your family, *et cetera*. He certainly would not let you marry one of them."

With that, John stood and announced that he was going to bed. William followed him out of the room, his thoughts heavy enough to slow his steps.

PERHAPS IT WAS Jeffrey's career that accounted for his speaking as he did the morning of his departure from Pemberley. William knew that politicians were often scrutinised and ridiculed in the newspapers. Whatever the reason, the encounter left him trembling and with a great deal to contemplate.

William met his uncle in the upstairs corridor by chance. Jeffrey's expression immediately put him on his guard. He pressed his heels into the floor to prevent himself from bolting.

"My brother will not speak plainly, but I shall," Jeffrey hissed. "You will be recognised as a Darcy, which is a very great honour. Nothing in your memory has prepared you for this. I can only hope it is somehow inside of you. I will not allow you to disgrace our family name or allow our economic or social position to be marred by any unfortunate connexions to your past. Do not think to hold on to sentimental alliances you had. Do not think I will tolerate anyone from that insignificant place you lived making a claim on you or any other Darcy. There are means to deal with such situations, and I *will not* hesitate to use them."

The last word had scarcely passed Jeffrey's lips before he turned on his heel and marched away. William was left shaking, sweat running down his back, and feeling like he was going to be sick. He returned to his room, dismissed his valet, and sat with his head between his hands.

William had heard much to dishearten him since meeting his family. George, Rebecca, and John had all at least implied that he was expected to marry very well; they would not approve of Elizabeth. Most distressing of all was what Jeffrey said. William did not know exactly what his uncle would do to the Lucases or Bennets or anyone else, but the threat had been obvious. Did George feel the same way? Could William risk the well-being of his loved ones by testing them?

That evening, when it was just him and his father again, George's words added to the weight William felt on his chest and shoulders.

"It was gratifying to see everyone and have them come to welcome you home. For the first time in many years, our family is complete. Only your mo—"

William assumed he was going to say that only his mother was missing.

George lifted a glass of crimson wine, then returned it to the table untasted. "Family is very important to me. We have a great deal to be proud of. Caring for one another, acting in unison, and in the best interest of the Darcys, doing good for the world around us because we have been granted so much—all of it is important.

"The Darcys are an ancient family. You have seen that yourself. Pemberley is the work of generations. We are stewards of it, you and I. Not just for our own well-being. We must always remember those who depend upon our prosperity. Caring for them is our duty, just as they owe us their hard work. Maintaining the family's reputation is the responsibility of all Darcys; keeping Pemberley prosperous is that of the few, the ones chosen to be master by virtue of their birth. To share it with you, with my son when I thought for so long... I am very grateful."

George had never spoken so plainly about his happiness at Fitzwilliam's recovery. Yet, underlying his present joy was sorrow.

Twenty-two, almost twenty-three years. That is a very long time to grieve. And it was because of me.

William walked around his bedchamber that night. He did not know why, but he had a sudden memory from his childhood in Shropshire and now could not stop thinking about it.

When all the while, I was the son of a wealthy gentleman. I should have been the customer, not the servant! His rightful life and the opportunities it afforded had all been stolen from him. He should have gone to school and university, travelled, experienced the best of everything and *belonged.* He could look at George, Jeffrey, or his cousins and see he was of the same blood as them, the same family. He had never had that feeling with the Lucases, as much as he had loved them and believed them to be his kin.

With my father, with this family, I can do so much. With what they have—Pemberley, Jeffrey in Parliament, Frederick and his law practice—they do so much good for the world. I am part of it. By comparison, the life of William Lucas seemed trivial.

"It was all a lie. The Lucases knew it was." If he had known, he could have worked to discover his true identity and reunited with George sooner.

As he looked into the night, the thought crept into his mind that if he had always been Fitzwilliam Darcy, he likely never would have met Elizabeth, let alone considered marrying her. To even have such a thought robbed him of part of his heart.

I was not always Fitzwilliam Darcy. I was, but I did not know it. Surely, that makes all the difference. I must write. I wish to. I miss— No. I cannot give in to that feeling, not if...

He sighed and pressed his eyes closed, hoping the resulting darkness brought stillness to his mind.

His eyes flew open, and he demanded of the black void outside his window, "Why has this happened? It is not fair to me or Lizzy. I did not even have a chance to say goodbye to her or Charlotte."

He began to pace, his footsteps muffled by the thick carpet. *The truth has come out. Some have gained by it, some have lost by it, and I am in the middle. I cannot possibly make everyone happy. No matter what I do, someone will suffer. No matter what I do, I shall suffer.*

He stopped moving and took three slow, deep breaths. His agitation eased. He sat by the fire and watched the flames dance for half an hour. He did not know how to reconcile his two halves, yet to select one, forever turning his back on the other, seemed impossible. Yet, something had to change; he would go mad if he continued on in this way.

I cannot be forever thinking about myself as William Lucas, who is a person who never existed. It is time to put him aside and accept that I must live as Fitzwilliam Darcy. As for those people I left behind... He ran a hand over his mouth. *Time will help me understand how to act. It is not so long since Frederick found me. Three weeks or thereabouts? Not long at all.*

In the early hours of the thirteenth of November, he penned a note to Sir William. After a few hours of repose, he told Quinn, his valet, to see that it was sent and asked for his discretion.

That task accomplished, Fitzwilliam Darcy joined his father for their morning ride.

CHAPTER 10

"KITTY, LYDIA, TAKE YOUR BOOKS AND GO ELSEWHERE," MRS Bennet ordered. "I want a word alone with your sister."

Elizabeth lowered her chin and allowed her eyes to close. She was sitting in the small back parlour with her sisters, attempting to read. It was a week after Sir William's return.

As the girls left the room, Lydia complained, "Why do we have to be inconvenienced because Lizzy did something awful to William!"

Elizabeth's nails dug into her palms and heat flushed through her body. She wanted to grab Lydia by the shoulders, shake her, and yell that *she* had not done anything to William; other people had. Sir William and Lady Lucas had kept the truth from him, and now who knew what the Darcys were doing to him!

With William's continued absence and the Lucases' inability to say when he would return, neighbourhood gossips had decided that Elizabeth and William's 'understanding' had ended, although no one could say for certain who had instigated the breach. The gossips had it that William Lucas stayed away until tempers calmed and the couple could meet again as nothing more than friends.

Mrs Bennet sat beside Elizabeth on the faded settee and tugged at her woollen wrap. "I was with Lady Lucas—"

Oh no.

"She still does not know when William will return. She acted very peculiar when I asked her what news she had from him. Lady Lucas said she was thinking of postponing, perhaps even cancelling, his birthday dinner! His *birthday*, Lizzy!"

Elizabeth would not speak. *She has not asked me a question, and until she does—*

"You *have* argued with him, have you not?"

Elizabeth clenched her teeth together until her jaw hurt. Mrs Bennet had hinted at this question before but never asked outright. Elizabeth had always been happy that her family loved William so well, but now she wished they loved her more and him less.

"It is the only explanation," Mrs Bennet went on. "William is the kindest, most loyal young gentleman anyone could imagine."

William was. Is Fitzwilliam? William's silence was far more distressing than anything her mother or sister could say. It was worse than everything her neighbours did, or how Charlotte avoided her or would only speak about Captain Farnon, or how Sir William patted her hand and shook his head. Elizabeth longed to go to her room, crawl under a blanket, and hide.

"I did not argue with him."

Mrs Bennet huffed. "Then why is he avoiding you? Has he changed his mind about marrying you? What man wants a wife who will always argue with him or tease him to death like you do?"

Tears burned Elizabeth's eyes as her mother continued along this vein for a minute.

"Now what will become of you? What shall become of me and your sisters when your father dies? You will become a spinster, and I shall not be able to keep you. You are not beautiful and gentle like Jane. Oh, Lizzy!"

Elizabeth could bear no more and leapt to her feet. "I have *not* argued with William or done anythi—"

The effort of not weeping or screaming robbed her of her voice. Without asking for permission to leave the room, she did, and headed straight to her father's book room. She entered without knocking.

"Whatever is wrong?" Mr Bennet went to her, took her elbow, and directed her to a chair. He sat on a footstool.

"I cannot bear this any longer," Elizabeth cried. "Everywhere I go, people stare and talk about me and William. It is insupportable! You do not know what it is like. No one looks at you and talks about you behind your back. No one blames you for William's absence."

He patted her hand. "Our neighbours may be fools, but they do not believe you are responsible for it."

"But they do! Am I to simply ignore it when someone says William left because he changed his mind and no longer wants to marry me?" She swallowed a sob.

"Who would say such nonsense?"

"My mother said it not ten minutes ago!"

He rubbed his forehead. "You cannot treat what your mother says about William seriously."

Elizabeth's cheeks burned. "Serious or not, I still hear it. When we visit our neighbours, I must listen to the questions and speculation, act as though nothing is wrong, and find a polite way to answer, one that does not betray what I really feel. Even Jane asks about him! She is gentle and kind, but she knows something is amiss."

"My dear girl."

He stroked her hand and sighed as she recounted her recent conversation with Mrs Bennet.

"What would you have me do? I have thought about ignoring George Darcy's wishes and sharing the truth with everyone, but I am afraid it would make him less amenable to allowing William to visit."

Elizabeth looked into his eyes and saw what he did not say. *He believes Mr Darcy will keep William away from us.* She sniffed and pressed her lips together for a moment before begging, "Speak to my mother. Make her stop asking me about William."

He nodded. "It does not mean we shall have peace."

"Do not make me go to Aunt Philips's tonight."

Again, he nodded. "I shall tell your mother you have a headache."

A tear ran down her cheek, and he wiped it away. When they stood, he pulled her into his arms and kissed the top of her head before sending her to her room.

ALONE, Elizabeth threw herself on her bed. She buried her face in her pillow to muffle the sound of her sobs.

How could she endure weeks more of this? Her heart broke whenever she thought about William's silence. In her hopeful moments, Elizabeth imagined William writing to Sir William and including a message to her. Every time she saw him, Elizabeth experienced a moment of expectation; *this* time he would remember. But when Sir William said nothing beyond the ordinary, Elizabeth's spirits sank. She could not ask him, because she saw how affected he and Lady Lucas were by the separation.

It is less than a fortnight since he left.

She had had a good life. It was not perfect, but she had William, and they had planned such a wonderful, happy future together. Now it was slipping through her fingers, and she could do nothing to stop it.

EVER SINCE LEARNING that Frederick Darcy was returning to Hertfordshire, Elizabeth had been in a dither. She hardly ate or slept, took long walks during the day, and paced her room at night. She longed for news of—and from—William. Her anticipation was diminished after speaking with her father the morning Frederick and Rebecca Darcy were expected.

"Darcy does not know about your understanding with

William. I see no benefit to talking about it now unless William has told his new family."

Elizabeth's body tensed. Part of her wished he would just say that he expected George Darcy would not consent to a marriage between her and William or that William no longer had any interest in marrying her. Once upon a time, she had been a very good prospect for him; now, his position in life was far above hers. If her father said such a thing, she would tell him he was wrong or that she had no interest in aligning herself with someone like George Darcy, who was too proud to accept her. Elizabeth did not know which argument would come out of her mouth if given the opportunity. Adding to her anger was that her mother and sisters, and even their neighbours, spoke about William less and less.

Mr Bennet made her promise not to say anything to either Darcy, then sent her on her way. She went for a long walk, hoping the autumn air would cool her temper. Her steps were fast, and she took little time to notice her surroundings until she stopped to admire a quartet of cows in a field. They ambled around, dropping their heads every so often as they searched for something to eat. The peaceful scene succeeded in calming her.

It is as though everyone is forgetting him. Except when they decide to tease me about him. It is either too much or too little with me! She chuckled and took a deep breath, the faint scent of manure and damp earth filling her nostrils. *I suppose too little is better under the circumstances. It makes it easier to bear being at Longbourn.*

Mr and Miss Darcy will come, spend two days with us, then depart. Mr Darcy will tell Papa about his cousin's plans and talk to him about William. Once they are gone, Papa will tell me. What cannot be cured, must be endured. I cannot change this situation. Thus, I shall find a way to bear it.

When the Darcys arrived that afternoon, she studied them to better understand the sort of people William was now among and for any hint that they knew what she and William had meant to each other. Miss Darcy resembled her father, although her dark hair was accompanied by bright blue eyes, rather than Mr Darcy's brown ones. When Elizabeth had first met Mr Darcy, she thought there was a resemblance between him and William; knowing Mr and Miss Darcy were his cousins, she could appreciate the sameness of their features and their tall, lean forms.

After dinner, Elizabeth sought a moment to speak to Miss Darcy alone, but none arose. Jane, Kitty, and Lydia asked Miss Darcy about living in London. Elizabeth wondered why she did not mention the sensation of her newfound cousin, but realised Mr Darcy must have cautioned his daughter against it. It was a shame, as it meant Elizabeth retired without so much as hearing William's name.

ELIZABETH INVITED Miss Darcy to take a turn in the garden before breakfast the next day; she readily agreed. It was mild, considering the time of year, and the sun was bright, making it pleasant. They talked about indifferent matters for ten minutes, before Elizabeth mentioned William, which she thought demonstrated remarkable restraint.

"I understand you recently met a new family member."

Miss Darcy stopped and regarded Elizabeth, her lips forming an 'o'. Her brow creased beneath the rim of her velvet hat.

Elizabeth smiled, linked her arm with Miss Darcy's, and directed their steps towards a wider path with few trees so that they could take advantage of the sun's feeble heat. "I know about your cousin Fitzwilliam, whom I knew as William Lucas."

"My father said only your father and the Lucases knew, and I should not mention him."

Elizabeth shrugged. "I learnt the truth, but no one else has. He is well?"

"I believe so, but since I know him so little, I cannot really judge."

"I appreciate the nuance of your answer. Most people would simply say yes and be done with it."

Miss Darcy chuckled. "True. My father has taught me to take more care with my words." She sighed. "I do sympathise with my cousin. I cannot imagine what he is thinking or feeling. To discover you are not who you always thought you were! We are all overjoyed, of course. Shocked too. It is like something from a novel!"

A horror-filled one, Elizabeth thought.

"My father told me about Fitzwilliam when I was fourteen or fifteen. I had asked why my uncle was always so sombre. My father said Uncle George never recovered from his grief. He is such a good man, so kind and generous, and I pray he will find happiness now, and peace."

Elizabeth directed them towards a stone bench. Her voice quivered as she asked, "Peace?"

"Not knowing exactly what happened to his son has haunted him. He still cannot know what Fitzwilliam endured when he was with the abductors."

Now sitting, Elizabeth tilted her head away from Miss Darcy and closed her eyes. She plucked at the fingers of her gloves and willed her stomach to stop somersaulting. "I have not heard you or your father mention Mrs Darcy, Wi-Fitzwilliam's mother."

"Lady Anne," Miss Darcy said. "Her father was Lord Romsley. Her brother is earl now. The heirs to Pemberley *always* make excellent matches. You know the sort of thing I mean. Lady Anne offered wealth and connexions. She died two years after Fitzwilliam was taken. I can only imagine how she suffered, believing her son was dead."

Elizabeth had a vague memory of her father mentioning some of this when he first told her the truth about William's past. *His mother was rich and titled. Two things I am not.* A sharp blade pierced her breast, killing a portion of her remaining hope.

They sat in silence for a moment before Elizabeth shook off her reflections and attended to her guest. She asked about books, feeling it was a topic she could participate in without much effort. By the time they returned indoors, Elizabeth had determined that Miss Darcy seemed very nice and that it was pleasant to be with someone who did not know about her and William; she did not look at Elizabeth with pity or suspicion.

ELIZABETH SPENT a considerable amount of time with Miss Darcy during her short visit. She asked about William's life. It was not always easy for Elizabeth to talk about him, but in return for talking about 'William Lucas', her visitor told her about the Darcys, which Elizabeth claimed would help her to understand what his life would now be like. They joked about it being a fair exchange. Elizabeth saw no humour in it, but she hid it as best she could.

Miss Darcy spent time with Jane, Mary, Kitty, and Lydia, too, but privately admitted to Elizabeth that there was only so much she could talk about fashion or living in town, "without pulling my hair out at the roots. My mother would disown me if I did. How could I ever hope to marry if I were half bald? Not that I am in a rush to marry. I am determined that only true love will tempt me to resign my name."

Elizabeth would not say she knew Miss Darcy intimately by the time she and her father left Longbourn, but Elizabeth liked her. *If I were not so miserable, I would rejoice to have a new friend,* she thought as she brushed her hair before bed one night. *I might like her even better if her name were not Darcy.*

She looked at her reflection in the mirror and was not pleased with what she saw. *Well, if I am unhappy, I believe I have a right to be. But I cannot dislike Miss Darcy or her father, regardless of their name. They are simply too nice.* She smiled to herself as she recalled playing riddles after dinner. Miss Darcy was quick witted, a trait Elizabeth appreciated.

Her thoughts turned dark again. *Frederick Darcy is just Mr George Darcy's cousin. He is the sort of person Papa met at school, the ones who were unkind to him because he lacked their wealth and consequence. He would hate to connect himself to people like the Lucases or Bennets, even through friendship. Mr George Darcy would never allow his son to marry the poor daughter of a country gentleman.*

He has changed my William already, convinced him that we are beneath his notice. My William would have written to me or Papa or Sir William by now. Was it easy to give us up after seeing how rich his rightful family is?

When such thoughts entered her mind, Elizabeth berated herself. William had not been gone a month, and while his silence was difficult, she vowed not to condemn him for it yet.

CHAPTER 11

As Fitzwilliam prepared for his morning ride, he remembered the date. It was the fourteenth of November, the day he knew as his birthday. *I have lost everything I knew about myself—my name, how I expected to live, the date of my birth.* He would have to peek at the family Bible his father had shown him to discover the correct date.

They rode to the top of a small hill that afforded them a view of the lands in all four directions.

George said, "It is a glorious morning."

Fitzwilliam agreed. The sky was uncommonly clear and the temperature not very cold. Before they climbed the hill, a gentle hint of wood smoke competed with that of horse and leather, but it was gone by the time they reached the top. Seeking an escape from the silence, he asked, "Are the winters severe here?"

"Some years. During difficult times, it is our responsibility to secure the well-being of our tenants and needy families in the neighbourhood."

"I shall help in any way I can."

George smiled and inclined his head. "Derbyshire is a beautiful place. We are fortunate to call a piece of it our home. You are heir to a great estate. I was younger than you are now when my father died. While it was difficult, I was prepared. You have learnt well while you were…away. Now you can take back the life that was stolen from you, from us."

They sat in silence for a minute or two. Fitzwilliam watched the mist from his and his horse's breath drift upward, slowly dissipating, and slipped into a trance. His father's voice startled him.

"So much has changed for you. I do not think I considered it as much as I should have. I was overjoyed, but for you…" His voice sounded strained, almost as if he had to force the words from his mouth. "I hope you begin to feel that this is where you belong."

Fitzwilliam did not know what to say. Elizabeth's name was on the tip of his tongue, but Jeffrey's voice in his head strangled him. John and Rebecca made him feel that his father would not like Elizabeth as a daughter-in-law—even George had done so— but it was his uncle's threats that caused him the most alarm.

He ran a finger inside his collar. "I do. I am glad to know the truth."

He saw George nod, a small smile on his face, and knew that his opportunity to talk about Elizabeth was gone.

THAT NIGHT, he dreamt of Elizabeth.

Jane and Charlotte were about fifty feet ahead of him and Elizabeth on the road from Longbourn to Lucas Lodge. His stomach was full as though he had just stood from the breakfast table, although the sun showed it was past noon. He was relieved to discover that he held a muffin. The walk was long, and he would need a snack. He was happy that Elizabeth was beside him; he enjoyed every minute he spent with her.

He heard birds singing and knew they were commenting

on the fineness of the weather. He lifted his face to the bright summer sun.

She said, "I am glad for the breeze. It would be horribly hot without it."

William bit into the muffin.

"You have been so quiet since Papa spoke about university this morning. Is that what is causing this introspection?"

He chewed and nodded.

"Would you like to go?"

The trees that lined the side of the road were thick with leaves. At their bases were grasses and white and yellow flowers. A butterfly passed them, dropped a bouquet into Elizabeth's hands, then floated away.

After swallowing the last of the muffin, he said, "Yes. Maybe. There is no question of it, so it does not signify what I feel. I believe my father likes the idea of sending his son to Oxford but does not like it as a practical matter. My mother would hate to see me go. Besides, I am needed at home to help my father with the estate, and the expense would be too much."

William felt her bump into his side. When he looked down at her, he saw that, like the butterfly, she floated above the ground. She emitted sunlight and her hair fell around her shoulders; the bonnet she had been wearing had disappeared, and he knew Mrs Bennet would scold her for losing it, but he preferred to see her this way.

She said, "I am sorry. You would do so well at university, and I know you would like it."

He would like to learn from the scholars but suspected he would otherwise hate it. Although he had not spoken aloud, she answered as though he had. "Because of what Papa has said about his time at Oxford. My father does not have a high opinion of those who belong to the ton. *There are very good people in it, no doubt, but he met so many who dismissed him because of his situation in life. He had that one friend he met at school—before university. I cannot remember the name.*

"He went to Cambridge. His family was high, not him. I will meet him one day. So will you."

Suddenly, they were standing by a fence, watching several sheep, a horse, and two cattle graze in a field. He took a deep breath and could almost taste the fresh summer grass the animals were eating. He was hungry again and took a bite of the apple that appeared in his hand.

Elizabeth said, "I maintain that the well-born show the same variety as the rest of us. Some of them are excellent people, while you would not want to know others. You must have seen that when you lived in Shropshire, even though you were so young."

William shook his head. He was not supposed to remember Shropshire, but then, for just a moment, he was at the inn again, seeing a quick succession of images—of people, rich and poor, being rude or kind to Mr and Mrs Lucas. He wondered why he did not call them Father and Mother, but they wore signs around their necks that proclaimed their names, and he was somehow bound to use them.

Back in Hertfordshire with his dearest friend, whose hand he held, although he usually would not dare to be so bold, he said, "Could you truly imagine me as one of those young men? If they discovered my past and that I actually worked at an inn..."

"You would have to choose your friends wisely. Find someone like Papa's old friend. If I were there, I would make sure no one treated you poorly or like you are not just as good as they are." She held up her fists in a fighting stance and grinned.

He guffawed. "They would laugh at you, make you miserable."

Fitzwilliam sat up and panted. The dream had been so vivid, almost like he was living the day again, for it had been based on a real memory. Mr Bennet's friend had been Frederick, though he had not made the association before. He climbed out of bed and went to poke the fire before falling into a chair. He had been worried about his treatment at the hands of people like those he now called family.

"Another time, perhaps in fifty years, I might laugh at the irony. For now, I..."

He closed his eyes and prayed for sleep to rob him of his gloomy reflections.

GEORGE'S LONDON ATTORNEY, Mr Pedlar, arrived as scheduled two days later and was suitably surprised by Fitzwilliam's appearance. Long into the evening, his father, Mr Pedlar, and Fitzwilliam discussed the circumstances of Fitzwilliam's life and return to the Darcys. The conversation continued the next day, as George sought the man's advice on a number of matters, from those related to money to the best way to inform society that Fitzwilliam had been discovered alive.

Fitzwilliam did not like the solicitor, whose squint-eyed stare gave the impression that he disliked and distrusted him; he escaped their company as much as possible. During one of those times, he studied the family Bible and its record of generations of births, deaths, and marriages. He discovered that he would become twenty-five at the start of July; it meant he was about four months older than he had always believed.

Mr Pedlar thinks I am not George Darcy's son. Fitzwilliam walked around the library, pulling the occasional book from a shelf to look inside of it before returning it to its place. *Either my father will remain firm in his belief that I am, or he will not. Either way, in time, I will accustom myself to the change in my life. I shall no longer feel I have lost so much; I shall, instead, think of what I have gained. The Lucases must feel they lost something. And my Lizzy. We have lost the future we dreamt of having. Even if George would accept the match, everything Lizzy and I imagined for our future is changed. We could never be Mr and Mrs Lucas and live in our little corner of Hertfordshire.*

His life was in Derbyshire now, as George Darcy's son and heir to Pemberley, and Elizabeth would have to accept that. *Would she even want this life?* In his soul, he knew this was where he belonged. He still had ties to Hertfordshire, which he could feel tugging him towards his old home. He hated to admit it, but they did not seem quite as tight as they had during those first days after Sir William left.

Fitzwilliam dropped into a chair and let his head rest against the back. *It is just that I have grown used to the sensation of being pulled in two different directions.* He turned to look out of a nearby window. Rain hit the glass; the staccato sound was oddly calming. He longed for a way to make everyone happy— from the Lucases and Elizabeth, to George and the rest of the

Darcys—but knew it was impossible. Someone would suffer no matter what he did. The thought left him lonely.

Two days after he arrived, the solicitor departed.

"Well, that is over with." George clapped Fitzwilliam on the back. "It was necessary, but not pleasant, eh? Pedlar has an excellent legal mind, and we settled a number of important matters. I shall explain it all later. I must meet with Potter this morning; he has been clamouring for my attention for days." Mr Potter was the steward. "But first, shall we go for a ride? Potter will not be here for another hour or so. If he gets here before we return, Mrs Reynolds will give him tea."

Fitzwilliam agreed. When they made their way to the stables a short time later, he was surprised when the stable master brought a new horse, a great grey stallion, for him to ride.

George cried, "Excellent! He has rested enough after his journey?"

Mausdley nodded. "He is a fine animal and will do well for the young gentleman."

Fitzwilliam walked around the beast, running his hand along his strong, smooth body. He had never seen a finer horse, and this one was *his*. Could it be?

After they had been riding for several minutes, his father said, "You must see what you think of him. He comes from a farm about twenty miles from here. You need your own horse, one selected for you and befitting your station. If you do not like this one, think nothing of saying so; we shall try another."

Fitzwilliam nodded. His mind screamed that it was impossible not to like the creature. If anything, he felt the horse was too good for him. Yet, this was what he *should* expect, and the cheapness of his life as William Lucas was distasteful. Thinking in this way disturbed him, and with an effort, he pushed all such reflections from his mind and enjoyed the ride and his beautiful surroundings.

THAT AFTERNOON, Fitzwilliam and his father sat by the fire in the library and reviewed the plans George had decided on. They would go to London before Christmas, at which time they would announce Fitzwilliam's return. There was no avoiding the fact that people would be very interested in their tale, but, his father said, they would try to see that as little fuss as possible was made of it.

His father said, "I wrote to tell my cousin Sophia, of course. She holds a ball on Twelfth Night every year, and we shall attend. The whole family will, I trust. Sophia always invites an enormous number of people, and we will introduce you to our circle then."

The thought of a large ball, at which he would be surrounded by strangers who wished to meet him, was not something Fitzwilliam could anticipate with any equanimity.

George also spoke about clubs they would visit and friends and acquaintances of his he wished to introduce to his son. "They wield a great deal of influence, and I intend to ensure they use it to ease your entry into society. They are from my generation, so not people who will be your companions, although some of their children may be. I am sure many of them even have daughters grown up; I cannot say I keep track of the goings on of their offspring. When the time comes, we might be able to arrange a favourable alliance for you from among them."

Fitzwilliam accepted that George had a right to approve of his choice of wife, just as he had acknowledged that Sir William and Lady Lucas did. There had never been any question of them accepting Elizabeth, of course. *For people like the Darcys, with great fortunes to consider, I suppose the matter of choosing appropriate spouses becomes even more vital.*

Mrs Gardiner, Elizabeth's aunt who lived in London, often wrote to her and Jane about the latest scandals she had heard about; many of them involved misalliances or affairs. He, Elizabeth, Charlotte, and Jane had laughed about how important it seemed to Mrs Gardiner or the people spreading the news. As he learnt more about the Darcys, he thought he understood the concern. This was driven home to him after his father received papers from Mr Pedlar regarding the arrangements they had made, from changing George's will, settling certain properties on Fitzwilliam immediately, and determining his allowance, which was staggering by the standards of William Lucas. He had known that his father was rich, but seeing the details of his estate laid out before him, Fitzwilliam was dumbfounded. Pemberley brought in a clear ten thousand a year—ten times what Sir William's estate did—and that was not taking into account the wealth he saw all around him, such as in the paintings and silver.

One morning, as he was changing after coming in from a ride, his father came to his room. Fitzwilliam dismissed Quinn, and as soon as the door closed behind him, George spoke.

"You are happy with him?"

"Yes." Fitzwilliam had dismissed the idea of needing a valet when Quinn first appeared, but he had quickly become accustomed to it. His wardrobe had grown since he came to Pemberley, which he suspected was Quinn's doing. In addition to new linen, several of George's older waistcoats and jackets had been altered to fit him. He had been dismayed at first to realise that some of the clothing he had brought with him from Meryton had disappeared, but seeing how much finer his new things were, he understood that the change was necessary so that he did not shame his family. Running his hands down the front of the blue jacket he wore, he appreciated the soft, thick wool of the fabric.

"Good," said his father. "I was remembering that we need to have your rooms renovated while we are in town. We have not talked about it since you first returned, but since we depart soon, decisions should be made. Mrs Reynolds will be able to help. She might have illustrations and samples you can look through now; she certainly knows the warehouses we use to order furnishings. We can visit them once we are in London."

Fitzwilliam nodded. "Of course. I shall talk to her this morning." He did not feel he needed to change the look of his apartment, but since his father made a point of it, he would not argue.

As they walked to the breakfast room, George chatted about other things they would do in town, such as purchasing new clothes for Fitzwilliam and ordering a curricle for him. He spoke a little too quickly, his voice taking on an almost frantic quality, as Fitzwilliam noticed it sometimes did. It did not surprise him when, after breakfast, as they sat in the library to read—a room and activity they both favoured—he caught George looking at him in such a way that would make one think he had just received bad news. He was ashen, and Fitzwilliam could almost feel how tight the muscles in his father's neck and shoulders must be as he held himself so rigidly. Fitzwilliam did not know exactly what was behind it, but at times he wondered if, in truth, George doubted whether Fitzwilliam really was his son. For the most part, he did not think so. There were more occasions when he believed his father was happy than when he appeared distressed.

But, like me, he does not show his emotions easily, Fitzwilliam reflected. *I begin to understand why Lizzy teased me about it being so difficult to know what I was thinking.*

Finding it a struggle to concentrate on his book—a tome of indifferent poetry—Fitzwilliam considered their upcoming departure for town. He was surprised to find that the more he thought about it, the less he dreaded the coming months. London offered many diversions. While he would not like being surrounded by so many new people, there would be the theatre and lectures and races and much more—activities the Lucases and Bennets were never able to enjoy. It felt almost as though he was leaving them behind. As a Darcy, so much was his for the taking. He had a right to all of it. He occupied a different sphere of society now. He and Elizabeth had laughed at such distinctions of rank, but that was when he did not really understand the differences between the Darcys and Lucases and Bennets of the world.

That night, like many others, his thoughts drifted to Hertford-shire as he lay between the fine linens on his spacious bed. His heart ached for the people he had left behind. Knowing he was telling himself that which made his life easier, he thought, *My father wants me to embrace* this *life, not retain what I had. Given everything my abduction cost him, how can I do that which I know will make him unhappy? Yet, I do long to see Lizzy and the others again.*

An image of Jeffrey as he had looked during their encounter just before he left Pemberley popped into Fitzwilliam's mind, and his eyes flew open. He could not catch his breath. Sitting up, he blinked until he saw the shadows created by the dim light in his room. When his chest continued heaving, he rolled out of bed and went to sit on the floor by the fire.

If seeing Sir William, Lady Lucas, Charlotte, Mr Bennet, Elizabeth, and all of her sisters meant incurring Jeffrey Darcy's wrath—which Fitzwilliam suspected he would aim at them rather than him—then he would do better to stay away.

CHAPTER 12

ONE FINE MORNING IN MID-NOVEMBER, ELIZABETH RETURNED from a solitary walk to discover Sir William had just arrived and was with her father in his book room; she was told to join them. *William! It must be about him.*

She tore off her coat, hat, and gloves and rushed to the gentlemen. As soon as Elizabeth finished saying good morning to Sir William, he cried, "A letter, Miss Elizabeth! You must read it."

He thrust a sheet of paper into her hands, and she dropped into her usual chair. Hope became dismay as she read the curt missive.

Pemberley House, Derbyshire
13 November 1811

My dear sir,

Rest assured I am well. Everyone has been very kind and is doing everything possible to make me welcome. I have met most of the family. Arrangements for the future are not yet decided upon. I had hoped to offer some information in that regard. I shall be in town at least part of the winter, but I do not know when I shall be able to go to

Hertfordshire. I find there is a great deal to learn and much to occupy me. My time is not my own.

Please accept my wishes for your good health and that of all my friends with you. I pray our separation will not be of long duration.

FD

"Do you see, Miss Elizabeth? He has not forgotten us! Not that I ever thought he had. He is busy meeting new people and learning his way."

Elizabeth's chin almost touched her chest, and she remained silent. She could not share his enthusiasm. She interpreted the letter to say that George Darcy did not want his son to visit his old friends. She wondered whether William had even told his father about her.

Sir William said, "We must give him time to know his family. Oh, but it is a great deal for him to take in! Pemberley is a grand place. Why, learning to find your way around it without getting lost would take a month."

As he spoke, Elizabeth stood and walked to the opposite corner of the room, picking up and playing with the books her father had left on a side table.

"It reassures me," Sir William said.

So he says, but his tone does not match his words! Elizabeth dropped a book and it hit the floor with a loud thud. "I am happy for you. Pray excuse me."

She bolted from the room and ignored her father when he called after her.

AS NOVEMBER WORE ON, there was renewed interest in William's whereabouts and his peculiar behaviour. The excuses for his absence grew thin, even when Elizabeth and her father began to say they had heard from him. She was desperate for the truth to come out, but it would not happen for some weeks still. When it did, people might pity her, but it would be better than the suspicion she currently confronted.

The Gardiners were coming to Longbourn for Christmas as was their habit, and Elizabeth would ask her aunt about returning to town with them. She wished she had somewhere else to go, but an aunt who was kind if not always sympathetic was better than remaining at home.

Mrs Bennet was on the verge of making herself sick with nerves over William's absence. "He is never coming back," she lamented daily. She accused Elizabeth and Mr Bennet of having secrets, along with the Lucases, and finding no other likely explanation, continued to assume it had something to do with Elizabeth. "Why has William abandoned us? Oh, what is to become of us?"

The new Netherfield tenants arrived, and everyone, Elizabeth included, agreed that they were a charming couple and would be an asset to local society. Jane soon befriended Mrs Linnington, and Elizabeth was pleased for her. *It is not as if I am such good company these days. Everything is so unsettled, and I hate having these secrets lurking around me, ready to explode.*

She tried to talk to Charlotte about William, but Charlotte's attention was fixed on preparing for Captain Farnon's impending arrival.

"You do not know what it is like at Lucas Lodge, Lizzy," Charlotte said. "My parents take this very hard, and they expect me to console them—when they are not so occupied with each other that they forget I am there. I long for a home of my own. Marriage to Captain Farnon would provide me with security, and I like him. I may even grow to love him. I pray what has happened will not change his opinion of me."

Elizabeth did not understand her and did not try to. *Perhaps in five or six years, I, too, shall be content to marry a decent man who can offer me security. But I, who expected to marry for love... No, I cannot imagine it.*

She received a letter from Rebecca Darcy in the second week of December. She hesitated before opening it, trying to decide if she hoped it mentioned William. *Regardless of what Mr George Darcy expects from him, he has agreed to pretend we do not exist. I should not want to know how he is faring, and yet, I do.*

It was bitterly cold and icy outside, so Elizabeth curled up on the window seat in her room, wrapped herself in two thick shawls, and read the letter. It was pleasant, but only one part of it drew her attention enough that she reread it several times.

A cousin of Fitzwilliam's father, Lady Sophia Newberry, has a ball on Twelfth Night every year, and we shall attend. It will mark Fitzwilliam's first appearance in society. I am very excited and shall order a new gown this week. I hope that my cousin is not anxious about it.

Elizabeth sighed as she folded the paper. She looked outside and pulled her shawls closer. She could almost taste the damp weather, and knew she should move away from the window, but it would require more energy than she had. She thought about William being in London and her hope to spend some months with the Gardiners.

"I need not worry about seeing him if I go. The Gardiners and the Darcys occupy very different circles."

She sighed, rested her head against the glass, and let her eyes drift closed.

THE FOLLOWING DAY, the Bennets attended a party at Netherfield and were introduced to Mrs Linnington's brother. Mr Hawarden was handsome, young, and single. Although he was polite to Mr and Mrs Bennet, Elizabeth, and Mary, he was clearly struck by Jane's beauty.

After several minutes, Elizabeth and Mr Bennet wandered over to greet the other guests. The Lucases were standing with

Mrs Long and Captain Farnon. Elizabeth caught Charlotte's eye, but Charlotte immediately turned her attention back to the captain. Elizabeth was not sure if she should feel insulted or laugh.

Mr Bennet asked, "What do you think of Mr Hawarden? He has your mother captivated already. And Jane, if I am not mistaken."

"He has attached himself to the prettiest lady in the room. At least we know his eyesight is good."

Mr Bennet narrowed his eyes, and she chuckled. Her tone had been more sarcastic than she intended, and she hoped to make it sound like she had been joking.

"If Mrs Linnington's brother is like her, he will be a pleasant addition to the neighbourhood while he is here. The distraction is good for everyone. Even you."

Elizabeth had no wish to argue with her father and nodded towards Captain Farnon. "There is another gentleman whose arrival has created happiness."

"I would say I am glad for Charlotte, but I am afraid of sounding too much like a matchmaking mama."

Elizabeth smiled at his jest. "Let us hope for Charlotte's sake that he comes to the point. Do you think the…situation will make him question his attachment? Mrs Long's tongue has been busy with it."

Mr Bennet lifted one shoulder. "Time will tell. Come, dear girl, let us try to be cheerful, for everyone else, if not ourselves."

CAPTAIN FARNON and Charlotte liked each other as much as they had upon their first meeting, and the neighbourhood began anticipating an announcement from Lucas Lodge, though many suspected Charlotte would want to wait until William was home. Elizabeth was asked about him ever more frequently.

Another couple also interested the local gossips: Jane and Mr Hawarden. By the time they had met at three or four parties, his preference for Jane was plain to see, and Elizabeth knew her sister had no objection.

"He is just what a young man ought to be," she told Elizabeth one morning when they were sewing in the parlour. "He is kind and sensible. His manners are so happy. He has been very attentive. I do not deserve it. I certainly did not expect it."

"Did you not? You are by far the most beautiful lady in the neighbourhood, and the sweetest."

Jane rolled her eyes. "You do not know me at all, Elizabeth Bennet, if you think I would have expected such a thing." She sighed and said, "I believe he is the most estimable young man I have ever met."

With difficulty, Elizabeth swallowed her bitterness. She wanted to say that Mr Hawarden was nothing to William, but that would not be fair to Mr Hawarden or Jane. She wanted Jane to be happy, and if Mr Hawarden was the man who could bring joy to her sister's life, then she would welcome him. "I am pleased for you."

"I could wish that my mother was not so enthusiastic in her expressions."

Elizabeth felt a spark of amusement and chuckled. Imitating her mother's high-pitched voice, she said, "Smile, Jane! No, Jane, not the yellow gown, the *blue* one! Stand straight! A gentleman can go a long time without seeing a figure such as yours."

Jane covered her mouth with one hand and pressed the other into her stomach as she laughed. "Oh Lizzy, stop! We should not make fun of Mama."

Elizabeth cleared her throat but could not help grinning. It felt good. "You are right, but I mean no harm."

Jane clasped Elizabeth's hand. "William will be home soon. I know that the separation has been difficult."

Elizabeth pulled her hand away and began to remove the stitches she had just made, although there was nothing wrong with them. She forced a smile onto her face but could not look at her sister. Her heart was so broken it would never recover. Her moment of pleasure had been chance, the product of the little part of her that had yet to give up hope of a happy future with William. Jane could not understand what that was like, and Elizabeth prayed she never would.

ON THE FIFTEENTH OF DECEMBER, Mr Bennet came to Elizabeth's bedchamber to show her the letter he had just received from Frederick Darcy.

The announcement about Fitzwilliam will be published on the twentieth. I regret, as does my cousin, that the delay has put you in an awkward position, but it has been for the best. The news will create a sensation. George and Fitzwilliam have benefited from this quiet period of adjustment.

"Not even a week away," Elizabeth murmured, as she folded the sheet and handed it to her father.

He sat beside her at the window and sighed. "I wish I had refused to keep the matter secret for so long. It has been less than two months, but it has felt like two years. At first, I was too surprised, too unsure what would happen. I did not want to make George Darcy unhappy. I do not know him, but these great men, Lizzy, you do not refuse them lightly. I worried about the consequences for William, for us, and the Lucases if I told everyone the truth."

Elizabeth nodded and played with the fringe on her shawl.

After a moment, he said, "I must go to Lucas Lodge and tell them."

Again, Elizabeth nodded. He squeezed her arm, told her not to sit in the window too long because it was draughty, and left. Elizabeth crawled onto her bed, curled up like a cat, and prayed no one would disturb her for the rest of the morning.

On the evening of the nineteenth, Mr Bennet called the family together and told them about William.

Lydia burst into tears. "William is gone? He is never coming back?"

Kitty looked at each of them in turn, her brow creased and mouth hanging open. Mary, her face drained of colour, remained silent and stared at Elizabeth. Jane tried to soothe Lydia, listen to her father, watch Elizabeth, and calm Mrs Bennet, whose response was loud and unrestrained.

"William is— What did you say? No, no, I have not heard you properly. William, *our* William is not— Tell me once and for all, Mr Bennet, are you saying that *our* William belongs to the family of that-that-that *friend* of yours?" She said it as if Frederick Darcy was the least reputable person in the nation. "It could all be a lie, some mischief to take William away!"

"It is no lie, no mischief, no mistake," Mr Bennet stated. "Mr George Darcy has accepted William as his son."

Lydia began to sob. Kitty soon followed her example.

Bright pink spots covered Mrs Bennet's cheeks, and she jabbed a finger in Mr Bennet's direction. "You have known for weeks and weeks and said nothing to me? What about Lizzy?" Her finger swung to Elizabeth. "You told her, did you not? Your favourite daughter had a right to know, but not your wife?"

Through it all, Elizabeth sat with her hands clenched in her lap; her knuckles were white. Blood roared in her ears, which dulled the sounds of her family.

Her father barked, "Lydia, Kitty, enough! Mrs Bennet, calm yourself. Mary, be so good as to get your mother a glass of wine."

Mrs Bennet covered her face with her lace-trimmed handkerchief and began to moan. "Who will have Lizzy now? Oh, why has this happened?"

It took several minutes to restore order to the room. Jane sat beside Elizabeth, took her hand and did not relinquish it as Mr Bennet told the whole story again.

After almost two hours of questions and explanations, he said, "We have exhausted the subject for tonight. I understand how shocking this is. It will be much talked of throughout the neighbourhood. We all have a responsibility to mind what we add to the gossip." He looked at his wife and two youngest daughters in turn, fixing them each with a hard stare. "I shall be very displeased if anyone named Bennet does or says anything that disparages the Lucases, William, or the Darcys. No one is at fault in this situation. Do you understand?" He waited until each lady assured him that she did before sending them to their beds.

Elizabeth was not surprised when Jane came into her room later that night. She was sitting with her back against the head-board. Jane joined her.

"How you must have suffered, Lizzy!"

Elizabeth held her tongue. What could she say that would not sound as angry as she felt?

"I cannot believe it. It will take days just to understand it is real."

"It does take some getting used to."

"Poor William! To have everything you believed about yourself taken from you like that!"

Elizabeth's eyes burned and the weave of the uppermost blanket blurred as she stared at it. "His life is entirely different now."

Jane laid a hand on Elizabeth's; she had not realised she was picking at the threading on the snowy counterpane.

"You have heard from him, have you not? How is he?"

Elizabeth felt the blood rushing into her cheeks. She inhaled, and the acrid scent of burning wood mixed with Jane's rose perfume filled her nostrils. "I have not. He sent a note to Sir William weeks ago, but we have heard nothing since."

Jane gasped.

Elizabeth pushed aside the blankets and climbed out of bed.

The coldness of the room surrounded her, and her feet felt scorched by the bare floor when she stepped off the carpet. It was oddly satisfying. "How quickly he forgets us."

Jane was behind her, trying to drape a shawl across her shoulders, but Elizabeth moved away, not wanting the comfort. "I do not believe that! He will return. Lizzy, William lov—"

She spun to look at her sister. "That is the point, Jane. He is *not* William. He is Fitzwilliam Darcy. There is a world of difference between the Darcys and the Bennets. Everything has changed. I am quite reconciled to it."

Jane could not accept it, and Elizabeth forgave her for her disbelief. In time, she would see that Elizabeth was correct. She allowed Jane to fuss over her and listened in silence to Jane's assurances of William's devotion. After Elizabeth swore she had been a great comfort, Jane left, and Elizabeth sat at her window and stared into the darkness.

THE NEXT DAY, her father again found her in her bedchamber. In his hand, he held that day's edition of a London broadsheet. Tears pooled in her eyes as soon as she saw him. She did not understand why she cried now, but she could not stop the tears as they fell down her cheeks. He sat beside her, put an arm around her shoulders and directed her attention to a headline.

Mr George Darcy of Pemberley, Derbyshire, wishes to announce the recovery of his son, Fitzwilliam.

CHAPTER 13

GEORGE AND FITZWILLIAM KEPT BUSY PREPARING THE ESTATE FOR the master's absence. Fitzwilliam admired his father's dedication to his duty; there was no denying that George Darcy was a good man. How much easier it would be if he were not so good! If he were immoral or careless of his responsibilities, it would be so much easier for Fitzwilliam to leave him and attempt to reclaim at least a part of his old life, changed, but perhaps not so entirely separated from the person he had been. As it was, he wanted to know his true father and learn from him about their family and the future that was Fitzwilliam's to claim.

By the time they departed Pemberley on the sixth of December, Fitzwilliam had started to feel as if his life before he went to Pemberley was a dream, and not quite real compared to sitting with his father in the fine Darcy travelling coach for the long journey to London. He had imagined another family. Elizabeth, Mr Bennet, his many friends were fantasies. *This* was the reality. He was Fitzwilliam Darcy, a rich young gentleman of impeccable birth and with great expectations. The life he was living now did not feel so strange any longer, although it still felt unfamiliar, which he realised was a contradiction. His name was an example. When he was first at Pemberley, he had disliked being called Fitzwilliam, even though he accepted it as his rightful name. He understood why George and the rest of the family used it and not William; they had always known him as the former. Now, however, it felt natural, and he no longer felt awkward when he heard it.

The Berkeley Square townhouse was just what Fitzwilliam expected: large and fashionable. He liked it and found that it took very little effort to be comfortable in its spacious rooms or with the manifold servants. For the first few days in town, they had many visitors, from George's tailor, who was tasked with providing Fitzwilliam with a proper wardrobe—which he enjoyed selecting, even as part of him cringed at the enormous expense—to Mr Pedlar with a thick sheaf of legal documents to review, to their family. Frederick and Rebecca were the first to call, and they sat together in the morning room, which he particularly liked; it had pale green and gold papered walls, an abundance of plants, and looked out onto the street.

"You have been keeping well, I hope?" Frederick asked Fitzwilliam.

"I have, thank you."

George said, "I think I speak for both of us when I say we are looking forward to making the news official. It appears none of the wagging tongues have learnt of it. Being gossiped about will be disagreeable, but the reason for it is one I could never regret." To Fitzwilliam, he added, "I suggest you adopt my practice and ignore what is said about the family. Spiteful people will spread lies simply to make themselves feel better."

"I hope it will not be too awful," Rebecca said. "London society can be harsh, even to those they most profess to love."

The spice cake Fitzwilliam had just finished turned to stone in his stomach. "I am sure I shall manage." At least he hoped he would. He had just three weeks to prepare for the first test—Lady Sophia's Twelfth Night ball.

A short while later, George and Frederick went into another corner of the room. For several minutes, Rebecca chatted about this and that. Fitzwilliam only half-listened until he heard her say, "Hertfordshire."

"You went to Hertfordshire?" He leant closer to Rebecca and lowered his voice.

She nodded. "Papa and I stayed at Longbourn for two nights before coming to town."

"Y-you stayed at Longbourn?"

"We did." She bit her lip then admitted, "I met the Lucases."

Fitzwilliam sucked in a breath and sat back. She had been with Elizabeth and the Bennets and Charlotte, Sir William, and Lady Lucas. While it would be going too far to say that he had not thought about them of late, his ties to them had seemed to lessen as he became more immersed in his new life. To hear Rebecca speak about seeing them so casually left him with the sensation of something pulling him forcefully in one direction while he remained rooted to the spot.

"My father assured them that you were well. The Bennet girls were all so kind to me. I particularly enjoyed meeting Miss Elizabeth."

It took all his strength not to beg Rebecca to tell him every word Elizabeth had said, to describe how she had looked and acted. Had Elizabeth said anything about him? Had Mr Bennet perchance told Frederick about his attachment to Elizabeth? It would have been the perfect opportunity for him to do so, if he wished the Darcys to know. But Mr Bennet had never had a high opinion of the *ton* and might not be happy to see his favourite daughter marry into it.

"Miss Elizabeth told me you were friends and studied together as children." Rebecca's voice was soft.

Fitzwilliam's mind screamed, *Friends? Studied together? Is that all she said?* He was confused and a little hurt. Belatedly, he realised Elizabeth knew what had happened to him. *Is it too much to hope that Rebecca and Lizzy are friends, even though she and Frederick were there for just two days? Then Rebecca might have her to stay, and I could see her.*

It was a ridiculous dream, and he dismissed it. *She called me a friend and did not even hint that we were so much more than that. Was it her way of saying that she feels we have no future now that I am not William Lucas?* Without volition, he recalled his last conversation with Sir William at Pemberley. Sir William had been prepared to say goodbye; was Elizabeth too?

WALKING DOWNSTAIRS TWO DAYS LATER, Fitzwilliam's progress was halted by the sound of raised voices in his father's study. One of them was George's; the other was deep and at times conciliatory or angry. From the words, Fitzwilliam supposed it was Lord Romsley, his mother's brother.

"I want to see my nephew."

"*My* son. You have no claim on him or me. If it had not been for your actions—"

"That was over twenty years ago! My God! Fitzwilliam has returned."

"Just because my son has been found alive does not mean I shall alter my opinion of you," George hissed. "I lost years with him; my wife withered away and died longing for her child, a child we lost because of you and your father."

"That is not fair! Listen—"

"I will not. You and your father had no right then to direct affairs that were *my* concern, and you have no right to do so now. Leave my house. Do not return."

As the door flew open, Fitzwilliam stepped back. He caught a glimpse of the earl as he stalked out of the house. A part of him wanted to follow Lord Romsley, not to talk to him, but just to see him. Instead, he retreated to his apartment.

At dinner, as Fitzwilliam helped himself to beef ragout, George said, "You may have heard I had an unexpected and unwelcome caller today."

"I did." Fitzwilliam kept his eyes lowered.

"I have estranged myself from that family. My reasons are just, and I ask that you respect my wishes in this regard."

He watched the movement of his fork and knife as he cut his

meat into ever smaller pieces. "Of-of course, sir. If that is your wish, I shall naturally do so."

THE EARLY DAYS in London were long for Fitzwilliam. He and George went riding some mornings, but it was not enough exercise to satisfy him. Other than their family and people who called on matters of business, they saw no one. Everything changed on the twentieth of December. Fitzwilliam was at the breakfast table when his father joined him. He placed a newspaper on the table and pointed at a place midway down the page before resting his hand on Fitzwilliam's shoulder and giving it a gentle squeeze.

A headline screamed from the page.

Mr George Darcy of Pemberley, Derbyshire, wishes to announce the recovery of his son, Fitzwilliam.

When he could at last tear his eyes from the words, he read the accompanying article. It was fair and kind.

George said, "It was important to say publicly that there is no blame attached to the people you were with. We shall be asked about your life. Say only what is necessary. The past is the past. We must think of the present and the future. We are not home to anyone other than family today, but no doubt many people will call."

Folding the paper so that he no longer saw the announcement, Fitzwilliam placed it on the table and attended to his breakfast. He tasted nothing, did not even notice if what he chewed was hard or soft. If he or his father spoke, he did not remember what they said.

At the end of the meal, his father slid a velvet pouch across the table. "I have been meaning to give this to you."

Fitzwilliam poured the contents into his palm and found a handsome, weighty gold watch.

"Like Pemberley, this watch is passed down from father to

son and has been for many generations. Let it be a reminder during difficult moments—and I suspect there will be many in the next weeks. You are a Darcy, my son, always have been, and always will be."

Fitzwilliam ran a finger over the rough, cool surface of the watch, and nodded. He glanced at his father. "Thank you."

Fitzwilliam suspected the watch was worth hundreds of pounds. What it represented was worth far more, and in that moment, he felt exhilarated.

FITZWILLIAM HAD KNOWN that the interest in him would be intense. Some of the people he met were polite, but some gaped and asked impertinent questions. He did not know how to act in the face of such behaviour and said as little as possible to them. His new wardrobe, made of the finest quality cloth and in the latest style, felt like armour. When he looked in the mirror, he saw Fitzwilliam Darcy, not William Lucas, and it made it easier to confront each new day.

There were times Fitzwilliam felt a frisson of excitement. He was able to do things he never imagined he would have the opportunity to do, and he had more money than he could imagine ever spending. Yet, there were moments, such as when he thought about Lady Sophia's ball, when he was liable to break out in cold sweat and need to sit before his legs collapsed beneath him.

I shall have my father and cousins with me. That will make it easier.

He wondered how Elizabeth, the Lucases and Bennets, and his neighbours in Hertfordshire were. John had made a sly comment at Christmas about the people he had known as William Lucas taking advantage of his good fortune, even showing up at the ball and demanding attention. His and George's attendance at what was always one of the *ton's* most anticipated Twelfth Night events had been advertised in the gossip pages. John's remark sounded too much like what Jeffrey said at Pemberley to do anything other than worry him. It was difficult to believe that any of his old friends would do such a thing, but who was to say what their fellow man might do? The story of his past demonstrated how terribly people could behave. The notion that Sir William had played some part in the kidnapping crossed his mind one day, but he dismissed it at once. The Lucases were all that was good, and as much as they may have wanted another child, they would never steal one or purposely keep one from their rightful family. Any mistakes they had made had been due to lack of education and resolution.

Nevertheless, Fitzwilliam began to feel that it was better that they, that all of them, remained in Hertfordshire. He told himself that it was in their best interest; they would not like the scrutiny they would confront from the Darcys and the *ton*. Even Elizabeth was included in this thought. Of everyone from his life as William Lucas, he knew that she could bear it, but even if he only presented her as a friend, his family would reject her; being dismissed in such a fashion would distress her.

MOST OF THE people in attendance at Lady Sophia's Twelfth Night ball agreed that it was her finest in years. Lady Sophia welcomed George and Fitzwilliam with the warmth of true affection and insisted they stand with her until at least a greater part of the guests had arrived.

"This way, you can be introduced to everyone from the very start," she explained to Fitzwilliam. "It might be easier than being constantly interrupted for an introduction. It will be quite the crush."

Frederick, Rebecca, and Freddie—lately arrived from Norfolk—were among the first guests, soon followed by Jeffrey and John.

After greeting them, Lady Sophia remarked to Fitzwilliam, "You are a handsome family. You will learn, if you have not already done so, that the Darcy name is valued in our circle. Yours will be particularly so. Every hostess shall wish to have you at her parties; every gentleman shall wish to be your friend. It is very good that John is so close to you in age and can guide you through the perilous waters of the *ton* and help you to make the right friends. I assume he is up to the task; I do not know him very well."

George said, "Pay no mind to her. She is not immune to the same follies as the rest of us. She is beside herself with glee that she is the first lady to have you attend one of her events."

Lady Sophia laughed and agreed.

The ballroom was exquisitely decorated. The walls were several shades of soft blue. The ceiling was covered in circular patterns containing fans and shells and other shapes in the same colours mixed with ivory and gilt. A multitude of candles illuminated the room, and fires roared in twin fireplaces at either end. Before removing to Pemberley, Fitzwilliam had seldom noticed how a room was furnished. He cared whether a chair or sofa was too hard or soft, and a painting might catch his eye. When he was first in Derbyshire, the richness of the décor signified the difference between the Lucases and Darcys. As the weeks passed, he had learnt to appreciate the quality of what surrounded him— how solid a table was and the look of its gleaming, smooth finish, the comfort of his large bed, the variety of foods and how well they were prepared. Lady Sophia was clearly a wealthy woman and did not hesitate to advertise it.

Looking around him, Fitzwilliam saw that the guests, too, were elegant, especially the ladies. Fitzwilliam knew little about fabrics and lace, but he could see how much finer the attire of the young ladies he met was compared to that of Elizabeth, Charlotte, and the other girls in Meryton. The colours were more vivid, the lace more delicate. And the jewels they wore! Diamonds and rubies and so much more. The whiffs of perfume that tickled his nose were soft, not harsh. The musicians were skilled.

He struggled not to show his awe. Everything he saw, smelled, and heard—and no doubt what he would taste at supper —was a hundred, *a thousand* times superior to any assembly or party he had gone to as William Lucas. *This* was his rightful place in the world; he could not deny that it excited him.

Fitzwilliam danced the first set with Rebecca. He met and partnered many other ladies as the night wore on. Although he did not like to dance, there was a certain pleasure in partnering a pretty girl. It was expected of him, and in some ways, he preferred it to standing and talking to a group of people he did not know. He asked and was asked the same questions with each set, but between the noise of the music, shoes striking the wooden floor as they moved through the steps, and the chatter of so many people, conversation was necessarily brief and general. Some of the ladies were titled, and although he did not yet under-stand the significance of the names of fathers or grandfathers used when they were introduced to him, he knew that even the mere 'Misses' were of impeccable birth. Most of them, he assumed, had substantial dowries.

My father will expect me to choose a bride from among them, or those who come out over the next few years. They have been educated in the ways of this world; no doubt they could help me navigate it, as well as be excellent mistresses of Pemberley.

Although the night was not as trying as he had supposed it would be, it nevertheless made him think about Elizabeth more than he was comfortable with.

She would have enjoyed the spectacle, and I would have relaxed and found greater pleasure in the ball with her by my side. But she is not here, and I must learn to do without her.

CHAPTER 14

"MY DEAR CHILD," MR BENNET SAID AS ELIZABETH CRIED OVER George Darcy's announcement in the papers of the recovery of his son. He remained silent until her tears abated and she had wiped her eyes with the handkerchief he pressed into her hands. "I know how difficult this has been for you, Lizzy. I fear I have I failed you."

"Papa." Elizabeth shook her head, stood, and went to look out of the window. It was lightly snowing, which at any other time she would have found pretty. Today, the snow and grey sky looked cold and lifeless.

"I did not think what it would do to you to keep this secret for so long."

When she spoke, her voice matched the icy world she was watching. "It is over now. We no longer have to live a lie. I believe I shall step outside for a moment." She left the room before he could say another word.

The unusually cold, snowy weather was not enough to keep the neighbourhood from gathering to discuss William's story. The initial talk was mostly about the connexion between William's true father and the either reviled or loved Member of Parliament Jeffrey Darcy, as well as his relationship to the Earl of Romsley. Elizabeth knew that sooner or later someone would say, 'What do you think this means for Miss Elizabeth?' but until they did, she would enjoy the respite from being the object of their interest.

On Christmas Eve morning, Mrs Bennet insisted Elizabeth come to her room after breakfast. The space was crammed with too much old-fashioned furniture and lace for Elizabeth to be comfortable, which added to her dread about what her mother would say. She fussed with her paisley wool shawl. Elizabeth thought the colour made her look wan, but Mrs Bennet liked it.

"You were supposed to marry William and live at Lucas Lodge, and now look at you! You are pale and unhappy, and I do not know what will become of you. You have no idea what I suffer to see you like this! The shooting pains up and down my arms, my head—"

"I am sorry to hear it. Should I send for the apothecary?"

"Apothecary? Whatever are you talking about?" In an instant, her mother's voice went from demanding to lamenting. "Oh, your father should have let you marry sooner!"

Elizabeth's stomach muscles stiffened as though preparing for a blow. The thought that she could have been William's wife when the truth was discovered had been in her mind as well. *There is no point dwelling on it because that is not what happened. I am relieved we were not married when the truth was exposed. I am not wanted by that family, and I would be miserable being among them knowing they saw me as an embarrassment.*

"I know your father says I am not to speak of it, but I must. These Darcys, who think they are so wonderful, have stolen William from us and will not let him return." She drank her tea and ate half a ginger biscuit. "What was I saying?"

Not for the world would Elizabeth remind her. As her mother again adjusted her shawl and cap, wiped at her nose with her handkerchief, and otherwise fidgeted, Elizabeth had to avert her eyes to avoid hissing at her to stop.

"Everyone says that rich people like the Darcys will never allow William to marry you. My girls are good enough for anyone, and those Darcys would be fortunate to have you. Oh, how rich you would be! But William has not returned in all these weeks, and he has not even written to your father about you. Whether we like it or not, we must accept the situation as it is, and take what life gives us. Do you not agree, Lizzy?"

Elizabeth met her mother's eye, nodded, then turned to examine a precarious pile of novels on a small, round table. *A gust of wind would knock it over. If I do, it will create a diversion, and I might escape this conversation!*

"You must think about the future and forget William. You were never as pretty as Jane, and if you are not careful, you will lose what looks you have. There must be another gentleman for you. But you have to remember that not all men are like William. They do not want bookish sorts of wives."

Elizabeth was mortified and unsure whether she should scream, cry, or laugh. *Definitely laugh. I have not done it enough of late. As though I would ever change so that a man would like me better!*

"Perhaps Mr Hawarden has a friend who would take you. There is no better cure for a broken heart than a new beau. Why before your father…"

Elizabeth kneaded the back of her neck and resigned herself to listening to her mother's story.

ELIZABETH WAS glad to see the Gardiners when they arrived that afternoon. She was certain they would agree to her passing the winter with them. She was impatient to make her request but could not do it immediately; the Gardiners arrived only an hour before dinner, at which time many of the Bennets' neighbours would join them.

After church the next morning, the Bennets and Lucases spent the day together as had been the custom for many years. Elizabeth had hoped, albeit only faintly, that Sir William would tell her he had received a letter from William to mark the holiday, but he did not.

He must be in London by now. From Derbyshire to London and he could not come to Hertfordshire even for an hour. I think nothing of myself, but to injure Sir William and Lady Lucas and Charlotte by ignoring them! I cannot believe that anything would prevent the man I knew from doing what was right.

"Come, Lizzy." Jane grabbed her hand which made her jump. "Join us."

Jane smiled so sweetly that Elizabeth could not refuse. She acted lively, and when Sir William announced Charlotte and Captain Farnon's betrothal, she wished them joy. The couple would marry at the end of January and immediately return to the captain's home in Kent.

IT TRANSPIRED that Mrs Gardiner was an unexpected source of information about the Darcys. One morning, just as Elizabeth was about to enter the sitting room, she heard her aunt say the name Darcy, and stopped by the door to listen.

"Pemberley is but five miles from the town in which I spent most of my childhood. The Darcys ran with a rather different set of people than my family did." Mrs Gardiner tittered. "They are *very* rich. Lady Anne did so much good for the neighbourhood when she was alive."

Mary asked, "Lady Anne?"

"Lady Anne Fitzwilliam Darcy, William's mother. She was sister to the Earl of Romsley."

"Our William's uncle is an earl?" cried Lydia.

"Pemberley is grand enough to belong to an earl's family, and all the Darcy heirs marry very, very well. I know you hoped that Lizzy and William would make a match of it, but..."

Jane opened the door and jumped when she saw Elizabeth, who shook her head and began to walk away. Jane followed her to her bedchamber.

"I know you mean well, but I cannot talk about it. Please do not ask me." As Elizabeth spoke, her voice broke. She stood with her back to Jane, one arm across her middle and her other hand covering her mouth. She did not know why her aunt's words affected her so deeply. What Mrs Gardiner said was nothing Elizabeth did not already know.

Jane stood behind Elizabeth and rubbed her arm.

Elizabeth said, "I have lived with this for weeks, and I am reconciled to it. I long for the day everyone finds something more interesting to occupy their conversation." She gave a hollow laugh. "Something happy. Charlotte's good fortune, or perhaps Mr Hawarden can be brought to the point."

"We have only known each other a month."

Elizabeth could hear the embarrassment in her sister's voice and turned to see that she was blushing.

"Very true. You would do well to spend your time getting to know Mr Hawarden instead of worrying about me." When a shadow passed over Jane's face, Elizabeth shook her head. "Neither of us can change what has happened. I shall conquer this and be happy again, especially if I do not dwell on it."

She kissed Jane's cheek. "The sun has come out, and I desperately need a walk. The fresh air will do me good."

Jane offered to come with her, and with a resolve to forget about anyone named Darcy for the rest of the day, Elizabeth agreed.

BEYOND OVERHEARING Mrs Gardiner speaking with other people about the Darcys, Elizabeth had a conversation with her two days before the Gardiners returned to town which convinced her she would not be comfortable staying with them. They were alone in the morning room after breakfast. Mrs Gardiner worked on stitching a floral motif at the edge of a tablecloth.

"It must be very difficult for you, Lizzy. The story would have been extraordinary enough, but to find that we know the young man? You can imagine what Mr Gardiner and I felt. I lived in Lambton when he was abducted, but I do not remember hearing about it. I recall Lady Anne dying. It must have been a year or two later. My mother made us wear black ribbons to show our respect." Her fingers did not stop their steady movements.

Elizabeth wished to change the topic but could not think of a polite way to do it.

"Mrs Philips says everyone has been talking about William since October and speculating that he went away because he no longer wished to marry you. How dreadful that must have been!"

"It was." Elizabeth opened her mouth to ask about returning to London with her, but Mrs Gardiner, with her head bent over her work, did not notice.

"All this talk will not end soon. I am going to say something which I am afraid you will not like. I have only your best interest in mind." She peeked at Elizabeth without lifting her head.

Elizabeth nodded. Her hands trembled, and she tucked them under her thighs.

"I know something of the Darcys and the sphere they belong to. William has not come to see you or written, has he?"

Elizabeth averted her eyes just as her aunt looked up from her stitching.

Mrs Gardiner sighed. "I wish I could say it surprised me. I have heard your mother talk about you finding another gentleman to marry, and she is not wrong to suggest it. It is perhaps too soon, but your uncle meets many very fine young men, and we have sometimes questioned if they would do for one of you girls. We did not think *you* would need our help. However, your situation has changed."

Elizabeth pressed her eyes closed. When her aunt did not continue, Elizabeth nodded once.

"I shall say no more about it today. Now, I cannot recollect whether I told you, but my Margaret is to begin pianoforte lessons soon."

For the next little while, Mrs Gardiner chattered on about her children while Elizabeth nursed dashed hopes. As much as she wished to be away from Longbourn, she would be no happier at Gracechurch Street where, no doubt, her aunt would introduce her to every eligible man she knew.

THE MORNING AFTER TWELFTH NIGHT, which Elizabeth spent at Netherfield, she sat at her bedroom window and looked at the snow-covered ground and trees. The house was quiet, and she felt more peaceful than she had since William first went away.

While I was doing my very best to enjoy myself, he was at a London ball given by his father's cousin who happens to be the daughter of a marquess.

She sighed, and her breath created a circle of fog on the window. She shook her head, stood, and went to poke the fire. As she struck the logs, she muttered, "Stop it, Lizzy. What purpose is there to regretting him or what you thought this year would bring you?"

She replaced the iron and sat at the table. Her reflection stared back at her, and she wondered what her family and neighbours thought when they looked at her. *That I am pale and lifeless compared to what I was? Allowing my disappointment to make me bitter? I do not suppose they are entirely wrong.* But she had loved William and the life they had dreamt of.

I shall find a way to leave Longbourn. I cannot recover while being here.

ELIZABETH'S twentieth birthday came and went with more fanfare than she wished. She did everything possible to appear to be in good spirits to avoid worrying Jane, Mary, and her father. *Perhaps if I feign good cheer often enough, it will become true.*

Two days after her birthday, her father called her into his

study. He sat in the chair next to hers and took her hand. Elizabeth felt the muscles in her back and neck go rigid.

"Lizzy, my dearest daughter, we must discuss William and your future. I do not know what is in your heart, because you will not speak of it, but please tell me you accept that he is not returning for you."

Elizabeth felt the hot sting of tears in her eyes. They were ones of anger as much as of pain. She kept her chin tilted away from him and bit her tongue.

"The Darcys are a different breed of people than we are. His life has changed in every way. Mr George Darcy has plans for his son, ones that do not include those of us he left behind."

She wrenched her hand from his, stood, and went to the window. Her eyes drifted along the curve of the road that led to the front door, and she wished she saw a carriage or some other excuse to distract her father. The sun shone and Elizabeth imagined the cool freshness of a winter's day in her lungs and on her face. It would be so much nicer than the heat and smokiness from the fireplace, which was as stifling as the conversation. "I concluded as much many weeks ago."

"What can I do for you?"

Elizabeth took a moment before replying. "I am not meant to be unhappy—I cannot bear people who always seek reason to be discontented, and I shall not be. I have not been myself, but enough is enough."

With that, she left the room intent on half an hour outside before she joined her mother, Jane, and Mary to call at Netherfield.

THE FOLLOWING DAY, Elizabeth received a letter from Miss Rebecca Darcy which contained an unexpected invitation.

I mean to convince you to come to town. My father agrees that it is an excellent scheme. I would so love the company of another lady. I promise you a variety of amusements but warn you that my acquaintance is limited since I spend so much time in Norfolk and my father has no interest in being among the ton. *We have seen no one in our family since Lady Sophia's ball, and I do not expect it to change. My uncle and Fitzwilliam are horribly busy, and we rarely see our other cousins. Write and say you will come unless you very much hate the idea.*

Elizabeth immediately sought out Mr Bennet.

"You wish to go to London to stay with Miss Darcy? Lizzy, I must caution you—"

Elizabeth interjected, "You cannot object to her. You speak highly of her father, and I know you and he exchange letters."

"But Miss *Darcy*?"

Elizabeth's cheeks burned, and her fist closed around the letter. "Do not suppose I hope to see him. Miss Darcy writes, here," she thrust the sheet of paper at him and pointed at the appropriate passage, "that they have not seen him since Twelfth Night and do not expect to."

"That could change." Her father took the letter from her and laid it on a pile of papers on his desk.

Elizabeth straightened her spine and looked down at him. "I do not care. After everything that has happened, I can see him and feel nothing like what I used to." Her heart skipped and resumed beating at a faster than usual rate.

Mr Bennet groaned and ran a hand over his face.

"If I find that we are in company with him and that I cannot see him and maintain my composure, I shall make an excuse to Miss Darcy, say enough so that I need not see him when he calls or avoid being where he is. But I am not so weak, Papa."

Her father encouraged, even demanded she sit, but she would not.

He said, "If you wish to leave Longbourn so greatly, go to the Gardiners. I shall write—"

"No! I will not go to my aunt. She will talk and talk about the Darcys and show me off to every young, unmarried man she knows. Unless you have another relation whom I can visit, Miss Darcy it must be. I need to go away, just for six or eight weeks. I like her. Please, I am begging you, grant me your permission to go."

Being where everything around her was new and busy was just what she needed. It would be better if her friend were not one of William's relations, but beggars could not be choosers. If other hopes lived in the recesses of her mind, she refused to acknowledge them.

He shook his head. "I am afraid this is a mistake. You may come to regret it."

The sadness in his expression failed to touch her.

"If it becomes too difficult, supposing I even see him, I shall go to the Gardiners or return to Longbourn. Please, Papa."

After a long minute of silence and sighing two or three times, he nodded. Elizabeth thanked him and went to write her reply.

CHAPTER 15

A WEEK AFTER THE BALL, GEORGE AND FITZWILLIAM SAT IN THE carriage as they returned to Darcy House from Brooks's. The week had been busy, with dinner parties, calls, clubs, and a concert. Fitzwilliam had met more people than he could count. For the most part, he found the adjustment to his new circumstances difficult. He never knew what to say or how to act when people stared at him or asked if he remembered anything about being kidnapped. He saw that his father disliked it too—the tightness of his jaw or the clipped manner in which he spoke to anyone who offended him was evidence enough. Sometimes, at the end of a long evening, his father would sigh and close his eyes in the carriage as they drove home or rub his head as if it ached. Yet, George also showed pride when introducing Fitzwilliam as his son.

His father said, "It was not the liveliest few hours, I know. Those men are important acquaintances, and some of them will be useful in directing the speculation about you along lines we prefer. I know little of their sons. As I mentioned, I have preferred to remain in Derbyshire and come to town as infrequently as possible. John can tell you which of them are worth knowing. He is a good lad. Jeffrey did a fine job with him. It was not easy after his wife died. John was just twelve—a difficult age to lose a parent. Did you know that John will take a seat in

124

Parliament? He has been preparing to follow in his father's footsteps since finishing university. I know of one or two very respectable boroughs where we can get him in. I own a small property in one of them. If John likes the neighbourhood, I shall settle it on him."

"I did know. John has introduced me to a number of his friends already, and he mentioned another party tomorrow."

George clapped his hands together. Naming the housekeeper, he said, "Excellent. I hope Mrs Northmore has arranged something special for dinner. I believe this is the last time we dine at home until late next week, and we are unlikely to get much to eat at the Carvers' card party tonight. Ah, here we are."

The carriage stopped, and Fitzwilliam followed his father inside. Fitzwilliam knew that George liked and approved of John —had known it even before his words in the carriage—and he was always eager to send Fitzwilliam into society with him, claiming it was good for him to spend time with people his own age. Surrounded by so much that was new and mystifying, following the path that his cousin led him down was the easiest thing to do. It would please his father too; it was right and proper for a child to wish for his parent's approbation, even when that child was an adult.

But Fitzwilliam soon discovered it would not be as simple as that. He knew that what was acceptable in town, at least among the *ton*, was very different to life in the country, certainly to his experiences, but to become like John would require him to discard many of the precepts by which he had lived. As William Lucas, he and the young gentlemen he called friends might go into one of the local public houses for a pint or a meal. One evening the previous spring, a group of them met at the Gouldings' house when Mr and Mrs Goulding and their daughters were away. Some half a dozen of them played cards, talked, and drank long into the night. It was the first and only time he had overindulged, and Elizabeth had teased him mercilessly, but with good humour, for several weeks.

The routs to which John took him made the Gouldings' party seem like tea with one's aged aunts and grandmothers. At the first one they went to, soon after Lady Sophia's ball, John clouted him on the shoulder and said, "Stop standing around gawking. You attract enough attention as it is. Try to look like you belong."

So he had.

"God, hardly anyone is here," John complained the same night. "But it *is* only January." He yawned. "The parties will improve as people return from the country."

The thought of more people crammed into the hall astounded Fitzwilliam. It was crowded enough that breathing felt difficult, and the mingling of so many different perfumes, to say nothing of bodies that needed better washing, was nauseating. It was enough to make Fitzwilliam want to turn tail and escape to the relative freshness of the street. Beyond that, it was what people were doing that made him want to bolt. Alcohol flowed freely, and at least a half of those in attendance were inebriated. Fitzwilliam saw a number of people sniffing from vials—ether, he supposed—or mixing powders in their glasses; he suspected it was opium. Fitzwilliam saw a man sway precariously in his chair before collapsing onto the table while his friends ignored him. In one corner, a woman laughed so much that her face grew red; she seemed incapable of stopping. Women who could only be whores walked around the room, their bosoms almost spilling out of their tight, crudely cut gowns. It was a scene of vice. Fitzwilliam, unfamiliar with such things, was horrified and could not understand how his cousin thought such a place would be amusing.

But this was where he belonged. Had he not been abducted, he would be used to this life.

The commotion of his increasingly active social life as January continued was its own escape. He slept little, both because he was busy and because he was haunted by dreams of his days as William Lucas. It left him without time or energy to think, let alone feel how uncomfortable and dazed he was. He and his father were out most nights. They would often begin the evening together, but George would send him off with John by ten or eleven o'clock, claiming he was too old and too accustomed to life in the country for so much busyness and such late hours. With John and his friends there were more parties, and after one of his companions pressed a few strong drinks into his hands, he saw and thought little beyond what John showed and told him. John would drop nuggets of information about the people around him, most of which he would, upon sober reflection, consider gossip, such as who was having an affair with whom, how in debt this person was, *et cetera*. It was all so typical for him, and Fitzwilliam sought to see it in the same light.

While he did not protest drinking more than he was used to, he was not yet prepared to cross other bridges.

"You *must* sit down for a game or two," John insisted one evening.

"I am not a card player. I would prefer to watch."

The parlour they were in was filled with tables of men gambling, smoking, and drinking. The scent of tobacco burned his nostrils. Fitzwilliam did not like the idea of gambling. Sir William and Mr Bennet both frowned on the activity, and he had adopted their opinion. He pulled out his watch, realised it would be impolite to check the time, and returned it to his pocket.

John laughed. "You forget. You are rich now. It is nothing to lose a few hundred, or even a few thousand, at a table now and again. My uncle would not be surprised if you overspent your allowance. Who among us has not? I am certain he did and Grandfather Darcy was perfectly agreeable about it."

Fitzwilliam was surprised that Jeffrey did not care if John lost large sums of money. *If that is the arrangement they have made, good for them; it will not alter how I behave.* He remained adamant in his refusal until John at last desisted.

Fitzwilliam was happy for the diversions John offered him on the eighteenth of January, which was Elizabeth's birthday. *I was going to propose today,* he thought almost as soon as he awoke.

He lay in his bed and stared at the ceiling for a long while. His limbs were too heavy to move. He heard the sounds of a servant outside his room and prayed it was not Quinn coming to rouse him. *I just need a little time to mourn what today was supposed to be.* His jaw ached as his eyes watered.

Somehow, he managed to stumble through the morning during which he and George went to two different gatherings; Fitzwilliam again and again pushed aside remembrances of Elizabeth and the people in Hertfordshire who had made up his world for so long. When John collected him to attend a soirée at the home of some family acquaintances—George and Jeffrey were dining with one of Jeffrey's colleagues—he went with him, although he wished he could crawl back into his bed and hide under the blankets.

A little over an hour later, John asked what was souring his mood. "You are even more serious than usual. There must be an explanation."

Fitzwilliam mumbled a reply that amounted to nothing.

"There is only one good cure for it. You need a drink. So do I, but not here."

John took him somewhere—he hardly noticed their change of location—and one drink had been followed by many others. He drank more that night than he ever had before, having agreed with his cousin that whatever was affecting his spirits excused a little overindulgence. With each glass of wine or spirits, he prayed for the strength to erase Elizabeth's face from his thoughts.

He was only vaguely aware of Mr Mallon, the butler, and Quinn helping him up the stairs and to bed in the early hours of the following day.

FITZWILLIAM WOKE up the next morning and wished he had not. His head throbbed, his stomach was sour, and his mouth was so dry he could hardly open it. When he rolled onto his back, the room spun, and he groaned. Why had he drunk so much?

The answer came to him in an instant. Elizabeth. In another life, he would have started the day as the happiest of men because they would finally be engaged.

Yesterday would have been one of celebration, not—

He covered his eyes with an arm, and as he fell into a state between wakefulness and sleep, his thoughts drifted back to one of his favourite memories. He, Mary, and Elizabeth were in the small back parlour at Longbourn. Mary excused herself for a few minutes.

Elizabeth slid into the place next to him on the sofa. William's heart began to race. They were often alone outside, but it felt different to be in a room with the door closed. It was three days after Christmas, and she had a thick wool wrap around her shoulders. The apricot colour did something to her complexion that made her look even lovelier than she usually did. Her eyes seemed brighter, too, although he would not have supposed it possible for them to ensnare him more than they usually did. She slipped her hand into his, and when she smiled at him, he almost forgot himself.

"I had a very interesting conversation with my mother yesterday," she said. "About the Stuarts' Twelfth Night party."

"What about it?

"So impatient this morning, Mr Lucas!"

He smiled at her teasing, covered his mouth with a hand to show he would not interrupt again, and nodded at her to go on.

"Mama has convinced my father that since I shall turn sixteen in a few weeks, I should be allowed to go. My first real party! I am to have a new gown for it, but I do not expect that to interest you."

He mumbled behind his hand, which she then pushed away from his mouth. "Am I allowed to talk now?"

She giggled. "Only if you say the right things."

"Which are?"

"That you are happy I shall be there and that you will ask me to dance."

"I hate dancing."

"Even with me?"

He wanted to scream, No! I shall do anything you wish me to; you need only ask. Nay, a hint will do. Instead, he shook his head and trusted his expression told her what he felt. He supposed it did, because her cheeks became pink, and her smile widened.

She returned to her former seat when they heard someone approach the room. It was Mary.

"I told William that I shall be going to the Stuarts' party," Elizabeth explained.

Mary said, "I do not see why that is so exciting. I hope Mama lets me put off going to parties until I am at least eighteen."

"While I want to dress up in pretty gowns and listen to the music and laugh and dance. Despise me if you dare!"

Her eyes were locked on his, and he could not look away. Although he knew she was teasing, he still wanted to reassure her that he could never despise her. He loved her and had for so long he did not think he knew how not to love her. She gave every sign of returning his affection, but he could never bring himself to ask. Elizabeth went to the window and proclaimed that the sun was out, and she wanted to go for a walk. Mary declined to join them.

Once they were outside, Elizabeth said, "I have never really considered myself in a rush to grow up, unlike Lydia who already longs for the day she can leave the schoolroom, but I know I am ready to belong to the world of adults. I blame you."

William snorted. "What?"

"My best friend is four years my senior. How could that not have a maturing effect on me?"

She grinned at him, and he pulled her arm a little closer to his side. He so wanted to hint at his feelings for her. Elizabeth said his name; her voice was soft and warm, and his heart began to beat so hard he felt dizzy. Had she seen something in his expression? His lips formed her name, but he was not sure if any sound left his mouth.

She stopped walking and stood in front of him with her head lowered. Once again, she held his hand. While he waited to see what she would do next, he wondered when she had first taken his hand in this manner, other than when she was very young. One year ago? Two? He knew what he wanted it to mean, but should he put their friend-ship at risk by believing it, let alone speaking of it?

"How long have we been friends?"

He was startled by her question and furrowed his brow as he looked at her. Her expression showed determination, and perhaps something else.

"Twelve years is it?" she asked.

He nodded.

She bit her lip. "Is that...is that all we are, William?"

"Lizzy."

In a rush, she said, "I love you. I think you feel the same—"

"I do! I-I love you. Of course, I do."

She grinned, and a soft laugh escaped her as he rested his forehead against hers. He asked, "How could I not? You are perfect."

She laughed. "Hardly so!"

"For me, you are. I could not imagine going through life without you, not just as my friend, but as..." He could not say the word 'wife.' It was going too far at the moment.

She whispered, "As everything?"

He nodded. They began to walk again.

"Would your father allow it? Not now, but when we are older?"

Elizabeth nodded. "He loves you."

"He loves you. *I am not a great match for you." She opened her mouth to protest, but he insisted, "I am not. You cannot say otherwise. Lizzy, your father is well aware of who I am. I was born at an inn in Shropshire. It was a nice enough inn, grant you, but I am no better than Mr Payne's son." Mr Payne was the proprietor of the inn in Meryton.*

"You cannot compare yourself to Tom Payne!"

"I was born to be no better than he is. All that separates us is good fortune."

They were at the side of the house, and William's steps faltered when he saw Mr Bennet watching them from the window of his book room. The blood drained out of William's face, even though Mr Bennet could not know what he and Elizabeth were discussing. He lifted a hand in greeting, and when Elizabeth understood his gesture, waved at her father. They walked in silence for a few minutes before she spoke.

"It is not only good fortune. You have lived the life of a gentleman's son since you were eight and moved to Lucas Lodge."

"An estate that, at its best, brings in half what Longbourn does," he argued.

"My father married the daughter of a tradesman, and her

brothers are both still in trade. Whatever your past or that of Sir William and Lady Lucas, your family is no longer in trade. He will allow it."

"I pray you are right."

"I am. We have time to make him see the rightness of it. I am not yet sixteen, and you just turned twenty in November. We are too young to get married."

They stopped by a stone sculpture that was so old the features had been worn down and edges had been knocked off by mischievous children—including the two of them—until it was impossible to tell what it had once depicted.

Holding her hands in his, and keeping his eyes fixed on hers, he vowed, "I will not change my mind."

Happiness made her eyes shimmer. "And my wishes will not change. You know how stubborn I am. I have decided that you *are my choice, and it is one I have made with my heart and my head. Two years, three, four—however long it is until we are old enough—will not change my mind."*

Fitzwilliam rolled over to bury his face in his pillow as sobs overtook him

CHAPTER 16

FITZWILLIAM, JOHN, AND SOME OF JOHN'S FRIENDS WERE SITTING at a low table in his cousin's preferred club. His father had not needed him that morning—after they had had breakfast with one of his old school friends—so Fitzwilliam had gone with John, seeing that it would please George. It was two weeks since Elizabeth's birthday; he still felt sick from the combined effects of alcohol and memories. He was determined to regain the equanimity he had felt before her birthday, slight though it may have been, and again give his attention to establishing himself in his new life. There were times it was easier to do than others, and the conversation taking place around him, as the young men relived their exploits with the fairer sex, was making him uncomfortable.

A man by the name of Walker asked Fitzwilliam about the availability of female companionship in Meryton. He winked to make sure Fitzwilliam understood the sort of woman he was talking about.

John sniggered. "My cousin is not used to…a life of pleasure, shall we say. The ability to do what one likes, whatever that might be. The people who had him were rather puritanical, from what I have learnt."

By comparison to you, yes. Fitzwilliam did not think there was anything wrong with the morals with which he was raised, but neither was he willing to condemn John. It would be the same as thinking poorly of his father, which would be wrong. John's next words seemed to confirm that George knew the sorts of things his nephew enjoyed and did not disapprove.

"I have been trying to make him understand that my uncle would not begrudge him a little fun. He is aware of the enticements young men face. He does not wish to know how we amuse ourselves. It is easier to ignore what you have not been told, and that is exactly what he will continue to do, as long as we avoid causing the Darcy name to be associated with scandal."

Fitzwilliam nodded. He lifted the glass to his lips, stopped before he drank, and returned it to the table. He told himself to give his attention to his cousin, not his nerves. *He is trying to be kind, and this* is *my life now.* He was trying to like John because it was important to George, but it was not an easy task.

Talk turned to plans for that evening. He, John, and their fathers were engaged to have dinner with Lord and Lady Rosewood. Walker suggested they join the rest of them at a theatre afterwards. He again winked, and Fitzwilliam was tempted to ask if he had something in his eye.

"Sweet, sweet Molly's?" John asked. "It is about time I introduced my cousin to it. We shall be there by eleven o'clock."

He chuckled in such a way that made Fitzwilliam want to squirm in his chair.

Do not be ridiculous, he scolded himself. *I know nothing about it, and surely I am capable of finding something to like wherever I am.*

THE THEATRE WAS LOCATED in a part of town mostly occupied by tradespeople and labourers, but they were not the only highly born men there. The theatre part of the entertainment involved a series of performers at one end of the large, crowded room. Patrons sat at unsteady, scratched tables drinking. The odour was nauseating, and the air was thick and dark with smoke from cheap candles and dirty chimneys. A cacophony of shrieking feminine voices and swearing masculine ones reverberated through his head. Fitzwilliam had to pull his feet off the sticky floor with each step they took deeper into the space until he and John found their friends. He felt like tiny insects were crawling up his legs and arms.

There was no wine, only gin or some other alcohol that burned his throat. Fitzwilliam sipped his drink to appear polite, but he was determined to remain sober. To avoid seeing the indecorous behaviour of the people around him, he kept his eyes locked on the performers, although it was impossible to hear what they said. He pretended not to notice when John followed a young woman out of the room or when he returned almost an hour later.

"Do you see that girl over there?" John's mouth was no more than two inches from Fitzwilliam's ear, and his voice was like a knife.

Fitzwilliam looked in the direction his cousin indicated. "Which one?"

"The one in the blue. She is pretending to be coy, but she has been watching you since we arrived. I could introduce you—"

Fitzwilliam's head whipped back to the entertainment. "No, thank you. I am perfectly content where I am." While his body made the normal demands of any young man, he had loved Elizabeth too long to have ever sought relief in a woman's arms. Even though circumstance had separated them, he could not dishonour the love they shared in such a way. In a year or two, he supposed he would look on the ladies he met with more favour, perhaps grow to love one of them, even if it could not be with the same depth of emotion he felt for Elizabeth. There was one lady he had been in company with several times—Miss Harriet Chaplin—whom he liked well enough; if the circumstances were different, he suspected he could develop a *tendre* for her or a lady like her. *She* was the sort of daughter-in-law o f whom his father would approve.

John sighed. "I did not suppose you would agree. I do not

know what your life was like before Frederick found you, but it is time you decide to either give it up or go back to it. This," he jabbed a fingertip onto the table, "is Fitzwilliam Darcy's life. You are either Fitzwilliam Darcy or William Lucas. You cannot be both."

Fitzwilliam sucked in a breath and held himself rigid, although his body still trembled. *What if I am not meant to be either man?*

CHAPTER 17

ELIZABETH SPENT THE JOURNEY TO LONDON THINKING ABOUT THE past few months and what the next weeks would bring. She might see William. Upon occasion, Elizabeth admitted to herself that she longed to see him, that in accepting Rebecca Darcy's invitation, she hoped to do so, and she dreamt that the young man she had loved was not lost. However, if he were as changed as she suspected, it would be devastating. Regardless of what happened, she was determined to hold her head high and not let his actions injure her any further.

The winter will pass away, and with spring, I shall be refreshed and ready for whatever life brings me next.

She arrived to such a warm welcome that she immediately felt better than she had in weeks.

"I am so happy you are here!" cried Miss Darcy. "Was the journey terrible? Are you fatigued? You must tell me what you feel like doing or if you need anything at all. I am afraid you will find me a disorganised hostess, but I shall do my very best."

Mr Frederick Darcy's greeting was almost as warm. He introduced Elizabeth to his son, who grinned and was so friendly that Elizabeth took an immediate liking to him.

As Freddie Darcy spoke, his words ran together, and he bounced on the balls of his feet. "Rebecca has told me so much about you. We shall have the most excellent fun."

Elizabeth was charmed by her bedroom when Miss Darcy showed her to it a short time later. The soft shades of pink and sage combined with white linens left Elizabeth with a sense of peace; she had been right to come, whatever did or did not happen with William.

She said, "I cannot thank you enough for your invitation. You saved me from a very dull winter at home. I have felt a little restless. The sameness of it all. My friend Charlotte has recently married and moved away, and Jane is occupied with our new neighbours. Romance abounds, but it has not touched me, and so..." Elizabeth shrugged.

"Let us wish for two extraordinary gentlemen to fall madly in love with us. We do not have to like them in return, mind you!" Rebecca giggled.

Elizabeth watched the activity of people, carriages, and carts from the window. "And your family? Are they well?" She felt her heart pounding.

Through the reflection on the glass, Elizabeth saw Miss Darcy nod. "We have not seen them recently, but they are all well. Oh! I have not had time to write to you about this, but we received an unexpected caller recently."

"Oh?"

"Viscount Bramwell, the eldest son of Lord Romsley, Fitzwilliam's uncle. The Darcys and Fitzwilliams have been estranged since the kidnapping, and no one saw any reason to resolve the disagreement, I suppose. But now that we know Fitzwilliam is alive, they want to know him. My father says that my uncle is not ready to forget his anger. Lord Romsley sent the viscount to talk to my father about Fitzwilliam, and Lord Bramwell returned with his brother, Colonel Fitzwilliam. They are just a little older than my cousin. I should have said that Lord Romsley and Uncle George were very good friends before everything happened. As much as I love my uncle and know I have no real understanding of what occurred all those years ago, the whole situation seems rather silly to me. Oh! I ought not to have said that. Pray, forgive my loose tongue."

Elizabeth smiled at her friend and assured her that there was no need for an apology. If anything, she appreciated learning more about William's new family, although she did not admit it.

"Now, let me tell you what I have planned, then you must tell me if there is anything you wish to do." Miss Darcy sat on the edge of the bed. "We have been receiving a great many invitations. Far more than I expected."

Elizabeth joined her. "As long as it involves lively conversation, walks in Hyde Park when possible, shopping, and if I am being very demanding, the occasional dance, I shall be well pleased."

Miss Darcy grinned. "I believe I can promise you that and more. Our first party, a ball, is in two days at the home of Mrs Jenner."

As her friend told her about the lady, who was a family friend, Elizabeth vowed to make the most of the next six weeks.

ELIZABETH AND REBECCA agreed to use each other's Christian names within a day of Elizabeth's arrival. She liked Frederick and Freddie Darcy very much and was comfortable in the Darcys' home on Curzon Street.

Mr Darcy was unable to escort them to the ball; in his stead, he had Mrs Doull, who was the widow of one of his former associates, act as chaperone and charged Freddie with also keeping an eye on Rebecca and Elizabeth. Elizabeth anticipated it as an agreeable way to pass the evening hours, despite Rebecca's warning that she and her brother might not know anyone there.

"Should no one ask me to dance, it will be a treat simply to watch the ladies and gentlemen in their London finery." Elizabeth smiled and tugged on her new silk gloves before running her hands down her gown.

"Could you imagine what our mothers would say if we went to a ball and not a single gentleman asked us to stand up with him?" Rebecca said.

"Thankfully, our mothers are not here to witness it!"

They shared a laugh and joined Freddie and Mrs Doull in the carriage.

As soon as they entered Mrs Jenner's ballroom, Freddie exclaimed that he saw someone and dashed off with a promise to find them again before the music began. Mrs Doull spent a quarter of an hour with Elizabeth and Rebecca before telling them to find her between each set and going to join several ladies she knew. Elizabeth and Rebecca linked arms and walked deeper into the room.

After a few minutes, Rebecca said, "I see three ladies I know. Let us go to them, and I shall introduce you. There are already so many people here!"

Elizabeth agreed. *Just the sort of diversion I need! I shall laugh, dance, and forget all about extraordinary events. If the coming weeks pass as peacefully as the past two days have, I shall be very well satisfied.* She felt better prepared to tolerate hearing Fitzwilliam's name, even seeing him, without being robbed of her composure. *Especially since no one will study me to see how I react or talk about how I was supposed to marry him. No one here knows, and I shall never tell them.*

Fitzwilliam had lost count of the number of parties he had been to since Twelfth Night. He preferred the quieter events—smaller dinners or morning events he went to with his father, exhibits and lectures, riding parties, and the like. Tonight, he and John were at a ball at the home of people named Jenner who were some sort of family connexion. George had decided not to come with them; having seen how little he liked crowds of people, Fitzwilliam was not surprised. He was even relieved. It seemed to him that with each large party, his father aged a year or two. *Or perhaps it is simply with each week we spend in town. He was not exaggerating when he said he did not like the Season.*

"Fitzwilliam!" He looked around to see who had called his name and discovered it was Freddie Darcy.

"I have not seen you in weeks. How are you?" asked Freddie.

As Fitzwilliam greeted his young cousin, he saw that John had stepped aside and turned his back. Fitzwilliam then noticed that two gentlemen stood behind Freddie. The way they looked at him sent a shiver up his spine.

"Rebecca is here too. Somewhere over there." Freddie turned slightly as he pointed and laughed. "How stupid of me! I brought Lord Bramwell and the colonel to meet you."

One of them held out his hand. "Viscount Bramwell. My brother, Colonel Fitzwilliam."

Fitzwilliam put his hand in the viscount's and froze when he heard the name.

"Your cousins. No need for formality; call us Sterling and Tom."

"I-I see." Fitzwilliam dropped the viscount's hand, and his eyes darted between the brothers. There was a strange buzzing in his ears as he searched their faces for some trace of familiarity. His mother was their aunt. His mother whom he would never know because she had died of grief after his presumed demise. *But I am not supposed to know them. The Darcys do not acknowledge the Fitzwilliams and vice versa.*

"This is not the best place for us to have met," said Colonel Fitzwilliam.

"No, it is not," John stated as he stepped to Fitzwilliam's side. With a sneer, he added, "Bramwell," and gave the colonel a curt nod.

"*Lord* Bramwell," the gentleman said, his tone haughty.

John directed his next words to Freddie. "I should not have

expected better from you." He took Fitzwilliam's arm and pulled him away.

Fitzwilliam was both glad and disappointed at John's interference. He looked over his shoulder to see the viscount and colonel watching him; he quickly turned away. They were a tie to his mother, and he felt such a burning curiosity about her, a longing for some connexion to her. Yet, his father had asked him not to acknowledge his mother's relations.

After a dozen or so strides, John said, in low tones, "I am sorry I did not see what was going to happen until it was too late. I would not be surprised to learn that Freddie and his father arranged the whole thing. My uncle will not be happy if he learns of it. Your father and Frederick are not such good friends, you know."

"Not friends? But, at Pemberley—"

"At Pemberley," John emphasised, "Frederick had just discovered you, and George was grateful. You have not seen him since Lady Sophia's ball, have you?"

Fitzwilliam frowned and shook his head. He remembered his father telling him about seeing Frederick just the week before. George said that they would see little of Frederick or his children at least until after Easter. Fitzwilliam had supposed it was because they were so busy rather than an indication of discord between the two gentlemen. Now, he wondered if there was more to it.

"Frederick is jealous of him." John thrust his thumb over his shoulder in the direction they had come from. "That was done to create dissension. Let me warn you that there are few things that would really disappoint my uncle. One is if you associate with the Fitzwilliams. The earl has a reputation for doing whatever he has to do to get his way. He is furious that George has maintained the breach for so many years. I believe he would dearly love to see George suffer for it, and if half of what I have heard about the Fitzwilliams is true, they would not hesitate to use you to see that it happens.

"The other is if you admit some entanglement from your unfortunate past. The Fitzwilliams are of sufficient status that it would be unwise to challenge them, but there are ways to deal with the latter problem and ensure it is not repeated."

Fitzwilliam felt the blood drain from his face. This was too much like what Jeffrey had said at Pemberley for him to be easy.

John indicated the direction he wanted them to go. Fitzwilliam followed and tried to regain his composure after meeting his maternal cousins and John's unsettling words. Just as it seemed that he had succeeded, he was robbed of his breath when he saw Elizabeth—his Lizzy—standing not twenty feet away.

ELIZABETH LET Rebecca lead the way as they sought a quiet corner in which to await Freddie's return. She was startled when Rebecca stopped. "Oh dear. My cousin John is here."

Elizabeth looked to see who Rebecca meant. Her heart stopped when she saw William, and she felt her lips begin to turn up in a smile. She longed to touch him, to feel his arms around her and hear his voice. An instant later, she remembered everything that had happened, and her heart began to ache as it hammered against her ribs; only politeness kept her from fleeing. He was tall, beautiful, oh so familiar, and yet so, so different. How could he look exactly as she remembered and at the same time like a stranger? The blank look in his eyes, the way he stared at her with his features as set as though they were carved in stone, the rigidity of his body, and the way his head jerked towards the man who stood by his side.

It seemed as though he hated seeing her. Ire rose in her throat, its bitterness choking her. William approached them as she and Rebecca walked towards him; the other man remained where he was.

Rebecca exclaimed, "Fitzwilliam! I did not know you would be here tonight. Lizzy, look; it is Fitzwilliam, and my cousin, John Darcy."

Elizabeth felt like crying out in anger and anguish at his coldness. *His cousin will not even look at me. He only nods at Rebecca.* John Darcy had turned away from them before Rebecca could introduce him to Elizabeth.

Rebecca said, "You remember Lizzy. How could you not?"

The noise of the ballroom faded away as Fitzwilliam remained silent. Despite the heat created by so many bodies, Elizabeth shivered.

"M-miss Bennet," Fitzwilliam said at last. He bowed.

"Mr Darcy." Somehow Elizabeth managed a stiff curtsey.

He glanced at his cousin again. John Darcy closed the distance between them, took William's elbow, and pulled him away, stopping after just a few steps. Elizabeth heard John Darcy ask, "Who is that?"

"She is…someone I knew. I…" Fitzwilliam's voice trailed off.

"You?"

"It is not important."

John Darcy glanced over his shoulder and met Elizabeth's eye. He smirked, then walked off with William's elbow still in his hand. Bile rose in her throat. She had accepted that William Lucas was no longer part of her life, but to be treated in such a fashion! *He is truly changed. My William, my dearest friend, the man I loved, is gone forever.*

"Lizzy?"

Rebecca sounded concerned, and Elizabeth forced a smile onto her face. "As you can see, your new cousin and I are not good friends. Were not. I would not presume to say we know each other at all now that he has discovered his true identity."

"Oh."

They stood in silence, as Elizabeth drifted back to her bitter thoughts.

Lizzy! Was it truly her? Was she real or a manifestation of his dearest wish? As John continued guiding him through the throng, Fitzwilliam thought about everything that had happened in the last quarter of an hour. His head throbbed.

When he had stood in front of her, it had seemed like he had slipped into a dream. During the day, he seldom thought about his life as William Lucas, although at night his unconscious mind reminded him of everything he had left behind. To see her felt wrong, discordant. He knew he had spoken but could not recall what he said. He had wanted to collapse into her arms and never let go; she could end the struggle he found himself caught in between his father, the Darcys, the Fitzwilliams, the past, and the present. At the same time, he was struck with dread at the prospect of introducing her to John and of admitting her to his new life; she was meant to remain part of his false past.

When he felt a hand on his arm, he imagined that it was Elizabeth's. She was reaching out to him and telling him that everything would be well now that they were together again, that somehow, he could have the best of William Lucas's and Fitzwilliam Darcy's lives without intruding where he was no longer wanted or disappointing anyone.

With a revulsion he had not experienced before, he realised the evening had just begun. *How can I tolerate hours more of John's company, especially knowing Lizzy is here?* His heart ached and only the strictest of self-control stopped him from succumbing to tears.

ELIZABETH DID NOT KNOW how much time passed before she heard Freddie calling his sister's name. She and Rebecca turned as one to face the direction of his voice, and Elizabeth noticed that Rebecca looked as discomposed by the encounter with Fitzwilliam and John Darcy as she felt.

"Look who I found." Freddie grinned at them, then the two gentlemen who accompanied him.

They bowed, and one said, "Miss Darcy. You look lovely this evening."

"Thank you, my lord." Rebecca's cheeks turned pink, and Elizabeth felt a prick of curiosity.

Freddie asked, "Did you see Fitzwilliam? John was not pleased when I introduced him to—"

"If I might interrupt," the gentleman said. "Would you do us the honour of introducing your friend?"

"Oh, of course!" Rebecca made Elizabeth known to Viscount Bramwell and Colonel Fitzwilliam.

"You are from Hertfordshire?" asked Colonel Fitzwilliam. "Is that not where Fitzwilliam lived?"

The brothers looked at Elizabeth who nodded. "He came to live near my father's estate when he was eight years old."

As Elizabeth answered the colonel's questions about her travel to town, length of stay, *et cetera,* Lord Bramwell stepped aside with Rebecca. From the viscount's next words to them, she supposed he had asked Rebecca to dance and she had tried to demur.

"If your brother or my brother were to ask Miss Bennet to dance, then would you? I believe you are the most stubborn lady I have ever met, Miss Darcy."

Colonel Fitzwilliam cried, "Sterling!"

"She does not like it when I compliment her, so I am trying a different approach," the viscount retorted.

In the end, it was decided that Lord Bramwell would get his wish while Elizabeth and the colonel danced.

ONCE RETURNED HOME, Rebecca went into Elizabeth's chamber to talk about the evening.

"The viscount and colonel seem very nice," Elizabeth said. The two gentlemen had asked her a great deal about William, which she had not particularly enjoyed. She had said as little as possible but assured them that their cousin had been happy.

Apart from that, they had been amiable, a marked contrast to John Darcy. She was inclined to place any blame for the estrangement between the Darcys and Fitzwilliams on the former.

Rebecca played with the cushion in her hands. Her eyes were on it, but Elizabeth could see a slight frown on her face. "I know no evil of the colonel."

"And the viscount?"

It took a moment for Rebecca to respond. "I am afraid he is rather fast. Or was. I hardly know. It is so strange to me that he has called upon my father twice and is so friendly with Freddie. I suppose it has to do with Fitzwilliam, though he will flirt with me. I have no intention of falling victim to any gentleman's pretty words. Well, I should let you sleep; you must be tired."

With that, Rebecca was gone. Elizabeth stared at the door. She was surprised by her friend's words about the viscount; his desire to spend time with Rebecca had seemed genuine. Rebecca's reluctance to speak about Lord Bramwell led Elizabeth to wonder if she felt an attraction to him but was hesitant to admit it. Rebecca had said enough about her parents' unhappy marriage to suggest to Elizabeth that she had a rather cynical view of romance. Given the situation with William, Elizabeth suspected she was close to feeling the same way.

By the time Elizabeth was in bed, feelings of grief and disappointment enveloped her. She lay on her back, staring at shadows on the ceiling. Hot tears pooled in her eyes and soon ran down the sides of her face. After several minutes, she rolled onto her side and threw her arm over her head to muffle the sound of her distress.

"William Lucas is truly gone forever," she whispered into the dark. She prayed that hearing the words aloud would make her accept them once and for all. "How could he look at me like that and call me Miss Bennet? I am ashamed of him, and ashamed of myself for loving him."

A part of her longed to return to Hertfordshire so that she

would not risk seeing him again, but she shook off her pain and allowed her courage to rise.

I shall not let him drive me away! I intend to enjoy these weeks. Nothing he or his horrible relations do will rob me of the pleasure of this time with Rebecca and away from Longbourn.

CHAPTER 18

THE NEXT MORNING, FITZWILLIAM AND GEORGE ATE BREAKFAST together. John had wanted to leave the ball half an hour after they saw Elizabeth, and Fitzwilliam had agreed. His cousin suggested they find their friends at some club or other, but Fitzwilliam could not bear the thought of witnessing the debauchery they seemed to favour. He never liked it, but after seeing Elizabeth, it made him sick to think of it. He had wanted to go home and be alone. If he had been able to separate himself from John, he would have gone to Elizabeth, even if only to spend a few minutes at her side. Somehow, he knew she held the answers he sought, even though he had not yet determined what the questions were. But he had seen that Viscount Bramwell and Colonel Fitzwilliam were with Elizabeth, Rebecca, and Freddie, and when he saw Elizabeth dancing with the colonel, Fitzwilliam had wanted to punch something. He had never felt jealous before, but now that he knew they could not, should not be together…

Elizabeth's image remained in his mind as he slowly moved forkfuls of broiled eggs from his plate to his mouth. She had looked so lovely and sad, and his arms had ached for her. All through the night, even now, he could almost feel her presence beside him—the warmth her body radiated, the tickle of her breath on his skin, her form pressed to his. In the early morning hours, he had awakened from a dream of being with her, and the pain of realising she was not there was excruciating.

He glanced at his father sitting across from him and reading his newspaper. *I cannot just forget about her and what she means to me. Have I not tried to do that these last weeks? But one second with her has brought it all back to me. What would happen if I told him about her?*

Recalling John's words at the ball and Jeffrey's months earlier, he felt a cold sweat on his forehead. He pressed his eyes closed and tried to calm his racing heart.

What of the Fitzwilliams and what John said about Frederick? Could it be true that Frederick is no friend to my father? I cannot believe it. Yet, his father had said they would not see Frederick for the next weeks. Knowing that Elizabeth was staying at Curzon Street, Fitzwilliam assumed his father knew, too, and that was at least part of the reason for the separation. If Frederick and George were close, as Fitzwilliam had assumed, would Frederick allow Rebecca to invite Elizabeth to town, knowing George would not like it?

He sighed. His life was complicated enough without adding Elizabeth and the Fitzwilliam brothers to the mix.

I must avoid them. Doing otherwise would be a betrayal of my father, and I cannot risk Lizzy or the Lucases and Bennets if my cousin or uncle were to take it into their heads that they must prevent our being...friends. It is what Lizzy wants, too. I do not know why she is in town, but it is not to see me, not after so long with no communication between us.

It is right and proper that I attend to what my father expects.

He recalled another man he had believed to be his father; he had hardly thought about Sir William in weeks. *But he also expects me to separate myself from all of them. He said as much when he left me at Pemberley to be with my true father.*

The sound of George's newspaper being dropped on the table roused him from his thoughts. Regarding his father, Fitzwilliam thought he looked thinner and paler than when they came to town.

"We have been asked to dine with the Earl of Wyncham," George announced. "He has a daughter to settle, and I suspect that more than anything else is behind the invitation. I do not know Lady Amelia, but she *is* the daughter of a peer and has a fine fortune. But that is for another time; it is soon to think of you marrying. You have only just returned. This is the time for you to accustom yourself to your new life and enjoy it."

Although Fitzwilliam had admitted the possibility of loving a lady other than Elizabeth not so long ago, having seen her, he thought, *There is only one woman I shall ever* want *to marry*. Before his father continued the discussion of marriage, he asked, "Have you any news from Pemberley?"

His father looked startled by the change in topic, but after sipping his coffee, said, "I had a letter from the steward just this morning."

After speaking about it for some time, they prepared themselves for another busy day, which would start with attending some sort of lecture on recent scientific discoveries. *If I can turn my mind to it, I know I shall find it interesting. At the very least, I must allow it to put Lizzy from my thoughts.*

DESPITE A BUSY AND rather pleasant day spent mostly with his father, Fitzwilliam was in no mood to find dinner enjoyable. That Lord Wyncham was not subtle about his desire to match Lady Amelia to Fitzwilliam made it worse. If forced to describe her, Fitzwilliam would say that she was in every way ordinary. Lady Amelia had little conversation beyond the banal, which made for a tedious meal. It was dizzying to think that an earl wanted *him* as a son-in-law, but not all of Lady Amelia's connexions or fortune could make her more attractive while his heart and thoughts were full of Elizabeth.

I wish she had not come to town. I might not have grown to like everything about my life, but I was becoming used to it. Seeing her again has disturbed it all; it might even be contributing to my father's unhappiness.

THE DAY AFTER THE JENNERS' ball, Rebecca, Freddie, and Elizabeth sat in the parlour. They had been receiving callers for several hours, and Elizabeth was happy that the last of them had just left.

Freddie yawned and said, "Last night was great fun, but I am so tired. I am still on country hours and was out of bed not long after I got into it."

The same was true for Elizabeth, but before she could say so, Rebecca spoke.

"I am sorry John was so rude to you, Lizzy. He is so conceited. We do not see him or his father much, as I told you, and I hope our paths will not cross again while you are here. I was mortified."

Freddie said, "He is always like that, always very proud. I suppose Jeffrey—that is his father—is, too. Being sons of Pemberley, and all of that. Unlike my father, who is just a cousin." He rolled his eyes and colour suffused his face. "Father is a hundred times the man either of them are."

Elizabeth did not doubt it for a moment. *Fitzwilliam will be just like them, if he is not already. He ought to take Mr Frederick Darcy as an exemplar, since he finds Sir William and my father no longer adequate.* "Do not mind on my account. Everyone I met was very kind, and I had, as Freddie said, great fun. Remind me, if you will, what we shall do this week."

After speaking about it for a while, they separated to prepare for dinner. During the meal, Rebecca mentioned seeing Fitzwilliam to her father. Elizabeth was determined to act as though it meant nothing to her.

"I hope you found him looking well, Miss Bennet?" Mr Darcy enquired.

"Y-yes." Elizabeth smiled and hoped it looked more genuine than it felt.

Rebecca glanced at her and said, "We did not talk to him beyond a few words. It is still so strange to me that you knew him all that time. The whole situation is peculiar!"

Elizabeth agreed. She took a bite of chicken curry and appreciated the spiciness. The heat of it was a perfect balance to her anger and disappointment. She would let it burn for a little longer before putting it away and remembering her resolve to leave William Lucas in her past. *With time, I might think about him with fondness once again and look back on our time together as one of carefree youth.*

Frederick Darcy's voice recalled her attention. "Miss Bennet, I am afraid I acted rashly by rushing Fitzwilliam away from Hertfordshire before he had a chance to say farewell to Miss Lucas or any of his friends, you included. I doubt Fitzwilliam understood what was happening until we were at Pemberley, if not for several weeks longer." The corners of Mr Darcy's mouth turned down and he pulled his eyebrows together. "Had I more presence of mind, I would have acted differently. But I dare say he has written to the Lucases and your father and his old friends. It is not easy for him to visit Meryton at the moment, but at least he can send as many letters as he likes."

Elizabeth thought, *His father does not want him to visit. Do not hesitate to say it; I had already come to that conclusion. I know what you do not, however. William has not written, and even if his father gave him leave to go to Meryton, he would not.*

"It is such a change for him," Rebecca said. "He went from being in such a happy little neighbourhood to London where his every move is scrutinised."

I am certain the compensations make it worth the while. Elizabeth refused to feel sympathy for him. If his new life was so disagreeable, he should do something about it. That he had not, and that he had shown no regret—or really any emotion whatsoever—when they met, told her he was perfectly content where he was.

As soon as dinner was finished, Elizabeth excused herself, saying she had a headache.

EARLY THE NEXT WEEK, Lord Bramwell called. Elizabeth joined the Darcys as they received him. Elizabeth soon noticed how the viscount's eyes drifted to Rebecca, and how she avoided looking at him. After the usual pleasantries were exchanged, Lord Bramwell turned to Elizabeth.

"I wanted to thank you for sharing your knowledge of Fitzwilliam the other night. My father and mother were pleased to hear your assurances that he was happy. You will be much in demand when people learn that you have known him for so long."

"Thank you, but I hope few people ever hear about my past acquaintance with him." She would walk back to Longbourn if it became common knowledge.

He inclined his head and addressed Mr Darcy again. "For now, my father is prepared to do as you recommend and exercise patience. Fortunately, my aunt, Lady Catherine remains in Ireland with her daughter and son-in-law."

Elizabeth's eyebrow quirked up in curiosity. The viscount satisfied it by explaining that his aunt was, "too accustomed to having her own way, and she would make the situation with my uncle much worse. As it is, she has written a dozen or more angry letters to my father, and I suspect my uncle has received a number of them too."

Frederick nodded. "I know that he has. They go directly into the fire."

"Very wise of him," Lord Bramwell said.

Mr Darcy soon took his leave, saying he had work to attend to. The viscount remained for another quarter of an hour. Watching him with Rebecca, Elizabeth thought she understood her friend's wariness; he was a flirt, and it behoved any young lady to be cautious around such a man until she was certain of his intentions. To her, he remained polite, and when he mentioned Fitzwilliam, she caught glimpses of what she took as remembered sorrow that hinted at more depth than Rebecca seemed to believe he possessed.

CHAPTER 19

WHENEVER SHE WENT OUT, ELIZABETH WAS FOREVER LOOKING this way and that. She was certain she felt Fitzwilliam's presence and convinced he would suddenly appear in front of her. The arrival of callers would make her chest tighten as she grew over-heated. It was never him, however, and as much as she told herself she was relieved, she was disappointed. Sooner or later, they would meet again, and each morning, afternoon, and evening, Elizabeth vowed to be unaffected by his presence and manner towards her.

Nine days after the Jenners' ball, she, Rebecca, and Freddie were shopping. It was a fine day which hinted at the coming spring, and they were not the only people who decided to take advantage of it. The street was crowded, which made it astonishing that Freddie noticed Fitzwilliam across the road.

"I see Fitzwilliam!" Freddie exclaimed. "Stay here; I will return in a moment." With that, he dashed towards him.

Elizabeth's breath caught in her throat. She watched as the men spoke and desperately tried to regain her equanimity. A part of her was thrilled to see him, but a greater part knew no good would come of it. The pair walked towards her and Rebecca. Feeling Fitzwilliam's eyes on her, Elizabeth undertook a pointed study of her environs.

Fitzwilliam greeted Rebecca first before saying, "Li—Miss Bennet."

Was she mistaken, or was his voice softer when he said her name? Had he almost called her Lizzy as he used to? *He simply forgot himself for a moment.* She glanced at him, her expression blank, and curtseyed.

Rebecca said, "Fitzwilliam, it is so good to see you! We hardly ever do. Is it not a lovely day?"

Fitzwilliam agreed with her, and he, Rebecca, and Freddie spoke about shopping and errands. Elizabeth remained steadfastly silent. He stared at her. She could not imagine why and wished he would stop. It was evident that Rebecca noticed, and Elizabeth did not want his behaviour to cause her to have to answer awkward questions. She feigned interest in the passers-by and a need to adjust her hat.

"We were headed towards a pastry shop around the corner," Rebecca announced.

No, no, no, no! Do not invite him to join us!

Rebecca continued, "My father takes me to it all the time. It has the most delectable cakes and tarts. Lizzy has never been. Have you?"

Fitzwilliam shook his head. Elizabeth wanted to hit him. He might glance at Rebecca or Freddie, but he kept looking at her. *Does he think I am here to interfere in his perfect new life? How little he knows me if he believes I would do such a thing. I would be much happier if I never saw him again.*

Her heart stuttered, and she wondered why she had accepted Rebecca's invitation. But she could not lie to herself; part of her had hoped to see him, despite the long weeks of his silence. Even more than she had realised when she first drove to London, she knew now that part of her had imagined that if—when—they met, he would be able to explain everything away, would vow that he still loved her, that they would get married and have the life they had dreamt of. He would assure her that he was only staying with

George Darcy for long enough to make the world see that he was the man's son; it was always the arrangement that he would soon return to his true home—Meryton—and resume the life he chose to live, that of William Lucas. Perhaps there had been letters that had gone astray; they would exclaim over what a shocking failure of the postal service it represented, and, in time, laugh over it.

None of that had ever been likely to happen, and she knew it had been imprudent to come stay with Rebecca. *Yet, I like her and Freddie and Mr Darcy, and I needed to be away from Longbourn. I would be completely contented at Curzon Street if I did not have to see him. Perhaps I am still deceiving myself and remain because unconsciously I believe this might end in something other than further heartbreak.*

"Come with us," said Freddie.

Fitzwilliam shook his head. "Forgive me. I-I must be home."

Both Freddie and Rebecca expressed their disappointment and tried to convince him that he could spare a quarter of an hour.

"I am sure your cousin has many demands on his time," Elizabeth said. She was disappointed to discover that he cared so little for Rebecca and Freddie; it had appeared that way at the ball, too. *They are not as grand as Mr John Darcy. How quickly he embraced the change in his circumstances!*

"Truly, I cannot," Fitzwilliam told Rebecca and Freddie. He said goodbye to his cousins, a soft, "Miss Bennet," to her, and walked away.

Elizabeth was glad to see him go. She pushed all thought of him out of her mind and devoted her attention to her companions and enjoying their outing. The tears that stung the back of her eyes would have to wait until later.

ELIZABETH CALLED on Mrs Gardiner several days later.

"Lizzy, my dear girl, let me look at you! Is this a new gown?"

Mrs Gardiner said within a minute of Elizabeth entering her sitting room. "Very pretty."

Elizabeth thanked her and said that it was. She prayed that she could keep her aunt talking about fashion, or other subjects which were not William or marriage, for the duration of her visit.

Her hopes were dashed twenty minutes later when Mrs Gardiner asked, "Have you seen William?"

"I saw him at a ball. It was crowded and noisy, and we hardly spoke." She had written almost the exact same words to Jane only two days earlier. To avoid looking at her aunt, Elizabeth smoothed a tiny wrinkle in her skirt.

"Oh. That is all?" She sighed and patted Elizabeth's hand. "How awful it must be for you. I am very sorry it has happened. It was never a very fine match for you, but with so much affection on both sides, considerations of wealth seemed unimportant. Who could have foreseen that such a thing would happen?"

Sir William and Lady Lucas both did.

"Your uncle and I have seen notices about him in the news. Hardly a day goes by without someone talking about Fitzwilliam Darcy and his sensational return to his family and his place in society. Have you seen any of it, or met his father?"

Elizabeth shook her head.

Mrs Gardiner squeezed her hand. "I should warn you that there has been some speculation about his marriage prospects."

Elizabeth pulled her hand away before her aunt noticed that her limbs trembled. "That does not surprise me."

"I cannot imagine his father will want to rush into making a match for him. Better to let the dust settle, so to speak, then... Well, perhaps I ought to hold my tongue."

Elizabeth was very thankful that Mrs Gardiner took her own advice and said no more about Fitzwilliam. "How are the children?" She asked, knowing it was a subject upon which Mrs Gardiner could speak for a very long time, and she did.

Before Elizabeth left several hours later, after seeing the children and her uncle, Mrs Gardiner said, "You can come to us at any time, should you decide you would rather not stay with Miss Darcy. We shall always be happy to see you."

It was a kindly sentiment, and Elizabeth appreciated it even as she reminded herself that she had no intention of letting Fitzwilliam Darcy make her unhappy.

THREE DAYS AFTER SEEING ELIZABETH, Rebecca, and Freddie while shopping, Fitzwilliam made his way to Frederick Darcy's house. He knew he ought not to go, but the part of him that still felt like William Lucas loved Elizabeth and needed to see her. Surely there was no harm in being near her for a few minutes? *It might even help me put aside the past once and for all.*

Rebecca and Freddie received him gladly.

"I, uh, was nearby." Fitzwilliam hoped he was surreptitious as he looked around the room for any sign that Elizabeth was there. "You are well, I trust, and your father?"

Rebecca smiled, while Freddie replied, "Father will be sorry to have missed you."

Fitzwilliam mumbled an appropriate response.

"Lizzy went to see her aunt this morning. Mrs Gardiner. You must know her," said Rebecca.

Fitzwilliam nodded. *The Gardiners who are in trade. How it would horrify my father and my uncle and John if they knew.* "I am sorry your father is not here. I have not seen him in some time."

Rebecca said, "I imagine you and Uncle George are very busy. We have been as well. I had no notion so many people would invite us to this or that amusement. I suppose it is because of you. They hope that if they are our friends, we shall encourage you to be their friends, too. Or that we will supply them with fresh gossip about you." Rebecca blushed bright red. "Oh, I ought not to have said that."

"I know it is true."

Freddie blurted, "Do you mind that I introduced you to Lord Bramwell and Colonel Fitzwilliam?"

"No." Fitzwilliam had no intention of furthering an acquaintance with his mother's relations, but he did not blame Freddie for making the introduction.

"The thing is, they want to know you. Not because you are a sensation—"

"Freddie!" Rebecca cried.

"Well, I am sorry, but I did not know how else to say it. Fitzwilliam knows what I mean. The thing is," Freddie repeated, "you *are* their cousin, and they wanted to meet you. Bramwell even remembers when you were little, before...well, *before*."

Fitzwilliam wanted to appease Rebecca, who looked mortified, and Freddie, who looked anxious. "I did not mind."

Freddie gave a sigh of relief. "It never occurred to me that you would not like it, but then afterwards, I thought you might not have. Their parents—Lord and Lady Romsley, you know—want to meet you, although I know my uncle would not approve. Bramwell came to see my father in January because they wanted to know how you were, what had happened to you, and all of that. More than what they could read in the news or get from gossip. Bramwell and the colonel are really very nice, and they have been awfully kind to me."

Fitzwilliam gradually relaxed as Freddie told him about a recent excursion he took with them. All ease disappeared ten minutes later with the arrival of a new caller: Viscount Bramwell.

As the viscount greeted them, his eyes remained on Fitzwilliam. "I had no notion I would see you here today."

Fitzwilliam stood. "Likewise." To Rebecca, he said, "I must be off. I have lingered too long already."

"Then I am fortunate I arrived in time to see you," the viscount said.

Fitzwilliam stared at him for a moment, then nodded curtly and left the room with quick paces. *I do not care that Freddie and Rebecca like him and his brother, I do not care that they are my mother's nephews, I do not care that they want to know me and are my cousins as much as John and Freddie and Rebecca are. I just wanted to see Lizzy for a few minutes!*

IT DID NOT TAKE LONG before Elizabeth's and Fitzwilliam's paths crossed again. Two days after he called on Rebecca and Freddie, Fitzwilliam happened upon Elizabeth, Rebecca, and Frederick while walking in the Hyde Park. The morning was overcast but not terribly cold, and he had been invited to join a group of young people he had met in recent weeks. A young lady whose name he was not confident he remembered had brazenly linked her arm with his.

Fitzwilliam stepped aside to talk to his cousins and Elizabeth, pleased to have an excuse to disengage the lady's arm. He was even happier to see Elizabeth. With trees and shrubs around them, it almost felt like they were walking near Longbourn, as they had done countless times over the years.

If only everyone else would disappear. It should be just her and me and the sounds of birds and the wind shaking the leaves, not this crowd of people to whom I am nothing but a curiosity or eligible marriage prospect. The air should smell of earth, not smoke and refuse.

"Good morning, sir, Rebecca." He turned to Elizabeth. She was curtseying, and her head was lowered which hid her face. Her reserve, her discomfort gave him an odd sense of relief. *She is as much affected by seeing me as I am to see her. How can I let her go? It is too much to ask of me. But I cannot simply go to my father and say that I want to marry Miss Elizabeth Bennet, a country gentleman's daughter with no dowry and connexions in trade.*

Frederick asked, "How are you? I have not seen you since Twelfth Night."

"I am well. Busy."

"I hear you called the other morning."

Rebecca said, "It was the day Lizzy went to her aunt."

"That is correct. I was not so fortunate as to see Miss Bennet, though I was happy to have a few minutes with my cousins."

Fitzwilliam's eyes naturally gravitated to Elizabeth when he mentioned her, and he caught her disbelieving glance. Was she surprised that he would seek her out? She had always understood him so well, and surely she knew how difficult all of *this* was for him. He knew it must have been hard for her too, this sudden change, but hers was the advantage. She, at least, had remained where she always had been, surrounded by people who loved her and the comfort of the familiar. He had been confronted with the fact that everything he remembered about his life was a lie, and he had to adopt a new name, new family, new way of life, new expectations, new everything.

At once, he felt he could no longer remain with them. It was too painful to be so close to Elizabeth, to see how unhappy she was because of what had happened to them, when he did not know how to make the situation easier for either of them.

"I must rejoin my party. Please, excuse me." With a bow, he left them.

CHAPTER 20

ONE EVENING AT THE START OF MARCH, JOHN BROUGHT Fitzwilliam to a music hall. It was not the same one they had been to before, neither were the friends they met the same ones they had been with at the last so-called theatre. Fitzwilliam had not even known where they going when they left the soirée they had been at. His father had been there too, and had told him to enjoy the rest of his night before making his own way back to Berkeley Square.

As soon as they were seated at a table, John pressed a glass into Fitzwilliam's hand.

"It is going to be a glorious night. The girls here are without equal."

Examining the establishment, Fitzwilliam was relieved to find that it was less disgusting than he expected, based on his previous experience. It was not pleasant, and he would be happier if it was cleaner and less crowded, but the other patrons were well-amused with the entertainment and each other, and he intended to be likewise, if only to prove to himself that he belonged to the fast set occupied by his cousin and his friends.

John leant in close to Fitzwilliam. "I intend to see to it that you enjoy yourself tonight. *Properly* enjoy yourself. You have been a stick in the mud, and it is time to get over your unfortunate past. If it is so impossible, perhaps you do not belong here at all."

I might not belong here, *but I do belong at Pemberley.* Like George, he had a responsibility and a right to it. *I was born to tend to it, to be a steward of the land and the people beholden to the estate, just as my father said last autumn.* Fitzwilliam both knew and felt the truth of it.

"Drink up!" John drained his glass and tapped Fitzwilliam's hand.

Looking at his companions, he saw a group of laughing, grinning young men, all of whom had had the sorts of childhoods he ought to have lived; all of them represented the friends he would have had, had he never been kidnapped. When he thought, *I wish I could be so free,* it was immediately followed by the conviction that he could do it. He *would* do it. After all, there was only so long any man could withstand temptation, especially when it seemed that no one expected him to show such restraint. He accepted the glasses of rum that were pressed on him, not caring that he was drinking far more than was his custom and that it would leave him feeling sick the next day. For now, it quieted his mind and let him banish Elizabeth's image from his thoughts. Each time he saw her, it was like the strings that bound him to William Lucas, the ones that had given way in the weeks he spent apart from her and his old life, grew stronger. If he was not careful, he would return to the dazed, confused child he had been when he first learnt the truth about his past.

John said something about a barmaid. Fitzwilliam had vague impressions of her leaning towards him, of his nose filling with a cheap, harsh scent. She touched his arm and bent such that he had a clear view down her bodice; her bosom shook as she laughed. It would be nothing to lift a hand and touch her there, where her flesh looked soft and tantalising. He felt something like lips on his jaw. It reminded him of Elizabeth kissing him, and he closed his eyes to revel in the sensation. He was on the point of turning his head towards what he believed, hoped was her waiting mouth, when he felt a hand high on his leg, almost at the fall of his breeches; it sent a shiver of revulsion through his body. He realised with a sickening clarity that, in a drunken haze, he had mistaken the barmaid for Elizabeth and was perilously close to doing something he would forever regret.

He was on his feet before he knew what he was about, fleeing, driven by an urge to be away from the music, the rum, John, the other men, the girl, the temptation, and the memory of Elizabeth. The cold night air hit him, and he shook his head, praying for sobriety.

A hand grabbed his arm. "Where do you think you are going?"

Fitzwilliam felt a moment's alarm, assuming John had followed him and would force him to return. He turned, hardly knowing what he would say to excuse himself, but instead of John, he saw Viscount Bramwell.

"You?"

"You did not notice me across the hall? How astonishing. This way, if you please. I know where we shall find a hack chaise."

"I do not require your assistance." In his current state, he had no stomach for the viscount. He was dizzy and unsteady, and his heart still pounded in his chest at his narrow escape. John would berate him the next time they met. John would laugh, insult his lack of worldliness, tell him he was a disappointment to his father. Because it was what Fitzwilliam feared, it was easy to believe.

The viscount said something, but Fitzwilliam did not understand the words. He blinked several times, hoping it would turn the three Lord Bramwells into one. His cousin shook his head and pulled him along by the elbow as he spoke.

"Unless I am mistaken, I am sober, while you are not. I shall see that you get home safely."

They entered a square. Lord Bramwell whistled and gestured with his free hand to alert an idle driver to their need. He pushed

Fitzwilliam inside the carriage, told the driver they would first go to Berkeley Square, then Grosvenor Square, where, Fitzwilliam assumed, he lived.

"Surprised I know where you live?"

Lord Bramwell's voice was even. Only shadows were visible in the darkness, so Fitzwilliam could not see his expression, but he thought his cousin might be mocking him.

"The Darcys have had the same townhouse since my uncle was a child. I have been inside of it many times. You and Tom and I played there together as children. Does that surprise you?"

Every muscle in Fitzwilliam's body tensed. He wished his mind was not clouded by alcohol so that he could understand what his cousin was saying.

"I am four years your senior. Tom is not quite two years older than you are. We were together at Darcy House, at Pemberley, at Fitzwilliam House. Our parents were dear friends."

"That was a long time ago." Lord Bramwell's words sounded manipulative, designed to evoke an emotional reaction from him. Here was someone who had known him and his mother and what his family had been like before he was stolen from his home, forced to live a different life for two decades, only to then have *that* all snatched from him. Somehow, he knew that this cousin would tell him anything he wanted to know, if only he had the courage to ask, and that added to his distress. "Our families do not—"

"A long-ago argument between your father and our grandfather. It has nothing to do with you and me."

Fitzwilliam snorted. "I rather think it has a lot to do with me."

"We were children. We did not make this decision and—"

"Nevertheless, I shall honour my father's wishes. What else can I do?" *Please, God, tell me what I can do that would not cause him, me, any of us, more anguish!*

He knocked his hat off his head as he ran his hands through his hair. It landed on the viscount, who returned it without comment. The ride continued in silence. Fitzwilliam tried to clear his muddled thoughts and, for the second time that night, prevent himself from doing something he would regret. The rocking of the vehicle made him feel queasy.

"There is no reason we cannot be friends."

"There is every reason. I *must* honour my father." Fitzwilliam hoped the words sounded less forlorn than he felt.

When they reached Darcy House, Fitzwilliam exited the cab without saying another word.

ELIZABETH'S FONDNESS FOR REBECCA, Freddie, and their father grew each day, and she was happy to get to know Lord Bramwell and Colonel Fitzwilliam, who were amusing and charming. Watching Rebecca alternately blush or grow exasperated when she was with Lord Bramwell made Elizabeth smile and occasionally laugh. From the late-night conversations they had, Elizabeth knew Rebecca was reluctant to give her heart to any man. She feared making the same mistake her father had by not choosing his spouse wisely.

Elizabeth had called on Mrs Gardiner the day before, and her aunt wanted her to stay at Gracechurch Street for a week or two before going home. Elizabeth had agreed but could not say when it would be. Rebecca spoke about Elizabeth extending her stay, and Elizabeth was tempted to do so; the only reason she hesitated to accept was Fitzwilliam. She could no longer even think of him as William; it hurt too much to do so.

As the weather improved, Elizabeth, Rebecca, and Freddie—and sometimes Frederick Darcy—began a regular habit of walking in the park before breakfast. When Elizabeth first saw Fitzwilliam there with his friends, she had taken it for coincidence. The second time it happened, he walked with them for a little while, and without her realising it, the others had fallen behind, and she was alone with him. Her arm twitched with desire to slip around his. The silence between them—who had always spoken so freely and easily—was distressing. It also made her angry—at him for intruding on her life when he had shown that he no longer wanted to be part of it, at his father for turning him against her, her family, the Lucases, and at the entire situation.

After two or three minutes, Elizabeth said, "We make it a point to come out each day, as long as the weather is fine. This is a favourite path of ours. It is not too busy, and it is very pretty." She hoped he would realise that the chance encounters would continue if he did not change his routine.

Fitzwilliam sounded distracted when he replied, "Very nice. Very pretty."

Despite her warning, it happened a third time. To Elizabeth's relief, two ladies she and Rebecca had befriended were with them. It looked like Fitzwilliam intended to walk with them, but then one of the ladies began to talk to him, asking questions about how he was enjoying his first Season and if she would see him at this or that party, and he soon made an excuse and left— but not before sending what seemed like a longing look at her. She did not understand him and did not try to; she was convinced it would only lead to a headache.

This morning marked the fourth time she, Rebecca, and Freddie encountered him, and Elizabeth felt a ball of frustration growing inside of her, threatening to explode. The cousins greeted each other, and Elizabeth curtseyed. Her jaw was too tightly closed for speech to be possible. *Everything about my visit would be perfect, if I did not have to see him*, she told herself for what was likely the hundredth time. *It serves no purpose except to remind me what I have lost and that I blame him for allowing it to happen.*

Once again, she ended up with Fitzwilliam by her side; Rebecca and Freddie walked ahead of them. The sky was blue, though there were clouds in the distance, the trees and bushes were becoming lusher each day and soon flowers would begin to blossom. Spring was her second favourite season, and with its impending arrival, she knew her spirits would truly recover. If only *he* would stay away from her!

I have given up quite enough over the last four and a half months already. Can I not at least keep these excursions?

They walked in silence for what felt like an hour. She was determined not to be the one to speak this time. Elizabeth did her best to take in her surroundings—the gentle sound of children playing in the distance and the faint odour of fresh earth—and ignore the man walking next to her. She jumped when he spoke.

"It is a fine day."

"Mm." *He is speaking to me about the weather?* That *is all he has to say for himself?* She waited for him to ask about the Lucases or her family; it would be a sign that her William was still part of him. Nothing would change between them, but it would ease her heart to know the good man he had been was not completely lost.

Fitzwilliam asked, "How do you like the park?"

"Very much."

"Are you enjoying your time in London?"

"I am."

A moment later, he said, "I am surprised to see you here."

Her jaw set, she replied, "Are you?"

She took several quick steps and caught up to Rebecca and Freddie. Elizabeth knew what he meant to say. He did not like to see her. Perhaps he was afraid she would tell someone about their past. If he had ever truly understood her, he would know that she would not.

FITZWILLIAM WATCHED Elizabeth join Rebecca and Freddie after her enigmatic final words. Freddie fell back to walk with him. As they strolled along, Fitzwilliam only gave half of his attention to their conversation. He kept his hands clasped behind his back to stop himself from reaching for Elizabeth.

His presence in the park was no coincidence. He walked

there every morning he could, hoping to see Elizabeth. As much as he liked Rebecca and Freddie, it was the thought of Elizabeth that had him refusing every invitation to a pre-breakfast outing. He had even stopped riding with his father. George said he understood and was pleased that Fitzwilliam was making so many friends and enjoying himself, but Fitzwilliam saw and heard his disappointment. His father's voice seemed to shake when he asked who Fitzwilliam was meeting and what they were doing. When Fitzwilliam prevaricated, a muscle near his father's eye began to spasm. He thought his father might insist on knowing more about his activities, but instead he gripped the teacup he was holding so tightly that Fitzwilliam was worried it might shatter.

He had been unable to stop thinking about Elizabeth since the night he and John went to the music hall. His near misstep was a forceful reminder that he loved Elizabeth and that his happiness was with her. He might exist without her by his side, might even, in time, find it in him to take a wife and do his duty to Pemberley and produce an heir, but only with her would he experience joy and fulfillment.

The morning she said they intended to be in the park whenever possible, the weight on his shoulders eased a little. He had told himself that she understood the barriers to their being together, that although she had wanted to be Mrs William Lucas, she was not interested in a life as Mrs Fitzwilliam Darcy. But now, his heart sang, the refrain repeating again and again: *She wants to see me. She still wants us to be together. That is why she is in town.* All he needed to do was find a way to reconcile his father to the match and to ensure his uncle understood that she, her family, and the Lucases were not taking advantage of his new situation, thus protecting them from whatever retaliation Jeffrey would otherwise inflict on them. The Darcys might not like it, might accept her only grudgingly, but it would not matter, because they would be together.

Watching her walk arm-in-arm with Rebecca made him

realise that Frederick and his children might not object to their marriage. *Or would their affection for her vanish if I introduced her as my betrothed?*

Mr Bennet might not insist on the match, despite the expectation that he and Elizabeth would marry, but if they did, the Bennets would benefit a great deal. Did he not owe them for the years of their friendship and everything Mr Bennet had done for him? Had it not been for Mr Bennet's interest in him, Fitzwilliam would have been completely unprepared for the role of a gentleman. Mr Bennet had been happy to think about Elizabeth marrying William Lucas; given his disdain for those in the *ton*, would he be as willing to give his daughter to Fitzwilliam Darcy?

He heard John's voice saying, 'You must choose. You are either William Lucas or Fitzwilliam Darcy—you cannot be both'. There was no choice to make. *I am Fitzwilliam Darcy. But, right or wrong, I still want to marry Lizzy.*

Even after five months, his life still felt so unsettled. He could not deny the comforts afforded him as Fitzwilliam Darcy. He liked the concerts and theatre, sitting in the Darcy boxes rather than the inexpensive seats he had occupied on the rare occasions he had experienced such diversions in the past. His father had bought him a new curricle with a matched pair of fine horses to pull it. Fitzwilliam had taken his father driving through Hyde Park one pleasant afternoon. He was able to spend money liberally—on clothes, books, new furnishings for his apartment at Pemberley—anything he saw that he liked and wanted. However, there were discomforts. It was beginning to feel like each time he left the house, there were more and more people who watched him, asked him impertinent questions, tried to befriend him, or pushed some young lady in his direction. He did not like the feeling that everyone wanted something from him. It was as if he were trapped in a room that was growing smaller and smaller; one day, it would crush him.

But then, there was Elizabeth. His dearest friend. The person who understood him better than anyone else. The woman with whom he had planned a future, and the one without whom the years ahead would be empty and grey. She alone could open the door and rescue him.

There must be a way to make my father accept Lizzy! If he met her, spent time with her, he would have to agree that she was not seeking to gain from an association with me. Recognising his folly, he sighed. *I am certain he knows Lizzy is staying at Frederick's and has refused to meet her. I do not know if it is a prejudice against people like the Bennets or because they were part of William Lucas's life, but the fact remains that it would take a great deal more than meeting her for him to accept her.*

Freddie said, "I am glad Rebecca asked Lizzy to stay. She is awfully nice. My father likes her, too, and is happy to spend time with both of them when I am busy doing something else and cannot take them where they want to go. Like tomorrow. He is taking them to an exhibit."

"Oh? Do you know what it is?"

A minute later, Fitzwilliam knew where his Elizabeth would be on the morrow.

CHAPTER 21

EACH TIME FITZWILLIAM SAW ELIZABETH, HIS DESIRE TO HAVE her became stronger until it was so powerful, so raw, he felt it scraping at the inside of his stomach. He itched with need for her. It did not escape him that, if he married Elizabeth, he would establish new connexions to the Bennets and Lucases, even the friends he had left behind in Hertfordshire. No matter what the Darcys thought about them, they would be unable to argue that Elizabeth should sever her ties to her family, and as her husband, he would naturally visit Longbourn with her. In his more rational moments, Fitzwilliam knew it was at least as likely that his father —and uncle—would demand that Elizabeth give up the Bennets as accept them as his in-laws, but, because he did not like the idea, he pushed it aside. All he required was the right way to explain to George that he *had* to marry Elizabeth. Then he *would* act.

It was not easy to remain firm when he saw his father. The longer they remained in town, the more evident his father's unhappiness became—he was less inclined to go out, especially in the evening hours, and his appetite suffered. When they were together, his father stared at him as he had when Fitzwilliam first returned to Pemberley. He asked what Fitzwilliam did less and less frequently, and when he did enquire, it was impossible to tell whether he was pleased with what he heard.

Or perhaps I am reflecting my own guilt. I cannot tell him that I do not like spending time with John and his friends and that I would rather be with Lizzy—he must know she is in town, even though he cannot know what she is to me—or that I would like to know Viscount Bramwell and Colonel Fitzwilliam.

The previous week, after returning from the park one morning, Fitzwilliam came across Jeffrey leaving Darcy House.

"Fitzwilliam," his uncle had said in reply to his greeting.

"You have seen my father?"

Jeffrey nodded.

Glancing around to make sure no one would overhear, Fitzwilliam asked, "I own, I wonder if he is quite well."

"Have you asked him?"

Fitzwilliam said that he had. "He says it is nothing except being in town for too long."

Jeffrey considered him for a moment before replying, "Yes. My brother has never much liked society. Being here this Season is a sacrifice he has made for *you*. Do not concern yourself; he is perfectly healthy. I talked to him about how he was faring, and I have no anxiety about him at all. If you wish to assist him...?"

Although insulted that his uncle questioned his desire to be of use to George, he said nothing other than that he did.

"What will do him the most good is to see that you are amusing yourself—spending time with John, making friends, getting up to the usual mischief young men enjoy."

Fitzwilliam would have thought suggesting they—or at least George—return to Derbyshire might be more to the purpose, but Jeffrey knew his brother best. "I see. Thank you, Uncle."

His uncle was stepping away but stopped and faced Fitzwilliam again. "One word of caution. Do not bother my brother with your concerns. He dislikes anyone hovering over him, fretting like an old woman. There is no need to talk about what is disturbing him." With a curt dip of his chin, Jeffrey left him.

Fitzwilliam was not entirely certain what to make of his

uncle's advice, but if Jeffrey was not anxious about George's health, Fitzwilliam supposed there was no reason he should be either.

After an early breakfast, he went to the exhibit hall where he expected to find Elizabeth; he soon saw her, Rebecca, and Frederick.

They exchanged the usual greetings, and Rebecca said, "We have only just arrived. You must join us."

Since he was there to see Elizabeth, he naturally accepted the invitation.

The hall was crowded and full of the low murmuring of voices. Elizabeth linked arms with Rebecca, and the two women walked ahead of Frederick and Fitzwilliam.

After five minutes of them looking at stone and bone tools and a colourful coat with beads and feathers, Frederick asked, "How are you doing, Fitzwilliam?"

"I am well." Fitzwilliam was distracted by the nearness of his beloved. How he wished he had the right to be at Elizabeth's side, her hand resting on his arm. He could imagine their conversation, her intelligent eyes and lively expressions as, together, they would wonder about the people who had made the relics. Had they given them up voluntarily? Did they mind their loss?

"Are you? It has been a difficult few months. If you are at all like your father, and I think you are, all the attention will not be to your liking."

"It is not."

"George talks of going to Pemberley at Easter," Frederick said a moment or two later. "Will you go with him?"

"I do not know." He had forgotten that his father mentioned travelling into Derbyshire. It was something to do with an escalating dispute between a group of tenants. *If he goes, I do not have to go with him, do I?* He would, should George ask. *But how can I leave London when Lizzy is here?*

They stopped to let a party of four ladies, one with a ridiculously tall hat decorated with so many feathers it looked like she had a bird roosting on her head, pass them.

"You have been spending a great deal of time with John. Do you enjoy his company?"

"He has been very kind." For the moment, Fitzwilliam gave Frederick his full attention. The question was strange. More and more, he disliked going out with his cousin, even though it pleased his father. The end of the Season could not come soon enough for him. By the next time he was in town, he would find a way to avoid John without his purpose being obvious. By then he would know more people and truthfully be able to say he was busy with other friends—friends he selected for himself.

Fitzwilliam was called upon to talk to this person or that several times. In truth, he did not always remember the people who claimed a right to greet him. He resented the way they demanded his attention. He liked feeling that he was with his family—people who saw him as more than the Season's sensation and a wealthy, unmarried young man.

He and Elizabeth had just a few minutes to talk. While Frederick was greeting an acquaintance, Fitzwilliam went to stand by her as she examined a piece of sculpture. When Rebecca saw him, she smiled, patted Elizabeth's arm, and joined her father.

"It is fascinating, is it not?" he said.

She kept her head bent to the object, but he watched her and saw the colour rise on the curve of her cheek.

"Indeed."

"Why do you think they made it? Was it only for artistic merit, or do you think it served some practical purpose?"

Elizabeth turned her face away from him for a moment before resuming her study. "I am sure I do not know."

When she walked to the next item, he followed and, like her, began a silent inspection of it.

As soon as he judged they had sufficient privacy, he lowered his voice and said, "We must talk."

Her eyes darted to him then to their surroundings; although

there was a quartet of people standing nearby, they were engaged in a lively conversation and unlikely to overhear their exchange.

Elizabeth said, "It would serve no purpose. There is nothing to say."

"I—"

"Miss Elizabeth," Frederick called as he approached, Rebecca by his side, "have you seen enough? Rebecca and I are ready to depart, whenever you are."

Fitzwilliam averted his gaze, lest his cousins see how annoyed he was by their intrusion. *I want—need—more time with Lizzy!* He felt stronger with her nearby, almost as if he could see a clearing in the fog that had enveloped him since that earth-shaking day in October.

Elizabeth said she was also ready to return to Curzon Street. With reluctance, Fitzwilliam declined Frederick's invitation to go with them. His father awaited him at home.

FITZWILLIAM TOOK his time returning to Darcy House. He was lost in thought imagining what it would be like to have Elizabeth with him always. Her insistence that they had nothing to talk about was another mark of her acceptance that his changed circumstances made their marriage unlikely. He wanted to assure her that he was working on a way to make it possible. It was not the life they had planned, but, somehow, they *would* be married. Had they not both said, more often than he could recall, that being together was of utmost importance to their happiness?

Once home, he and George sat in the study drinking coffee and eating honey cake while they discussed business. After twenty minutes, George asked, "Where were you earlier?"

The question was innocuous, but there was a tightness in his father's voice that made Fitzwilliam sit up straighter.

"I went to an exhibit."

"Oh? What was it?"

Fitzwilliam described it to him and mentioned several of

the relics he remembered. From the look on George's face, he was disappointed Fitzwilliam had not invited him to attend, and perhaps suspicious, though about what, he could not imagine.

"Did you see anyone you know?"

Fitzwilliam hesitated. "A few people."

"It has been very busy, these last weeks."

Fitzwilliam nodded.

"Are you enjoying your time with John? You are getting along with him?"

Must everyone ask me about him today? "He has been very kind." Inwardly, he rolled his eyes at saying just what he had to Frederick earlier. Fitzwilliam forced his hands apart and picked up his coffee. Drinking it gave him an excuse not to talk, but in any case, he seemed to have placated his father.

George cut the remainder of his cake into small pieces with his fork, but he did not eat any of it. "I must go to Pemberley at Easter. The trouble will not be resolved from here."

After one more sip of cold, milky coffee, Fitzwilliam asked his father to explain how he foresaw settling it. The conversation then returned to business, to Fitzwilliam's relief.

THE FOLLOWING WEEK, Elizabeth attended a ball with Rebecca, Freddie, and their father. She was alone in her room preparing, and as she examined her face in the mahogany dressing mirror, her mind drifted to Fitzwilliam. She wondered if she had stayed too long in London. *I cannot bear to continue seeing him. He has not asked about the Lucases, my family, or his friends. He is not happy to see me, not that I expected he would be, and...and it is time that I not only* say *that I am going on with my life but that I* actually *do it.*

Half of London was expected at the ball, since it was the last one before Parliament took a recess for Easter. She was wearing a new Pomona-green gown with a golden net overlay; it was the most fashionable dress she had ever owned. She looked pretty in it, and she intended to enjoy the evening.

After they remarked on the number of people and decorations, Frederick Darcy expressed a desire to seek out some friends who were in attendance.

Freddie assured him, "I shall stand guard on Rebecca and Lizzy and make sure they do not dance with anyone you would not like."

"And who will protect you?" Elizabeth asked.

"Me?" His expression became one of horror; she knew he only partly meant it. "I have no interest in dancing except for the one you promised me."

"If you like, I shall step on your toes so that you have a ready excuse to avoid dancing for the rest of the evening."

Her companions laughed, and they separated. The young people walked through the room until they found an exit to the terrace. They stepped outside to enjoy the fresh air.

"I did not see Bramwell and the colonel, but I know they are coming," Freddie announced.

Rebecca demanded, "How do you know that?"

"Bramwell and I spoke about it the other day. He was not certain they would arrive in time for the first set."

"Do you tell him everything we do?"

"Why should I not? He is my friend."

"That does not mean you have to tell him where he can find m-us."

Elizabeth smiled, albeit with a tinge of sadness; she would miss them when she left. "Come along, you two. Let us continue our walk and see all the wonders there are to see."

ANOTHER BALL, Fitzwilliam thought as the carriage slowly jostled along the busy street. He had never anticipated Easter so much as he did this year. *No balls or parties for several weeks at least. If*

Lizzy was not in town, I would gladly go to Derbyshire. How I am growing to despise London.

John was his only companion. They, along with George and Jeffrey, had been to dinner with Lady Sophia. His father had intended to accompany them, but changed his mind, claiming he was too fatigued.

"You will have more fun with just John there, I dare say," his father had said.

There had been an odd expression in his eyes; Fitzwilliam could not name it, and he tried to find reassurance in his uncle's recent words. That might be easier, he speculated, if he liked Jeffrey.

Fitzwilliam hoped that Elizabeth would be at the ball. *If she is, I shall spend time with her, but I must first separate myself from John. They have not met yet, and I intend to put off introducing them for as long as possible.*

When they arrived, John suggested they look for their friends. "There are so many people here, we might not see them, but it will help to pass the time."

As they walked around, Fitzwilliam looked for Elizabeth but did not see her. He heard his name on the tongues of the people they passed. Like so much else about his new life, he had thought he was becoming used to it. However, after seeing Elizabeth more, he was beginning to find the gossip—and his cousin's company—intolerable.

One person said, "He is very proud, is he not? Cannot be bothered to say above two words to anyone other than his family!"

Proud? Just because I shall not answer their impertinent questions, I am condemned. How ought I to respond to the false friendships offered by people who want to use me because they think I am naïve, a fool that lived a lesser life? Fool. I feel like a fool. What am I doing here, completely separated from everyone I love?

John stopped and moaned. "Oh God, I see Rebecca and Freddie. I suppose we must acknowledge them."

Fitzwilliam's heart pounded as they walked towards his cousins and Elizabeth. She was lovely, her cheeks dusted with colour as she turned her head this way and that, taking in her surroundings. When she spotted him, her eyes locked on his.

He did not want her anywhere near John. His cousin would dismiss her, even mock her for her position in life. His head jerked between them. *No, no, no, no. I do not want to introduce them. Please, no!*

He stood stiff and tall and tried to calm himself as Rebecca made the introductions. To her credit, Elizabeth seemed as reluctant to know John as he was to know her. Within two minutes, John was pulling him away. Fitzwilliam took one last look at Elizabeth and vowed to return to her side that night.

Just as Fitzwilliam and John Darcy walked away from them, Viscount Bramwell and Colonel Fitzwilliam joined them. Elizabeth noticed that Lord Bramwell watched Fitzwilliam walking away with John Darcy; the expression on his face seemed to be one of exasperation. She returned Colonel Fitzwilliam's greeting.

The colonel nudged his brother with his elbow. "We are very glad to see you, are we not?"

The viscount sputtered, greeted them, and fixed his eyes on Rebecca. Elizabeth thought she looked particularly charming that evening. She wore a coral gown with a lace overlay, and under Lord Bramwell's scrutiny, her cheeks soon turned rosy. "Miss Darcy, will you do me the honour of dancing the first set with me?"

"It is very kind of you to ask, but it is not necessary." The colour in her cheeks grew darker, and she opened her fan and began to wave it in front of her face.

"Are you engaged to dance with another gentleman?"

Elizabeth suppressed a giggle. *At least watching their romance develop distracts me from Fitzwilliam.*

Colonel Fitzwilliam sniggered. Elizabeth and Freddie exchanged a look that showed he shared her wish to laugh.

Elizabeth gave Rebecca's hand a reassuring squeeze. "What Rebecca meant to say is that she is not engaged for the first set, it is very kind of you to ask, she is most honoured, *et cetera,* and thank you."

Lord Bramwell grinned. "Excellent!"

"Will you do me the honour of dancing with me, Miss Bennet?" asked Colonel Fitzwilliam.

She smiled at him. "I would be most happy to, Colonel."

They arranged to meet Freddie and find Frederick after the set, and the couples went to take their places in the lines. Elizabeth vowed to forget that Fitzwilliam was there and enjoy the remainder of the evening. After all, she was in the company of amiable, handsome gentlemen who, unlike him, did not see her as beneath their notice.

CHAPTER 22

"WHY SO HASTY?" FITZWILLIAM SHOOK OFF JOHN'S HAND AS they walked away from Rebecca, Freddie, and Elizabeth.

"You did not see Bramwell and his brother?"

Fitzwilliam remained silent. He had not seen either of them since the night the viscount had taken him home in a cab. Fitzwilliam had been angry at the time, but the next day he was grateful for his cousin's assistance.

"Did you wish to stay with Freddie and Rebecca?" John's tone was verging on mocking, and it made Fitzwilliam's fists curl. "Or is it their friend you wished to be near? You knew her before, did you not?"

"I did." He held John's eye until someone jostled his arm, almost daring him to say something more about Elizabeth.

A feminine voice said, "Oh, please do excuse me."

Fitzwilliam inclined his head at the lady and stepped aside to make room for her and her party. She smiled at him and opened her mouth to speak, but before she did, a young man said, "Come along, Caroline."

They were hardly out of hearing range when John said, "Trust Caroline Bingley to 'accidentally' bump into you. You have not had the honour before, have you?"

Fitzwilliam gave a curt shake of his head.

John sneered. "She was with her brother, and their older

sister and her husband. Hurst is someone, but the Bingleys are not. She was hoping you would be more gallant. Perhaps beg the favour of an introduction or offer her marriage. Their father sold his business when they were children, but the stench of trade is still rather ripe. They are rich but…" He shrugged. "Could you imagine what my uncle and father would say if one of us wanted to marry a lady so closely tied to trade?" With that, John guffawed.

Fitzwilliam thought about the Lucases, Philipses, and Gardiners and felt his cheeks heat. They were all excellent people, as was Mrs Bennet, who had always been so kind to him. In mocking the Bingleys, John might as well have been speaking about Elizabeth. Fitzwilliam could not abide John's intolerance; really, he was beginning to realise just how much about John he found unbearable. "You might not think their friendship or marriage to one in their position would be suitable, but that does not mean they deserve your contempt."

Even though he had not intended to speak, he did not regret having done so. To remain silent was to suggest that he agreed with his cousin. Nothing would convince him that people in trade, or with family connexions in trade, deserved such scorn simply because of their circumstances.

After an uncomfortably long silence, John said, "We should find something else to discuss."

Fitzwilliam said nothing further. A short while later, he found an excuse to separate from his cousin.

SOON AFTER LEAVING JOHN, he ran into the Fitzwilliams. Colonel Fitzwilliam nodded towards a quiet corner. With a mix of reluctance and curiosity, he went with them.

"You know there is no reason you cannot talk to us," the colonel said.

"I can think of one."

Lord Bramwell grumbled but said nothing.

Fitzwilliam said, "This is a very public space. I have no wish to—"

"Be seen with us?" Lord Bramwell interjected.

"You know very well that my father—"

"Would not like it."

The colonel was matter of fact, which was better than argumentative or dismissive, Fitzwilliam supposed.

"Did it ever occur to you that we would simply like to be your friends and leave the strife to our parents?" the colonel asked.

"Friends?" An involuntary bark of disbelief came out of Fitzwilliam's mouth. The notion that he had any friends felt more ludicrous with each day.

"Yes, friends," Lord Bramwell hissed. "We were once."

"Perhaps, but it was long, long ago. You have new friends now. Freddie. Rebecca." *Lizzy. Would* they *object if I married her, or would they be allies?* Fitzwilliam held up a hand, palm out. "I do not pretend to understand what happened when our parents had their falling out, and neither can you. We were all too young. What I do know is that my father has suffered enough. I *will not* cause him more grief." As the words left his mouth, Fitzwilliam felt like a hypocrite given his inability to stay away from Elizabeth.

"Choose your companions wisely," Colonel Fitzwilliam advised.

"Consider what your return means for him. You know whom I mean," the viscount added.

"And how he expects you to behave."

The advice made something stir inside of Fitzwilliam, but he could not grasp its nature. His brow furrowed, and his eyes met first one brother's then the other's before he walked away.

FAR INTO THE NIGHT, Fitzwilliam returned. After their last encounter, Elizabeth had forced all thought of him from her mind so that she could enjoy the evening. It was successful, and she had danced and laughed and partaken of every other amusement one could find in a ballroom. His reappearance was like a dark cloud suddenly appearing to block the sun.

Freddie asked, "Where is John?"

"I do not know." Fitzwilliam turned to her. "Li—Miss Bennet, will you do me the honour of a dance?"

Elizabeth knew her expression showed her surprise, but she was powerless to stop it. "I-I do not, that is—"

Freddie and Rebecca encouraged her to accept, and as the music for the set was just commencing, she and Fitzwilliam went to join the lines.

Why would he ask me to dance? Every time we have seen each other, he has been silent and severe. I am content to go our separate ways, yet he singles me out in such a public setting.

In happier times, they would chat and laugh as they danced. There was none of that this time, and she once again blamed George Darcy for ruining her William. She could taste the bitterness of her disappointment in her mouth and was angry with herself for not being stronger.

When the dance was at the midpoint, he spoke. "I hope everyone in Hertfordshire is well."

"Those I have an acquaintance with are quite well." *After all the times we have seen each other, he only now asks about the people he once loved best!*

When the dance next allowed them to speak, he said, "How came you to be staying with Rebecca?"

"Are you so surprised that she would see value in my company?" *Not all Darcys think me beneath their notice. You may, your cousin, your father...*

"I had not thought you liked London."

As they had discussed many times, they both preferred the pleasures of the countryside.

"I am as capable of changing my opinions as anyone else is."

It was only when their dance was almost at an end that he

spoke again. This time, his voice was little more than a whisper. "Why are you here?"

"Because I did not wish to be at Longbourn." If he had given any thought to what she suffered in his absence, he would not have had to ask. Elizabeth's heart sank when it was clear that he did not understand.

SHE DOES NOT WISH to be at Longbourn! Fitzwilliam's mind cried. *She wants to be with me. She hopes, even expects me to honour those wishes I expressed when I was William Lucas.*

John caught up to him while he was woolgathering. "There you are. I have had quite enough of this. Let us find our friends and go seek some real amusement. Some place with friendlier girls and better music."

Consumed by his own thoughts, Fitzwilliam hardly heard John speaking. They were near the exit when Colonel Fitzwilliam pulled him aside. John did not notice as Fitzwilliam was trailing behind him, his thoughts still on Elizabeth.

The colonel asked, "Where are you going? Do you have any idea what he is up to?"

"What?"

His cousin shook his arm, which dispelled some of the haze in which Fitzwilliam was caught.

"Think about those men you have been spending your time with. I do not care that John is your cousin, or how much Uncle Darcy or anyone else tells you that he should be your best friend. Do you like him? Do you truly wish to emulate him?"

"What gives you the right—?"

Colonel Fitzwilliam interjected. "Sterling and I have both seen you looking less than happy in his company."

"Do not presume to tell me how I feel!" A sudden rush of resentment and frustration burned in his chest. He was tired of everyone telling him what to do or think or like or what he must be feeling since finding out he was a Darcy. None of them stood a chance of understanding him; only Elizabeth did.

"I will not, but I shall presume to give you a piece of advice, one I think you sorely need. Consider what you want and what will make you happiest in this reclaimed life of yours. Think very carefully about the people you are befriending. I cannot imagine what the last few months have been like for you, but it is clear to me that you need someone you can confide in, someone you can trust. I do not think it is John Darcy."

Colonel Fitzwilliam disappeared into the ballroom. His words rang in Fitzwilliam's ears as he stared after him. *I do need someone who knows me and understands me and whom I can trust. I need Lizzy.*

John returned to find him, and they went to join the men John called friends. Once outside, the cool night air revived Fitzwilliam, and he was surprised to realise that he was about to step into a carriage. The others were already seated within it.

Fitzwilliam retracted the foot that had been upon the step and let his arms fall to his sides. "I do not believe I shall go with you."

In response, there were several cries of protest.

He shook his head. "I do not want to." A corner of his mouth jerked upward as he said, "I am going home."

Fitzwilliam closed the door and turned his back to it.

CHAPTER 23

FITZWILLIAM WAS LOOKING THROUGH THE NEWSPAPER AT breakfast the next morning. He was aware of his father's eyes upon him, and after several minutes, George broke the silence.

"You were home early last night. Was the ball not to your liking?"

"It was like any other large ball—too crowded, too loud, too hot. John went elsewhere afterwards, but I was not inclined to join him."

"I see."

Fitzwilliam heard doubt or perhaps disquiet in his father's voice but did not know why. He did not understand his father. Questions were on the tip of his tongue, but he hesitated, whether because of his uncle's advice or because he was afraid of the answers—or a combination of the two—he did not know.

"I have a mind to depart for Derbyshire the day after tomorrow."

Fitzwilliam pushed the remains of his breakfast around on his plate. "Do you particularly wish me to go with you?"

There was a pause before his father asked, "You prefer to stay in town?"

"I had thought I might. Friends have mentioned doing this or that." *Lizzy is here. I cannot leave until I have settled things with her.*

Again, there was a pause, this time it felt like five or ten minutes, before his father responded. Guilt ripped at Fitzwilliam's heart. His shoulders drooped, but he could not do what his father wanted, not this time. *I cannot go on as I have been. I shall surely go mad if I do.* He had been awake almost the whole night thinking about Elizabeth. *The only way I shall be able to marry her is if the situation is forced. I hear enough warnings about ladies or their families seeking to compromise eligible gentlemen, though I cannot believe it happens as often as people say it does. If somehow it appeared that I had dishonoured Lizzy... It would have to be that way; if it seemed that she had compromised me, my father, Jeffrey, John, all of them would hate her forever, perhaps even seek to ruin her and the Bennets rather than allow a marriage. But how does one compromise a lady?* An image of him grabbing her by the shoulders and kissing her in the middle of Hyde Park or, better yet, a crowded ballroom came to mind. *Stupid, stupid idea. While it would be effective, Lizzy would never forgive me.* After a second, he added, *And I could never shame her, my father, or myself in such a way.*

At length, his father said, "If that is your wish, then, of course, you must stay."

George left London two days later, saying he would return in a fortnight. It was a short amount of time, given how long it took to travel to Derbyshire, and Fitzwilliam suspected his father would have remained longer in the country if Fitzwilliam had agreed to go with him.

"I shall be here," Fitzwilliam promised.

As much as part of him wished to go to Elizabeth at once, he found his time was not his own. He was engaged to dine with Jeffrey and John one night. He spent another evening with Lady Sophia and a large party of her friends. Frederick asked to see him and came to dinner at Darcy House one day. It was pleasant, if awkward, because Fitzwilliam expected Frederick to talk about Elizabeth or ask him further questions about John which, since his thoughts about his cousin were unsettled, he did not want to answer. Frederick did not; however, he did speak about the Fitzwilliams and his belief that George would soften towards them with time. Although Fitzwilliam did not say it aloud, he was pleased; at the very least, it would mean he no longer had to worry about being seen talking to them.

ELIZABETH HAD BEEN out of sorts since the ball. She informed Rebecca that she could not remain after Easter. From the way Rebecca looked at her, Elizabeth suspected she knew there was more to Elizabeth and Fitzwilliam's past than Elizabeth had told her, but Elizabeth could not speak of it. She arranged to go to Gracechurch Street for a few days the Wednesday after Easter. Elizabeth prayed she would not see Fitzwilliam again before she left, but he appeared at church on Good Friday. He arrived before they did, and Frederick caught his eye and waved him over.

Fitzwilliam said, "How good to see you. I have often walked past this church. With my father at Pemberley, I thought I would come here this morning."

"I hope you will join us," Frederick said.

Freddie and Rebecca echoed his invitation.

Elizabeth was relieved when Rebecca took the seat beside her before there was any possibility that Fitzwilliam might.

After the service, Frederick invited Fitzwilliam to join them for breakfast. "It will be no trouble, and we would welcome your company."

Elizabeth spoke before Fitzwilliam could. "He should know that Lord Bramwell and Colonel Fitzwilliam will be there."

He gave her a look that seemed grateful. "I cannot, but thank you for asking."

There were expressions of regret from Rebecca, Freddie, and their father, but Elizabeth said nothing. *He has spared us being forced into company together. Five days and I will be gone. We shall both be happier then, and I shall be myself again, not the sad, resentful creature I am near him or that I was before I came to town.*

FITZWILLIAM WAS grateful for Elizabeth's warning, which showed she understood the difficulty of his position regarding his maternal cousins. Her further silence told him that she was disappointed they were losing this opportunity to spend time together.

Soon we shall talk, my Lizzy, he thought as he left the church. *As soon as I can possibly arrange it!*

The time came the very next morning. While walking in the park, he saw Frederick and Rebecca, who informed him that Freddie was with friends and Elizabeth was at home writing letters. He made his excuses and hastened to Frederick's house.

She is alone by design! She knew I was likely to see Frederick and Rebecca and they would tell me that she was alone. How much happier I shall be once this is settled. Finally, we can be together as we planned. My position is very different now, but I will make her my wife as I have always wanted to. I shall say that I am obligated to her. My father will understand. He must. I will make him, somehow. It is a matter of honour, not through compromise, but through expectation. He is proud of the family name, and it would be a dishonour not to live up to my obligations, even if it was William Lucas who entered into them. No one will blame me or her or the Bennets or Lucases. There will be no cause for Jeffrey or John to-to— Fitzwilliam pushed these thoughts aside and imagined the joy of having Elizabeth by his side once again.

At Frederick's, he was shown into the morning room. Elizabeth put down her pen and stood when she saw it was him. She looked pale, but so beautiful, and his arms began to reach for her before he stopped himself. There would be time for that after he had proposed and she accepted. How good it would feel to have her body pressed into his once again. His head swam with anticipation. After flinging his hat onto a sofa, he took several long strides towards her.

"At last!"

"At last?" she echoed.

When she held up a hand, palm forward, he stopped walking.

"At last, we are alone and can talk properly. At last, I have resolved my dilemma. It may not be easy, but-but he *will* understand. I know how to explain it so that none of them can say you are taking advantage and— I am bound by honour."

"I am afraid I do not take your meaning." Elizabeth's cheeks flushed, and he could see her chest rising and falling rapidly. One of her hands rested on the table behind her.

He pulled off his great coat, tossed it on top of his hat, and began to pace. "It has plagued my mind for weeks. So much has changed; I knew that almost as soon as I arrived at Pemberley. You have no idea—"

She said something, but he did not hear the words and kept talking.

"Everything I heard, everything I saw, showed me how much different my life was supposed to be. My father would hate it if he knew I was here. I do not want to cause him more pain, but I will find a way to explain it to him, to make him understand—"

Elizabeth spoke loudly enough that her words made it past his agitated reflections. "Pray tell me, what it is that Mr George Darcy is to understand?"

Fitzwilliam stopped to gaze upon his dearest, loveliest Elizabeth. "You. Our marriage." His voice was raspy and heavy. "You are not the sort of woman Fitzwilliam Darcy of Pemberley—but everyone in Meryton expects it. Had I not been abducted, I would marry a lady of rank and fortune, but this is a matter of honour. Jeffrey, John, maybe others in my family, will hate it, but they can do nothing about it, not given the circumstances. I shall assure them that I am obligated."

Elizabeth's mouth fell open, and she stared at him for a moment before her expression hardened. "You are *not* obligated to me. I will not hold you or myself to a foolish promise made when we were children and too ignorant of the world to know better."

The oddest sound came out of his mouth, and his hand flew out to grasp the back of a chair before he fell to his knees. "W-what? I do not understand— Are you saying that you will not marry...?"

He must have misunderstood. How many times had he longed for her? Even in the face of Jeffrey's and John's warnings, had he not sought a way for them to be together? Now that he was here, telling her that—despite everything that had changed—they could be together, she would not have him?

Her lips pressed into a thin line, Elizabeth nodded.

"Just like that, I am refused? After all the times you told me—?"

Elizabeth interjected, "I made promises to William Lucas, *not* Fitzwilliam Darcy. I scarcely know Fitzwilliam Darcy, and what I have seen of him, I do not like."

He sucked in his breath as if someone had kicked his stomach. He had struggled to understand who he was and the consequences of losing his identity twice before his twenty-fifth birthday. Her words were a reminder of how much he still did not understand and of how lost and alone he felt. "But why are you here?"

"Why do you think? William Lucas would know."

He shook his head, hoping to dispel the dark shadow that engulfed him. "To see me. To-to show that if I could find a way to overcome the expectations of my family, my duty to them—"

Elizabeth scoffed. "You think I came to London to seek you out? Rebecca said they never saw you, else I would not have accepted her invitation. I needed to be away from Longbourn. How could you forget me? Have you no consideration for what I had to endure?"

Fitzwilliam was angered by her words, hurt by her rejection. "You? Do you have any idea what it was like for me? I was

197

stolen from my family as a baby and left to die. When Frederick found me, I had to leave behind everything I knew and confront the truth that my life, my name, all of it was a lie. My father—"

"Your father!" Elizabeth cried as she threw up her hands in dismissal. "I am sure he wasted no time telling you that what William Lucas had was not good enough for you, whether it be clothes, your family, or-or me!"

He had no time to respond even had he known what to say; she waited but an instant before continuing.

"You speak of your family. What about the family you left behind—Sir William and Lady Lucas and Charlotte? Do you even know that Charlotte is married?"

It felt as if someone had hit him in the chest. "Married?"

"To Captain Farnon in January. You did not know because you abandoned them along with me and everyone else who loved William Lucas. One letter! That is all the time you could spare for us. One short letter in all these months for those who have loved you and cared for you all your life.

"I am sorry I came to London, sorry I ever saw this creature you have become. I do not claim to know you now, but I do know that Fitzwilliam Darcy is the last man in the world I would wish to marry! You are free to choose a rich, titled lady who, unlike me, is suited to be the wife of Fitzwilliam Darcy of Pemberley, free to forget about those you left behind in Hertfordshire." Her eyes were like steel, her laugh bitter. "You already have, by all accounts."

With as much dignity as he could muster, and it was precious little, Fitzwilliam said, "You have said quite enough. I did what I thought was right, and I shall never be ashamed of it." He gathered his things. "Good day, madam."

With that, he was gone.

CHAPTER 24

HOW COULD ELIZABETH SAY SUCH CRUEL THINGS? HAD SHE truly not understood how full of turmoil the last months had been for him? He had been desperate to find a way for them to be together, and she rejected him. Elizabeth had condemned his father without ever having met him. Never would he have supposed her capable of such actions.

As soon as he arrived at Darcy House, he told Mallon he was going away as soon as a bag was packed. "Have my curricle brought around at once."

The butler asked if he was well, but Fitzwilliam waved off the question and instead directed him to inform Lady Sophia—with whom he was supposed to dine the next day—and the housekeeper that he would be out of town. "I shall return before my father is expected."

His eyes fell on a calling card which sat on a glossy walnut table near the front door.

John! His cousin had likely come to drag him off to who knew where or to drape himself languidly in a chair and berate Fitzwilliam for not spending more time with him. The more Fitzwilliam thought of such an interview, the more desperate he felt. *I must leave London!*

He ran up the stairs to his bedchamber. When Quinn entered

the room, Fitzwilliam thrust two books into the valet's hands and ordered him to pack a bag.

"I do not need much. I shall not be dining out or going to this party or that blasted ball. You will stay here."

Quinn did as he was ordered. While his valet packed, Fitzwilliam wrote a few lines to his father to inform him about his absence from town. In a reasonable amount of time, though it was still too long for Fitzwilliam's liking, he was properly dressed for driving and leaving the house.

Fitzwilliam drove, heedless of the direction, for the better part of an hour before he felt he had put enough distance between himself and Elizabeth. Not far outside of the city, he stopped by the side of the road and breathed deeply, as if he had been running. He rejected several offers of assistance and thought about what to do. Leaving town was unequivocally the right decision. He *needed* to be away from Elizabeth and his cousins and uncle and everyone else who knew him.

I want to be alone, just for a few days.

His heart felt like it would burst with the weight of emotion resting on it, and he entertained a fantasy of standing in the middle of the street, screaming at everyone to leave him alone. *If one more person tells me how wonderful it is that I discovered my true identity, I shall beat them with a stick.* It was *not* wonderful. Nothing that had happened to him since Frederick Darcy's visit to Longbourn in October was wonderful.

No, that is not true. It was good to know the truth. But so much had happened to him since he discovered who he really was, and he could bear no more.

Where can I go? Not north. Hertfordshire lay in that direction, and it was the territory of William Lucas. Brighton was an easy enough distance, but it was too lively and full of people who would recognise him.

East. It is early enough that I can go some distance, perhaps even make it to the seaside. I shall find a town where I can stay for a few days and, please God, find some peace.

He had one week before he must return to being Fitzwilliam Darcy, and he would take advantage of every minute.

FITZWILLIAM DROVE TOWARDS ESSEX, not certain where he would end up and not particularly caring. In the early afternoon, he stopped at an inn to eat a meal when his body reminded him that he had consumed nothing but toast that day. The proprietor's wife served him herself. It was just what Lady Lucas had done years ago when they had a particularly wealthy customer.

Fitzwilliam said, "I wish to spend a few days by the seaside. Somewhere quiet, but not too quiet. Do you know of such a place?"

"Southend, sir. It can be lively enough, but there will not be many about at this time of year. I happen to know just the place to suit you."

With this recommendation, Fitzwilliam continued on his journey and reached the town before night fell. The establishment was well-maintained, and the owner was friendly and accommodating. As he ate dinner, Fitzwilliam realised that it reminded him of the Lucases' inn in Shropshire. *The first home I remember.*

They were happy times. He had helped around the inn, played with the sons of their neighbours and, whenever he could, lost himself in reading. Everyone remarked on his intelligence, and Sir William often said, 'It seems our humble William was meant for great things'.

The words, long forgotten, took on new meaning now.

Then their fortunes had changed. Sir William earned a knighthood by providing assistance to the king's travelling party when one of the carriages had an accident. How awestruck he, then a lad of seven, had been to get a glimpse of the sovereign. *To think that now I dine with princes and dukes and am the grandson and nephew of an earl!*

The Lucases had sold the inn and moved to Hertfordshire to

take on the mantle of gentlefolk. Fitzwilliam still could hear Sir William's awed voice saying, 'You will be a gentleman, William my lad, a real gentleman!'

A real gentleman. Much good it has done me.

Immediately after eating, he retired. He was exhausted, in body and heart and mind.

THE NEXT MORNING, Fitzwilliam went to church and listened to an indifferent sermon. Because it was not terribly engaging, he reflected on the Easter holiday and the idea of sin and rebirth. He had sinned. All men did, whatever their intentions. But he knew he had more to atone for than most, even though he could not order his thoughts enough to understand where, let alone why, he had gone wrong.

As for rebirth, he almost laughed aloud when he considered that he had already been reborn twice—first when he became William Lucas and again when he resumed his real identity.

After taking breakfast at the inn, he went for a walk. His body wanted activity, and he intended to wander for as long as possible. The bitter exchange with Elizabeth was foremost in his thoughts. He had yearned for her when they were apart and mourned when he realised his new position meant they could not be together. Then he had seen her again and understood just how much he wanted and needed her by his side. He had known that it would take some delicacy to explain their attachment to his father, and to Jeffrey and John and perhaps others in the family. He had wanted to ensure that they saw that Elizabeth was not taking advantage of him, that although they viewed the match as a degradation, it must take place. But then, just as he knew how to explain it to them, she had rejected him.

She has forsworn every promise she made to me. He sat alone on a bench under a tree in a pretty spot Elizabeth would like. *How could she forget everything we were to each other, everything we hoped the future would bring?*

Her voice saying that she had made promises to William Lucas, not Fitzwilliam Darcy, reverberated through his head until he pressed his fingertips to his temples to ease the pain.

"William Lucas, not Fitzwilliam Darcy," he whispered.

His eyes burned, but he was too empty for tears. He gave a short, humourless laugh. *Have I not often said that I never was William Lucas?* He took a deep, steadying breath to ease the tightness in his chest. *But for so long that* was *my life. I did not know I was Fitzwilliam Darcy. I believed I was—*

He growled, stood, and resumed his walk, but it was not enough to stop his thoughts from going in circles—William Lucas, Fitzwilliam Darcy, William Lucas, Fitzwilliam Darcy. The confusion he felt after first learning the truth returned. This time it felt even stronger, perhaps because now it was not masked by shock.

Elizabeth looked at him and saw Fitzwilliam Darcy, an entirely different person from the William Lucas she had known and loved. But he did not *feel* like a different person. He still felt like William and struggled to understand who Fitzwilliam was.

He fell against the side of a thick oak and slid to the ground. With his knees pulled close to his chest, he buried his face in his hands and groaned. "Oh God, help me. I do not know who I am."

ON MONDAY AND TUESDAY, his strongest emotion was one of sorrow. The weight of everything that had happened since the day Frederick recognised him threatened to crush him. He was devastated by the loss of Elizabeth. He felt friendless, without even the comfort of knowing himself. It hurt to learn that he had been kidnapped. This terrible thing had happened to him, even if he could not remember it, and the knowledge of it made him cry out in anguish. He had almost died, certainly would have had not the Lucases found him. Everything he had experienced in his life had almost never been. It was an unsettling thought.

There was the loss of a mother he would never remember and

the pain of knowing she died without learning that he had survived. The emptiness of a past people told him had happened, but that meant nothing to him.

He could not know what had happened during the time he was with his abductors, but he must have been afraid and confused. *Just as I was when I returned to Pemberley over two decades later. I was like a small, unsure child. Which is how I felt when we moved to Hertfordshire.*

But then he had had four-year-old Elizabeth who had offered to play with him and who had become his first—and best —friend.

He walked along the water's edge and kicked a stone as his mind screamed, *How I wish they had told me I was adopted!* If Sir William and Lady Lucas had explained any part of the past to him, it might have spared him some of the grief he now felt for William Lucas and everything it meant to be him—his home, his family, his friends, his memories.

As he sat in his room at the inn Tuesday night, his thoughts returned to the moment he first saw George Darcy. He had known in an instant that George was his father. There was the startling resemblance, but there was something more that told him he belonged to George and Pemberley and they belonged to him. It resembled the connexion he felt to Elizabeth.

The weather remained fair on Wednesday, to his good fortune, and he continued on as he had spent the previous two days. He walked or rode, ostensibly to explore the neighbour-hood, although he knew he would remember nothing of what he saw. That afternoon, as he viewed an old abbey, he thought again about the early weeks at Pemberley.

What else could I have done? I had to allow my father and Frederick to guide me. I was a stranger in a strange land. So alone and unsure and—

Feeling like he had hit a wall, he stopped and stood as motionless as possible for a long moment. Then his heart began to race, and his eyes darted around to take in his surroundings.

The memory of meeting the Darcys made him afraid. He had been confused by the whole situation, and being surrounded by new people had made it worse, but *afraid*?

It was Jeffrey. He was displeased and hostile. Jeffrey had cautioned him about holding on to sentimental attachments from his past.

Fitzwilliam began walking, taking long, fast strides not knowing where he was headed. "I did what I had to do," he muttered. "For my father and to protect Lizzy and Sir William and Lady Lucas and Charlotte and the Bennets. Lizzy should understand that. They all should. How *she* suffered? What about my father and his suffering or that of my family when they thought I was dead? What about me, and what *I* have suffered? I did what I had to do," he repeated.

He walked for less than a minute before stopping and staring at the landscape ahead of him.

Did I not?

CHAPTER 25

Elizabeth stamped around the morning room for ten minutes after Fitzwilliam's departure.

"The arrogant—I cannot believe he would come here, say such things to me, and expect—!"

At last, she dropped onto a settee and covered her face with her hands. She was horrified and devastated by what had happened.

"Oh, why did I come to London? And to stay with his relations! How could I be so stupid?" *I cannot bear the thought of seeing him again. I would leave today, but that is not fair to Rebecca or her father and brother.*

After several minutes of reflection, and a large drink of her now-cold tea, she decided to go to the Gardiners on Monday rather than Wednesday. She sent a note to her aunt to inform her and requested that Mr Gardiner make arrangements for her to return to Longbourn on Wednesday.

She had just finished this task when Rebecca and her father returned. After seeing Elizabeth, Mr Darcy looked at Rebecca and left the ladies alone. Rebecca sat beside her and took hold of her hand. Elizabeth averted her eyes and held her lips shut between her teeth. Rebecca was so sympathetic; it would be too easy to succumb to tears or to blurt out the whole wretched story.

"What happened? I know Fitzwilliam called."

With reluctance, Elizabeth nodded. "We quarrelled. We just... I..." Elizabeth covered her eyes with her hand and held her breath to stop herself from saying more.

"I am so sorry."

Elizabeth shook her head and looked at Rebecca. "I knew I might see him if I accepted your invitation, but I did not know it would be this hard."

She wanted to slap herself for sounding so weak. She was hurt by what had happened with Fitzwilliam, but she was also angry. It would be better, she felt, to think about that feeling for the moment. Wiping a stray tear from her cheek, she stood and went to the window. It overlooked the street, and she tried to focus on the people who were walking by.

With her back to her friend, she said, "Nothing happened that I did not expect."

Rebecca expressed her disappointment, which Elizabeth compounded a moment later by telling her about her altered plans.

"I cannot see him. We might argue again, and I would not embarrass you or Freddie or your father by behaving in such a manner."

She returned to her seat beside Rebecca, whose shoulders were stooped, her eyes lowered. Elizabeth hated to injure her friend, but there was nothing else for it. "I have been very glad to see you. All of you have made me so welcome, and I cannot thank you enough."

"You will write to me, will you not? Whatever happened between you and Fitzwilliam—"

"Has nothing to do with our friendship, which I would hate to lose."

"As I would yours."

As the ladies embraced, Elizabeth closed her eyes. *At least one good thing has come out of this terrible time. I would have to be a fool indeed to reject such a friend.*

MRS GARDINER and her four children greeted Elizabeth with appropriate familial feeling. After half an hour spent crawling over their cousin and telling her vitally important things, such as that Frances had just lost a tooth, the children were sent to the nursery.

"You are not happy, Lizzy," Mrs Gardiner said. "Was it William?"

"Please, Aunt, do not ask. I do not wish to talk about it."

Mrs Gardiner sighed; it was a loud, heavy noise. "If there is anything I can do to help, I hope you will ask or at least relieve your feelings by talking to someone who, I trust you know, has only your best interests at heart."

Elizabeth nodded and felt a surge of affection for Mrs Gardiner. However, she had no wish to talk about Fitzwilliam with anyone. *Soon I shall be at Longbourn. It is spring, and I can lose myself in long walks.*

The next day, Mrs Gardiner said, "My dear niece, I shall be sorry to see you go tomorrow. You know you can stay with us for as long as you like or return at any time."

Elizabeth smiled and nodded. She was helping her aunt sew clothes for the children and was pleased for the distraction. "I should return to Longbourn. My father has begged me to do so more than once these last few weeks."

"Jane wrote that Mr Hawarden was expected at Netherfield by Easter. None of us doubt what the outcome of that friendship will be."

And no one doubted what the outcome of my friendship with William would be, either! Elizabeth understood what her aunt was hinting and knew it was kindly meant. "I am very happy for Jane. I shall endeavour to be of use to her. Perhaps I can give them time alone so that he might propose." She chuckled. "I have been in town too long. The fresh air and being able to ramble about the countryside will do me a world of good."

"I shall say nothing more about it." Mrs Gardiner patted her hand. Two minutes later, her aunt said, "I do not know if I told you, but your uncle and I plan to go to the Lakes. We shall leave in June."

Elizabeth lay the white cotton chemise in her lap and smiled. "The Lakes! How wonderful. You will have such an adventure. You must tell me all about it."

"Would you like to see them for yourself, instead of relying on my poor powers of observation?"

Elizabeth shook her head and furrowed her forehead.

"We would like you to come with us, Lizzy. We need not talk about...what has happened, and it would be a good distraction for you. If you could bear to spend five or six weeks with me and your uncle."

It was an extraordinary offer, and as much as she did not want their pity, Elizabeth knew she could not tolerate being at Longbourn for the entire summer. She smiled and clasped her aunt's hand. "If you are certain you wish it."

"It is quite settled then. Your uncle will write to your father about our arrangements. Now, what say you to cake and tea? I shall tell you the particulars while we eat."

A grin covered Elizabeth's face as she nodded.

ON WEDNESDAY MORNING, Elizabeth left London. She felt she had aged five years or more since coming to town. Then she had been angry that the truth about her William had emerged. *I even went so far as to wish Mr Frederick Darcy had never come to Longbourn so that we could have gone on in ignorance. How stupid I was!* Even as she told herself and her father that she refused to be upset about it any longer, she had been. Now, after the terrible confrontation with Fitzwilliam, she was truly ready to mourn the past and go on with the future. *I will never love another man as I loved him, but I shall find happiness in this life. God willing, I shall have a family of my own.* The thought of marrying anyone other than William was distasteful, but she knew that would change, even if it took six months or six years.

The Bennets' carriage was waiting to take her the last leg of the journey home. She was not surprised to see Jane waiting with it. The sisters greeted each other warmly.

"You did not need to come meet me, but I admit I am pleased you did," Elizabeth said during the drive. "Tell me the news from home I would not have heard yet. How is Mr Hawarden?"

Jane smiled and tilted her head away, but Elizabeth saw the blush on her cheeks. "Mr Hawarden arrived last week, and he hopes to remain until May."

Elizabeth opened her mouth to tease Jane about the gentleman but refrained. Instead, she watched the familiar buildings and countryside outside the window. She was pleased to be back, but also knew that, even apart from her trip with the Gardiners, she could not remain long. *I do not know what my future will be, but I know it will not be here.*

She asked, "When shall I see him?"

"He and the Linningtons call tomorrow."

"I look forward to it." *But please let the Lucases delay coming for a few days at least. Whatever shall I say to them about him?*

Once at Longbourn, the housekeeper sent her to her father's book room. Elizabeth knew he would wish to talk to her alone and prayed she was prepared for it.

Mr Bennet held her in his arms for a minute before they sat together in the worn green wing chairs. "I encouraged your mother to visit her sister so that we would have a little time together when you first arrived. I thought you might prefer it."

"It was not necessary, but I thank you, nevertheless. You are well, Papa?"

He shrugged. "Well enough. Little has changed since you went away. Tell me truly, Lizzy, how are you?"

Elizabeth patted his arm and went to the window. The trees

and shrubs were gaining their leaves, and she saw a few spring flowers.

His tone gentle, he said, "I can see that you are unhappy."

She turned to look at him. "I am not unhappy, Papa. I greatly enjoyed spending these past weeks with Rebecca and her father and brother. I like them very much."

"But?"

She looked over his head at the shelves filled with rows of mismatched books. This room held so many memories of William. Before her time in London, her heart ached whenever she was in it, but she believed the sensation was dulled. *That must be a hopeful sign. I am truly ready to put him behind me.* "I admit it was difficult to see him, but it has helped. I know, really, truly know in my heart that my William is gone, and I can move on. I do not mean to be unhappy about it any longer."

"You have said that before."

Elizabeth shrugged. "I was angry then. Now, I know it is different. I am pleased to be home, and I shall go for a long walk tomorrow morning, even if it dares to rain. You know how much good that will do me. And, I have something to look forward to." She told him about the trip with the Gardiners, then excused herself to change and refresh herself before seeing the rest of their family.

SINCE ELIZABETH DID NOT HAVE a chance to speak privately with her mother before dinner, Mrs Bennet's chief object during the meal was to ask about London. Elizabeth did her best to keep the discussion to generalities—the parties she had been to, the people she had met, and the shops she had gone into.

Mrs Bennet demanded, "But did you see William?"

Mr Bennet spoke before she could. "She did. We need say nothing more about it."

Mrs Bennet protested, but he insisted. Elizabeth was grateful for his interference. *I shall have to talk to her about him some-*

time but not just yet. Let me accustom myself to being home again.

Jane came into Elizabeth's room that night and, as Elizabeth knew she would, asked about Fitzwilliam. "Is he well? How was it to see him?"

Jane was sitting on the bed, and Elizabeth joined her. She sat facing her sister but looked at the bedcover. Her fingers ran over the rough surface as they traced the outline of the floral pattern.

"It was not easy, but I am glad I saw him. It has allowed me to truly understand that his life is there now, with those people, not here with us."

"His circumstances have changed, but—"

Elizabeth shook her head and glanced at her sister. "It is more than that. I was right all those months ago when I told you everything had changed. I suppose part of me had hoped I was wrong, but I was not."

Elizabeth peeked at her sister, seeing a variety of emotions cross her countenance—confusion, sadness, concern, and disbelief. At length, Jane said, "He is still William—"

As gently as she could, Elizabeth insisted, "No, Jane, he is not William. He never really was."

"Mr Darcy and Miss Darcy were very kind when they were here. William's fam—"

Elizabeth stood and went to the window. She drew back the curtain to look into the moonlit night.

"Yes, they are very kind, and Freddie Darcy is as amiable a young man as you are like to meet. But his other Darcy cousin would hardly look at me. I was beneath his notice. He is one of them now."

"I *cannot* believe that of William."

"Believe it of Fitzwilliam Darcy." Elizabeth turned to face Jane, whose face was shadowed by the candlelight. "The world outside of Meryton is very different. Going to Gracechurch Street does not prepare you for it. The more I see of it...I cannot say that I like it very much."

And yet, I cannot stay here. I am already counting the days until I leave again!

THE NEXT MORNING, Elizabeth was out of the house before breakfast. She took a long walk, stopping to touch the soft new leaves, watch the water flowing over rocks in the stream, take in deep lungfuls of crisp, cool air, and listen to the lowing of cows in their pasture. After breakfast, she went for another walk, this time accompanying Jane, Mrs Linnington, and Mr Hawarden into Meryton. Each warm greeting from her neighbours, each moment of sun peeking through the clouds, revived her spirits.

Upon their return to Longbourn, Elizabeth found a letter from Rebecca. She brought it to her bedchamber to read and was embarrassed that her hands shook as she broke the seal and unfolded the sheet. After the usual remarks, Rebecca wrote:

I apologise if the following causes you discomfort, but I thought I ought to tell you. No one has seen Fitzwilliam since the day you and he quarrelled. The butler at Darcy House told my father that he left suddenly and only said he was going out of town for a few days. Freddie saw our cousin John, and John claims not to know where Fitzwilliam went. I think he must have been as affected by your argument as you were.

You know I have little to do with John, but I was alarmed when Lord Bramwell told me he does not like him. The look in his eyes when he said it told me much more than his words did. He would only say that he believes John is upset about Fitzwilliam's return, and when he and his brother have seen Fitzwilliam with John, he appeared ill at ease. Can he be a good friend for Fitzwilliam? These last months have been a struggle for him. I would hate to think anyone is making it more difficult.

Elizabeth dropped the letter onto her bed and went to sit at the window. She remembered Fitzwilliam saying something about losing everything, but her temper had been too high to fully take in his words. She had never really thought about it, had she? She had missed him and been exceedingly angry at what the discovery of his past meant for her life. *I might not have thought enough about what it meant for him.*

She shook her head, stood, and went to the table where she occupied her hands with rearranging her things. *It does not matter any longer. He has made his choice—a life with the Darcys. Everything that passed between us while I was in town, and his ignoring us for weeks before that, lessens any guilt I might have felt.*

THAT EVENING, Sir William and Lady Lucas came to dinner, along with half a dozen other neighbours. Their eyes sought Elizabeth as soon as they entered the parlour. She drew the couple to a damask sofa. They sat close enough that their legs and arms almost touched, while she sat across from them on a fauteuil. Before speaking, Elizabeth smiled at Jane and Mr Bennet, who were watching. *They are worried this will be difficult for me, but they need not. I do this for Sir William and Lady Lucas. That is all the comfort I need.*

"You will like to know that I saw him." Lady Lucas reached for Sir William's hand. "He is well, and the Darcys are very happy to have this time with him." To forestall their questions, particularly awkward ones she could not answer, she spoke about the busyness and excitement of being in town during the Season before insisting they tell her the latest news from Charlotte.

During dinner and afterwards, Elizabeth was repeatedly asked about her time in London. She said as little as possible about it and changed the topic to local events. William and the Darcys were mentioned many times. While it was not pleasant, neither was it particularly difficult.

"In that way, going to stay with Rebecca did what I hoped it would," she said to her reflection as she prepared for bed that night. "I also have a new friend, and I danced with a viscount!"

She smiled, though her heart still ached, and would for some time. Nevertheless, she was determined to be happy again. "And once I have decided to do something, I am bound to succeed!"

CHAPTER 26

FRIDAY MORNING, FITZWILLIAM SAT UPON THE HARD, COOL ground, looked at the ocean, and thought about returning to London the next day. The question of whether he had acted properly gnawed at his conscience. He might be excused for not knowing what to do immediately after hearing Frederick's tale or meeting George, but as the days and weeks slipped by, he realised he should have done more. He had been selfish and thought about what he suffered; he had not considered what Elizabeth and everyone who had loved William Lucas had endured.

I wrote to Sir William only once. I thought about writing to him and Mr Bennet again and again, but I never did. I turned my back on them, told myself they belonged to a life that was not mine, and convinced myself they did not belong in my new, proper sphere. I had the temerity to be angry with Lizzy for not knowing how difficult the last five months have been. How could she?

Anger gave way to a sense of shame and disappointment in himself. He had ached for George and Lady Anne and himself and everything they had lost. He had given little thought to those who had rescued an abandoned baby, taken him into their home, and loved him as a son. He had failed the Lucases—who, blood relation or not, were his parents—Elizabeth, and the Bennets. Fitzwilliam allowed himself to feel how much he missed them. It hurt deep in his soul, but he knew it should. Hiding from the pain, as he had in the past, did none of them any good.

My sister is married, and I did not know. Is Charlotte my sister or was she my sister?

He watched the waves gently break for several minutes. The rhythmic sound was soothing. When he licked his lips, he tasted salt from sitting so close to the water.

I cannot go on as I have been doing since Twelfth Night. I do not want to live the life John and his friends do. Would my father be unhappy if I hinted that I want something different? There must be a way for Fitzwilliam Darcy to retain the best part of William Lucas. All that was good, everyone I loved, everything I believed, should not be tossed aside in favour of the principles of men like John.

Fitzwilliam laughed and shook his head. He did not like the things John said were expected of young men of their station and worried that admitting it meant disappointing his father.

Would I fail him because I prefer the country to the city, because I shall not drink to excess or gamble or treat women so indifferently? I could not be like John and retain my self-respect. I know my father esteems him, but he views him as a nephew, not as a young man who sees how he amuses himself.

In addition to not wanting to follow his cousin's example, Fitzwilliam did not like him. He did like Freddie and Rebecca and Frederick—people he knew John cared nothing for—and they were friends with Viscount Bramwell and Colonel Fitzwilliam. The Fitzwilliam brothers had no love for John, a feeling Fitzwilliam knew was mutual. What was he to make of it? He grunted in disgust, stood, and began to walk back towards the inn.

Perhaps what I should make of it is that I should not let people tell me who I must like or not like. Did I lose my ability to decide for myself somewhere on the road between Hertfordshire and Derbyshire? My father may have wished me to be friends with John, but I cannot. It does not follow that I have failed him or that I do not deserve to be his son. How could I have been so stupid?

I had friends, people I loved—Lizzy, my family and hers, the Gouldings, and so many more—and I gave them up. Dear God, how could I ever give up Lizzy? He gave a mirthless laugh. *How many times did I long for her? At least I was never so foolish as to think that I no longer loved her.*

And now he had lost her. It was his own fault.

Back at the inn, Fitzwilliam ate breakfast, then sat by the fire to chase away the damp sea air. He pretended to read as his thoughts drifted to his father. Fitzwilliam saw himself in George, not just physically, but also in character.

In good and bad ways, it seems. Both he and George were quiet, introspective people. While there was nothing wrong with it *per se*, it could create problems. There were things he had not said to George, and it was possible the reverse was true, too.

My life is with him now. That is both right and what I want. We were apart for so long, and I want to know my father. It is not just that I have a responsibility to him.

Fitzwilliam knew that George believed it was better for him to leave Hertfordshire in the past, but it was not as simple as that. Until six months ago, he had lived with other people, had another family and other friends, all of whom he loved dearly. For so many years, he had been William Lucas, not Fitzwilliam Darcy.

Staring into the fire, he knew what he had to do.

FITZWILLIAM LEFT SOUTHEND IMMEDIATELY. He had made so many mistakes. Righting them and setting a proper course for the future would not be easy.

I am the one in the middle being pulled apart by everyone else's beliefs and expectations. Somehow, I will find a way to do right by as many people as I can and to the greatest extent possible. I alone have to face my conscience and God and justify my choices. With luck and effort, I shall manage it without feeling like I am being cut into a hundred pieces and scattered among everyone from Derbyshire to Hertfordshire to London.

The roads were a little slow due to recent rain, and Fitzwilliam was impatient; he had an important task to complete before the morrow when he had to be in London to greet his father.

"I have time," he murmured again and again to reassure himself.

It was growing dark when he reached his destination. He climbed out of the curricle, secured the horses, went to the door, and knocked. The girl who answered gaped at him.

"How are you, Meg?"

She made a faint, incoherent sound.

"If I go into the sitting room, will you tell them I am here?"

Meg walked away, so he entered the house and closed the door. He did not need the maid to show him the way; after all, it had been his home for sixteen years. Standing at the entrance to the parlour, he ran a hand over his mouth. After removing his great coat and placing it, his hat, and gloves on a chair, he walked around the room. The few drawings and small ornaments, a plant which looked like it was being neglected, were all so familiar and yet so strange.

This is not my home any longer, yet a part of me will always be here. It was the height of stupidity to think that I could or should deny that I shall always be William Lucas as much as I am Fitzwilliam Darcy. They are one and the same. Somehow, I shall help everyone understand. He felt calmer than he had since he was last in this room listening to Frederick Darcy tell an incredible story of a decades-old kidnapping.

When the door opened, he turned to see Lady Lucas and Sir William. His heart stopped beating for a moment before it began to race. It was strange to see them and know they were not truly his parents yet feel in his heart that they were. *My adoptive parents. Surely, they have earned the right to be my mother and father.* His mother's mouth was covered by her hand, in which she held a linen handkerchief. Even from across the room, he could see the tears falling down her cheeks. In an instant, she was across the room and in his arms. His father stood beside them murmuring nothings and patting his back.

They sat, Lady Lucas's hand clasping Fitzwilliam's, and he said, "I am sorry I did not come sooner."

She dabbed at her face. "It does not matter. You are here now."

"We always knew you would write or visit as soon as you were able," Sir William added as though there was no doubt.

The two Lucases repeated themselves for a minute, assuring Fitzwilliam that they had not felt neglected. Fitzwilliam knew it was untrue, but also that it would injure them if he continued to say they should be hurt by his behaviour.

"If you will not hear an apology, then at least let me say that I wish I had written more and come sooner."

Sir William pulled a large, wrinkled cloth from his pocket and ran it over his face. "We know that— Well, you have your proper family again. Your-your true father. We are very happy for you and for Mr Darcy."

Fitzwilliam interjected. "But *you* are also my family. I am happy to know the truth. It has brought joy to people who deserve it, especially George Darcy. But I cannot, I *will not* forget what you have been to me. I was happy and well-cared for and I am very grateful for all of it. Any goodness in me is because of the two of you."

His mother smiled through her tears and touched Fitzwilliam's cheek.

"H-h-how long do you…?" his father asked.

"I am afraid I must be in London tomorrow."

The change in conversation must have reminded Lady Lucas of the hour. She insisted on having food prepared for him and seeing that his room was ready for the night. While he ate, they made him tell them everything he had done since he 'went away'. They kept him speaking long after his plate was empty, and when at last he had said enough to satisfy them, he asked about them and Charlotte.

He said, "I must have her direction. I hope she will welcome a letter from me, late as it is in coming."

"Of course she will!" Sir William cried.

Fitzwilliam was not quite so certain. He expected Charlotte would feel some of the same anger Elizabeth did.

Sir William and Lady Lucas said little about the weeks when his identity was still a secret, and he had the impression there had been some difficulty. *It is yet another mistake I made. I did not consider what it was like for them or Charlotte or Lizzy and Mr Bennet before the announcement of my recovery. There must have been questions about my whereabouts.*

The trio spoke long into the night and only called an end to the day after Sir William fell asleep in his armchair.

"I must return to town tomorrow," Fitzwilliam reminded them. "I should leave earlier rather than later, but before I go, I would like to call at Longbourn."

He hoped he might see Elizabeth. He believed she intended to return to Hertfordshire soon after Easter, but her plans might have changed. He dreaded the prospect of seeing her as much as he longed for it. She had accused him of forgetting them all, and she was right to do so. He was not trying to win her regard or forgiveness by coming to Hertfordshire, but if it made her hate him less, so much the better.

Mrs Bennet stopped Elizabeth before she could escape the house the next morning. As they walked into the small back morning room with its fussy floral wallpaper, Mrs Bennet said, "You will have time to go wandering this afternoon. I have no notion what you find so interesting about being outside. Now, where is that—?"

"Someone is coming!" Kitty called from the window.

Elizabeth suppressed a moan. If they had visitors, she would have to give up all hope of a walk before breakfast.

Lydia rushed to the window. "There are three people walking and a wagon. No, a curricle!"

"Three people? A curricle? At this hour? Well, there is nothing for it. Quickly girls, tidy up. Lydia, that table." Mrs Bennet pointed to a wooden table overflowing with books and pencils and paper.

"Lydia, Kitty, come away from the window," Jane insisted.

The ladies were just sitting down when Mrs Hill opened the door and stepped aside to let Sir William, Lady Lucas, and Fitzwilliam Darcy enter the room.

"William!" Lydia exclaimed, as she flew to him.

Elizabeth's book hit the floor with a thump as she stood. She was conscious of her mother and sisters jumping to their feet and everyone speaking at the same time, but it was just movement and noise to her. Mrs Bennet's loud, high-pitched voice cleared Elizabeth's fog, and she fell back into the chair.

"Oh William! Oh my! Why did no one say you were—? When did? Oh, come give me a kiss. I cannot believe—!"

In a moment, Mr Bennet entered the room and called out his greetings. Elizabeth's chest hurt as she struggled to pull air into her lungs.

Jane sat next to her and took her hand. "Lizzy?"

Elizabeth shook her head, while her eyes remained fixed on Fitzwilliam who sat between Lydia and Kitty on the long yellow sofa.

Lydia demanded, "Why did you not come sooner? You have been away for months. Everyone said you would never return!"

Elizabeth did not care why he had not come sooner. She wanted to know why he had come now.

"Lydia!" hissed Mary.

Fitzwilliam offered Mary a small smile, then turned to meet Elizabeth's gaze as he said, "I am afraid I do not have a good answer. I ought to have visited or written."

Mr Bennet said, "We all understand how busy you have been. Do we not, Lydia, Kitty? Let us speak of the present, not the past. How long do you stay?"

"I am afraid I must return to London this morning. I wished to see you before I left."

Elizabeth wished he would stop staring at her. Yet, she could not look away.

"Tell them what has kept you so busy," Lady Lucas urged. "What adventures he has had! He met the Prince Regent!"

For the next while, Fitzwilliam answered a great many questions from her sisters and mother, some of which were rather impertinent. Elizabeth remained silent and still. She was not sure she could force her lips apart or do something as simple as stand when he was sitting across from her.

Why is he here? It cannot be because of what I said! She remembered Rebecca's letter and the news that he had left town. It only served to confuse her further.

After several attempts to take his leave of them, Fitzwilliam succeeded. "I promise I shall write or come again as soon as possible. I *will* write. It may be some weeks before I can return."

With this promise, he climbed into his curricle and drove off.

CHAPTER 27

FITZWILLIAM ARRIVED IN TOWN LATER THAN HE HAD HOPED, BUT it had been difficult to leave Longbourn. He felt so much better, so much more like himself after spending time with the Lucases and Bennets, but wished he could have spoken to Elizabeth.

His hope that he would reach Darcy House before his father did was dashed by Mallon, who told him that George was in the morning room. Fitzwilliam took a deep breath, told himself that everything would be well, and opened the door. George stood as Fitzwilliam walked towards him.

"Father, I regret I was not here when you arrived. My journey took longer than I anticipated."

His father waved his hand as though dismissing the apology, and they sat across from each other. He looked wan, but his colour improved a little as he ran his eyes over Fitzwilliam. Fitzwilliam suspected the separation had been difficult for him. He prayed what he had to say would not cause his father more anxiety.

"Your trip from Derbyshire went well?"

George nodded. "It was as easy as it ever gets."

"Good. I look forward to hearing the news from Pemberley."

"I look forward to telling you. And your time away? Where were you?"

"Essex. Southend. I needed a few days of quiet, to be alone."

224

His father's eyes flickered over him. "I see."

"I was in Southend until yesterday, that is." Fitzwilliam cleared his throat. "Then I went to Hertfordshire. I saw the Lucases and, this morning, the Bennets."

Because he was studying his father carefully, Fitzwilliam saw the tension in his jaw and the way his hands trembled. After running his hands down his thighs and again clearing his throat, Fitzwilliam said, "I realised that, when I look back on the months since Frederick found me, I have not wanted to admit it, but it has been very difficult at times. I cannot be proud of how I have acted, mostly towards those from my past life. I know the circumstances have been extraordinary, but I ought to have done better by them, by myself, and by you."

George exclaimed, "Me?"

Fitzwilliam nodded. "I was raised with better principles than I have been living by these last months. One in particular—to honour my parents and my family. I know you feel as I do that family is very important. You told me that once, when we were at Pemberley."

His father nodded, his brow furrowed.

"I have not honoured my family. Since October, I have not really known who I was. I lived for so long as one person only to learn that I was always someone different."

George swallowed heavily. "But now?"

"'To thine own self be true,'" he quoted. "I know that I *am* Fitzwilliam, your son, the boy who was taken. But a part of me is also William Lucas. I cannot pretend the years we were apart never happened or that they were unimportant or forgettable. I am so grateful to know the truth and to have this chance to know you and my family. That does not diminish the role other people have played in my life.

"At times, I have thought my life then was a lie, but it was not. I was very fortunate to be surrounded by good people. Sir William and Lady Lucas are kind and honest. I would not have survived had they not found me. They, Charlotte, Mr Bennet, all the Bennets—they all loved and cared for me. What happened to you and me was terrible. Horrible. But it did happen, and now we are left with this messy, complicated situation."

Fitzwilliam paused to see if his father would speak, but he did not.

"My life is here, with you, as a Darcy. I have no doubt about that. It is what I want and what I know is right."

George appeared to exhale a mighty breath, and his shoulders relaxed. His lips moved, and Fitzwilliam had to strain his ears to hear his words. "You will stay. I will not lose—"

Fitzwilliam continued, "My home is with you, but I cannot forget or ignore them. William Lucas, with all those memories and attachments, is part of me. They are good people and would never seek to gain advantage from knowing me. I hope you can accept that. I know I cannot easily express what I feel, and all of this is still confusing to me, but I must try to unite both parts of my life."

He fell silent, and after a long moment, George began to nod; he seemed to gain strength each time his chin dipped and rose. He appeared to be thinking about everything Fitzwilliam had said.

After two minutes during which neither of them spoke, Fitzwilliam said, "It is almost dinner time. I should go to my room; I am still dirty from the road."

He stood and was just turning towards the door when George leapt to his feet and placed a restraining hand on his arm.

"Fitzwilliam," his father gasped. His eyes were pink and wet, and after staring at him for a moment, he enveloped Fitzwilliam in his arms and murmured, "My son. My precious boy. I understand. I do. I am— Whatever you need to be happy, I will do. I see now that…you are recovered, and we will never be separated again. I will not lose you again."

FITZWILLIAM AND GEORGE did not revisit the conversation that day or the next. They spoke about Essex and Derbyshire, went to church, and spent a quiet day at home to avoid the rain. Sunday afternoon, Fitzwilliam wrote to Charlotte. He apologised, told her about his visit to Lucas Lodge and Longbourn, and expressed the hope that, should she be willing, they would see each other soon.

His father asked no questions, and Fitzwilliam took his silence as a tacit acceptance of Fitzwilliam's intention to retain his ties to Hertfordshire, although part of him feared it would be difficult for his father to accept. Fitzwilliam saw George watching him as they sat together at meals or in the morning room. He seemed more contemplative than anxious, however.

That evening, they had dinner with Jeffrey and John. Talk was dominated by politics. John was polite when George addressed him but said little to Fitzwilliam.

After the meal, with their fathers sitting across the room from them, engrossed in their own conversation, John asked him where he had gone. "You left London so suddenly."

"I went to Essex for a few days." Even two weeks earlier, Fitzwilliam was likely to have experienced a tightness in his muscles, a faint nausea, or throbbing in his head when faced with John's sarcastic tone. Now, he felt nothing.

"Did something happen to drive you out of town?"

Fitzwilliam arched his eyebrows. "Whatever could you mean by that? I wished for a few days to myself. My father was in Derbyshire, I had no important engagements, so I went."

John pressed for more information, but Fitzwilliam had no intention of telling him about his argument with Elizabeth or that he had gone to Meryton. He was not sorry to see the evening end. In his disclosures to George, he had not mentioned John, and he hoped he would not have to. *I shall simply stop going out with him. We shall become the sort of cousins who see each other at family dinners and such. There is no need to make a point of my not liking him or being uncomfortable with how he acts.*

MONDAY MORNING WAS OVERCAST, but since it was not raining, Fitzwilliam decided to go for a walk in the park. He wandered for a while and thought about Elizabeth. *If I detect any hint that she might forgive me, then I will do what I ought to have done months ago; I will tell my father and pray he understands. It was the height of stupidity to suggest I would call her an obligation. If I do have cause to talk to my father about her, I shall admit that I love her and cannot see how I will ever be happy with another woman as my wife.*

He did not notice much about his surroundings other than that he could feel the dirtiness of the air after his days at the coast. Even though it was quieter than usual, there were still too many people for his mood. He longed for a walk through a grove or to Oakham Mount or that hill at Pemberley whose name he could not remember. Before he saw it happening, the Fitzwilliam brothers were standing fifteen feet in front of him. He almost tried to evade them but stopped himself.

He approached them and said, "Good morning."

The brothers exchanged a look then turned to face him, their expressions wary.

"Fitzwilliam," Lord Bramwell said.

"We did not know you had returned," Colonel Fitzwilliam said. "Frederick Darcy, Miss Darcy, and Freddie were alarmed when you left town without telling anyone."

Fitzwilliam nodded and almost shoved his hands in his pockets. He did not know what, if anything, Elizabeth had told Rebecca. "I needed to be away, and since my father was in Derbyshire, it seemed like a good time. I am sorry to have distressed them." He cleared his throat. "I wanted to thank you both."

The brothers again exchanged a look. They seemed to share a silent communication, just as he used to with Charlotte and Elizabeth.

"I could not really see it at the time, but I know you have sought to be of use to me, in different ways and—"

The colonel interjected, "We wanted to be your friends."

"I know, and I appreciate it. I wish—"

"That circumstances could be different," Lord Bramwell said in a sarcastic tone, while his brother rolled his eyes.

Fitzwilliam sighed. "You know my father's opinion. He asked that I respect his wishes. I do not pretend to understand the intricacies of what happened, but I know Frederick believes my father will change his mind in time, and he has told your father this."

They nodded in unison.

"I *cannot* be the cause of more distress to my father. I live with him. I see, as you cannot, how difficult this has been for him." *And I have just asked him to accept my connexion to the Lucases and Bennets.*

"What are you suggesting?" Colonel Fitzwilliam asked.

Fitzwilliam regarded his cousins for a moment and resisted the urge to pull at his hair. "Patience, I suppose. I will talk to Frederick about it and see if he has any suggestions for how we can...hurry the situation along." It was a weak response, but he had no other.

The colonel then said, "What do you truly want?"

Lizzy. I wonder if she likes these cousins of mine. "I would like to live an uncomplicated life."

They all chuckled.

Fitzwilliam continued, his tone serious, "I would like to know my family. *All* of it."

The viscount said, "Our fathers were very good friends once. I would like to see them be that again, or at least not have this animosity between them."

"I would like to see Pemberley again," the colonel offered. "There was a tree I very much wanted to climb, but I was forbidden to do so. I think I am old enough to have a go at it without my mother scolding me."

The cousins shared another laugh and soon went their separate ways.

FITZWILLIAM SAW John and his father again that night when they were at the same dinner party. It happened that Fitzwilliam was busy with other guests and did not talk to John. When their host indicated they should join the ladies after the separation of the sexes, John remarked that he and Fitzwilliam had other plans for the evening and would soon leave.

Fitzwilliam announced, "My cousin has a prior obligation, but I do not."

As the party left the dining parlour, John pulled him aside and hissed, "We are meeting our friends at the club."

Fitzwilliam removed his arm from John's grasp. "I did not agree to the scheme. I do not wish to go."

"We have hardly seen you of late. A few of them were remarking on it the other day."

"That was very kind of them, but not tonight."

"My uncle expressly wishes you to spend time with me," John insisted.

"He will not object to my going home with him. I do not wish to go, John, and I would not enjoy it."

Fitzwilliam nodded and left his cousin.

UPON RETURNING TO DARCY HOUSE, George asked him to come into the study and have a drink before retiring. Fitzwilliam admired the room's dark mahogany panelling and perfectly stuffed wing chairs as he sipped brandy. He was pleased he had spoken up and refused to go with John. His rumination ended when his father spoke.

"You did not wish to join your cousin tonight?"

Fitzwilliam shook his head. "I shall see him and some of the other gentlemen tomorrow morning. We are going riding."

Seeing John at such an excursion—when the intention was to get exercise, explore the nearby countryside, and enjoy the spring weather—was very different than going out with him in the evening. It might satisfy everyone that he was not avoiding his cousin, yet not require Fitzwilliam to speak plainly about his dislike of John's dissolute habits.

"I have been considering what you said the other day. I did not think enough about what it was like for you to leave behind everything you knew. No. It is not quite as simple as that."

George pressed his eyes closed for a moment, and Fitzwilliam waited with as much patience as possible even though he felt anxiety bubbling in his stomach. He set aside his glass, knowing he would be sick if he drank more of the amber liquid.

"It is difficult for me to think about the years we were apart. I cannot, shall not, attempt to explain— But, it happened, and I accept how important it is to you to remain…friends with the Lucases and Mr Bennet. There are others, too, no doubt."

Fitzwilliam relaxed against the back of his chair, and his lips curved upward in a small smile.

"I know I did not treat Sir William with the consideration I should have when he was at Pemberley. He was not to blame for what happened, and I regret my rudeness. I think," George ran a hand over his mouth, "it is past time I paid my respects to the Lucases and Mr Bennet. I would like to go to Hertfordshire. We shall be busy in the coming weeks, but I thought we could go the day after tomorrow." George finished the last of his drink and looked at him.

"Of-of course, sir." Fitzwilliam was too astonished to say more.

"If we left in the morning, we could dine with the Lucases and perhaps visit Mr Bennet. He is Frederick's friend, and more to the point, he was of great service to you."

"The whole family was good to me."

George nodded. "I assume there is a respectable inn where

we could spend the night. I would not wish to impose on Lady Lucas, especially at such short notice."

"There is." *And Lady Lucas would be nervous about having a man of your standing staying in her home.*

"Good." His father nodded. "I shall leave you to write to Sir William. We should keep our visit quiet."

He stood, and Fitzwilliam did likewise.

"Thank you, Father. I… Thank you. Good night."

George smiled and patted his arm before leaving the room.

CHAPTER 28

FITZWILLIAM SPENT A LARGE PART OF THE DRIVE TO MERYTON thinking about Elizabeth; he would soon be introducing his father to the woman he loved. It was enough to make beads of sweat form on his upper lip. *Not that I intend to tell him that I love her and would do just about anything to make her my wife. What would be the purpose when she despises me?*

The closer they got to Lucas Lodge, the more Fitzwilliam's agitation grew. The initial meeting was bound to be awkward, and he would be glad when it was over. Sure enough, he felt like a fidgeting schoolboy when they arrived and he had to make the introductions.

Surprisingly, it was George, who suffered the same discomfort when in company that he did, who made everything easier. He bowed and said, "Madam," then turned and held out his hand to Sir William. "Sir William."

Lady Lucas curtseyed for a second time. "M-mr Darcy."

"Well, ah, do come in, make yourselves comfortable," Sir William said.

They sat, and Fitzwilliam tried to see the room through George's eyes. It was nothing to Darcy House or Pemberley, but it was neat, even if the sofa was a dozen years old and the colour too reminiscent of dry mud.

"I would like to apologise," George said. "Sir William, I was unkind to you when we first met. I can offer no excuse other than the effect of the same shock we all felt. I had believed my son dead for so long, and to know that he had been alive the whole time… My feelings were great, and I am afraid you bore the brunt of them. It was inexcusable."

Sir William was shaking his head before George could finish speaking. "I understand. Quite so. What you said to me, I have asked myself many times if I could have done more to find out who he was, where he came from."

George begged, "Pray, Sir William, do not. It serves nothing to revisit the past. My second apology is to both of you. I ought to have thanked you before now. I am very grateful that you found Fitzwilliam and took such good care of him."

"Georgina and I always did our best." Sir William's chin was lowered, and he scratched his nose.

Fitzwilliam said, "I never wanted for anything."

At the same time, George said, "It was very good indeed. We can see that in the fine young man he is."

Fitzwilliam felt his cheeks grow warm at the fond looks all three of his parents gave him. The tears beginning to form in Lady Lucas's eyes made it worse.

"Nevertheless, the last months have been trying," George added.

When his father could not go on, Fitzwilliam understood. He said, "It has been a difficult time for all of us in different ways, I suppose. It was inevitable, given the extraordinary circumstances. I hope that we can put the unhappiness behind us."

"Well said, my boy!" Sir William exclaimed.

"Yes, indeed," George agreed.

Lady Lucas's smile broadened as a tear fell down her cheek.

As much as Fitzwilliam was pleased to bring the two parts of his life together in this way, he soon began to anticipate it being over. The years ahead would bring more meetings, he supposed; he trusted they would get easier.

Dinner was awkward with everyone trying to please and be

pleased. Fitzwilliam spoke more than he usually would. Sir William would start to say something, look between George and Fitzwilliam, and change his mind. Lady Lucas sent George shy looks and, as had happened when they first arrived, there were often tears in her eyes. His father did his part in trying to keep the conversation easy. Fitzwilliam was relieved when it was over and he and George climbed into the carriage for the drive to Longbourn. Sir William assured him that Mr Bennet knew they were coming and had arranged for the whole family to be home to greet them.

MR BENNET TOLD Elizabeth in the morning that the Darcys were expected after dinner but waited until the evening meal to inform the rest of the family. They were gathered around the old oak table, eating their mutton with turnips and carrots, when he made the announcement. Amid the expressions of surprise and happiness, Mrs Bennet's voice rose to the top.

"After all this time? There is some meaning behind it, and I would wager that you and Miss Lizzy know, just as you knew for months where William was and kept it from me. Does this have something to do with Lizzy's staying in London?"

"No, Mrs Bennet," her father replied. "It has nothing —nothing—to do with Lizzy. Mr Darcy has decided that he would like to meet us. It is as simple as that. None of you are to mention or hint or say anything whatsoever about the past friendship between Lizzy and Fitzwilliam. The only people who should speak of it, if they wish to, are Fitzwilliam, Lizzy, and me as her father. Is that understood?"

Elizabeth prayed that her sisters and mother would obey him and that the visit would be brief. Too soon, she was sitting with her father, mother, and sisters in the parlour waiting for the Darcys' arrival. Jane was beside her and said one or two things, but Elizabeth was lost in her thoughts and could not respond.

I do not know if I can see them. I could tell Papa that I

cannot, and he would excuse me. Her heart felt like it was flutter-ing, and her head buzzed. *You will remain in your seat, Elizabeth Bennet! No one needs to know how much you hate it.*

Seeing Fitzwilliam at Longbourn just four days earlier had been a shock. She did not understand why he had come and thinking about it was making her mad. Now, Mr Darcy wanted to 'pay his respects' to them? Proud, arrogant Mr George Darcy who had turned her William into Fitzwilliam Darcy and stolen all her hopes for the future, would soon be there. *I shall stand before him, look him in the eye, and know I am better off being away from him* and *his son.*

With such thoughts firmly planted in her mind, she was not prepared for her first sight of Fitzwilliam's father. When the gentlemen entered the room, she felt as though every bit of air was pulled from her body. She saw and heard nothing other than George Darcy.

She had known that he would look like Fitzwilliam, but it was so much more than the arrangement of their features or colour of hair. *They are, they are...* She could not think. A heavy weight pressed down on her chest at the same time that some-thing inside of her head ballooned.

What William must have felt when he saw him for the first time! What he *must have felt!*

Elizabeth vaguely realised that introductions were made and felt Jane tug at her sleeve when it was time to sit.

Elizabeth's eyes remained fixed on Mr Darcy. Her heart beat faster and faster as the minutes passed, and she heard the rushing of blood in her ears. She was struck not only by his physical resemblance to Fitzwilliam; there was something in his manner that reminded her so strongly of her William, her beloved William, that it made her eyes burn as tears formed behind them. She, who knew his son so well, could easily discern what Mr George Darcy was feeling. He was as uncomfortable as it was possible to be, but struggled not to show it. Elizabeth could not blame him for feeling ill at ease. How could he not be with the way her mother and younger sisters were behaving? Mrs Bennet had hardly stopped talking since the Darcys arrived, and Lydia and Kitty were being loud, despite Mary's attempts to calm them.

Elizabeth knew that she needed to shake herself out of her dream-like state, but the mist surrounding her grew thicker, not thinner, leaving only one clear patch so that she could observe the man she had blamed for every minute of her misery since the previous autumn. She saw that, although Mr Darcy looked at whoever was speaking, he glanced at Fitzwilliam over and over again, seeking reassurance; he *needed* to know that Fitzwilliam was by his side. It was not enough that Fitzwilliam was sitting next to him, Mr Darcy had to remind himself that his son was still there.

When Lydia or Kitty called Fitzwilliam 'William', Mary corrected them.

Lydia proclaimed, "I do not care. He has always been William to me and always will be!"

Mr Bennet reprimanded her, although Elizabeth did not know exactly what he said. What she did know was that hearing his son called 'William' injured George Darcy. *He does not like the reminder of the past. There is more, too. Fear? Why would he be afraid?*

Suddenly, Elizabeth was hit by a massive wave of grief and the awareness that she had been horribly, inexcusably selfish. *He lost so much—his son—his only child—his wife. What does it matter that Fitzwilliam did not die? He did not know that. Mr Darcy is afraid of losing him again, not to villains, but to the life he led.* It was so simple, but having believed only that which allowed her to feel anger, not pain, she had thought nothing about what Mr Darcy had suffered. Indeed, she had longed for Fitzwilliam to abandon his true father and return to living as William Lucas.

She stood, muttered, "Excuse me," and fled the room.

ELIZABETH RETURNED to the parlour after ten minutes. She sat beside Jane and said nothing. When it was time for Mr Darcy and Fitzwilliam to leave, she stood along with the rest of her family and curtseyed.

Once they were gone, Jane whispered, "Lizzy," as Mr Bennet joined them and said, "Lizzy, my dear."

"Not now. Please. I have a headache, and I would like to retire." Mr Bennet nodded and kissed Elizabeth's forehead.

Jane escorted Elizabeth to her bedchamber and helped her prepare for bed. As Jane brushed her hair, she asked, "Lizzy, are you quite well?"

Elizabeth shook her head. She tasted saltiness from her tears as they reached her lips. "Oh Jane, can you imagine what he must have felt to learn that his son, whom he had thought dead for so long, was in truth still alive?"

Jane's face became a mask of pity and sorrow. "I have thought about it."

Which is more than I have done. Elizabeth felt like hitting something or stamping her foot or running until she was so exhausted that she could not move another inch. "I am such a terrible person."

"Lizzy!" Jane dropped the hairbrush, pulled her sister from the chair, and brought her to the bed where they could sit together. "Why would you say such a thing?"

Elizabeth shook her head again and again. "I have harboured such animosity for Mr Darcy. I blamed him for turning William into someone I did not know, for separating us. I told myself that he was arrogant and proud and"–she gave a dark, sad laugh–"and never once did I think about his years of grief or what he must feel to have Fitzwilliam with him again. I never thought I could be so uncaring. I have wronged him."

"You are too hard on yourself. The circumstances—"

"Have been difficult for all of us." Elizabeth squeezed Jane's hands to apologise for interrupting. "I have thought only of my pain and how my life has changed. I wished that Frederick Darcy had never come to Longbourn. *Never* did I think of Mr George Darcy." She used the corner of her shawl to wipe her eyes. "What a muddle I have created."

"You are being too hard on yourself," Jane repeated.

Elizabeth shook her head. "I promise we shall talk, but not tonight. I truly do have a headache, and my thoughts are too confused to make sense."

Jane caressed her arm. "Come. Let us get you into bed."

Elizabeth allowed Jane to fuss over her for the few minutes it took to get Elizabeth settled for the night. Jane then kissed her cheek and left her alone. Elizabeth closed her eyes, and cried for George Darcy, Fitzwilliam, and herself.

THE CARRIAGE RIDE from Longbourn to the inn was silent. Fitzwilliam was thinking about Elizabeth and trying to understand why she had been so distressed. Did she despise him so much that she could not be in the same room with him? It was also evident that his father had been anxious, although he had remained polite. Fitzwilliam did not blame him; Mrs Bennet had hardly stopped talking from the moment they appeared, and Lydia and Kitty were overly excited. He loved them and found nothing disturbing in their behaviour, but he understood why one unaccustomed to their manner, particularly if they were reserved by nature, would find it taxing.

Once at the inn, his father said, "Come into my room, Son. Let us talk."

Quinn, who had accompanied them to Meryton, had left a decanter and glasses on a small wooden table. It sat between two stone-coloured armchairs which were by the fire.

George said, "I am glad we came. It was good to meet Lady Lucas and the Bennets. I regret that it has taken me so long to accept that they are not to blame for the years we were apart. They do not deserve to be punished when they did nothing wrong, and I know not seeing you has been difficult for them."

He sighed before continuing, "I have been jealous, which is not something I have ever felt in my life. While I grieved, you were here, with them. You spoke of it being an adjustment for you, and the same is true for me. I was envious and...fearful. I thought I would lose you to your past. How could I compete with people you lived among for so long? Just when I had found you, I would lose you again."

Fitzwilliam laid a hand on his father's arm. When George looked at him, Fitzwilliam said, "That will not happen. You are my father, and I *need* to be with you. I cannot explain my feelings, but anything else is simply not possible."

George smiled and patted his hand.

After taking a long drink of wine, George said, "The Lucases and Bennets are friends of yours. More than friends. It is natural for you to wish to see each other. Sir William and Lady Lucas also have a daughter."

"Charlotte."

Fitzwilliam felt on edge knowing there was something particular his father wanted to say. He watched as flecks from the fire floated into the air and turned from bright red to black.

After a long silence, George said, "Miss Elizabeth Bennet. Am I right that she is the lady who was lately with Rebecca?"

"Yes." Fitzwilliam's voice trembled.

"You saw her when she was in town?"

Fitzwilliam hesitated before nodding.

George loosened his cravat and rubbed his forehead. "Who is she to you?"

Fitzwilliam groaned and covered his eyes with a hand. How could he explain? He did not know the words to use, especially after tonight's visits, which had left him feeling numb and ashamed of how he had treated her and everyone else.

"Elizabeth...Lizzy is, or rather was, my dearest friend. As children, we spent a great deal of time together." Fitzwilliam told him about taking lessons with Mr Bennet and then-four-year-old Elizabeth insisting she be allowed to join him. He chuckled. "She was so happy and full of spirit. She would stamp her foot and get such a look on her face when she was angry or frustrated. A quarter of an hour later, she would be laughing again. She taught me to be less serious."

Fitzwilliam looked into the corner of the room. *And I ruined it all. Please, God, let her give me a chance to make it right.* His eyes darted to his father, who sat, neither smiling nor frowning.

George nodded, and, in an encouraging tone, asked, "You and Miss Elizabeth are more than friends?"

"I do not know what we are at the moment." Fitzwilliam dipped his chin and played with the fabric of his trousers. "I love her. I have loved her most of my life. I knew when I was twelve that I would marry her."

"Twelve?"

Fitzwilliam tilted his head until it was resting against the back of the chair and he was looking at the shadows on the ceiling. "She was eight and had said something teasing. I cannot remember what it was. She made me laugh at myself and understand the ridiculousness and beauty of the ordinary. I knew that life would be wonderful with her—exciting, full of love and loyalty, friendship and learning."

"Do you and Miss Elizabeth have an understanding?"

"No. Well, yes, but not-not formally. Or we did." Fitzwilliam's sigh was heavy this time. His shoulders slumped.

"She does not return your affection?"

Fitzwilliam ran a hand over his mouth and finished his wine. "Lizzy and I were never betrothed, but we wanted to be married. Several years ago, Mr Bennet told us he would not allow her to become engaged before she was twenty."

"And she…?" George interjected.

"Had her twentieth birthday in January."

George stood and walked towards the opposite side of the room where there was a desk. He rested his hands on it. "Why did you never tell me?"

"What I saw and heard at Pemberley suggested that Lizzy would not be an acceptable wife for Fitzwilliam Darcy."

"What did you hear?"

"That the heirs of Pemberley always make brilliant marriages. It was my duty to you and to my family to do the same. I knew none of you would see it as a good match, and-and I wanted to reclaim my place as your son. I felt that I should think and feel just what I would have had I never been taken."

"But you were." George sighed, returned to his chair, and refilled their glasses.

"But I was. I gave her up. I thought I had to, so I tried to push her and everyone else out of my mind."

"I knew a Miss Bennet was staying with Rebecca, but I refused to meet her. I did not want the reminder of your past."

Fitzwilliam slowly nodded. "I suspected as much."

"Where do things between you stand now?"

It felt like someone reached in and pulled Fitzwilliam's heart out of his chest. "I could not stay away from her when she was in town. That is why I did not go to Pemberley at Easter. I desperately wanted to find a way to marry her. I decided I would tell you that I felt obligated to her. If it was a matter of honour, you might not like it, but I believed you would accept it."

George gave a short bark of laughter. "So I would."

"We argued. She was angry, and I cannot blame her. I had neglected her and hurt her. I was selfish and did not think about what she felt. I was hardly eloquent when I presented my scheme to her." He paused, swallowing hard. "She rejected me."

Fitzwilliam glanced at his father and saw that he was rubbing his forehead again.

"That is why you left London."

Fitzwilliam nodded. "I thought about what she said, realised I had to find a way to bring both parts of my life together, and came to see the Lucases and Bennets."

"Do you believe she still cares for you?"

Fitzwilliam slid low in his seat and extended his legs in front of him. "I hope so."

"Then you must go to her and apologise. Tell her everything you have told me—about how difficult these last months have been, what is in your heart, all of it—then beg for her understanding and forgiveness. If she grants it and accepts you, then I will accept her as your wife."

Fitzwilliam sat up and faced his father. "She has almost no fortune, and...Mrs Bennet's brothers are in trade."

There was a moment during which George did not speak or move. "I see. The money is nothing, but... Well, I shall not lie and say I like it, but it does not alter my resolution. If she will have you, then you have my blessing."

Fitzwilliam could not suppress a smile which soon became a grin. "Thank you. I do not know if she can forgive me, but thank you."

George looked at him for a long moment. His voice was quiet and soft when he said, "All I want is your happiness, as maudlin as that sounds. I have my son. I never thought I would, but I do, and that is *my* happiness."

Fitzwilliam felt a rush of heat in his cheeks.

"Tell me about her."

The two men were awake for hours, talking as they never had before. Fitzwilliam told him about Elizabeth and his life in Hertfordshire. There were moments when it was evident that it was painful for George, but at others he laughed. For the first time, Fitzwilliam truly began to believe that everything would turn out well.

CHAPTER 29

THE BENNETS WERE JUST FINISHING BREAKFAST WHEN THEY WERE surprised by callers: the Darcys, Sir William, and Lady Lucas. Elizabeth had slept very little and eaten almost nothing; she felt like begging them to leave her alone. She would fall to her knees and sob if it would convince them.

After apologising for calling so early, Mr Darcy said, "I wished to thank you once again for your kindness to my son. I am leaving him in your care, yours and the Lucases, for a few days."

Everyone began to speak at once. Lady Lucas and Sir William expressed their surprise and delight to Mary and Mrs Bennet. Lydia and Kitty chatted excitedly to Fitzwilliam. Jane and Mr Bennet stood with Mr Darcy. All the while, Elizabeth stood on her own with her eyes fixed on Fitzwilliam. She failed to notice Mr Darcy approaching her and jumped when she heard his voice.

"It has been an honour to meet you, Miss Elizabeth. I regret that it has taken this long."

Elizabeth stared at him. His tone and demeanour were formal, but in his awkwardness, she once again saw a reflection of her William.

"I hope we shall meet again soon." He bowed and went to make his farewells to the others.

Elizabeth stared at him and tried to understand why he had singled her out. She watched as he left the room with Fitzwilliam and was once again startled by a voice at her elbow.

Jane asked, "Lizzy, are you well? What did Mr Darcy say to you?"

"I hardly know. I must— I shall return later." Elizabeth rushed from the room and out into the garden.

FITZWILLIAM RETURNED from seeing his father to the carriage. Mr Bennet stood in the corridor and wordlessly pointed towards the side door. Fitzwilliam thanked him and hurried outside again. He found Elizabeth pacing back and forth on the gravel walkway that led into the grove. When he called her name, she stopped and glared at him. As he approached, she stepped backwards. He could see the flare of her nostrils and anger in her eyes.

"Lizzy." He reached for her, although the distance between them was six or seven feet.

"What did you say to him? Why are you here?"

"I told him about you."

"What?"

"I told him about us, that I love you and—"

"Oh? Did you tell him you were *obligated* to marry me however little anyone would like it? That your honour was engaged, and though I am not the sort of lady Fitzwilliam Darcy of Pemberley should take as his wife, I would have to do because of stupid promises you made when you thought you were William Lucas? Did you tell him that?"

"Yes." He regretted the response when Elizabeth looked as if she would throw a rock at him, if she had one at hand. He was never very good in the face of her ire. "No. Not-not like that. You cannot truly believe I think—"

"Yes, I can! After months of ignoring me, of ignoring all of us, you came to me and said I was not the sort of lady you should marry."

"Lizzy, please." He was not above begging if that was what it took for her to listen to his apology.

"Why did you not just tell him I was someone you used to know?"

"What?" His eyebrows drew together.

"The evening we first met in London, when you looked at me —*me!*—and called me Miss Bennet, and told Mr John Darcy that I was simply someone you used to know. How could you say such a thing?" Her voice rose until it was almost a whine. She stamped her foot, turned on her heel, and stalked away. Her steps were loud on the stones, and she reached out a hand to slap the bushes as she rushed by them.

He followed her, and called, "Would you please listen to me for a minute."

She stopped but kept her back to him. Her hand tapped the side of her leg as he spoke.

"I told my father because he asked about you after we returned to the inn. I do not know exactly what he saw, but he knew you were more than an acquaintance I left behind."

Elizabeth scoffed.

"I ought to have told him months ago. I made so many mistakes. You cannot know how much I regret them."

Elizabeth shook her head.

"I am ashamed of how thoughtless I was." When she did not speak or move, he halved the distance between them. "After I was last here, a visit that was long overdue, I told him where I had been—"

"You did not come directly from London."

He shook his head even though she could not see him. "I wanted to be alone for a few days. So much has happened since October. I did not realise how desperately I needed time away from everyone." He sighed. "Or how selfishly I have been acting."

Elizabeth made a noise that suggested she agreed with him, though it was weak.

"I went to Essex. After a few days, I started to understand where I had gone wrong. You know what I did next. I went to Lucas Lodge to see my parents."

"No doubt they accepted you with open arms and would not hear a word of apology."

"I did try to make them hear it."

Elizabeth turned to face him. "They will not tell you how difficult it was for them, but I shall. It was terrible. They love you, and you disappeared from their lives, dismissed them as though they were unimportant once you were with the Darcys. How could you do that to them? Did you give any thought to what it was like during those long weeks before Mr Darcy decided he was ready to tell the world that you were found? You know what people are like! Everyone talked about your odd absence, everyone had an explanation for it, and few of them were kind or understanding."

"I am so sorry."

"It is not enough! It does not make what we-*they* had to endure any less painful."

"I wish I could go back and do better by all of you. When I returned to town, I told my father I could no longer neglect everyone who was important to me when I believed I was William Lucas."

Her expression changed just a little—the anger in her eyes faded and was replaced by wariness, and her frown was less severe.

"He accepted it more readily than I thought he would. It was his idea to return with me."

Elizabeth demanded, "Why?"

"He wished to meet Lady Lucas and your family."

Elizabeth shook her head. Fitzwilliam was not certain what she meant by it, but he would take advantage of her silence to say as much as he could.

"I should have told him months ago that I could not simply forget the life I had here. I should have told him about *you* months ago. I do not know how it happened that they assumed there was no one, but I did not correct them. I cannot say he would have been happy—"

Elizabeth gave a bark of disgusted laughter.

"But he would have accepted us. That is what I attempted to say to you that morning. You know I have always loved—"

Elizabeth brushed past him and began running towards the house. "No! I cannot listen to any more."

He hung his head and sighed.

FITZWILLIAM ENTERED Longbourn several paces behind Elizabeth. Mr Bennet stood by the door. Elizabeth walked past him.

She announced, "I am going to my bedroom. Alone."

Mr Bennet nodded slowly and regarded Fitzwilliam with one eyebrow cocked. Fitzwilliam swallowed and felt the sudden urge to loosen his neckcloth.

"Perhaps we might have a few minutes' conversation before we join the ladies and Sir William," Mr Bennet said.

Fitzwilliam scrubbed at his face as Mr Bennet led the way into his book room. He was exhausted, having been awake far into the night talking with George, and the scene with Elizabeth had left him feeling battered. Before speaking, Mr Bennet studied Fitzwilliam for a moment.

"It has been a most shocking week. Lizzy returned earlier than anticipated and refused to talk about you except to say that she had seen you. Then *you* turned up unexpectedly. Despite what Sir William and Lady Lucas opine, I know it was not because of Lizzy, at least not in the way they assume. She accepted months ago that her future is not with you."

Fitzwilliam did not act quickly enough to stifle a moan of dismay.

"What else could we think? A man in your position seldom marries a lady without fortune or connexions, neither of which my Lizzy has."

Fitzwilliam rolled his shoulders to ease some of the tension.

"And then, yet another surprise! Sir William shows me a letter announcing your imminent arrival with Mr George Darcy, who I assumed wanted to separate you from us! I cannot think so many startling events are good for me at my time of life.

"Throughout it all, my dearest girl has said not a word to me or Jane. This morning, she raced out of the house almost as soon as you and Mr Darcy left the room. What did he say to her?"

Fitzwilliam's hand drifted towards his face, and he stuffed it under his leg so that he would not run it over his brow or tug at his collar. "I-I-I do not know."

"Oh?" Mr Bennet regarded him, his right eyebrow arched.

Fitzwilliam reminded himself that he deserved far worse from Mr Bennet, considering his recent behaviour. "I suppose enough to tell her that he knows about, well, about my feelings for her."

"I am afraid I must ask: what are your feelings? Forgive the impertinence, but I am her father."

Fitzwilliam's cheeks grew warm. *Dear God, this is worse than when he first made me discuss the subject with him.* "They have never changed. I know you have good reason to wonder, and I can only beg forgiveness or at least understanding. The…"

He faltered and was grateful when Mr Bennet offered him a glass of juice. Fitzwilliam finished it before continuing. He spoke for some time, starting with how dazed he had been in October, to his argument with Elizabeth and time at Southend.

Mr Bennet let out a long, slow breath. "I begin to understand the situation. You did not tell your father about Lizzy until yesterday?"

Fitzwilliam nodded.

"I take it she had a few pointed words for you just now?"

Fitzwilliam could see Mr Bennet's lips twitching. He liked to laugh at the follies of others, and Fitzwilliam knew he had been exceedingly foolish. He nodded again.

"Oh, well. When she is willing to listen, and she will be if you give her time, tell her what you told me and whatever else you can more easily say to her. Am I right that your father would countenance a match? I will not see Lizzy further disappointed or injured."

"He will." Fitzwilliam hardly believed that Mr Bennet was not warning him away from Elizabeth or telling him that he would not permit an engagement for a year or two to give him time to prove himself.

Mr Bennet grunted. "Good. I leave the resolution of this mess in your hands and those of my daughter. Off you go, my lad. This excitement has exhausted me, and I have kept you too long to myself."

ELIZABETH RAN up the stairs and into her bedchamber. She flung herself onto her bed and buried her face in a pillow. She did not know whether to cry or scream, and did both. Every shred of peace she had found was lost.

Why would Fitzwilliam tell George Darcy about their past after all this time?

How could she have failed to think about Fitzwilliam or his father and what they had suffered?

How dare Fitzwilliam say that he loved her?

After punching her pillow, she got out of bed to find a handkerchief and sit at her window. It overlooked the path she and Fitzwilliam had just been on. She shook her head violently, determined not to give in to her tears again. *They do me no good.*

Elizabeth was by turns angry and disappointed in herself for being so selfish regarding Fitzwilliam, but especially his father. She had condemned George Darcy without ever meeting him and wished the truth had remained buried.

"Stupid girl," she muttered to her reflection in the glass before forcing her eyes to the trees in the distance. Their delicate new leaves waved gently in the breeze, and white clouds crawled across the blue sky. It helped to calm her. *Upon what did you base your opinion of him? That he is rich and highly born? That he ruined your perfectly happy life? Not that* he *is responsible for it.* "It is time to grow up, Elizabeth Annabelle Bennet. Confront this like an adult. I thought I was mature enough to get married and have a family, but when the truth was revealed, I acted like a spoilt child whose favourite toy was broken."

She shook her head and blew her nose. *How can I just forget Fitzwilliam and move on with my life? It was easier when I could tell myself that my William was lost to this new creature whom I could not like, but that was a silly thing to say. He is still William. I did not want to see it, because I did not want to believe my William could injure me in such a fashion.*

Her understanding of what he had faced and felt over the last six months was limited, although he had hinted at difficulties. She would have to let him tell her, but only once she believed she could listen without feeling as angry as she had that morning.

"I ought to have done better, at least by William, whom I have claimed to know and love so well. At the very least, I should have been more sympathetic to what he was experiencing, to say nothing of Mr Darcy. I shall do better. I just need a little time." *And sleep.*

She curled up like a cat and closed her eyes.

ELIZABETH EMERGED from her room to discover that Sir William and Lady Lucas had departed to arrange an evening party for later that day so that Fitzwilliam could see as many of his old neighbours as possible before returning to town. Although there was some discussion of the young people going out, their departure was delayed because the Linningtons and Mr Hawarden were expected to call. Watching Fitzwilliam with her sisters and mother, Elizabeth thought it almost seemed like nothing had changed.

Elizabeth continued to study Fitzwilliam when the Netherfield party arrived. He was as friendly and affable as William

Lucas ever was with people so new to him. *If anything, he seems more relaxed than he used to be in similar circumstances.* She supposed it was because he had met so many people over the last half a year that he had grown more accustomed to conversing with strangers.

Elizabeth, along with the Linningtons, Mr Hawarden, Fitzwilliam, Jane, and Mary went for a walk, which gave her more time to observe his manner. She could find nothing to fault. She was not ready to talk to him herself, however, and continued to avoid being in a position where she might have to. It meant linking her arm with Mary's for most of the excursion, which was a trial because Mary walked slowly.

The party at Lucas Lodge that evening was a great success. Everyone was pleased to see Fitzwilliam again, and he was happy to see them. He smiled and listened patiently to her mother and Aunt Philips. He joked and laughed with the Goulding brothers. He and some of the local gentlemen, including her father, spoke for quite a while.

She even said a few words to Fitzwilliam, although she had not intended to. Their conversation started as she was moving from one part of the room to another. Elizabeth did not see him before it was too late to avoid his path.

"Are you enjoying yourself?" he asked.

Elizabeth felt many pairs of eyes on them. "There is a certain comfort in being with people one knows as well as I do those here."

"I agree. It is wonderful to see everyone."

He looked at the assembled crowd, while Elizabeth restrained an urge to kick him.

"Oh? Did you miss them? They have been here all along." No doubt her annoyance was evident in her arched eyebrows, if not her sarcastic tone.

"Lizzy…"

She held up a hand and shook her head. "This is not the time or place."

"Then when and where?"

Elizabeth watched Jane and Mr Hawarden for a moment. Their affection for each other was plain for all to see. "I do not know. Not yet."

Before he could respond, she walked away.

Back at Longbourn, she had two visitors to her room. First, Mr Bennet came to assure himself that she was well. He encouraged her to talk to Fitzwilliam and said that they had an 'illuminating' conversation that morning. Second, Jane came to talk about the day and, of course, Fitzwilliam.

I appreciate Jane's caring nature, but if she plans to ask me how I feel every hour, I shall succumb to nerves. She chuckled. *I believe I require a lock for my door and a little sign that says I am not at leisure to have well-meaning but rather annoying conversations about Fitzwilliam Darcy!*

With another quiet laugh, she blew out the candle and closed her eyes for the night.

CHAPTER 30

FRIDAY MORNING SIR WILLIAM, LADY LUCAS, AND FITZWILLIAM spoke about the party. It was a relief to Fitzwilliam to see that his parents were increasingly like their old selves. They ought to be angrier with him, but it was not in them to hold such sentiments. They accepted that he would live with George Darcy and were happy to anticipate his future visits especially, as Sir William said, 'when a certain desirable event' took place.

Fitzwilliam said, "I was pleased to see everyone doing so well. My only wish is that Charlotte might have been with us."

Lady Lucas sighed and looked wistful.

"Has she spoken about visiting? When do you expect to see her?" Fitzwilliam asked.

Sir William furrowed his brow and shook his head. "It is too soon to think about such things. She and the captain have their life in Kent."

It was evident in their long faces that they felt Charlotte's absence. *Especially since I was not here.* He did not want to risk upsetting them further, but there was a matter they needed to discuss. He had often assisted Sir William with the estate and suspected his adoptive father was unsure what to do given the changed circumstances. *And has lost his enthusiasm for the work, since he no longer has a son who will rely on it to support his own family.*

He said, "I asked about Charlotte and Captain Farnon visiting because it would do them good to become more familiar with how the estate is managed."

His parents looked at him with puzzlement on their faces.

With as much delicacy as possible, he explained, "As we know, my life is in Derbyshire now. I shall visit and always do what I can to assist you. As often as we talked about me one day being master here, that is no longer our future."

Lady Lucas looked on the verge of spilling a tear or two at this reminder, but she managed to restrain herself.

"Lucas Lodge should be for Charlotte, or her eldest son, if you prefer. They might make their home here when the captain is ready to give up his career."

Sir William proclaimed it an excellent notion and Lady Lucas agreed, adding, "To think of my dear girl one day being mistress here!"

The three of them discussed it and other estate matters for the next several hours.

FITZWILLIAM WENT to Longbourn shortly after breakfast; he found the entire family together in the small parlour. Mr Bennet read the newspaper in his preferred chair, which was old and worn but, he claimed, particularly comfortable. Mrs Bennet sat with her two youngest on a sofa, and the other three girls were arranged in seats around the room. Elizabeth was occupied with needlework and hardly looked at him when he entered.

Lydia asked, "You will stay the whole day, will you not, William?"

"I shall."

Fitzwilliam glanced towards Elizabeth. He longed to go to her as he would have in the past. Mr Bennet noticed, and given the older man's guarded expression, Fitzwilliam decided it would be prudent to take the chair near Mrs Bennet. He was returning to town the next day and longed to talk to Elizabeth before he did.

Mr Bennet had given Kitty and Lydia leave to set aside their studies for the day, and after Fitzwilliam and the five Bennet girls agreed to walk into Meryton, Mr Bennet left them to visit a tenant. Mrs Bennet kept them with her for another half an hour by asking about the titled and otherwise famous people Fitzwilliam had met. He answered as best as he could, all the while trying to find a way to change the topic, but it was difficult for anyone other than Mr Bennet to stop Mrs Bennet saying what she liked.

She showed the truth of this when she asked, "Why did you not return for Lizzy sooner? There were some that said you were too good for her now. I suppose you and Mr Bennet and Lizzy arranged for her to go to your cousin long ago so that, although *we* have not seen you, *she* has. They did not tell me where you were for weeks. My poor nerves—"

Elizabeth announced, "I shall go prepare for the walk." With that, she stood and left the room.

Leaving Mrs Bennet to her other daughters, Fitzwilliam excused himself and followed Elizabeth.

In the corridor, he called, "Lizzy, I am sorry."

"Because my mother is being just as she always is?"

She walked away. Fitzwilliam sighed.

LYDIA AND KITTY commandeered Fitzwilliam's attention on the walk into Meryton. Fitzwilliam insisted Mary join them after the first little while, which left Jane to walk with Elizabeth. In between noticing signs of the advancing spring—a new flower here, the low buzzing of insects—or commenting on the temperature, which was perfect for their walk, or to say that the cloud cover was just enough to provide relief from the bright sun, Elizabeth watched Fitzwilliam interact with her sisters and the people they met in town.

She came to two conclusions. The first was that he seemed very much like her William, albeit it in finer clothes and with something more of seriousness about him. *Which is saying something since he has always been a serious person. Perhaps it is that he has matured. I feel as though I have aged a decade since the autumn, two or three years in the last fortnight alone, and it must be the same for him.*

The second conclusion was that everyone, with the possible exceptions of her father and Jane, expected that she and Fitzwilliam would soon be married.

The realisation confused her. So much had happened since they argued in London. She knew his wishes, and Mr Darcy had implied that he would accept the match. But what did she feel? It was too much of a leap from her present hurt feelings to wanting to be his wife. She could hardly talk to him. She knew her father was correct to encourage her to speak with him, yet she hesitated. Even when she could have walked beside him on the way back to Longbourn, she did not.

SIR WILLIAM and Lady Lucas joined them at Longbourn for a family dinner. Elizabeth used the time to study Fitzwilliam as he took a spoonful of cabbage soup, or a bite of celery and wine ragout, or a mouthful of steak and potatoes. The potatoes were particularly creamy and delicious and were the only thing on her plate she really tasted. Not even the bread pudding, a particular favourite of hers, could distract her.

Earlier, as they had prepared for dinner, Jane had spoken to her privately. "Lizzy, when will you speak to Fitzwilliam?"

Elizabeth sighed. "I do not know what to say to him."

Jane gave her hand a gentle squeeze. "You do still love him, do you not? It is plain to see that he loves you. Speak to him before he returns to town. You will regret it if you do not."

Elizabeth nodded, kissed Jane's cheek, and ended the tête-à-tête.

Now, as she sat at the dinner table and watched him, she chastised herself. *Have I not always prided myself on my courage? Yet, when I need it most of all, it has abandoned me. If Fitzwilliam tells me something I find distressing, well, it cannot signify. My heart has felt broken for months. Having everything out in the open would be better than continuing on in this way.*

It was thus that, not long before Elizabeth judged the Lucas Lodge party would leave, she found a moment to say a few words to Fitzwilliam.

"Tomorrow morning, before you leave, meet me. You know where."

He met her eye and whispered, "Of course."

ELIZABETH LEFT EARLY for her rendezvous with Fitzwilliam. She made her way to a clearing by the stream that ran between Longbourn and Netherfield. There was a slight chill and dampness to the air which was refreshing. Her footsteps were dull thuds as they hit the ground on the narrow path she preferred.

Once at her destination, she paced in front of a broad log that had fallen several years earlier. She saw a few wood sorrels growing from the moss at one end of it. The other side remained solid enough to bear their weight, but she would not sit, because it would invite Fitzwilliam to do likewise. A large cluster of star-shaped flowers grew by the bank of the stream, their bright yellow contrasting with the deep shade of the plants' leaves.

When Elizabeth heard Fitzwilliam approach, she turned to face him.

"Lizzy."

He appeared relieved to find her there and stepped towards her. She maintained a distance of about ten feet.

He said, "Thank you for meeting me."

Elizabeth shrugged. She felt awkward and wary. A part of her knew she would forgive him—she loved him too well not to—but she had questions about what had happened and how much she would have to forgive. Could she trust him again as she once had?

As though afraid she would not let him speak, he launched into his apology and explanation.

"I am sorry, Lizzy. There are so many things I regret, and I regret them all deeply." His hand lifted as though to touch her. "I felt like I was in the middle of such a conundrum without ever knowing how I got there. I am ashamed of myself and...I do not know how I made such a mess of everything.

"I hardly remember leaving Hertfordshire or travelling north or really anything until I was at Pemberley, staring at a man who looks so much like me that I might as well have been looking in a mirror twenty or thirty years in the future."

"Your father," Elizabeth whispered. Had she not also been struck by the resemblance between them, even after knowing the truth for months?

Fitzwilliam nodded and ran his hands through his hair. "Everything Frederick and Sir William had said about me being kidnapped and adopted by the Lucases crashed down on me. I was numb. Overwhelmed. All of a sudden, everything I had believed about myself was wrong. I felt like my life had been a lie. I did not know what I was supposed to do or think, or even who I was. I only really understood that last month. After what you said—"

"Pray, do not remind me." With her own thoughts in disarray, Elizabeth did not want to examine how she had behaved towards Fitzwilliam when they were in town.

"What did you say that I did not deserve? I behaved terribly, and I shall not attempt to excuse it. What I say now is to try to explain. The weeks we were apart were, without exaggeration, the most difficult ones of my life. I missed you every minute of every day. I felt alone and surrounded by strangers, but they were people who should *not* have been strangers to me. No sooner did my shock begin to recede then I started to understand how different the lives of the Darcys are to those of the Lucases and Bennets. I thought that because I was Fitzwilliam Darcy, not William Lucas, we could not be together. Because my life as

William Lucas had been a lie, I had to give up everything that had been a part of it. None of that makes sense when I say it aloud, but during those awful weeks and months it did.

"But, Lizzy, I never stopped thinking about you. I missed you and needed the comfort of your presence, the way you make me see everything more clearly, the strength you give me. I loved you the same. I just did not believe I would be permitted to have you."

"And yet, you sought me out," Elizabeth said.

Fitzwilliam nodded. "How could I not? In my desperation, I was certain I could make my father accept you, even if he did not like it. I ought to have told him the truth about you last autumn. I do not know why I did not."

Elizabeth glanced at him to find that he was looking at the ground and shaking his head. She, too, wondered why he had allowed the Darcys to remain ignorant of their attachment. Her father could have told Mr Frederick Darcy, but she understood that he thought it best for Fitzwilliam to disclose the truth. Mr Bennet had also mentioned the possibility that Fitzwilliam had informed George Darcy and been told a union with Elizabeth was impossible.

She asked, "And now?"

"My father knows I love you and have always dreamt of a life with you."

Their eyes met, and Elizabeth sought to understand whether Mr Darcy gave his consent grudgingly or wholeheartedly.

"When I was in Essex—oh, the relief of being alone!—I understood what I had to do if I ever hoped to be happy again. I cannot think of myself as being either William Lucas *or* Fitzwilliam Darcy. I am both men and always will be. I cannot pretend part of my life never happened. That is why I came to Hertfordshire, and that is what I explained to my father when I returned to town. He has accepted it."

Elizabeth nodded and let her eyes fall to the ground. "I owe you an apology, as well."

Fitzwilliam cried, "What? Lizzy, no—"

"I do, and I ask that you listen to me." She was conscious of sounding cold but knew not how else to keep her emotions in check. "I did not consider how terrible these months have been for you. I was hurt and angry when you did not write, and I thought the worst of you and Mr George Darcy."

"Even if that is true, it does not excuse how I—"

"No, it does not," Elizabeth interjected. "But I should have thought about what it was like for you. The same is true for Mr Darcy. I did not truly consider what it must have been like for him to learn that you were alive all this time. I thought about what *I* suffered in losing you, but never of what *he* suffered. I wished that the truth had not been discovered, not thinking what that would mean for the Darcys, especially your father. I cannot believe I was so unfeeling, and I pray I have learnt from this."

"Lizzy," Fitzwilliam whispered. "The fault is mine and mine alone. Had I done more—"

Elizabeth shook her head and waved away his words. She did not deserve to have her misjudgments dismissed.

"I love you so much."

Elizabeth made a noise that was somewhere between one of disbelief and a sob. It felt like her heart was breaking all over again. *Or perhaps it is the pain of it mending.*

"I do," he insisted. "Regardless of my name or my expectations—"

"But they *have* changed," Elizabeth stated.

"That does not matter."

He stepped towards her, and this time, she did not back away.

"Your life is very different now. I saw that when I was in London." Elizabeth expected him to understand what she meant. They had both listened to Mr Bennet speak dismissively about the *ton* and their licentiousness. Even to think of her William behaving in such a manner made her stomach roil. She watched him as he spoke, determined to face whatever he told her next with courage.

Fitzwilliam rubbed a hand over his mouth. "In town, I was surrounded by... There are some places I went to which I shall not ever, voluntarily, return to. I admit that, upon occasion, I drank more than I should have. I longed for some way to find relief from the oppression I felt. But I was always true to you. I could not be otherwise, not when my love for you has remained unchanged. I longed for *you*, for your comfort and company. Constantly." He blinked several times, and his voice grew thick. "For most of my life, I did not live as Fitzwilliam Darcy. I lived as William Lucas, and when I tried to deny it, I made myself, you, my father, the Lucases, your family, all of us so unhappy and-and unsettled."

Elizabeth felt the sting of tears in her eyes.

Fitzwilliam pressed his hand over his mouth for a moment before continuing. "I will always love you, just as I did when I lived here as William Lucas. How could I not? I am the same man I always was, older, wiser, more conscious of my weaknesses, but in essentials, I have not changed. My love for you has never altered, and in my heart, in my thoughts, in *every* way, I could not be other than true to you."

His voice faded away, and Elizabeth closed the distance between them. She felt a tear slide down her cheek as she slipped her arms around him and rested her head on his chest. In a moment, his body began to shake as he released his anguish.

CHAPTER 31

FITZWILLIAM WAS HAPPIER UPON HIS RETURN TO TOWN THAN HE had been in months, possibly since the morning he first left Hertfordshire to travel to Pemberley. George asked about his visit, and Fitzwilliam told him how much he had enjoyed seeing his old friends.

"And Miss Elizabeth? Where did you leave things with her?" his father asked.

Fitzwilliam averted his eyes and felt his cheeks warm. "We talked. This morning. I apologised."

"And?"

"And now I feel quite sanguine." Fitzwilliam avoided meeting his father's eye. "I hope to return soon. While we remain in London—"

George chuckled. "Of course. The distance is much easier from town than it is from Pemberley. But now, I am afraid we must turn our attention to this evening's…amusement. We cannot keep the duke and duchess waiting."

It was not a particularly enjoyable evening, but it was at least uneventful. There were a number of eligible young ladies at the party; some of them, or their relatives, attempted to secure Fitzwilliam's notice.

"It will not end until you are a married man," his father said as they made their way home. "Then the attention will change, not disappear. You are a Darcy of Pemberley. People will always wish to know you. You have experienced it already, no doubt."

"I have," Fitzwilliam grumbled.

With hesitation in his voice, his father asked, "Has it been very arduous to become accustomed to the *ton*?"

"It can be difficult to know who to trust."

"Fortunately, you have John to help you tell the difference between friend and foe."

In the growing darkness of the carriage, Fitzwilliam squirmed before he nodded.

THE NEXT DAY, George and Fitzwilliam joined Frederick and his children at church before taking breakfast at Darcy House. Fitzwilliam soon learnt that they knew about his and George's trip to Meryton. He wondered if his father had told Frederick about Elizabeth.

Freddie asked, "Did you enjoy it?"

Fitzwilliam nodded.

Rebecca said, "They must have been delighted to see you."

"You saw Lizzy, of course," Freddie added. "I liked her very much. Did you, Uncle George? I hope so. It was wonderful to have her in town."

"I had the pleasure of meeting her and her family. They were all very agreeable."

Freddie continued as he reached for another piece of toast, "Lizzy is so nice and seemed to—oh, how do I say it?—she seemed to *fit* so well, almost like she was part of the family. I hope she comes back, or that we can go to them."

Part of the family? I pray she truly will be soon. Fitzwilliam glanced at his father, who was looking at him. Frederick was too, and wore a reassuring smile.

George said, "I suspect we shall see a great deal more of the Bennets in the future. Tell me, you young rascal, what have you been doing with yourself? Are you enjoying your time in London?"

"Oh, very much!" Freddie cried.

Freddie and Rebecca spoke about their recent activities. Although Fitzwilliam knew they saw Sterling and Tom Fitzwilliam regularly, neither mentioned the brothers.

I wish they would. I believe I could be friends with them— more than I am with John, without a doubt. I can never know my mother, but I can know her brother, with whom she was particularly close, and my aunt-in-law. Somehow, I shall have to find a way to discuss it with my father. Fitzwilliam wanted to sigh and considered loosening the buttons on his waistcoat, as if that would ease the heaviness he felt in his chest. He had already asked his father to bear so much. Knowing that he wanted yet more and that it was sure to make George unhappy renewed Fitzwilliam's feelings of guilt.

SEVERAL DAYS LATER, Fitzwilliam and John dined with friends of the family, while their fathers were occupied elsewhere. The party then went to the theatre. Once there, John asked Fitzwilliam how he had enjoyed the company of Miss Yardley, whom he had sat beside during the meal.

"She was amiable."

John cocked an eyebrow at him. "She has a handsome dowry. It would not be a brilliant match for you, but I suppose you could convince my uncle to accept it if you developed a strong attachment to her."

Fitzwilliam had no interest in discussing marriage. "My father is an excellent man. What he most desires is my happiness."

After a long moment, John said, "I can conceive of nothing more important to my uncle. He might wish your wife to have fortune and connexions, but if you truly love a woman who does not have them, he will acquiesce. If, for instance, there was a lady from before. Oh, he will say it is impossible, and that he will not accept the lady. But if you persist, if you *insist* upon having her, he will relent. Your very persistence demonstrates firmness of mind and resolution, which are traits he appreciates."

Fitzwilliam ceased paying attention to the performance on stage. He listened carefully and with more than a little surprise and pleasure, to John's words. He dismissed the latter part of his speech, knowing that he already had his father's approval. John had often told him that George had great expectations for him and that they included a carefully selected bride. Whatever the reason, John now seemed to think differently. It was gratifying to feel that John would support his right to choose his bride in a disinterested manner.

Perhaps I misjudged him. I was convinced that he would think me a fool for forgoing the opportunity to marry a rich peer-ess. Now, so many months after my true identity was revealed, perhaps he and his father have learnt to think better of my past.

After the theatre—an indifferent show, in Fitzwilliam's opinion—they went to a ball. Like all such parties, Fitzwilliam found it too loud and hot, and there were too many clashing scents which made his nose itch. He looked around to see if there was anyone he recognised in the rapidly swelling crowd.

This sort of situation is far preferable to other evenings I have spent with John. I cannot always avoid him, and I would rather be at a ball such as this than at one of the clubs or dreadful so-called theatres he took me to. After knowing what sort of places he liked to frequent, why did I continue to go with him? Did I truly believe I had to in order to gain my father's approbation? Never again!

Fitzwilliam spotted Frederick and told John.

John scowled. "Must we go to him, do you think?"

"He has seen us."

"Rebecca and Freddie will be with him," John said as if in warning.

Facing John, Fitzwilliam said, "I like them. They are excellent people and good company in my opinion."

John's lips twisted in disgust.

Fitzwilliam shook his head. "I am going to see them."

As he walked towards Frederick, Rebecca, and Freddie, John following him, he suddenly remembered John saying that Frederick and George were not friends. *Why would he say such a thing? He must know they are. It is evident to me after our recent meetings, even just hearing how Frederick speaks about my father. John must have seen them together scores of times over the years. How odd.*

The middle of a busy ballroom was not the place to think about it, and he set it aside for the moment. When they reached their relations, Frederick offered each young man a smile. When he asked about their evening, Fitzwilliam mentioned the dinner party and theatre.

Frederick asked, "Did you enjoy the show?"

Fitzwilliam shook his head. "It was not much to my liking."

"I enjoyed it vastly," John said with an edge in his voice. "I imagine, Cousin, that it is your ignorance of what good society finds pleasing that makes you speak thus."

"John, that was unkind!" Frederick cried.

"Was it?" John sounded amused more than anything else.

Fitzwilliam's face heated, and he tried to think of something to say. John's words reminded him of his sense of not belonging and worries that he never would. *What a strange mood he is in. At the theatre, when he talked about my father wanting my happiness, I thought I had misjudged him, but...*

John said, "I see a friend. We really must greet him." He gave Frederick a quick nod and took Fitzwilliam's elbow as though to guide him, but Fitzwilliam pulled his arm away.

"I shall stay here. I hope to convince Rebecca to dance with me if she has a set free."

John glared at him.

"I am sure we shall see each other again before the night is over," Fitzwilliam said, though he hoped they would not.

He watched as John stalked off.

They were silent for a moment until Freddie asked, "What is the matter with John tonight?"

Knowing he was expected to reply, Fitzwilliam stammered, "I can hardly... I am afraid it is my fault. I expressed an opinion contrary to his." It sounded ridiculous, but the words were out, and it was too late to recall them.

"What?" Freddie exclaimed, while Rebecca cried, "He was rude because you said something he did not agree with?"

Frederick ran his eyes over the crowd. "Let us *not* discuss this here."

That suited Fitzwilliam, who decided he was grateful for John's rash words. It gave him an excuse to remain with relations he liked far better.

Several minutes later, Lord Bramwell and Colonel Fitzwilliam joined them. Fitzwilliam had not seen them since the encounter in Hyde Park a week earlier.

The brothers smiled and greeted Freddie, Rebecca, and Frederick before addressing him. They remained wary, and he did not blame them. *They might think me hesitant to talk to them so openly. I must find a time to discuss the matter privately with Frederick.*

The viscount turned his attention to Rebecca. "Am I permitted to compliment you this evening or not?"

Fitzwilliam was surprised to see Rebecca blush.

"Far be it for me to tell you what to do."

Freddie guffawed. "What nonsense! I have heard you tell Bramwell what to do a dozen times at least!"

Frederick chuckled. "Do not tease your sister, Freddie. Tell us, colonel, how do you do? How are your parents?"

Although he occasionally glanced at Lord Bramwell and Rebecca, Fitzwilliam devoted his attention to the others. *Between*

Freddie's familiarity with them and Rebecca's manner, I must conclude they are better friends than I had supposed.

Frederick allowed the couple to speak privately for several minutes before asking the viscount a question. Until the music started, and Lord Bramwell and Rebecca went to dance, the entire party had a pleasant conversation. The brothers requested Fitzwilliam call them by their Christian names.

I begin to suspect I shall enjoy this ball more than any other I have been to this winter. It only wants Lizzy's presence.

In response to Tom's questioning, Fitzwilliam told him how he came to be with Frederick and his children. He did not repeat John's insulting words.

"Ah, you were here with John Darcy." Tom's voice dripped with contempt.

Fitzwilliam stepped closer and lowered his voice. "I would be interested to know why you and your brother dislike him."

Tom regarded him through narrowed eyes. "Then I would be happy to talk about it when we are in more suitable surroundings."

Fitzwilliam accepted this with a nod.

"How is your father? Or, as Sterling would insist on saying, Uncle George. I trust he is in good health?"

Fitzwilliam said that he was. "About what I said last week, more has happened, and I am hopeful."

"You remain determined to tell him that you wish to know us?" Tom asked. "You know my parents greatly desire it, my father especially."

"I do. If I am not mistaken, there are other reasons why it is important. I had not realised what good friends all of you were, especially Rebecca and Bramwell."

Tom chuckled. "It is impossible not to like Freddie, and Sterling is *very* fond of Miss Darcy's company."

"Well then, something must be done about this breach." *And I am the one to do it. All I need is a little advice!*

FOR THE MOST PART, Fitzwilliam enjoyed his time at the ball. However, he had a disagreeable encounter with John several hours after separating from him.

John said, "You seem to be enjoying yourself. I cannot see why, but clearly some of your tastes are not mine."

Fitzwilliam saw no need to respond.

"You have done your duty by Rebecca?"

"I have." Fitzwilliam knew what was coming next.

"Good. It is time to go. Say your farewells. I shall go with you."

"My farewells? But I am not leaving." He spoke as though surprised and prayed that John soon understood that he would not be able to direct Fitzwilliam's actions any longer.

"I just told you that we are. We are joining our friends so that we can squeeze some pleasure out of this wretched evening."

"I am sorry you are not enjoying yourself. I find it perfectly agreeable. Go on without me."

With a clenched jaw, John retorted, "We talked about looking into the club tonight."

"You spoke of going, but I did not say I would. I shall see you again in two days at Lady Mildred's."

John attempted to argue him into leaving; the conversation ended when Frederick joined them.

Fitzwilliam said, "John is leaving. I explained that I would remain here and get a ride home with you."

"We are pleased to have your company. Where are you off to, John?"

John prevaricated, and Frederick did not push the issue. Fitzwilliam noticed Frederick's brow was furrowed as he watched John walk away, but Fitzwilliam felt only relief.

CHAPTER 32

THE FOLLOWING MORNING, GEORGE ASKED ABOUT THE PREVIOUS evening when they were at breakfast. Fitzwilliam said that he had enjoyed the dinner party and ball but had not liked the theatre.

"It was not a particularly late night. You and John did not go elsewhere afterwards? I thought that was what young men commonly did."

"John met friends at one of the clubs. I preferred to stay with Frederick, Rebecca, and Freddie and came home with them."

"I see." George frowned. "Which club?"

"I do not know. How was your evening, Father?"

George looked up and shook his head as if clearing his thoughts. "It was a group of old men talking about politics. It was pleasurable, I suppose, and it was necessary to help maintain our family's interests. Jeffrey and John require our support. Having connexions to gentlemen such as the ones I dined with yesterday is a part of it."

"Of course. Will you tell me about it?" One day, it would fall to him to nurture such ties, whether he liked it or not.

His father spoke for some time. Fitzwilliam did his best to absorb the lessons he offered. *I do have a great deal to learn. Fortunately, it does not seem like such an arduous task any longer.*

After breakfast, Fitzwilliam went to call on Frederick, having arranged to do so the evening before.

"I am glad to see you looking so well. George, too," Frederick said once they were settled in his library with a tray of coffee and cakes.

Frederick continued, "He told me about your visits to Meryton and your understandable wish to maintain your connexions with the Lucases, Bennets, and your friends. I admit, I thought you were exchanging letters with them all along. He told me about Miss Elizabeth, too. That was not such a surprise, although it was only at Easter—right before she left us—that I suspected anything."

Fitzwilliam blushed. "I know it is a great deal for my father to take in, and I wonder if he is truly…" He lifted his shoulders, feeling too awkward to continue.

"I have rarely seen him as happy as he was when he told me he feels the two of you have grown much closer. Indeed, looking back on it, I think all the times I have seen him so full of joy and optimism have had something to do with you."

Fitzwilliam was mostly pleased by the sentiment, but part of him was still worried. Frederick's next words helped.

"You should not worry so much about what he thinks. It is kind and generous that you do, but I am afraid you feel it too much. He wants your happiness and well-being. That is what is important to him. He told me the two of you spoke a great deal when you were in Hertfordshire."

"I believe we spoke more that one night than we had in the previous five or six months." He sipped his coffee.

"Good. Now the two of you need only remember to keep doing it. I dare say it will not always be easy." He laughed, and Fitzwilliam joined him.

Frederick then sighed and said, "I suppose you know we saw so little of you this winter because he was not pleased to learn Miss Elizabeth was staying here?" Fitzwilliam nodded. "I regret that it meant I missed a great deal. I knew George would not like being in town, but it seems it was even harder on him than I expected. These last months, I suspect he has not always believed that your return was real or that it would last. He says he will be well now that you and he understand each other better. No doubt, once the Season is over and he can return to Pemberley, he will soon be his old self. Better than his old self, now that he has so many reasons to be happy."

They spoke about Hertfordshire for a little while, after which Fitzwilliam said, "I would like to ask about my mother's family. I would like to know them."

"Naturally. I spoke to your aunt, Lady Romsley, just last week. You know she and your uncle were very close friends with your mother and father?" Fitzwilliam said that he did, and Frederick continued, "I would like to see them reunited. I believe your father will learn to want it, too. Now that he has such a joyful future to look forward to, he will see that it is possible and desirable to forgive the past. That is not to say that we should remain inactive. At the least, we can help him to see there is no harm in you knowing your cousins. You should not have to hide the fact that you have met them." He snapped his fingers. "I know just the thing. The three of us are going to the Hawkridges' together soon. We shall find a way to raise the subject of your cousins. It will be a start; we shall tackle the subject of Lord and Lady Romsley next. Your other aunt, Lady Catherine, is a different matter, but we need not worry about her until she returns from Ireland.

"Now, that is enough of that for the moment. Before you rush off, as I know you must so that you can attend one of the hundred or so parties or excursions or lectures you will go to in the next few weeks, there is something I would like to ask you."

"Sir?" Fitzwilliam knew he ought not to feel anxious, but he did.

"Tell me truly, Fitzwilliam, how do you get along with John? I admit, I was unhappy with his manner yesterday."

"We...we get on well enough together."

"Do you?"

"Our tastes are not similar, no doubt because our lives have been so different."

Frederick regarded him for perhaps ten seconds, but Fitzwilliam would say no more. He was starting to see his cousin in a new light, and what he saw was disturbing. Before he said anything about it, he had to be sure.

After assuring Fitzwilliam that he could talk to him at any time and about anything, Frederick seemed content to let the subject drop. They spoke of other matters until Fitzwilliam took his leave a short time later.

GEORGE, Frederick, and Fitzwilliam went to the Hawkridges' outdoor fête as scheduled; Rebecca was with friends, and Freddie was doing something with Lord Bramwell, although Fitzwilliam did not know what. The day was hot for mid-April, and they were drinking tart lemonade while observing the crowd from their seats near the river.

Frederick pointed across the lawn. "Look, by that stand of oak trees."

George asked, "At whom or what am I to look?"

"Tom Fitzwilliam is here."

George said nothing.

Fitzwilliam said, "I met him and his brother at a ball recently."

His father turned to regard him. His face showed no hint of his feelings. "I see. Their parents?"

Fitzwilliam shook his head. "No, just-just them. We have spoken a little, but not what I would call a great deal."

George nodded and looked at the colonel again.

"They are very amiable," Fitzwilliam added.

George did not respond. Frederick caught Fitzwilliam's eye and gave him an approving smile.

THE FOLLOWING DAY, Fitzwilliam received a long-hoped-for letter from Charlotte. He had not heard from her and assumed it meant she was not ready to forgive him. Charlotte commented on her surprise that he had been to Lucas Lodge and that she had never expected to hear from him again. She did not spare him her vexation about his past behaviour. Fitzwilliam could read her disappointment with each line.

> *I have returned to my letter after taking some time to consider my words. I cannot regret what I wrote. I understand that the last months have been difficult for you, and for that, I am sorry. It does not alter what any of us suffered. But you have made my parents happy by visiting. My mother claims your father was very kind. My father told us about his decision to make my son— supposing I am so fortunate as to have one—his heir, and says it was your idea. Captain Farnon and I shall go to Hertfordshire to discuss it further. My father hopes you can be there when we visit. It would be helpful, if it is possible. If not, I hope you will give Captain Farnon leave to write to you. I would not be displeased to see you.*
>
> *Yours, &c.*
> *Charlotte Farnon*

Fitzwilliam folded the letter and set it beside his breakfast plate, which was still full.

"I trust you have not received bad news."

The sound of his father's voice startled Fitzwilliam. He looked across the table and said, "The letter is from Mrs Farnon, Miss Lucas before her marriage." He explained Charlotte and Captain Farnon's upcoming visit to Lucas Lodge. "I would like to be there. My hope is that the Farnons will remove to Hertfordshire within a year or two. They would be company for Sir

William and Lady Lucas, and Captain Farnon could assist Sir William with the estate."

"You could see Miss Elizabeth as well."

Fitzwilliam nodded and attended to his breakfast. His spirits were affected, and not even the prospect of seeing Elizabeth lifted them at the moment. He did not blame Charlotte, but it was a difficult letter to read. He picked at the food on his plate and wondered how he would be able to finish it.

After a few minutes, George said, "You should go."

Fitzwilliam nodded again and thanked his father.

CHAPTER 33

Escaping from the busyness of London was a relief to Fitzwilliam. He hoped that in future years, he could avoid spending so much of the Season in town. *Lizzy might wish to partake in part of it. I would enjoy it more with her by my side.* He imagined the way they would laugh at the spectacle of it all and fall into a long debate about a lecture they had heard or the way a new invention would change their lives.

I must believe that the years we spent together and the love we shared means she will forgive me. He would do whatever it took to show her that she could trust him and that he was, in essentials, the same man he had always been.

George had wished him safe travels and an agreeable visit, but beneath the ease of his exterior, Fitzwilliam saw traces of apprehension.

Perhaps once a little more time has passed and he has truly become accustomed to everything, we can talk about it further. We shall both be happier if I can find a way to make him like my union with Lizzy, not just tolerate it, and to see that I can love both him and the Lucases and think of all three of them as parents; it is not one or the other.

He sighed. *And I must reconcile him to my wish to know the Fitzwilliams. I want to be friends with Bramwell and Tom. Having spent more time with them, I like them.*

For a few minutes, he focused his attention on the road, allowing his mind to clear. There was another problem, one he had not appreciated until recently: that related to John.

With a heavy sigh, he banished these thoughts from his mind. Once he returned to London, there would be time to worry about the people there.

AFTER AN AWKWARD DINNER during which Charlotte's disgust with him was plain for all to see, Fitzwilliam found an opportunity to talk to her alone. They walked in the wilder parts of the garden before breakfast. It was a fair day, and the temperature was perfectly agreeable for the season. Cowslips and violets were blooming, and Fitzwilliam hoped the renewal of spring would be matched by one in his personal connexions, especially those with Charlotte and Elizabeth.

He said, "I know there is little I can say that would truly express how sorry I am, but I am. I know I made a great many mistakes." He explained as best he could, feeling rather fatigued of the story but knowing she deserved to hear it.

Charlotte listened, shrugged, and said, "It does not matter any longer. I suppose we should put it behind us and look to the future. It must be breakfast time. We go to Longbourn afterwards. I assume you are anxious to see Lizzy. My mother and father believe you are already engaged but must keep it secret for some reason or other."

"We are not."

Charlotte's brusque manner indicated that the easy bond they had once shared was lost forever, which saddened him.

"Was she very angry with you?"

Fitzwilliam nodded.

"Good." Charlotte turned her back to him and returned to the house.

TWENTY MINUTES AFTER FITZWILLIAM, the Lucases, and Farnons arrived, Elizabeth saw her father speaking to Fitzwilliam, who then left the room. Mr Bennet joined her and said that he was waiting for her outside.

"No one will miss you for a quarter of an hour."

Elizabeth thanked him and went to find Fitzwilliam.

"Lizzy." A broad smile overtook Fitzwilliam's face.

Elizabeth took a deep breath and appreciated the hint of sweetness in the air that came with the spring vegetation growing around them. She smiled but did not know what to say. She had spent hours thinking about him since his last visit, often lying awake long into the night. Her father had asked if she wanted to return to London so that she could have more time with Fitzwilliam, but she had said no, adding a silent 'not yet'. Elizabeth felt she had been absent from Longbourn too much, even before she went to stay with Rebecca. She wanted time with her sisters, especially since it was likely Jane would soon marry and move to Surrey.

Staring at Fitzwilliam now, she remembered her other reason. *I wanted time to breathe easily and let my thoughts and feelings about him settle. I was so angry and hurt. Even now, I do not understand how he could have acted as he did, confused or not.*

"How are you?"

His voice was soft and warm. It reminded Elizabeth of the many wonderful moments they had shared when it seemed as though they were alone in the world and nothing mattered except that they were together.

"Well. And you?"

"The same. London has been busy, as you might expect."

"Not so busy that you could not return."

"With Charlotte coming..." He shrugged. "I wanted to see you. Every day, I have wanted to be here, with you."

"Charlotte's visit was an excuse."

"It was." He sighed; it almost sounded like a huff. "Everywhere I turn, there is someone else who wants to or must be introduced to me, yet another party to go to. My father and Fred-erick assure me it will not be so burdensome in the future."

Elizabeth nodded.

"As it is, I had to rearrange several engagements and give my excuses for others."

"Nothing too pressing, I trust." A mischievous little smile curled the corners of her mouth. "No dukes or princes?"

Fitzwilliam chuckled. "My mother?"

"I congratulate you for your quick, and accurate, guess. Lady Lucas takes great pleasure in sharing your letters with everyone in the neighbourhood."

"Can we not talk about it? I have not seen you for so long and I would rather…" He held out a hand to her.

Elizabeth's eyes moved from his hand to his face and back again. She did not take his hand, although a part of her wished to. Instead, she led the way to an iron bench sheltered by an old blackthorn tree. Elizabeth and Fitzwilliam had sat on it many times over the years. It was a little cool in the shade, and the bench itself was cold, but she did not mind.

"Tell me what you have been doing since I was last here," said Fitzwilliam.

She did as he requested. When he asked whether Jane and Mr Hawarden had reached an understanding, she shook her head and chuckled.

"If he does not come to the point soon, my mother truly will develop a nervous complaint. Mrs Linnington, with whom I am cultivating a friendship, told me that her brother understood that Jane preferred to wait a little longer. When I asked Jane about it, she did her best not to answer."

"And you persisted."

Elizabeth nodded. "Jane, my silliest of sisters, does not wish to think about marrying until she knows that I am no longer as unhappy as I was this winter. Naturally, I told her she was being stupid and that if she did not settle things with Mr Hawarden within the fortnight, I would go to him and force him to propose."

"You would."

"I most certainly would!"

They laughed then fell into a silence that lasted for the better part of a minute.

"We have a great deal to talk about."

Elizabeth nodded and lowered her eyes to the ground. She drew shapes into the dirt with the tip of her shoe. "Not the first day you and Charlotte and the captain are here."

"Tomorrow."

Elizabeth agreed.

"Charlotte is very angry with me. I do not know if she will ever forgive me, or if she even wishes to try."

Elizabeth slipped her arm around his and slid closer to him. "It is different for her. She has her life as Mrs Farnon. I have..."

"Me," he said when she stopped. "Always."

Elizabeth rested her head against his arm. They said nothing more and returned to the house in a few minutes.

CHAPTER 34

FITZWILLIAM'S TWO FULL DAYS IN HERTFORDSHIRE WENT BY much faster than he would have liked. Although he was busy with his family and seeing friends, he spent every possible minute with Elizabeth. It was beyond wonderful to be in her company again. They met before breakfast the second morning of his stay, again going to their favourite spot by the stream.

After a brief greeting, Elizabeth said, "I understand how confused you were last autumn, but… Why did you think you had to forget all of us? Was it really simply a matter of the Darcys' station in life being so different from ours?"

He suggested they sit. Their log was a little damp, and he pulled out his handkerchief to protect Elizabeth's gown. He took her hand in his.

"I do not think I can adequately explain how…turned around I became. It was as though I was lost in a dark forest, unable to find my way out, and I had no one to help me. I knew you could, and you did."

Elizabeth let out a surprised bark of laughter. "Hardly."

Fitzwilliam shook his head. "You did. I can hide nothing from you. By the time my father and I went to town—I speak of my Darcy father, which, I suppose, is evident—I *did* expect that my life would remain separate from all of you. Yet, night after night, I dreamt of my life as William Lucas. It was as if I was haunted by memories. Now I would say my unconscious was reminding me that I was William as much as Fitzwilliam. Then you were there, and the more we saw each other, the more I knew I was a fool to think I could ever forget my life here. I imagined that you would take my hand and lead me through the forest to a clearing where I could see my way again. Instead, you gave me a hard kick in the backside—"

Elizabeth slapped his arm. "William!"

He chuckled. "That is what it was like. It said, 'you know very well what you have to do, and I shall not and cannot do it for you'! In Essex, I was able to be quiet and devise a plan for getting un-lost."

"It does not explain why or how you became so lost," Elizabeth said. "Part of it is easy to understand, but, I admit, I am struggling to accept it."

Fitzwilliam kissed her hand. Challenging him to explain would help both of them make sense of everything that had happened.

"There were times when I was angry that Sir William and Lady Lucas had never so much as hinted that I was not their true son."

"I see nothing wrong with that," she said. "Upon occasion, I wished they had not been so secretive about it, but I understand why they were."

"As do I. Of late, I have wondered if that influenced my behaviour. If it did, I do not believe it was a significant factor." Fitzwilliam sighed and squeezed her hand. "How I longed for you, Lizzy! I needed your comfort and your strength and your ability to talk so easily." He chuckled. "You would have demanded answers, told everyone you were confused. I was silent. I watched and listened. I started to tell myself that, instead of being raised as the heir to a grand estate and bearing a name with so much history and respect attached to it, I was the son of innkeepers from an obscure town in Shropshire who had the great fortune to move to a small estate in a quiet corner of Hertfordshire."

With surprise in her voice, Elizabeth asked, "You resented not having the wealth and position?"

Fitzwilliam shook his head, although he knew the answer was more complicated than that indicated. "There were moments I certainly appreciated what came with it, such as knowing I shall never have to worry about money. My father does a great deal of good with his position, for the poor, or those dependent on the estate. *That* I appreciate. In time, I grew concerned about what learning the truth would cost me. I told Sir William to tell you I would write as soon as I could, but—"

Elizabeth interjected, "Did you? Before he left Pemberley?"

Fitzwilliam nodded.

"He said nothing when he returned. I wonder if it would have made a difference. I know I used your silence to tell myself you forgot us as soon as you saw how rich your new family was."

Fitzwilliam shrugged. "It does not matter. I *was* silent. At first, I did not know what to write, so I delayed and delayed. I met the Darcys, and, well, I started to believe that I had to stop being William Lucas. And Fitzwilliam Darcy would not marry—"

"Someone like me."

He nodded.

"When Rebecca was here, she told me about Lady Anne, and we spoke about the sorts of marriages someone in your position makes. It affected me greatly. I believe I allowed it to influence my opinion of the Darcys, particularly your father, which was not right."

"You can have nothing to regret."

Elizabeth smiled. "I assure you, I do not dwell on my errors nearly as much as I do those of other people."

Although she teased, he could tell she was upset with herself.

"Despite it all, as soon as I saw you again, I felt how much I wanted, *needed* you. But I believed that, if I were to truly honour my family and be the man I was always supposed to be, I should not."

"Honour your family." Elizabeth slid down the log and turned to look at him. "Honour your *Darcy* family. You forgot about honouring your *Lucas* family. Why did the Darcys become so much more important than those of us who have loved you for years?"

She stood and took a few steps away from him. Fitzwilliam rose to his feet, but remained by the log, his eyes fixed on her. When she looked at him, her brows arched in impatience, he shrugged.

"I do not know what to say. I have a duty to my father— George, I mean. Lizzy, he has suffered. For over twenty years, he thought I was dead. Lady Anne died grieving for me, he argued with her family." He could feel his father's sorrow like a cold hand around his heart and hung his head. "It is because of me, and the knowledge of it feels oppressive at times. I told myself it meant that I had to be the son he deserves, the one he would have had, had I not been taken."

When he looked up, he discovered Elizabeth glaring at him. "You have to compensate him for what he did not have while you were apart?"

Fitzwilliam opened his mouth to answer, but nothing came out. After a moment, he nodded. In a weak, weary voice, he said, "No one else can. It is my responsibility. Or so it feels. Felt."

"Hmm."

Elizabeth relaxed her rigid stance, and to Fitzwilliam's bemusement, began to search for something.

"What are you doing?"

In an offhand manner, she replied, "Looking for a stick."

"A stick?" A tiny bubble of laughter, combined with a sob, formed in his throat. Elizabeth often broke tense situations with her humour.

"To beat you with. Perhaps it will shake the nonsense out of you or knock some sense into you." She spied his gloves on a nearby rock and snatched them up.

"Lizzy." She took several quick steps towards him.

With the gloves, she began to hit his arm. "Do you honestly believe that *you* have to make up for his grief, as though it were somehow your fault, that *you* are to blame? I have never heard such utter foolishness in my life. Fitzwilliam— Oh, what the devil is your full name?"

"Fitzwilliam George Alexander."

Elizabeth let her hand fall to her side and hissed, "Fitzwilliam George Alexander Darcy, you were a child, a *baby*, when evil, vile people stole you from your home. You had no memory of it, no way to prevent it, or to return to your parents. Blaming yourself for it is the stupidest thing I have ever heard you say, and I am willing to wager that your father would agree with me! Whatever duty you owe George Darcy, let it be because he is your father and because you care for him, not because he grieved for you or to recompense him for what others did."

Fitzwilliam took her face between his hands and kissed her. She was surprised but did not seek to escape from his embrace. Feeling Elizabeth's lips against his, so soft and responsive, with her hands around his body, her teasing tone, all of it showed that he had what he had prayed for. She loved him still and could not deny it, even to herself.

Elizabeth pulled away, but only enough to laugh. His hands fell to her shoulders.

"My dearest, loveliest Lizzy. I love you so much, and I have needed you to help me see reason. I am utterly lost without you."

"Stupid," she whispered, as his lips again descended onto hers.

Their kiss soon became passionate. Fitzwilliam clutched her to him, and she reciprocated by locking her arms around his waist. Half of the local population could have walked by, and they would not have noticed. Realising their precarious position, he groaned and rested his forehead against hers. Neither spoke for a minute as they caught their breath and cooled their ardour. Elizabeth then stepped away from him. She collected their hats and gloves and gave him his.

"My father said I was to bring you to Longbourn for breakfast. He caught me leaving the house and guessed where I was going."

Fitzwilliam held out a hand to her, which she took, and they began the walk back.

ELIZABETH AND FITZWILLIAM met again the next morning. She brought buns filled with raisins and sweetened with honey for them to share. Since he was returning to London after breakfast, it was their last opportunity for a private conversation. Elizabeth had thought about what he said, especially his feelings of guilt, and raised it as they sat on their log.

"Almost as soon as I saw your father, I was struck by the resemblance between you. Knowing you as well as I do, I thought I understood his feelings. He suffered. Of course, he did! What parent would not? It also seemed to me that he was afraid he would lose you again. When one of my sisters called you William, he looked as though someone had struck him."

Fitzwilliam's shoulders slumped, and he gave a light grunt. "It is important to him to know that I shall not abandon him."

"That is natural, under the circumstances."

"You do understand?" He held her eyes and covered her hand with his. "My home is with him, at Pemberley."

Elizabeth nodded. "You need to tell him how you feel. Talk to him." She clasped his hand. "If you do not, I shall write to him myself and tell him what you told me. Or, if I find that too frightening a prospect, I shall write to Rebecca and tell her, she will tell her father, who will then tell yours. You know that is likely to result in miscommunication, and I shall not be held responsible for what happens after that!"

Fitzwilliam's chest shook with quiet laughter. He then sighed so loudly Elizabeth thought it frightened several small animals.

"I have had so many serious conversations of late. I am exhausted by it all."

"I know." She caressed his forehead, smoothing out the lines, and his cheek. They shared a gentle kiss.

"That helps." He took a deep breath and scrubbed at his face with his hands. "I am afraid I must have another awkward, disagreeable, possibly devastating conversation with him."

"What do you mean?"

"My cousin John. Early on, my father encouraged me to think of him as a friend. John would introduce me to his friends, we would do the things young gentlemen of fashion do. By the end of January, I began to be uncomfortable with him."

"Why?"

A light blush crept onto his cheeks. "I do not like how he and his friends behave, how and where they find amusement, or how they speak about people. Of late, I have come to see... Something is not right in how John acts with me."

Elizabeth watched as he stood and began to pace.

"Oh God, Lizzy! I hate to think it. My father places such trust in John, who is his godson. I do not even know what I am accusing him of!"

He told her how his cousin encouraged him to participate in activities he found disagreeable. He gave no details, but she was not naïve and knew the sorts of things he had been exposed to. If Fitzwilliam were correct that his cousin had been trying to trick him, she would be furious on his behalf, and that of George Darcy.

"Even when I said I did not wish to, he told me I should, even must, that it was what my father expected. He had to know I was ill at ease. It seems like he encouraged me to feel that I did not belong or was disappointing my father."

"But why?" she cried.

He shrugged. "At different times, he told me I was either

William Lucas or Fitzwilliam Darcy; I could not be both. I had thought it, but he kept saying it, and it just… There was a point to it, but I am not sure what." Fitzwilliam sat down again; he opened and closed his mouth twice before speaking. "My uncle, John's father. When I first met him, he was cold and suspicious, even after he claimed to accept that I was Fitzwilliam. Something he said to me when we first met at Pemberley…"

When he failed to go on, Elizabeth laid her hand on his knee. "Tell me."

Looking apologetic and embarrassed, he said, "He told me I was very fortunate to be a Darcy and I should not think they would tolerate anyone I knew before making a claim on me. It sounded threatening. John said something similar in town. I believe it was the night you and I first saw each other. I know I felt little short of panic at the thought of introducing you to him. It affected me greatly. I did not realise how much until recently."

"What a muddle!"

She rested her head on his shoulder, and they sat in silence for a few minutes.

"You need to tell your father all of it."

Elizabeth felt him nod, but he did not speak for another minute or two.

He said, "We should return to Lucas Lodge. They will be waiting for us to have breakfast."

"And you should begin your journey back to London."

Again, Fitzwilliam nodded. "Lizzy, Rebecca told me she would be happy to have you stay again. Will you?"

She sat up, looked at him, and shook her head. "Everything you have told me, between the Fitzwilliams, your cousin and uncle, you and your father—you must address it. My presence would not help." When he opened his mouth to protest, she pressed a finger to his lips. "It will not. Tell me, how many people know about me?"

Fitzwilliam, with evident reluctance, said, "My father, Frederick, and, I assume, Rebecca."

"If I were there, people would suspect, and you know as well as I do that some of your family will not like it. Even, and perhaps I am mistaken, your father does not."

"He accepts—"

"Accepts, yes," Elizabeth interjected, "but that does not mean he likes it."

He lowered his head and attempted to shield the distress in his eyes from her view.

Elizabeth said, "I hope he will think better of it in time."

"Once he knows you, I am confident he will."

"I shall be glad if he does, but we are not having that conversation today. You have quite enough to cope with as it is."

He walked away, keeping his back to her, for ten or twelve paces before returning. "Will you let me write to you? Your father would act as an intermediary, if you asked it of him."

Elizabeth nodded and smiled in a manner meant to convey an apology and encouragement.

"And will you consider returning to London once the situation settles down?"

Elizabeth's smile broadened just a little. "I shall."

Fitzwilliam slowly drew in a deep breath and released it. He held out a hand and helped her to her feet. After one last kiss, they returned to face their families and the reality of another separation.

CHAPTER 35

WHEN FITZWILLIAM ARRIVED HOME THE FOLLOWING DAY, HE AND George had only a few minutes to talk before preparing for an evening engagement. Fitzwilliam enjoyed it even less than he usually would. He was impatient for it to end so that he could speak to his father privately.

Upon their return to Darcy House, Fitzwilliam said, "Sir, if you are not tired, there is something I would like to discuss with you."

George agreed, and Fitzwilliam trailed behind him as they went into the study.

Sitting across from his father, his eyes on a spot beyond his shoulder, Fitzwilliam admitted, "I am afraid what I have to say will upset you. It is about John."

"I do not understand." George sat back in his chair and pulled his eyebrows together.

"I must be honest and say," he stopped and licked his lips, "I do not like him. I do not like his behaviour or manner towards me."

Fitzwilliam told him tale after tale of his cousin exposing him to debauched activities and encouraging him to participate in them even when he expressed a firm wish not to. George's visage grew white then grey before becoming red. His hands gripped the chair's arms.

Enunciating each word carefully, his father said, "He encouraged you to-to—?"

Fitzwilliam nodded and kept his voice low. He took no pleasure in making these disclosures and felt tears pricking at the back of his eyes to see how affected his father was. "There were many, many occasions on which he urged me to drink more than I liked or gamble or-or," he felt his face heat, "enjoy the company of women."

George stood and walked across the room; he kept his back to Fitzwilliam. "He *urged* you?"

"He told me my discomfort was because I had grown up among lesser people, and that it was what you would wish."

His father spun around to face him. "What *I* would wish?"

"I hardly remember everything he said, but yes, he told me again and again and in many different ways that I should be more like him and that it was what you expected."

"I would never!"

"Once I had the time to reflect on everything, when I was in Essex, I began to realise that it was unlikely you would truly feel that way. It has become even clearer since then."

His father stared at him. His lips moved, but he was speechless.

Fitzwilliam said, "Thinking about it now, I believe he was manipulating me."

George returned to his chair. Fitzwilliam saw that his hands trembled and wished he knew what to do to make this easier for him.

The truth shall set us free. With that thought in mind, he continued. "Before I left for Meryton, the ball I went to with him, but returned home with Frederick?"

George nodded.

"I told Frederick, in John's hearing, that I had not enjoyed the theatre. John said it was because I had not lived in good society. He has suggested that, if I could not act like Fitzwilliam Darcy— meaning more like him—perhaps I should return to my old life, which I would not do." His father's visage became pale. "And this winter he told me you and Frederick were not friends and that Frederick was jealous of you. I am sorry to have to tell you this, Father."

George shook his head and reached a hand to Fitzwilliam. Fitzwilliam caught it and held it for a moment. His father sat back, and they were silent for several minutes.

"They told me," his father said, then stopped, pressed his eyes closed, and shook his head before again looking at Fitzwilliam. "John and Jeffrey both talked to me about you. They hinted that you had habits I would not like. It started in January." His voice dropped as though he were talking to himself. "Dear God, were they manipulating me at the same time they were manipulating you? No. Not my own brother and nephew."

Fitzwilliam had not known that his uncle and cousin had met with George to talk about him. *It should not surprise me. But why?*

"Fitzwilliam, why did you never tell me about Miss Elizabeth? Why did you feel you had to give up your past? Was there more than what you told me in Hertfordshire?"

He tilted his head back until he was looking at the ceiling; his eyes traced the plaster ornaments. After loosening his neckcloth, Fitzwilliam admitted, "When we were at Pemberley, just before they left, Jeffrey found me alone and said I was very fortunate you would recognise me as a Darcy, and I should endeavour to be worthy of the name. He also said I should not think he, and I suppose you by implication, would allow anyone from my past to make a claim on me. John has said the same thing."

Before George could respond, he added, "I am responsible, too. I believed I had to do everything I could to be the son you ought to have had and to live as though we had never been separated. It left me—"

"Vulnerable," George interjected.

Fitzwilliam nodded.

"Did he... Did you feel threatened in some way?"

With some reluctance, Fitzwilliam said that he had. "I do not remember the exact words he used, but he said there were ways to deal with people who tried take advantage of my new position, and he would use them."

George buried his face in his hands and rested his elbows on his knees. When Fitzwilliam knelt beside him and placed a hand on his shoulder, he could feel his father's body shaking.

"Father—"

"I am sorry. I was blind, too lost in the past. I failed you. I failed you."

Fitzwilliam draped his arm across his father's back and rested his head on his shoulder.

FITZWILLIAM TURNED his father over to Ashford half an hour later. After a restless night, during which he reminded himself that George deserved, even needed, to know everything he had disclosed, he was not surprised to learn that his father had left the house before breakfast.

He has gone to Jeffrey's. There is no other explanation. Fitzwilliam paced in the morning room and resisted the urge to go after his father. *This is something he needs to do. Please, God, keep him safe.* He knew his uncle and cousin posed no physical danger to George, but the emotional toll might be severe.

Almost an hour later, his father returned. His complexion was ashen, and his breathing laboured. He fell into a chair and waved away Fitzwilliam's offers of a beverage, rest, or anything else he could think to name.

"Sit." His father pointed to the sofa next to him and waited until Fitzwilliam had obeyed. "I went to see my brother." He made a disgusted noise. "Always, *always* I have made it a practice not to listen to gossip about the family. People will talk about us, often in unflattering terms, simply because of our position. How I wish I had paid more attention! I do not know if I would have heard anything, but perhaps—" He waved a hand. "That does not signify. I confronted them. John was in such a state. I could smell the alcohol on him still, and he wore the clothes from last night. But I am not telling it properly. You, of anyone, have a right to understand."

George rubbed his eyes with the balls of his hands. Fitzwilliam watched, feeling helpless. He leant forward in his seat as though that made him more prepared to assist.

With a sad bark of laughter, his father admitted, "It was all about money. I do not know if you are aware of this, but some in the family, maybe outside of it, too, believed John was my heir before your recovery. I never said he was, but I never said he was not. He is the elder of my nephews and my godson, and Freddie is already well provided for. I was careful not to treat John any differently than Freddie, or even Rebecca. I, who knew what it was to lose a son, could not take him from Jeffrey to raise as my heir, especially after the death of his wife." His voice grew thick with sorrow. "I could never look upon another as your replacement."

"Father," Fitzwilliam whispered and grasped George's hand.

George squeezed it and continued. "I charged Jeffrey with what you told me. At first, he pretended not to know what I was talking about, but that did not last long. He knew what John was doing. Dear God, my own brother, who saw what I suffered, how I struggled, he knew and even helped him!

"And John! I shall not tell you the vile names he called you. I would have done anything for them. I *have* done everything possible to support my brother's career, and I would have done the same for John. But they wanted more." George opened his eyes to look at Fitzwilliam. "They sought to show me that you did not deserve to be a Darcy or my heir, believing that I would, I do not know, get rid of you somehow. That is what John said. I could never conceive of something I am less likely to do. Had you been ignorant, still an innkeeper's purported son—none of it would have mattered to me. You are my son, mine and Anne's, and *nothing* could make me give you up."

Such a strong statement of affection might have embarrassed Fitzwilliam had the circumstances not been so distressing. His father dropped his hand, stood, and walked to the window. Fitzwilliam saw him take several deep breaths before he continued his recitation.

"Jeffrey was so certain you and your connexions from before would bring disgrace to our family, when it is he and his son who have done so. I am finished with them. I shall not openly break with them—it would injure us and Frederick and his children—but I shall not pretend we are on good terms."

George turned to look at him, and Fitzwilliam was relieved to see that his colour was a little better.

His father said, "We have Frederick and Rebecca and Freddie, and we have each other. I do not forget the Lucases and Bennets, especially your Elizabeth. We do not need those who will seek to harm us, just those who will love us."

FITZWILLIAM WAS PLEASED his father slept for over two hours after telling him about his interview with Jeffrey and John. He wrote to Elizabeth and was reading an agricultural treatise when he received word that his father was awake. He went to join him in his chambers.

"I sent our regrets for today's engagements," Fitzwilliam told George as he prepared a cup of coffee from a tray Ashford had just delivered. "I used the excuse of a family matter but said it was nothing serious. If there is anything else I can do, I am happy to. Just tell me what you need."

The corners of George's mouth lifted just high enough to be called a smile. "How fortunate I am. I wish your mother could see what a remarkable man you became."

Fitzwilliam lowered his eyes to hide his embarrassment.

His father tapped a piece of toast on the table. He looked over Fitzwilliam's shoulder to where a landscape painting by Gilpin hung. Fitzwilliam always found the coastal scene to be a strange combination of light and gloomy.

"I shall not say that this is not difficult. For your sake, I wish I had been less blind, less trusting."

"Do not distress yourself on my account," Fitzwilliam begged.

"How can I not? I put you in John's care and encouraged you to trust our family above everyone else. Then, out of my own... fear of your past, and just when we needed them the most, I separated us from those in our family who are most caring and honourable." He sighed, shook his head, and took a bite of toast before dropping the remainder on his plate.

With reluctance, Fitzwilliam admitted that Jeffrey had called.

George grumbled. "I am not surprised. Did you speak to him?"

"No. Since you were not available, he left a note."

Fitzwilliam withdrew it and passed it to his father who, after quickly perusing it, stood and threw it into the fireplace.

"I am not interested in his justifications. I may be called resentful, but I cannot forgive that they tried to hurt you."

After Jeffrey made another attempt to see his father an hour later, Fitzwilliam wrote to Frederick to tell him what had transpired. Frederick was at Darcy House even sooner than Fitzwilliam expected him. While his father told Frederick what had happened, Fitzwilliam sent notes to cancel their engagements for the next day. Frederick promised to talk to Jeffrey, if only to convince him not to return to Darcy House.

At dinner, George announced that he had sent for his solicitor. "There are several matters I wish to see to immediately. Pedlar will call tomorrow." He grimaced. "Unless we wish to encourage yet more gossip about us, I do not think we can avoid going into company much longer. As it is, I take little pleasure from being indoors for so long. You should not feel obligated to remain with me all the time."

After he swallowed a mouthful of rich beef and mushroom ragout, Fitzwilliam said. "Let us see what tomorrow brings."

They were just finishing their meal when Frederick returned. They went to sit in the study while he told them about his interview with Jeffrey.

"He was anxious to unburden himself to me. I believe he thought that once I understood his situation and reasoning, such as it was, I would intervene on his behalf. You would see that it was all, if not innocent, not nearly so dreadful as you suspect."

His father scoffed, and Fitzwilliam almost did likewise.

Frederick told them that Jeffrey was experiencing money problems. "There is nothing left of what he inherited. It seems that he relied upon John inheriting from you."

George demanded, "Debt?"

Frederick nodded. "I am afraid so. I do not know the exact extent of it, but I gather it is substantial. Jeffrey did not wish to admit it to you or ask for your assistance, knowing you would disapprove. I suspect he was also afraid you would want to know *why* he is in debt. I did not enquire; there was only so much of his conversation I could tolerate. In any case, I understand that he and John had agreed that, after this last season for John to—in Jeffrey's words—enjoy himself, they would convince you to begin letting John help you with the estate, *et cetera*. In other words, John would start acting like your heir, and in so doing, somehow—I do not presume to understand how—get you to give them enough money to satisfy their creditors. You need never have known how much trouble they are in."

George said, "And if it looked like he was my heir, even if I still said nothing about it, that, too, would appease whomever they owe money to, perhaps even allow them to borrow more?"

Frederick agreed and added, "Fitzwilliam returning spoilt their plans, and they hoped to get rid of him—either convince him to return to his previous life or you that he did not deserve to be your heir. Jeffrey is worried about the future, particularly if you do not continue to support his career. Without your influence working for him, he will find it harder to make a good living at it. I dared not enquire about John's prospects."

"Did you see him?" Fitzwilliam asked.

"No, and that is just as well. I could hardly keep my countenance when talking to Jeffrey. Had I seen John, there is the strong possibility I might have boxed his ears."

Draining the last of his wine, Frederick stood. "I shall take my leave. I am so dreadfully sorry for what has happened. You both know that I shall do whatever I can for you."

His father scowled as he stood. "Thank you, Frederick. You are, as always, more valuable to me than I can say."

"Not at all, George. You would return the favour. There is no one more loyal than you. Jeffrey is a fool to have used you in this way."

Once alone, Fitzwilliam said, "Will you retire, Father? It has been a long and trying day."

George nodded. "Will you?"

When Fitzwilliam said he would, George placed a hand on Fitzwilliam's shoulder and kept it there as they climbed the stairs together.

CHAPTER 36

THE NEXT MORNING, FITZWILLIAM AND GEORGE WENT FOR A ride, despite the weather being indifferent. The cool morning air, which was just damp enough to suggest rain, was reviving. Spring was well-established and birdsong and the scurrying of small animals accompanied the clip-clop of their horses' hooves as they went by trees now full of leaves.

George remarked on the pleasantness of their ride and added, "Pedlar will arrive soon after breakfast, and I expect Frederick later in the morning. He intends to talk to Tom Fitzwilliam about John. Sterling has gone to Worcestershire to attend to some minor problem at Romsley Hall."

Although surprised by George's words, Fitzwilliam only replied, "I, too, had planned to talk to the colonel or his brother. I know they have no love for John, and I wished to know why."

George grunted. "Frederick told me that Sterling spoke to him weeks ago about John. You saw him at some...establishment?"

Fitzwilliam shuddered at the memory and felt heat creep into his cheeks. "A theatre of sorts. I admit I drank more than I should have, especially since I was so uneasy there. John was pressing me to— Well, it does not matter. I left. Bramwell followed and insisted on seeing that I made it home safely." He did not know how to describe his early impressions of Sterling and Tom.

"There were other occasions. When I look back on it, it is obvious that they were trying to be useful and kind."

After doffing their hats to greet an acquaintance, George asked, "Did you know that Sterling and Rebecca are fond of each other? Frederick told me."

Fitzwilliam tilted his head such that the brim of his hat hid his face. It was difficult enough to talk to his father about his love affair with Elizabeth; he could not talk about his cousin's. "I-I thought I noticed something when we were last together."

George again grunted and kicked his animal into a greater speed.

THE ONLY DISTRACTIONS they had throughout the day were the two expected visitors; George had the knocker taken off the door. After dinner, they sat in the library and read. Fitzwilliam's book was on the history of South Wiltshire. It was enough to hold his attention, but he knew that his father more often looked at the fire or at him than at the volume in his hands.

When it was close to ten o'clock, George said, "Fitzwilliam."

Fitzwilliam looked up. His eyebrows arched in question.

"What say we go to Pemberley for two or three weeks? We could return in time for the races next month. I know you are looking forward to them." His father sat up straighter, and his voice gained strength. "Indeed, there are several matters I would like to see to at the estate, and you would have a chance to meet more of our neighbours. I know you do not wish to be separated from Miss Elizabeth, but we could spend two or three days in Hertfordshire on the way north and break our journey there on the way back to town."

Fitzwilliam's mouth hung open for a moment before he spoke. "You wish to visit Meryton again?"

With a resolute nod, his father said, "Yes. I want to know Miss Elizabeth better, as well as the Lucases and your friends."

While Fitzwilliam did not exactly wish to jump up from his

chair and rush to pack a bag immediately, his feelings came close to it. "I would like to be away from London for a time. When we return, it will be easier to encounter my uncle and cousin."

"It will not be pleasant, but I pray a few weeks' separation will help us know how to act when we do see them. Come. Let us talk about arrangements."

THE NIGHT FITZWILLIAM returned to London, Elizabeth and Jane once again talked in Elizabeth's room. Elizabeth found she greatly enjoyed the growing intimacy with her elder sister. They had always been close, but with William and Charlotte there to be their best friends, she and Jane had not relied on each other as much as they otherwise might have.

It is one benefit of remaining here for now. I shall miss her when we are both married.

Elizabeth confided that she and Fitzwilliam were not engaged, "But I feel much, much better after our last talk."

Jane tried to smile, but it was at best tremulous.

Laughing gently, Elizabeth sat beside Jane on the bed. "I can honestly say that I believe everything will be as it should be between us. It is a matter of time. I have given him leave to write to me. And…Jane, has your Mr Hawarden ever kissed you?"

Jane's cheeks turned bright pink, and she squeaked, "Lizzy!"

"Hmm, I cannot tell if that means yes or no." Elizabeth eyes remained wide and unblinking and her brows arched as she waited for Jane to answer.

Playing with the end of her plait, Jane whispered, "Just on the cheek and on my hand."

Elizabeth poked her arm. "If you will take advice from me, my dear sister, keep it at that until you have a wedding date in the not-too-distant future. One kiss can quickly lead to more."

Jane's eyes flew to her sister's. "You are not saying that you and William—?"

"No, of course not!" Elizabeth cried. "But we have kissed, and not just on the cheek. With each one, I want more. It is far better for us to be apart until I am convinced the time is right to announce a betrothal."

Jane's eyes returned to the blanket. "Is it really so...?"

Elizabeth grinned and nodded. "It would be horrible to kiss a man you did not really like, but with Fitzwilliam..." She giggled. "I confess I like it very much." Elizabeth was determined to call him by his true name, out of deference to George Darcy, except when she was with the Lucases, although they seemed to be increasingly comfortable with their son's change of name. She put her arm around Jane's shoulder and adopted a stern tone. "Now, Jane, I have another piece of advice for you. Get yourself engaged! I shall not have you wait out of a misplaced sense of concern for me. If you do not, Mrs Linnington and I are resolved to arrange the whole of it between us, and you will deprive Mr Hawarden the great anxiety that must be part of a gentleman's proposal. It is no way to treat the man with whom you intend to spend the rest of your very happy life."

TWO DAYS LATER, Jane and Mr Hawarden came to an understanding, and Longbourn was filled with Mrs Bennet's joyful cries and Kitty's and Lydia's pleas to be bridesmaids and have new gowns.

"Your turn next," Mr Bennet whispered to Elizabeth as they watched the lively scene.

"I am very happy for Jane."

Mr Bennet grumbled, but Elizabeth knew he meant nothing by it. "Before I know it, Mr Hawarden will take her away to Surrey. Then Fitzwilliam will come for you, and you will be even farther away in Derbyshire."

Elizabeth linked her arm with his and rested her head on his shoulder. "How fortunate that you have three other daughters to keep you company."

He groaned. "How am I ever to make sensible women out of Lydia and Kitty?"

Father and daughter were quiet for a moment as they watched the two youngest Bennets pester Mrs Linnington, Jane, and Mrs Bennet about the wedding, mindless of the fact that nothing had yet been decided. Mary sat nearby and observed.

"And Mary! I must find her a proper husband, or she will accept the first fool who offers for her." Mr Bennet feigned distress.

"I recommend that you find a biddable young man and mould him into a son-in-law you can be proud of. Come, Papa. Go talk to Mr Hawarden and rejoice in the knowledge that you will soon have a very likeable son-in-law."

He kissed her hand. "Two, when you at last send Fitzwilliam to me."

Elizabeth smiled and went to talk to Mary.

ONE MORNING, as Elizabeth and Jane strolled through the gardens, which were bursting with spring flowers, Jane said, "I am glad you remained at Longbourn instead of returning to town. It is so much more pleasant to plan my wedding with you."

"I am invaluable for keeping Mama from making every decision herself and distracting Kitty and Lydia so that they do not tease you to death."

Jane laughed. "That is not what I meant, as you well know. But, Lizzy, you must not sacrifice your happiness for mine. Go to Fitzwilliam when you feel you are ready."

Elizabeth assured her that she would.

The matter was on her mind the following day when rain prevented her from walking out. She stood at the window in Mr Bennet's book room and remarked on how much more vibrant the world looked with a sheen of water covering it. *How much brighter I feel. I am as giddy as the cuckoo flowers waving in the wind. Well, perhaps not quite that silly!*

"Papa, I have made a decision. Two, actually."

"Have you indeed? That is very decisive of you."

Elizabeth rolled her eyes and turned to face him.

"I shall write to Mrs Gardiner and tell her that I will not go to the Lakes with them. I should remain where I might more easily see Fitzwilliam."

"Yes, you should be close at hand so that you might catch him, as your mother would say." Mr Bennet chuckled.

Elizabeth shook her head at him. "And I shall soon return to London."

Her father sighed. "Very well, Lizzy. I expected you would follow him to town. However, I am pleased to have you at Longbourn for as long as possible. It will not be your home much longer."

"Oh, Papa!" Elizabeth sat by his side and rested her head on him, as he draped an arm across her shoulders.

"My dearest girl," he murmured. "I cannot tell you how thankful I am to see you happy again."

"I assure you, I am very thankful to *be* happy again. Now, what shall we talk about so that we do not become maudlin?"

That afternoon, she replied to a recent letter from Fitzwilliam and expressed her relief that the truth about his uncle and cousin was out, as difficult as it had been for George Darcy. At the end, she added,

I must close soon, but before I do, let me tell you some of our other news. First, there is talk of Jane going into Surrey with the Linningtons next month. Second, I have written to Mrs Gardiner to say I shall not go with them on their northern tour. Third, before Charlotte and Captain Farnon returned to Kent, I had a good conversation with her that I hope will help her resolve her anger towards you. Fourth, I told my father today that I shall soon return to London.

Do you see how I slipped that in? You might even miss it, if you do not attend to my letter with the close attention it deserves. I must finish this now and prepare for dinner at the Gouldings. I miss being with you.

Lizzy

CHAPTER 37

Mrs Bennet's happiness was second only to Elizabeth's when they learnt that Fitzwilliam and George Darcy were returning. George Darcy would remain two nights before travelling on to Derbyshire; Fitzwilliam would remain longer before joining his father at Pemberley.

As soon as they were alone, Mrs Bennet insisted, "Now, Lizzy, you will listen to me very carefully. It is imperative that you make William propose before he goes away again! Forget whatever nonsense you have in mind about hurt feelings or what have you. There is time to worry about that after you are properly betrothed!"

Despite the strong part of her that wished to argue with the dubious value of her mother's advice, Elizabeth replied with a demure, "Yes, Mama."

She then made her escape and went for a short walk to rejoice in private. While she anticipated seeing Fitzwilliam again, she was nervous about George Darcy remaining two nights in the neighbourhood.

Stopping to lean on a fence and watch a cow pull at the grass, she murmured, "It is perfectly ridiculous. There is no reason I should be afraid to see him. He loves his son, as do I. We have that in common, and it is the ground upon which we can build."

She sighed and scratched the cow's head when she

approached. Elizabeth did not want to forever live with a father-in-law who merely accepted her to make his son happy. It would be taxing. More than that, it would distress Fitzwilliam.

"For his sake, I shall try to love George Darcy, and if Fitzwilliam is correct about his father's goodness, he will try to love, or at least like, me, too!"

THE DARCYS and Lucases came to dinner the day Fitzwilliam and his father arrived. After the usual greetings, Elizabeth stood with Mr Darcy and Fitzwilliam.

"It is good to see you and your family again," said Mr Darcy.

Elizabeth stumbled over her words and felt exceedingly foolish. "And you. I hope the journey from London was uneventful."

"It was. Well, I shall leave you to my son. I am sure you have much to say to each other."

He inclined his head and clapped Fitzwilliam's shoulder. Elizabeth watched as he went to stand with her father and Sir William, then turned to her companion.

"Lizzy," Fitzwilliam whispered.

Elizabeth's cheeks grew warm at his tone and the way he was looking at her. Surreptitiously, she pinched his arm. "Remember we are in company!"

He chuckled, and his eyes drifted back to the gentlemen.

Elizabeth said, "Father, father, and—"

Fitzwilliam interjected, "Father-in-law soon, I hope. I know that after everything that happened, everything I did, I have no right to assume, and yet—"

"And yet." She laid her hand on his arm. "Let us have done with apologies. I am desperate to hear your news, such as why you and Mr Darcy decided to visit."

When it was time to go through to dinner, Elizabeth grasped Fitzwilliam's arm and whispered, "Take my mother in and sit next to her. Jane and I have it all arranged."

The scheme worked, and Fitzwilliam and Jane sat at one

side of Mrs Bennet, while Elizabeth and Mr Darcy were at the other. Mrs Bennet made many remarks on weddings despite Jane's and Elizabeth's attempts to turn the conversation.

No doubt, she believes she is being sly, but we all take your meaning, madam!

Dinner and the remainder of the evening passed without incident, though Elizabeth could not relax. She worried that her mother or younger sisters would shock Mr Darcy, and she and Fitzwilliam had little opportunity to talk.

"So close and yet..." Fitzwilliam whispered to Elizabeth as he was preparing to depart.

"You are here for several days. I must not be selfish and keep you all to myself."

"Tomorrow," he promised just as his attention was demanded elsewhere.

FITZWILLIAM AND GEORGE met Mr Bennet to go riding the next morning. Elizabeth was waiting outside with her father, who sent them off to say good morning to each other.

"Just for a minute, mind you!"

Fitzwilliam took Elizabeth by the hand and led her a little distance from the house where they could have privacy. They stopped in a small clearing, and Elizabeth leant her back against an oak tree.

"At last," he said.

Elizabeth smiled. "At last? You are impatient. It has been twelve hours since you last saw me."

"A few hours in your presence, which I had to share with our families, after far too long a separation—"

"Of not even a fortnight!"

"Far too long." He spoke each word deliberately. They were only returning to themselves after seven months and needed more time together. Nothing could truly make up for their separation, but he felt more and more like himself with her by his side and suspected she would say the same.

Elizabeth's smile softened, and she caressed his cheek. "Mr Darcy seems in good spirits, despite everything."

Fitzwilliam did not wish to talk about George or anyone else at the moment. "He will be well in time. Enough about that for now. I finally have you to myself—"

"Do you know, I never realised that you have such a vein of selfishness in you?" Elizabeth teased.

Fitzwilliam rolled his eyes and rested his forehead against hers. "I missed you."

"I missed you, too," she whispered.

He kissed her. "Thank you for missing me." He kissed her again.

"Ridiculous," Elizabeth whispered, as she pressed her lips to his for another kiss.

ELIZABETH WAS in the morning room with her younger sisters when Fitzwilliam joined them. There was little time before breakfast.

Lydia demanded, "Come sit with us! We hardly ever see you, and when you are here, you spend all your time with Lizzy."

Mary huffed. "Why would he want to talk to you when he can talk to her?"

"Girls!" Elizabeth cried.

"We shall have time together before I go to Derbyshire. I promise," said Fitzwilliam.

"Go on. Talk to them now," Elizabeth said for his ears only. "Kitty and Lydia will be occupied after breakfast. My father promised."

Elizabeth watched him with her sisters from across the room. She felt content, as though something that had been wrong had now been righted. When she heard the door open, she turned to see Mr Darcy entering, and invited him to sit with her.

"Did you enjoy the ride?" asked Elizabeth.

"Yes. It was very—" He stopped speaking when Lydia's and Kitty's voices filled the room.

"William! How can you say such a thing?" said Kitty.

Lydia added, "You *must*. It would be too cruel of you not to."

Mary protested and glanced nervously towards Elizabeth and Mr Darcy, as Fitzwilliam said, "I make no promises."

There were no more outbursts from the girls.

Elizabeth glanced at Mr Darcy and chuckled, though it was forced. "I can only imagine what treat my sisters are demanding. They are young and, I am afraid, spoilt. Their spirits are high, too, with Fitzwilliam here. He is as dear as a brother to them."

Mr Darcy looked as though he truly thought about her words, which she appreciated, and murmured, "Of course."

"I am sure it is very strange for you. Rebecca, Freddie, and I spoke about it several times. How odd it is." She could kick herself for being so inarticulate.

A soft smile adorned Mr Darcy's face. "Yes, but I trust it is getting easier."

Elizabeth nodded but was prevented from speaking by Lydia calling, "Lizzy, tell William he *can* go with us into Meryton after breakfast. He says that he cannot, but—"

"And he is correct. You and Kitty have to study, and I hope to prevail upon Fitzwilliam and Mr Darcy to take me for a walk." She shot a warning look at her sisters and faced Mr Darcy. "There is a favourite spot of ours not very far from here. The walk is pleasant, and if you are agreeable, sir, I can show you such sites as where Fitzwilliam nearly broke his arm falling out of a tree and where he caught what, I am told, is the largest fish that ever resided in Hertfordshire."

Fitzwilliam joined them and laughed. "You would not recount all my childhood misadventures."

"Oh, but I would; you know I would."

A moment later, Mrs Bennet came to tell them it was time for breakfast.

Fitzwilliam, George, and Elizabeth set out from Longbourn shortly after eating. For a little while, nothing was said other than a few quiet words of direction. The sky was nearly free of clouds, and there was a light breeze to provide relief from the heat. With spring flowers blooming and the sounds of birds to delight their eyes and ears, it was very pleasant. Fitzwilliam was relaxed and happy. It was good to see favourite places again and to bring his father to see them. *To say nothing of being here with both him and Lizzy. In time, they will love each other.*

Elizabeth practically skipped along, always looking this way or that, touching a leaf or watching a small animal, when she was not looking at Fitzwilliam. He was always pleased to know that she had not lost her childhood *joie de vivre*. Not even the last seven months had destroyed it.

She asked, "Where did you ride to this morning?"

Fitzwilliam explained, and his father said, "I have not spent much time in this part of Hertfordshire, and it was pleasant to see the country."

"It is certainly very different from Derbyshire," said Fitzwilliam.

George asked, "I do not believe you have been to that county, Miss Elizabeth?"

"I have not. However, I have read a great deal about the northern counties."

"Particularly the rocks," Fitzwilliam said in a droll tone.

Elizabeth laughed merrily. "Quite right!"

"I do not understand," George admitted.

"Lizzy is a rather ardent student of geology."

"I am afraid it is true. It is an interest your son does not share or appreciate. I have spent many an hour boring him about it."

Fitzwilliam tried to disagree, but she slipped her arm around his and said, "I have, and I am not afraid of you owning it. I have seen you trying to disguise your yawns and struggle against eyes that did not wish to stay open. It does you credit that you would take so much trouble to spare my feelings. Not that I am ashamed for how I acted since you have done the same to me with fishing." She gave an exaggerated shudder and turned to George. "I think it a fair trade, sir. Do you not agree?"

Fitzwilliam chuckled.

His father smiled and said that he did. "You will have much to explore when you come into Derbyshire."

Elizabeth blushed and grinned at Fitzwilliam.

Several minutes later, his father asked Elizabeth if she rode.

"Yes, but seldom willingly," she replied.

Fitzwilliam explained, "Lizzy prefers to keep her feet on the ground. She is a better rider than she thinks she is."

Elizabeth shook her head. "You must forgive us. It is an old argument, and you," she turned to Fitzwilliam, "would do well to let it alone, thank you very much. A day such as this should not be disrupted by discussion of such contentious matters. We can revisit it on a rainy, miserable morning."

"There is nothing to argue about. You *are* a better rider than you profess to be."

To his delight, George chuckled. "There are places around the estate one really does need to ride to, Miss Elizabeth."

"If they are of particular beauty or scientific interest, I shall endeavour to become more comfortable atop a horse."

"Good. I do not like to sound presumptuous, but perhaps your discomfort is because the horse has not been the right one for you. Mausdley, the stable master at Pemberley, is an excellent judge of horseflesh. With his help, we shall see you properly mounted, and you may find you enjoy the activity in consequence."

She smiled at Fitzwilliam and George. "I shall do my very best. Perhaps the glories of Derbyshire will distract me enough that I can cease to worry that I shall fall off or that the beast will take a dislike to me and throw me off before kicking or biting me. I would not mind the injury to my person, but I would never recover from the injury to my dignity."

Fitzwilliam did not know how to interpret the way his father was looking at Elizabeth, but he believed it was speculative. His father's questions and statements were an attempt to know her and showed that he accepted that Elizabeth would be his daughter-in-law. *All we are missing is an actual engagement. Lizzy must see what he is doing and soon agree to marry me.*

His father next enquired about Elizabeth's past travels. She admitted that, like Fitzwilliam, she had done little.

She added, "I enjoy reading about different places and imagine visiting them. Fitzwilliam and I used to talk about it quite often. Do you remember?" Fitzwilliam nodded, and she continued, "We dreamt of where we might go, what sights we would see."

"Where did the pair of you wish to travel?"

Their answer took some time as they had, at one time or another, talked of seeing places as diverse as the Scottish Highlands, many areas in Europe, the Americas, and Africa, to say nothing of Asia.

"The practicalities of the more exotic locations meant that we talked about them less as we grew older," Elizabeth told George.

She stepped away from Fitzwilliam and said, "Now, I believe I promised to tell you tales of Fitzwilliam's misbegotten youth, should you wish to hear them."

Fitzwilliam laughed and said her name, as his father said, "I would."

"I shall tell your part in any mischief you report," Fitzwilliam warned. "Indeed, I believe you, dear Lizzy, were often the instigator of it."

Elizabeth gasped. "How ungallant of you! You would ruin me in your father's eyes simply to make yourself look less culpable?"

Her bright, beautiful eyes sparkled, and the sound of her laughter rang through the air. Had they been alone, Fitzwilliam would have kissed her. Instead, he smiled in return, as did his father. Their walk continued, and Elizabeth and Fitzwilliam told George stories of their life together. His father grew more relaxed as the morning passed, and Fitzwilliam began to believe that the future would be one of comfort, companionship, and happiness, just as he had long dreamt. *The place and people involved are not quite the same, but I shall have my Lizzy. I can endure anything as long as she is by my side.*

CHAPTER 38

ELIZABETH AND FITZWILLIAM WANDERED AROUND THE GARDENS after returning to the house. Mr Darcy went inside to join Mr Bennet in his book room.

Elizabeth said, "I was happy to have the time to talk to your father. I like him."

Fitzwilliam raised her hand to his mouth and pressed his lips onto it. "He likes you, and as you must have noticed, he has no reservations about us."

Elizabeth laughed. "I would have to be very thick-headed not to have caught his implications that Pemberley will be my home one day."

"Soon, I hope."

Elizabeth walked with her hands clasped behind her back. The time with George Darcy had done a great deal to relieve her anxiety about the future; she was confident that he was prepared to welcome her and would not always be thinking that his son's marriage was an evil. She was on the cusp of deciding that she was ready for her and Fitzwilliam to move forward. *After everything, I suppose I have to simply trust. This is my William we are talking about—the person I have trusted the most since…I hardly know how long.* She took a deep breath, taking in the scent of damp earth from newly turned beds the gardeners had prepared for planting.

"When Jane goes to Surrey next month, I shall return to Rebecca."

Fitzwilliam took one of her hands in his. "Have you written to her?"

Elizabeth shook her head. "Not yet. I shall, as soon as an opportunity arises."

They continued their slow walk and stopped only to admire a crab apple tree that was covered in delicate white flowers. Elizabeth was lost in thought and furrowed her brow or nibbled her lower lip as she reviewed the reasons she had not been prepared for Fitzwilliam to propose. One by one, she realised they were no longer relevant.

Fitzwilliam stepped in front of her. "Lizzy, tell me what is worrying you."

Elizabeth gave a light laugh. "I am not worried. I have been thinking."

"About what?" he implored. "I know it is about us, or the situation with my new family, but unless you tell me, I can do nothing to address it."

As he spoke, Elizabeth's smile broadened. Whether it was the tone of his voice or the look in his eyes, and whether it was just the moment or a culmination of moments, she felt such certainty that, despite everything that had happened since Frederick Darcy's first visit to Longbourn, all would now be well. She could trust him, and George Darcy, to ensure that it was.

She said, "I love you."

Fitzwilliam stared at her.

She smiled and laughed. "I love you, my William. My *Fitz*william."

His confused air changed to one of relief. "You truly forgive me."

Elizabeth rolled her eyes. "Yes, of course I do. I love you too much not to, I suppose. The past is the past. I shall not think of it any longer, except those parts of it that give me pleasure. What happened, oh, my love!" She cupped his cheek with her hand and wished she had taken off her gloves so that she could feel his warmth. "What a horrible time you had of it, I had of it, your father, your *other* father and mother, our families had of it. I should say our family. It is large and unconventional, but it will do."

"I love you. So, so dearly." Fitzwilliam took Elizabeth's face between his hands and pressed his lips to hers in a fervent kiss.

After a moment, Elizabeth pushed him away. "Is there not something else you have to say to me?" She arched her eyebrows, tilted her head to the side, and regarded him.

Standing so that there was only a small space between them, he said, "Will you marry me?"

Elizabeth laughed. "Is that all the proposal I can expect?"

Fitzwilliam shrugged and looked apologetic. "At the moment, yes. I cannot think of anything else to say."

Elizabeth flung her arms around his neck and exclaimed, "Yes!"

As she kissed him, Fitzwilliam lifted her off her feet until his back was straight. A sudden noise broke them apart, and he lowered Elizabeth to the ground.

Elizabeth's giggle and Fitzwilliam's deep chuckle filled the air.

"That was a bird or rabbit, was it not? Not one of my sisters or, heaven forbid, a caller?"

Fitzwilliam looked around and shrugged. "If it was a person, they have gone." He returned his eyes to hers, and a broad grin overtook his face. "My dearest, loveliest Lizzy."

"My dearest, handsomest Fitzwilliam."

Once again, their lips met in a soft kiss.

WHEN THEY CONTINUED THEIR WALK, Elizabeth said, "Someday, perhaps on our first anniversary, I expect a proper proposal." His simple question had been enough, but she did like to tease him.

Fitzwilliam huffed, and in the tone of a henpecked husband, said, "Yes, my dear."

They walked, and Elizabeth suggested they not announce their understanding immediately. "You should tell Mr Darcy. We cannot let him leave for Derbyshire without knowing such vital information. We might still find him and my father together. I *think* Papa shall give you his permission to marry me."

Copying her mocking tone, he said, "Let us pray he does."

"I shall tell my mother after your father has left the neighbourhood. He does not need to hear her enthusiastic reception of the news. Besides, we go to Netherfield for dinner, and I do not wish to disrupt Mr and Mrs Linnington's party by making an announcement this afternoon."

Fitzwilliam kissed her hand. "As much as I would prefer to tell the world immediately, I agree. Let us go see if our fathers are at liberty. I must tell someone!"

Unfortunately, Mr Darcy and her father were in the morning room with the Bennets and Lucases enjoying refreshments. There were a few remarks about how long they had remained outdoors, and Mr Bennet closely regarded Elizabeth, but nothing more was said about it. The Darcys and Lucases soon left to prepare for their evening engagement. Mr Bennet caught Elizabeth's eye and told her with a look that he would like to talk to her. They went into his book room where they would not be disturbed.

Her father took his customary place behind his desk, and she sat in her usual chair.

"I take it your walk with Fitzwilliam and Mr Darcy went well. He and I had a very pleasant chat."

"Did you? I am glad, and yes, I would say our outing was successful."

Mr Bennet cocked an eyebrow as he regarded her. "I was happy to find that he takes it as quite a settled matter that you and Fitzwilliam will marry. Almost a *fait accompli*, really. We even went so far as to discuss the settlement."

A laugh burbled out of Elizabeth. "Truly? Well, if you and

Mr Darcy had had the good sense to be alone still when Fitzwilliam and I returned to the house…" She affected a demure manner.

"Like that, is it? Well, well." Elizabeth saw him swallow heavily before he cleared his throat. "But, Lizzy, this is a very odd way for a father to learn that his daughter is engaged."

Elizabeth smiled and went to sit on the arm of his chair; she gave him a kiss on the cheek. "Forget I told you. I would not rob you of the right to make Fitzwilliam work for your permission. Make him doubt it for at least a quarter of an hour. Question him closely on how he means to provide for a wife and family and what sort of husband he intends to be."

Mr Bennet caught Elizabeth's hand and pulled it to his mouth for a kiss. "Let us be serious for a minute. Are you prepared to take this step? Nothing will give me greater pleasure than to know that Fitzwilliam will be my son-in-law, but do not let that or anyone rush you into a betrothal. These last months have been difficult ones. If you need more time or—"

"No, Papa!" Elizabeth cried. "I am, oh, I am so happy. I love him. You know I do, and I have for years. He is still the same person he always was. You have seen it. After spending time with Mr Darcy, I am confident that there is nothing to stop us from being the happiest of couples, just as we always intended to be."

Her father patted her hand. "If you are satisfied, my dear."

"I am," she insisted. "It is as if a terrible storm hit our lives. The damage has taken some time to repair, but now the sky is clear, the roofs have all been put to rights, the bridges rebuilt, and, although a road or two has had to be redirected, we can all go back to where we left off before the storm."

Mr Bennet smiled. "You used to like to watch storms."

"I shall never like them again!" She laughed. "I should say, I hope never to experience one quite like this again."

He groaned. "I do not think I could bear it."

AT NETHERFIELD, Mr Darcy took the first possible opportunity to inform Elizabeth that Fitzwilliam had told him about the engagement.

He said, "I understand you and my son had a most agreeable conversation this morning."

Elizabeth could not prevent the broad smile that overtook her face or the light blush.

"It is news we can all celebrate. I am expected in Derbyshire to see to some matters of business, so I cannot prolong my stay, but Fitzwilliam shall remain longer. Celebrate with your friends and family here, and when you come to London next month, we shall celebrate again."

Elizabeth thanked him for the kind sentiment and proceeded to introduce him to those people she thought would be pleasant company for the length of the party. It was only as the Darcys and Lucases were leaving that Elizabeth and Fitzwilliam were able to exchange more than a few words.

He whispered, "I hate that we could be in the same house for so many hours and have so little time together!"

"I know," she murmured. "But you will be here for some days still, and we shall steal lots of time to ourselves."

"Promise?"

The look in his eyes made her blush. "Yes, but only if you promise to behave in a gentleman-like manner, Mr Fitzwilliam Darcy."

He chuckled and said no more as his attention was demanded elsewhere.

Mr Darcy bowed over her hand in a manner that dared anyone to say he did not approve of her. "I shall not keep Fitzwilliam long at Pemberley so that he has sufficient time to return before we must be in town. Goodbye, Miss Elizabeth."

"Safe travels, Mr Darcy." Elizabeth curtseyed.

The Bennets left soon after. In the carriage, Mrs Bennet spoke on and on about what a fine gentleman Mr Darcy was and added, "What did he say to you, Lizzy? Your father refuses to tell me what he has said about you and William marrying—"

Mr Bennet interjected, "I am right here, my dear. Granted, it is quite dark inside the carriage, but I am surprised and not a little wounded that you have forgotten my presence already."

"Oh really, Mr Bennet!" his wife cried.

"I have said as much about the matter as I intend to. Mr Darcy does not object to the match. We would all do best to hold our tongues and let Lizzy and Fitzwilliam settle it between themselves. When the time comes, Fitzwilliam will do as he ought and ask my permission to take Lizzy away from us."

Jane said, "It was a lovely party. What do you think of Mrs Linnington's new cook, Mary?"

Elizabeth could have kissed her for changing the subject.

"Please, do tell us, Mary. I had much rather talk about food than marriage," Mr Bennet said.

THE DARCYS HAD ELECTED to stay at the inn in Meryton, just as they had upon their last visit. With his father's departure, Fitzwilliam removed to his old home. After breakfast, and once Fitzwilliam had shared the news of his and Elizabeth's betrothal —which delighted Sir William and Lady Lucas—they walked to Longbourn. Fitzwilliam immediately went to Mr Bennet, who was waiting for him in his book room.

"Ah, Fitzwilliam. I had wondered when you would turn up. Take a seat, my boy. We could go through the usual routine of you begging me for my daughter's hand, *et cetera*, or we could have a friendly chat and save ourselves the bother since we both know what the outcome will be."

Fitzwilliam sat and waited for Mr Bennet to continue.

"Lizzy assures me this is what she wants, not that I had any cause to doubt it, and now that I have spent more time with your father, I can be easy in sending her to Derbyshire with you. Why did your true family have to be from so distant a county? If it were anyone other than you, I would refuse to let my dearest girl settle so far away from me."

Fitzwilliam smiled. "You will always be welcomed at Pemberley."

Mr Bennet nodded his thanks. "Since I understand the library is magnificent, I might see my way to making the trip, despite my abhorrence of travel. I believe I shall like your Darcy father as much as I do your Lucas one, though not nearly as much as I do your future father-in-law. My goodness, you are surrounded by paternal figures, are you not? I know my friend would be happy to fill a similar role. You will have to find a way to be your own man, despite all of us. I do not doubt that you will, for Lizzy's sake, if not your own.

"Now, tell me, what good books have you read of late?"

WHILE FITZWILLIAM SPOKE to her father, Elizabeth was with her mother. Having heard the news she most wished to hear, Mrs Bennet could not contain her joy. Elizabeth blushed at her references to Fitzwilliam's wealth and consequence.

"And his father!" Mrs Bennet cried. "I have never met such an elegant gentleman. To think that you, my own dearest girl, will be his daughter-in-law! I always accepted that you would marry William, even when he was just a Lucas, because you were so attached to the idea, but this is so much better! Oh, my dear, dear girl!"

Mrs Bennet fluttered around her room, her handkerchief looking like the delicate wings of a dove as she flapped it. Elizabeth listened to her mother in silence for several long minutes as Mrs Bennet spoke about them getting married before anyone could stop it.

"Mama, we have hardly had time to think about when we shall marry. We must consider Mr Darcy's feelings—"

"That is what I am doing, Lizzy!" Mrs Bennet insisted. "He might change his mind. We must get you married as soon as possible, because once you are married, there is nothing he can do about it. Perhaps by special licence?"

Elizabeth protested this vigorously.

Mrs Bennet next spoke about the rightness of Elizabeth and Jane sharing a wedding day. Elizabeth refused to consider it or to discuss the timing of her wedding. She would only say that it would be after Jane's. Another quarter of an hour passed before Elizabeth convinced her mother to join the rest of the family below stairs.

AFTER LETTING their family fuss over them and ask about their wedding plans for an hour, Elizabeth and Fitzwilliam escaped to the gardens.

He said, "I am very glad to have you to myself."

Elizabeth, whose arm was tucked into his, smiled.

"Are you happy, Lizzy?"

"I am. I do not need to ask you if you are. I can see it in your eyes."

Fitzwilliam placed a gentle kiss on her lips. They continued to wander around the wilderness at the rear of the house for a while before sitting on a bench. With their hands clasped together, they exchanged tales of their conversations with their parents.

Elizabeth laughed. "I suspect I shall have to tell my mother several more times that we shall not share a wedding day with Jane and Mr Hawarden. It is their day. It is not even as though you and he are good friends."

"In time, I hope we shall be."

"I did have a thought."

Fitzwilliam kissed her hand. "If it involves a long engage-ment, I shall not agree."

Elizabeth leant into him. "It does not. The third week of July would be perfect. You, Jane, and I are all travelling between now and then. My mother, Lady Lucas, and I can make arrangements for our wedding before I go to town. I shall return before Jane and Mr Hawarden's wedding in the middle of July, and there will be time to do whatever else needs to be done then, particularly if we remain resolved on keeping the whole event small."

"Two months."

"It will pass in the blink of an eye," she assured him.

He was silent until she looked at him. He then pressed his eyes closed for a few seconds. Once he opened them, he stared at her. "We are still not married, and the date you propose is still two months away."

With a fingertip, she poked his chest. "Be reasonable. And serious!"

He tossed his head back and huffed. "If you insist. It is not so far in the future, and we shall be busy. The third week of July it is."

He put an arm around her waist and kissed her temple. "I cannot tell you how much I love you or how happy you make me. I would wait as long as necessary to marry you, but now that you have agreed, I want you to be my wife. I cannot wait to *see* you as my wife. More than anyone, you know I was satisfied as William Lucas. As much as I dreamt of travelling the world or what it would be like to have the freedom of wealth, I did not long for those things. I was happy to anticipate our life together at Lucas Lodge, with our family and friends nearby.

"There is so much more ahead of us now. I know you will blossom like one of the flowers you love so much. I cannot wait to see the success you will have, the enjoyment you will find in our life. We can travel. I can buy you things I never could have afforded—"

"I do not need any of that," Elizabeth protested.

He nodded. "I know you do not, any more than I do. I cannot deny that there are pleasures to being in my position. You are too intelligent, too sensible, to deny it. The knowledge that I shall never have to concern myself with money or how I shall provide for our children's futures, especially that I can give all of it to you, is so gratifying."

They kissed, breaking apart before either of them became too heated.

Elizabeth whispered, "Two months does seem like a long time. I love you so much. I cannot wait to be your wife; for you to be my husband."

They held each other for a few minutes before deciding they should return to the house before they forgot themselves.

CHAPTER 39

FITZWILLIAM'S TIME IN MERYTON WAS OVER TOO SOON FOR Elizabeth. He was at Longbourn as much as possible, but the Lucases and his friends had a right to his company, too. Mr and Mrs Bennet forbade Elizabeth to meet him away from the house, Mrs Bennet deciding such behaviour was unseemly now that they were engaged. Thus, the couple lost the comfort—and temptation—of their unchaperoned walks. Before they knew it, the morning of his departure was upon them, and they faced another separation. Fortunately, it would not be a long one.

There was still a quarter of an hour or twenty minutes before breakfast, and Elizabeth was anxious for the time to pass. Fitzwilliam, Sir William, and Lady Lucas would join them for the meal, after which Fitzwilliam would be on his way north. She wanted to see him as soon as possible and make the most of every second until he left.

She was on her way to wait for him and the Lucases outside when she heard her father whisper her name. Turning around, she saw him by the door to his book room. He held it open and ushered her inside.

"I shall give you no more than ten minutes."

As soon as he closed the door, she felt arms around her and heard a voice murmuring her name in her ear.

She laughed. "Wha—?"

Fitzwilliam pulled her towards the sofa. He held her face between his hands, and they kissed. Elizabeth wrapped her arms around his waist and moved several all-important inches closer to him.

"Lizzy, my love," Fitzwilliam said as they sat, still wrapped in each other's arms.

"Fitzwilliam, my love."

"How long until we meet again?"

"You should be the one to tell me," Elizabeth said with a smile in her voice. "I am but a simple female, destined to wait upon your convenience."

Fitzwilliam snorted. "That describes you perfectly. I shall be back in a fortnight, or a few days after that, but not for long."

"And I shall follow you to London soon after," Elizabeth reminded him.

They sat in silence for a minute or two until Mr Bennet made a gentle tapping sound on the door, alerting them to the end of their time alone. Elizabeth sat up and turned to face Fitzwilliam.

"I do love you, and in seven—I pray very short—weeks, we will be man and wife."

"And I shall never, *never* be separated from you again!" he vowed.

FITZWILLIAM ARRIVED at Pemberley in good time. He saw evidence of strain in his father, who looked tired and as if he carried a large weight on his shoulders. Fitzwilliam told himself it was because of the situation with his brother and nephew rather than anything to do with him or Elizabeth. After all, George had looked better of late—except for the period immediately after Fitzwilliam's disclosures about Jeffrey and John. His supposition was confirmed by his father's talk of which rooms might suit Elizabeth best and what they should do to make Pemberley ready for the new Mrs Darcy. They took Mrs Reynolds into their confidence so that she could ensure that everything was prepared properly. They made and received a number of calls, and his father often commented on which ladies might make good companions for Elizabeth.

While his father's outward mood improved, Fitzwilliam remained concerned. As much as he accepted that he and his father should speak openly, especially given how much unhappiness their reticence had created over the last months, he hesitated. Towards the end of his fortnight at Pemberley, he hinted that he knew something was disturbing George.

His father waved away the idea but sighed. "I am afraid it is nothing you can help me with, no more than by being here." After a moment, and with evident reluctance, he admitted, "I have been thinking about your mother a great deal."

They were riding, and it was an effort to hear him when his voice became thin. With George's eyes pointed towards the horizon, Fitzwilliam was not certain his father's next words were directed at him.

"I wish...I wish she were here to share in our joy. I wish I had been able to convince her that I did not blame her for writing to her father. She never forgave herself. I wish I knew what she would want me to do." He sighed again and lowered his chin.

After a minute or two, he nodded his head and seemed to regain a measure of his vigour. "There is nothing for you to concern yourself with, Son. The shadows of the past. I must find a way to settle them. Thinking about the future helps. I noticed that your Miss Elizabeth likes to laugh; I look forward to hearing laughter at Pemberley again. It has been too quiet for too long."

GEORGE'S MOOD remained sombre when they left Pemberley, but it lightened when Fitzwilliam asked about the Darcy family's history and his boyhood, including his long friendship with Frederick.

The morning they were to start the last leg of their journey, his father said, "Fitzwilliam, I shall not go with you to Meryton.

There is something I must attend to in town. It would be better to do it before you arrive and Miss Elizabeth goes to Rebecca."

"Do you wish me to go with you? Lizzy would understand—"

"It is not necessary. It is something I must do alone. Please make my excuses to the Lucases, Miss Elizabeth, and her family. Let us not talk about it further. Now, before we part, I have something I wish to give you."

From his pocket, he pulled a small, green velvet bag, which he gave to Fitzwilliam. As Fitzwilliam opened it and extracted a diamond and ruby ring, his father explained, "It was your mother's. I gave it to her to mark the one-year anniversary of our betrothal." His cheeks coloured. "A bit of romantic nonsense. Your mother would have liked to know that your bride has it. One day, you might pass it along to your son to give to his intended."

Fitzwilliam held the ring reverently between two fingers. It was a delicate, elegant piece, and he knew Elizabeth would like it. Of greater significance, his father wished her to have it. It was a symbol of his acceptance and her inclusion in the Darcy family. For those reasons, she would love it.

"Thank you." Fitzwilliam's voice was rough and his eyes grew moist as an image came to mind of Lady Anne wearing the ring, laughing and smiling as her husband presented it to her. "I wish I could remember her."

He heard his father sharply inhale. He stepped closer to Fitzwilliam and squeezed his arm.

"I wish she were with us. She is, in a way, but I so wish she were physically with us. She adored you, and would have rejoiced, just as I do, to know you survived. She—"

Fitzwilliam was surprised to see tears in his father's eyes. George cleared his throat and continued, "Your mother would have been happy to know that you had a mother's love, even though she could not be the one to give it to you. She would have been grateful to Lady Lucas, just as I am grateful that you had Sir William and Mr Bennet."

It was an extraordinary speech and touched a special place in Fitzwilliam's heart because he understood how difficult it was for his father to acknowledge the years of his grief and loneliness. He closed the small gap between them and embraced his father.

"I love and honour *all* of you, Lady Anne included. Even though I do not remember her, I *feel* her."

His father held him tightly, and Fitzwilliam felt his chest expand as he inhaled deeply.

As he released his hold on Fitzwilliam, he said, "Tell Lady Lucas. I think she needs to know."

Fitzwilliam nodded.

"Enjoy your time in Hertfordshire, even though it is not for long. You will hate to leave Miss Elizabeth, and she will not like to see you go, but I must ask you to return as we arranged."

"Of course, Father. Lizzy has been busy with her mother and Jane. She will not mind sending me on my way." In an attempt to bring levity to their conversation, he added, "I suspect she will be glad to have me gone, since I am of no use when she asks about wedding arrangements or talks about the gowns and bonnets she and Jane have purchased." Elizabeth had written about both, and he had begged her to excuse him from commenting on either.

His father dutifully chuckled, and the gentlemen spoke about Elizabeth and Fitzwilliam's wedding and plans for afterwards for a few minutes before parting.

FITZWILLIAM WAS impatient to see Elizabeth and went to Longbourn before going to Lucas Lodge. He remained with the Bennets for two hours, taking his leave only as dusk began to turn to night. Elizabeth escorted him outside. The couple embraced.

Fitzwilliam sighed and tightened his hold. "I have longed for this."

Elizabeth nestled her head against his shoulder. "I am so happy you are here."

Fitzwilliam glanced towards the house and did not see any figures lurking in the windows. Nevertheless, he dared not kiss Elizabeth. "I wish I could remain longer and escort you to London myself, but my father says there is something we must attend to before you arrive."

Elizabeth looked at him and smiled. "Are you up to mischief, Mr Darcy?"

Fitzwilliam shook his head and furrowed his brow.

"What is it?"

He shrugged. "My father's mood was odd. Not precisely odd. He was not unhappy, he was even quite cheerful at times, but there was something weighing on his mind."

Elizabeth's expression softened and she played with a lock of his hair.

Fitzwilliam closed his eyes for a second to enjoy the caress. "I ought not to keep you out of doors, and I should get to Lucas Lodge before it grows darker. My mother will be anxious. I will see you tomorrow, my darling, and I shall tell you everything that happened. I have something for you."

"Oh? A kiss?" She laughed.

Fitzwilliam shook his head. "Something special, but I shall not tell you what it is. I want to give it to you when we are alone."

Elizabeth touched his cheek then stepped back. "I shall not tease you. You should be on your way before Lady Lucas rouses the neighbours to search for you."

"Tomorrow morning?"

Elizabeth nodded and moved away from the horse. "Come here. I was reminded not to sneak out to meet you. We can find privacy in the gardens, even if it is not as much as you or I would like."

Fitzwilliam nodded and with a quiet, "My love," was away.

THE NEXT MORNING, Fitzwilliam told Sir William and Lady Lucas what George had said about Lady Anne. Predictably, his mother cried. His father, too, was moved by George's expression of gratitude. Before the mood became maudlin, Fitzwilliam mentioned the letters he and Charlotte had exchanged and explained that they spoke about him and Elizabeth visiting Kent. Fitzwilliam showed them the ring George had given him for Elizabeth and left for Longbourn, where he would see them later in the day.

Elizabeth was delighted with the ring. When he explained its significance, she said a soft, "Oh. To know that it was Lady Anne's…"

Fitzwilliam bowed his head. He held Elizabeth's hand in his. They sat on a favourite bench in the Longbourn gardens.

"He accepts you; us. Me, even, and my past. As serious as he was before we parted ways, he also seemed more at ease. I know it sounds paradoxical, and perhaps I am being fanciful. I shall see how he is when I am in town."

"Very wise, Mr Darcy."

They held hands, and she said, "Let us talk about this wedding of ours."

They reviewed what had been decided for their wedding day, and Fitzwilliam explained that his father wished to take on the task of arranging a wedding trip for them. Elizabeth agreed, but she suggested it be no longer than a fortnight.

She explained, "I am anxious to see Pemberley."

They continued to discuss how they would spend the coming months until Mary called them into the house.

As they walked inside, Fitzwilliam said, "Once we are married, I shall not be separated from you for more than an hour or two at a time."

Elizabeth laughed. "You always say that. Am I to be allowed so little time to myself?"

"Perhaps I shall allow you three, if you are being particularly vexing."

Elizabeth laughed again, and the merry sound filled the air around them. It was soon mixed with that of Fitzwilliam's deeper voice.

THE MORNING FITZWILLIAM returned to London arrived far too soon for the young lovers. They agreed to ignore Mr and Mrs Bennet's strictures and met away from Longbourn. Elizabeth suspected her father knew and was not greatly disturbed. They kissed as they sat on the fallen tree in their favourite spot before deciding it was more prudent to talk than embrace.

Fitzwilliam said, "I shall be glad when we can just tell everyone we are at last engaged. I have not seen one person who did not take it for granted that we shall soon be married."

George Darcy wished to inform his family before the news became more widely known. In particular, Fitzwilliam had told her that his father wanted to ensure Jeffrey and John Darcy understood that he would not tolerate any attempts to denigrate the match.

Elizabeth laughed. "You can hardly wonder at the assumption. Not only have I been frequenting the shops in Meryton in a most particular manner, but the sight of this lovely, lovely ring on my hand can only be interpreted in so many ways."

Fitzwilliam kissed her hand where his mother's ring rested. He twisted it around Elizabeth's finger. "We shall have the size adjusted when you are in London." It was loose but not likely to fall off.

Elizabeth nodded. "I must thank your father. The gesture of passing Lady Anne's ring to me is..." She chuckled. "Words fail me, which, as you know, is unusual. It is beautiful, and the significance of it makes it even more dear to me."

"I knew you would feel that way."

Elizabeth smiled and teased, "No doubt, you also anticipated my mother's raptures, Lydia's and Kitty's wishes for such jewels, Mary's attempt to hide her interest, and Jane's happiness for us."

"Naturally. I am very intelligent, when I am not being incredibly stupid."

Elizabeth laughed again. *I am making up for all the laughing I did not do last autumn and winter!* She stood and tugged him to his feet. "Let us walk along the river before we return to Longbourn. While we do, you can tell me how much you adore me."

CHAPTER 40

FITZWILLIAM ARRIVED AT DARCY HOUSE TO THE ASTONISHING news that his father had reconciled with Lord and Lady Romsley, and that they were expected at Fitzwilliam House for dinner.

George said, "It is what your mother would have wished. It is what I want, for you and Miss Elizabeth, for myself, for Tom and Sterling and Rebecca. Not knowing if I should or could was the matter that was occupying my thoughts when we were at Pemberley. I was not certain how your uncle would receive me; considering my obstinacy, he—and your aunt—were kinder than I deserved."

"Are Sterling and Rebecca—?"

His father shook his head. "No, there is no engagement yet. Not one that your uncle and aunt know of, at least. I did not see your cousins." He took a deep breath and released it in a rush. "It is time to put the past in the past. You, I, many others have said it recently. Frederick has been urging me to do it for months."

"I know it has not been easy for you, Father."

George rubbed the back of his neck. "No, it has not been easy, but the rewards for doing it will be substantial. Your uncle and I were once good friends. I do not know if you are aware of that."

Fitzwilliam nodded.

"I have reason to hope we can be again. He loved your

mother very much, and she and Margaret were the best of friends. Your mother thought of her as more of a sister than she did Lady Catherine, who is her sister by blood. I suppose she will return from Ireland eventually, and you will have to meet her, but we need not cross that bridge just yet."

Fitzwilliam was on the edge of his seat when George next told him that he had called on Jeffrey. "I told him about your betrothal, as I said I would. He was not happy, but I do not care, and neither should you. I suppose we—I include Miss Elizabeth in this—shall meet him and John upon occasion. As long as they behave appropriately, we shall, too."

With a smile, his father said, "Go prepare for dinner. Your aunt and uncle and cousins await us. Philip and Margaret are anxious to meet you."

They walked to Fitzwilliam House since the day was fair and the distance short. The butler showed them to a comfortably proportioned withdrawing room that, Fitzwilliam suspected, was used by the family, rather than for guests. The four Fitzwilliams stood and regarded them, and an awkward silence lasted until Tom spoke.

"Cousin, I believe I speak for all my family when I say how good it is to see you here." Tom addressed George next. "You as well, sir."

His father said a soft, "Thank you," before introducing Fitzwilliam to the earl and countess.

Lord Romsley took a step closer to Fitzwilliam and stared at him. His uncle's lips were parted, and his chest rose and fell heavily. He turned to George and cried, "My God, George! Anne's—"

The earl spun around and marched to the fireplace. Leaning against it, he kept his back to them. Sterling met Fitzwilliam's eye, shrugged, and went to his father.

The countess held out her hands to him, and Fitzwilliam took them in his, even though he felt unsure and awkward.

"I cannot tell you how wonderful it is to meet you. Do not

mind your uncle. He loved your mother very dearly, as did I, and seeing you, well, it is quite overwhelming."

Fitzwilliam stammered, "Thank you. I am very happy to meet you as well."

Lady Romsley released one of Fitzwilliam's hands, and held her hand out to George. "Now we can be a family again."

His father kissed her hand, let it fall, and turned to Tom. "Some of us are yet strangers to each other. I hope to rectify that."

"As do I, sir."

Lord Romsley and Sterling joined them.

Bramwell asked his brother, "As do you what?"

Lady Romsley chastised him for being rude. "Will you not greet your uncle and cousin properly?"

"I apologise. Uncle." He gave George a slight bow, then faced Fitzwilliam and held out a hand to him. "I am glad this day has arrived."

"As am I."

Lord Romsley suggested they sit and indicated that Fitzwilliam should take the place beside him. No one seemed to know what to say, and Fitzwilliam exchanged looks with his cousins. In a moment, Lady Romsley began to recount what she said was one of her favourite memories of them being together at Pemberley, and until they went into dinner, they spoke of the past.

During dinner, his father announced the news of Fitzwilliam and Elizabeth's engagement and plans to marry in July. Congratulations were offered, and Fitzwilliam told the earl and countess about Elizabeth.

By the end of the meal, the earlier awkwardness was a thing of the past, and the rest of the evening was enjoyable. When Fitzwilliam and George took their leave, it was with the understanding that they would bring Elizabeth to meet the earl and countess as soon as it could be arranged. Lady Romsley agreed to assist Elizabeth in any way she could, such as by introducing her to the ladies in their circle and taking her shopping.

"Lady Sophia will, as well. I called on her yesterday," George told Fitzwilliam. "With their acceptance, no one will dare question the suitability of your marriage."

"I shall not permit it." Lady Romsley turned to her eldest son. "I am as happy to help *two* young ladies as I am one. Miss Da—"

"Thank you, Mother, I take your meaning," Sterling interjected.

Tom, who was standing next to Fitzwilliam, sniggered and whispered, "He has not yet worked up the courage to ask her. I think it is because she disliked him so much when they met in January. It is an amusing tale. Remind me to tell you, another time."

"From what Lizzy told me, he should not worry so much."

"Oh?" Tom cocked an eyebrow.

Fitzwilliam shrugged and went to join his father, who was ready to depart.

THE TWO DAYS after Fitzwilliam's return were extraordinary. Meeting his aunt and uncle made him feel closer to his mother. He had a true sense of family with them, something he had never felt with Jeffrey and John. Fitzwilliam spent one morning with his uncle and Tom, and he and his father had dinner with Frederick, Rebecca, and Freddie. Frederick informed them that Sterling had proposed, further solidifying the ties between the Darcys and Fitzwilliams. Now, Fitzwilliam could count the hours until Elizabeth arrived. They would see each other at dinner.

Two or three months ago, I never would have dreamt that everything could be so happy and so...right.

He went to a jewellery shop to buy Elizabeth a gift to commemorate their betrothal. As he was looking at a display of earrings, he realised that the gentleman standing several feet away was staring at him. Taking a surreptitious glance at him,

Fitzwilliam felt a flicker of recognition. He appeared to be a few years Fitzwilliam's junior. His smile was affable but shy.

Fitzwilliam inclined his head. "Good morning."

The other man returned the greeting but made no attempt to say more.

"Forgive me, but are we acquainted? I have met so many—"

This was met by a vigorous head shake and a grin. "We have not been introduced, but we have been at the same party more than once."

"Ah. I am Fitzwilliam Darcy." He supposed the other man knew this already.

A light dusting of colour bloomed in the young man's cheeks. "Charles Bingley."

The name was not familiar to Fitzwilliam, and he could not account for Mr Bingley's surprise at the introduction.

"I gather you are seeking a gift for a lady, as am I," said Fitzwilliam.

Mr Bingley nodded. "My sister. For her birthday."

They helped each other select gifts. Mr Bingley was an easy talker and soon confided the situation of his family which sparked Fitzwilliam's memory. At a ball, John had insulted the family because of their close association to trade.

Before they parted ways, Fitzwilliam said, "I shall be in town for a few more weeks. Send a note around if you like. We can meet at the club or go riding one morning."

Mr Bingley smiled and took the card Fitzwilliam held out to him. "Thank you. I shall!"

ELIZABETH ARRIVED in London without delay. After spending a few minutes with Mr Frederick Darcy and Freddie, Rebecca took Elizabeth to her room, and they settled in for a good chat.

"I am so happy you are here!"

Elizabeth laughed and embraced her friend. "As am I. I shall not thank you for welcoming me again, because I know you do not wish to hear it."

"I would just as much thank you for returning."

Elizabeth held one of Rebecca's hands. "I must be serious for a minute. I do thank you. Your friendship has been a great solace to me these last months. This winter, I needed distraction and to be away from Longbourn. I was happy here with you and Freddie and your father."

Rebecca blinked away a few tears. "But now you are *truly* happy."

Elizabeth grinned. "Indeed, I am. Part of my joy is knowing that you will be my cousin-in-law."

A light blush stole onto Rebecca's cheeks. "In the not-too-distant future, we shall be double cousins-in-law."

"You and Viscount Bramwell are engaged?"

Rebecca grinned. "Just yesterday. Oh, I hope I am doing the right thing!"

Elizabeth offered her congratulations, insisted she had made the correct decision in accepting the viscount and on knowing all the particulars. They talked about their young men—and a few less-interesting matters—for so long that Mr Frederick Darcy had to remind them to prepare for dinner.

ELIZABETH HAD NOT EXPECTED to be nervous about going to Darcy House, but she was. Her eyes flew around the entry hall and the passages to the withdrawing room. Seeing the richness of her surroundings made her realise, as she had not before, what a change her William had confronted when he learnt the truth of his identity. Fitzwilliam's presence helped to steady her as she was introduced to Mr Darcy's cousin, Lady Sophia. Her manner towards Elizabeth was warm, which put her at her ease.

Mr Darcy encouraged them to sit, and Fitzwilliam tucked Elizabeth's hand into his elbow to guide her to a sofa.

He whispered, "Lizzy, my love."

Before Elizabeth could speak, Mr Darcy said, "I am very pleased to have you all here today, especially to welcome Miss Elizabeth."

The butler approached with glasses of champagne, and Mr Darcy said, "I am not one for making speeches, but I wish to offer my congratulations to Fitzwilliam and Miss Elizabeth. Your betrothal is a mark of the happy times ahead of us."

Elizabeth smiled at him and hoped he understood how much she appreciated his effort.

Congratulations were offered and doubled when Rebecca and Lord Bramwell's engagement was announced a moment later. For several minutes, the room was full of happy chatter as they spoke about the two upcoming weddings. Throughout it all, Fitzwilliam remained by Elizabeth's side. They exchanged frequent looks, but the only opportunity they had to speak privately was during the walk to the dining parlour.

"I have missed you, my love," he whispered.

"And I you."

"I met my uncle and aunt. Lord and Lady Romsley."

Elizabeth's step faltered, and she gaped at him. In a few words, Fitzwilliam explained.

"I am so pleased for you, Mr Darcy, and Lord and Lady Romsley," said Elizabeth.

They entered the dining room, and Fitzwilliam led her to a seat beside his father.

During the first course, a creamy asparagus soup Elizabeth found delightful, Mr Darcy told her and Rebecca, "Lady Romsley is expecting both of you tomorrow morning. I understand she has many plans for the two of you."

Elizabeth looked at Rebecca who confirmed this with a nod. "I forgot to tell you, did I not?"

Elizabeth nodded.

"And I must have some time with her, George," Lady Sophia said. "Miss Elizabeth, there will be a very lively interest in you once your engagement is known."

"Of course." Elizabeth was on the verge of finding it overwhelming but decided it would do her no good and reminded herself that she possessed a prodigious amount of courage.

After they ate, Elizabeth was introduced to the housekeeper, and they arranged a time for Elizabeth to tour the house. The party then settled themselves into the withdrawing room, and she and Fitzwilliam finally had a chance to speak.

Fitzwilliam said, "It will be a very busy few weeks, as you no doubt have realised from our conversation at dinner."

She exhaled slowly and regarded him with wide eyes. "I had no notion. I suppose I did not think about what these weeks would be like, other than seeing you and Rebecca and Freddie and your father and theirs." She grimaced and laughed.

"We shall see each other as much as possible." Fitzwilliam held her hand. "I will go to Frederick's tomorrow morning, and you, Rebecca, Bramwell, and I shall walk in the park before breakfast. Bramwell and I then take breakfast at Frederick's before you and Rebecca go to my aunt."

Elizabeth glanced at Mr Darcy and in a lowered voice said, "Everything is truly well with Lord and Lady Romsley? It seems incredible. Too easy, almost."

He shrugged. "They used to be very good friends. Perhaps that helped."

She studied Mr Darcy again and nibbled her lower lip. He was more at ease than she had ever seen him, though that could be because it was the first time they had met away from Hertfordshire. Whatever the reason for it, she was pleased.

Elizabeth turned her eyes from the father to the son. "There is some sort of party tomorrow evening, too. Everyone must understand we want as much time together as possible. We shall not be in town for long. Before we know it, we return to Hertfordshire—"

Fitzwilliam interjected, "And get married!"

Elizabeth laughed. "Yes, my love, and not a day too soon!"

ELIZABETH AND REBECCA were awake until the early hours of the morning. Rebecca shared what she knew about George Darcy's reconciliation with the Romsleys and said that she had yet to meet either the earl or the countess.

"Are you anxious about it?" Elizabeth asked.

Rebecca shook her head, to Elizabeth's relief. "Sterling—he insists I call him by his Christian name—assures me they are pleased. I shall be glad to have the initial meeting over with. You do realise she will keep us very busy while you are here?"

Elizabeth nodded. "The reality, my dear friend and soon to be double cousin, is that neither of us were brought up to marry men such as the viscount or Fitzwilliam. I pray Lady Romsley and Lady Sophia allow me to solicit their advice when I need it." She waved off Rebecca's attempts to reassure her, saying they were not necessary. "It will be a very different style of life from the one Fitzwilliam and I imagined. Their advice may prevent me from making too many blunders! Now, before we both fall asleep, I shall leave you with a question to ponder. There are some things I must buy before I return to Hertfordshire."

Elizabeth listed a few items and asked Rebecca to consider the best warehouses in which to find them. Rebecca returned to her bedchamber, and Elizabeth climbed into bed, extinguished the last candle, promptly fell asleep, and had very pleasant dreams about her Fitzwilliam and their life together.

CHAPTER 41

THE TWO YOUNG COUPLES HAD A PLEASANT WALK THE following morning. During a moment alone as they waited for breakfast, Fitzwilliam presented Elizabeth with the earrings he had bought for her. They were in the shape of flowers and decorated with pink and green gemstones. After the meal, Lord Bramwell—Elizabeth was not yet comfortable calling him anything else, despite his request that she do so—and Fitzwilliam escorted Rebecca and Elizabeth to Fitzwilliam House.

Once there, they went to Lady Romsley's private sitting room, where they found a smiling countess and Colonel Fitzwilliam.

He welcomed them and said, "I offer you both my congratulations. My brother and cousin are fortunate gentlemen. If I did not love them, I would be wildly jealous."

Lord Bramwell punched his brother's shoulder, while Elizabeth and Rebecca thanked the colonel.

Lady Romsley cleared her throat, and the viscount performed the introductions.

The warmth of her voice and smile enveloped Elizabeth. "My dears, I am very pleased to meet you. As lovely as it is to see you," she looked at Lord Bramwell, "and especially my nephew—"

Both of the lady's sons protested, but she just smiled at them, walked to Fitzwilliam's side, and touched his arm; he kissed her cheek.

"As I was saying, I intend to banish you. Away with you, my darlings. Do not look so wounded, Sterling. It was you who told me that you and Fitzwilliam had something to occupy your time while I was with your young ladies, and Tom has a meeting with his general."

Elizabeth knew that Lord Bramwell, Fitzwilliam, and Freddie were attending a lecture by a man recently returned from a tour of plantations in the West Indies.

The gentlemen bade them good day, and the ladies sat upon elegant ivory settees. The countess served Elizabeth and Rebecca barley water. Elizabeth twirled the glass around and around while telling herself she was not nervous.

"Now, let us get to the business of becoming acquainted," Lady Romsley announced.

They spoke about general subjects for a few minutes, before the countess said to Elizabeth, "Lady Sophia and I have agreed that we shall introduce you as Fitzwilliam's betrothed. My nephew has been an object of curiosity, as I am sure you understand. You, my dear, will also be. Do not let it make you anxious. We shall see you through."

Elizabeth thanked her, and Lady Romsley then asked Rebecca, "You wrote to your mother?"

Rebecca said that she had. "My father sent the letter express, so I suppose she has it by now."

"Do you think she will come to town?"

Rebecca blanched. "I do not know." Elizabeth knew that Rebecca and her mother had a contentious relationship, and Rebecca dreaded Julia Darcy's scolding and demands.

Lady Romsley patted Rebecca's hand. "If she does, we shall manage, my dear. Never fear."

She asked Rebecca when she would like to get married, then asked Elizabeth what had been decided for her wedding.

"You have known Fitzwilliam for some years, I believe."

There was a slight tremor in her voice which reminded Elizabeth how much his loss and recovery meant to his family.

"I have known him for sixteen years."

The countess sighed and whispered, "Sixteen years. Was he...was he happy?"

"He was very happy. The Lucases are good, kind people, and they love him as though he were their own."

Lady Romsley pressed her fingers to her eyes, but Elizabeth saw no tears. "Forgive me. His mother was a dear friend as well as a sister, and she has been much in my mind these last few days. It would have given her such comfort to know that he was alive and happy." She shook her head, chuckled, and put on a brave smile. "Let us think about more pleasant matters. I have been making plans for us, my girls." She rattled off a list of calls to ladies she wished them to meet and outings they were to attend with her and shopping they had to do.

By the time the gentlemen joined them that afternoon, the ladies were getting along famously. With some discussion, Rebecca and Lord Bramwell decided they would marry in London in early September. Their betrothal would remain secret until they understood Julia Darcy's plans.

That evening marked the beginning of their very busy days. The mornings were spent shopping, making and receiving calls from more ladies than Elizabeth thought she would ever remember, and attending a variety of breakfast parties and outings with Lady Romsley, Lady Sophia, and as often as possible, Fitzwilliam and the viscount. Elizabeth and Fitzwilliam would have appreciated more time to be together. They longed for the relative quietness of life in the country during which they could take long walks or sit in the gardens and talk.

"We shall have that after we are married," Fitzwilliam said.

"Which is another reason I say our wedding cannot be soon enough!"

Among the various ladies and gentlemen Elizabeth met, she particularly liked Mr Bingley. He had an easy charm and liveliness that reminded her of Freddie and the Goulding brothers, with whom Fitzwilliam had long been good friends.

Not all meetings were pleasant, however. Elizabeth was introduced to Jeffrey Darcy one evening when they happened to be at the same concert. George Darcy stood by Elizabeth's side, and she could feel how rigid he held himself as he said the necessary words. Jeffrey Darcy hardly looked at her or Fitzwilliam. He seemed desirous of speaking to Mr Darcy and remaining with them, but one look from Mr Darcy had him disappearing into the crowd.

To Elizabeth and Fitzwilliam, Mr Darcy said, "There has been enough strife in this family. I shall do everything in my power to ensure no one robs us of a moment of comfort and happiness again."

AT THE START OF JULY, Lady Sophia held a party to commemorate Fitzwilliam's twenty-fifth birthday. Aside from various Darcys and the four Fitzwilliams, the guests included a number of people Fitzwilliam had met and liked during his months in town. Among them was an appreciative, excited Charles Bingley. He and Freddie were fast friends by the end of the evening.

Elizabeth decided it was her most favourite party during her time in London. She felt more and more comfortable with George Darcy, and very much liked Lady Romsley. Lord Romsley was intimidating, but he was friendly enough. It was clear that knowing Fitzwilliam was very important to the earl, and equally that it meant a great deal to Fitzwilliam, who confided that he felt like he was getting to know his mother by listening to Lord Romsley's stories about her.

With so many people present, Elizabeth and Fitzwilliam had little time together that evening, although they did steal a few minutes by slipping into a corridor while the remainder of the party was in the withdrawing room. They spoke about the evening and how odd it was for him to celebrate his birthday in July instead of November.

Elizabeth said, "It had not occurred to me that I am marrying a much older man than I had anticipated. Oh dear." She furrowed her brow and nibbled her lower lip.

Fitzwilliam rolled his eyes. "Four months older."

"Almost four and a half!"

She giggled, and Fitzwilliam smiled and ran a finger along her jaw.

Just as he was leaning forward to kiss her, they heard Colonel Fitzwilliam's voice.

"My mother says you have been alone long enough. Back to the withdrawing room with you. You will be married before you know it."

"I beg to differ," Fitzwilliam grumbled.

The colonel laughed at them.

Elizabeth said, "One day, it will be your turn, and we shall take great pleasure in laughing at you! You have been warned."

There were other moments Elizabeth enjoyed, too, including the conversations she and Rebecca had late into the night during which they shared their hopes for the future. Elizabeth liked to think she was of particular use to her friend the day a letter from her mother arrived. Julia Darcy was angry that Rebecca had not told her she was being courted by a viscount, and demanded that Rebecca and Freddie return to Norfolk immediately; she insisted Freddie had been absent too long and that the wedding take place there.

Freddie ignored his part of the missive, saying, "She has been telling me as much since January. I was not in town a week before they told me that my grandfather missed me, and it has only gotten worse since then. They will have to accept that I am old enough to make decisions for myself. I shall not always ignore them, of course, but spending part of the year with my father is not so much to ask. And I have friends I might like to visit, in addition to going to Pemberley and Romsley Hall."

"As for me," Rebecca said, "if she wishes to see me wed, she can come here. I told Sterling that it was possible she would do something like this. He says that, if I like, we can go see them later in the year."

Although Rebecca sounded like the letter did not distress her, the bright spots of colour in her cheeks said otherwise. After returning to Curzon Street from an evening party, Elizabeth listened to her complaints about her mother with all the sympathy she possessed. In the end, Rebecca vowed that she felt better and would be able to turn her mind to enjoying the period of her betrothal.

"Planning the wedding will be more pleasant without my mother here. It is a terrible thing to say, but there it is."

THE DAY before Elizabeth's departure, Lady Romsley sought a private interview with her.

The countess said, "We have only known each other for several weeks, and yet it seems much longer. I mean that in the very best of ways, as I trust you understand."

Elizabeth thanked her. "I am grateful for your help. I feel much better prepared for my new role."

Lady Romsley patted Elizabeth's cheek. "I am happy to know I did you some good. I have no doubt you will do well at Pemberley."

"I shall certainly try to."

"False modesty, Elizabeth."

Elizabeth laughed. "I intend to do well, but I do not pretend it will always be easy."

"Very wise." Lady Romsley reiterated the chief of her advice, including that she was not alone and should not hesitate to ask for assistance from George Darcy, Lady Sophia, or herself.

When the countess presented her with a wedding gift, an exquisite diamond jewellery set, several tears fell down her cheeks. Elizabeth had discovered that the closer her wedding approached, the less she could control her emotions. She laughed and excused herself. "I think it is knowing my sister is getting married soon, then it is our wedding, and after the dreadful weeks last winter... Oh, I am absolutely ridiculous!"

Lady Romsley gave a soft laugh. "If you think you are prone to outbursts now, dear girl, wait until you find yourself with child!"

CHAPTER 42

JANE'S WEDDING DAY WAS EVERYTHING SHE AND THOSE WHO loved her could wish. Mrs Bennet cried and was both grateful to have a daughter so well settled and sad to know that her dear Jane would no longer be close by. It left those with her unsure whether to congratulate or console her. Mr Bennet abandoned the attempt to understand his wife within a quarter of an hour.

Two days after Jane's wedding, George Darcy, accompanied by Colonel Fitzwilliam, arrived. Elizabeth and Fitzwilliam were in perfect agreement that the next four days passed quickly and were exceptionally pleasurable. The weather cooperated, which allowed entertainments and calls to proceed without interruption. Mrs Bennet demanded hours of their time each day to attend to a flurry of final wedding preparations she insisted were necessary. Elizabeth was relieved to discover that once Mr Darcy had assured Mrs Bennet six or seven times that she had arranged everything to suit his tastes perfectly, she calmed sufficiently to be as rational as she ever could be. To Elizabeth and Fitzwilliam's delight, their fathers were soon on their way to being good friends. Then, with one final dinner party, kindly hosted by the Linningtons, Elizabeth and Fitzwilliam said goodbye to each other and went to their separate homes for the last time.

THE NEXT MORNING, Fitzwilliam was in his bedchamber at Lucas Lodge fussing with his neckcloth while his valet stood nearby holding his coat. When his father entered the room, Quinn placed the coat across the back of a chair and left them alone. Fitzwilliam's voice shook when he said good morning.

His father said, "You will ruin it if you keep at it like that." George straightened the folds of the cloth. "There. Leave it. It is just as it should be."

Fitzwilliam took a deep breath and slowly blew it out his mouth. He nodded and went to a table on which sat the Darcy family watch.

"What has you worried, Son?"

Fitzwilliam sat and rubbed his hands over his face. "I do not know. I am not at all anxious about marrying Lizzy. God knows it is what I want."

"You cannot doubt her sentiments. Any fool could see how happy she is." His father sat on the small bed.

A brief smile graced Fitzwilliam's face. "I know that she shares my wish. I..." He sighed. "I cannot get away from the knowledge that I came so close to losing all of this."

"Fitzwilliam. My son. I still cannot believe I am sitting here with you. I suspect it will take many years before I fully rid myself of the sense of disbelief. All of us have been on a remarkable journey these last nine months, and it is bound to leave wounds that will take time to heal. Fortunately, the ones your Elizabeth suffered, like those of Sir William and Lady Lucas, have healed quickly and well. She loves you and has forgiven you."

Fitzwilliam nodded, but he remained troubled.

"The past *is* the past. Perhaps we should adopt it as a new family motto." George chuckled. "Do not dwell on your regrets, especially today. Take that energy and use it to make your wedding and honeymoon joyful for Elizabeth, if not yourself."

Fitzwilliam sat up and nodded.

His father cleared his throat. "If it is your wedding trip that adds to your anxiety, I shall offer this advice: take your time. Your relationship is about to change enormously, but the two of you will do well. Talk to each other, laugh together, just rejoice in having each other through life's ups and downs."

They stood, and George said, "Let us finish making you handsome for your bride."

LONGBOURN WAS alive with voices and footsteps as people rushed from one room to another and as doors were opened and closed. Amid it all, Elizabeth sat at the dressing table in her room, her maid standing behind her, arranging her hair. Jane, who had insisted on being at Elizabeth's wedding, sat on the bed. Wishing to have a few days alone, Jane and Mr Hawarden had spent the time since their wedding in London. They would be leaving for Surrey after staying a week with the Linningtons.

"Lizzy," Mrs Bennet's voice boomed as she walked into the room. "Why are you not yet ready? Oh, Jane! I did not see you. I must speak to your sister. I am sure the girls could use your help."

Elizabeth was too happy to be anything other than calm. She smiled at Jane, knowing she would regret being unable to distract their mother, and dismissed her maid.

Mrs Bennet sat on the bed and, while fussing with the edge of her lace shawl, said, "I do not imagine you need me to tell you what will happen when you and William are alone. I know him too well to suppose you have practical knowledge, but…" Mrs Bennet let out a sharp huff of air. "It *is* William. I have no doubt you will be happy together. You always were such good friends. But you will be married now, Lizzy, and that does change things."

Elizabeth was startled to see an expression of fondness and sadness on her mother's face. "Mama."

"It is very hard to see you and Jane leave. Your father feels it, you know. I always supposed that at least *you* would be settled nearby."

Elizabeth knelt on the floor by her mother and took hold of her hand. "We shall visit, and you will come to Pemberley."

Mrs Bennet sniffed. "It will not be the same."

Elizabeth did not know what to say. Fortunately, Jane returned a moment later and announced that it was almost time for them to leave for the church. Mrs Bennet flew from the room to finish her preparations.

Jane smiled. "Did she cry?"

"No, but only because you returned too soon."

They giggled. Jane retrieved Elizabeth's gown and ran her fingers over the soft, white fabric before helping Elizabeth into it.

"I am so happy for you and Fitzwilliam. You and he belong together."

Elizabeth embraced her sister. When they broke apart, a mischievous smile crept onto Elizabeth's face.

"Do you have any advice, oh married sister of mine?"

Jane appeared to consider for a moment until she could no longer contain a broad smile. "Enjoy!"

Elizabeth laughed merrily. "I intend to!"

THE CHURCH WAS as full as it could be as the neighbourhood came to wish Elizabeth and Fitzwilliam joy. Throughout the ceremony, Elizabeth smiled so broadly that her cheeks hurt. After the ceremony, the newlyweds climbed into an open carriage for the short drive to Longbourn for the wedding breakfast.

"At last," she whispered.

"At last," Fitzwilliam echoed.

Elizabeth felt a laugh gurgling up her throat. "I can hardly believe it."

"Neither can I. You are beautiful, Lizzy. I thought I would forget myself and kiss you in the church."

She giggled. "In front of all those people? Shocking!"

They decided to take a few minutes alone and ordered the driver to stop before they reached Longbourn. Leaving the road, they entered a thicket which afforded them privacy. Fitzwilliam stopped, took Elizabeth's face between his hands, and kissed her. Elizabeth's arms slipped around his back and tightened.

"I love you more than I can say, Lizzy, and I am so grateful that we are here now, like this." He kissed her and, with their eyes locked on each other's, said, "I was lost without you. Those dreadful, dreadful weeks. You give my life purpose and make me a better man."

"You are the best of men." She kissed him, then rested her head on his chest. "All I have wanted and dreamt of for years is to be your wife. I could never imagine my life without you as my husband."

They stood, silent and embracing, for a long moment before going to join their family and guests.

Neither Elizabeth nor Fitzwilliam remembered much about the wedding breakfast. They knew they ate good food and spoke to many people, but what remained with them was a sense of contentment and joy. Everyone from Lydia and Kitty to Tom Fitzwilliam and George Darcy was pleased with the day. Elizabeth and Fitzwilliam took the time to speak to as many people as possible, particularly those they would not see for some time. The couple missed Charlotte, but the impending arrival of her first child kept her in Kent.

Elizabeth had a conversation with George Darcy in which he surprised her by talking about the day they met.

He said, "I do not believe I ever told you, but the first time I saw my son truly smile was when he told me about you. We had come to Longbourn, and when Fitzwilliam introduced you, there was something different in the way he looked at you and the tone of his voice. As soon as we returned to the inn, I asked about you. I knew immediately that for him to be happy, he needed you. You understand when I say that my most fervent wish is for my son's happiness."

Elizabeth looked into his face, which was so like that of her beloved Fitzwilliam. Only knowing it would make him uncomfortable kept her from embracing him. Instead, she relied on words. "That is what I wish for, too. Together, we shall see that he is happy."

Her father-in-law smiled and gave her arm a gentle squeeze before sending her off to talk to someone else.

The other moment she knew would remain with her was speaking with Lady Lucas. After the usual remarks on the day, they spoke about the Lucases and Bennets visiting Pemberley in the spring, which George Darcy himself had proposed.

Lady Lucas then startled Elizabeth by saying, "You must take care of them, Lizzy. Oh, I know you will be good to William, but Mr Darcy, too. He has so much heaviness in him, so much sorrow and responsibility. You are bright and strong, and I know you are just what both of them need."

It was not often that Lady Lucas showed so much insight, and Elizabeth appreciated both her concern for George Darcy and the compliment she paid her. Elizabeth embraced the older woman.

"Mr Darcy has had a great deal to bear. I shall do everything I possibly can to keep them both well and to make them happy." She kissed Lady Lucas's cheek. "And I shall write to you often, Mama Lucas."

"Oh," Lady Lucas squeaked with a smile on her lips and tears in her eyes.

GEORGE DARCY HAD ARRANGED for the newlyweds to stay at an estate in Cambridgeshire for two weeks. Once there, they went to their rooms to refresh themselves. Alone, they faced each other. A smile slowly formed on Elizabeth's face, growing until it could be no wider. Fitzwilliam took a deep breath, exhaled it in a burst that left a grin behind. Laughing, Elizabeth threw herself into his arms. He lifted her off her feet and swung her around as the sound of her joy rang in his ear.

"Oh, my Lizzy," he whispered.

Elizabeth stopped laughing so she could say, "I believe you meant to say, 'Oh, my wife.'"

He chuckled. "Do not ever stop teasing me." He set her on her feet, kept his hands on her waist, and looked into her eyes. "My wife."

Elizabeth caressed his cheeks. "I promise I shall not. My husband."

ELIZABETH AND FITZWILLIAM spent the following fortnight exploring the local environs and enjoying each other's company and the freedom of being husband and wife. They read together and laughed and loved and, as much as neither had believed it possible given how close they had been for years, grew to know each other better. The couple was full of excitement and anticipation for what the future would bring and the absolute conviction that they would succeed in this new endeavour because they were in it together.

The weather was agreeable for their journey to Pemberley, and they made the trip in good time. Fitzwilliam revelled in Elizabeth's appreciation for everything they saw and her excitement when they reached the estate. He had the coach stop at a likely spot and announced that he and Elizabeth would walk the rest of the way.

It was a glorious summer day. The sky was deep azure with sparse, soft wisps of clouds gently floating in the distance. Holding hands, Fitzwilliam led Elizabeth around a small stand of trees. They stopped and looked across a well-tended deep green lawn. A soft blue stream, whose banks were covered by lush shrubs, separated them from the house. In the quiet of their surroundings, they could hear the gurgling of water and the carriage rolling down the road as it headed towards a wide stone bridge. Fitzwilliam and Elizabeth would use the smaller wooden footbridge. Individual trees—silver birch, maple, willow, and ash —dotted the landscape, which was divided by hedges closer to the white stone house which shimmered in the sunlight. Behind it lay groves and rolling hills.

Elizabeth gasped. "Oh my."

He pulled the fresh, clean-smelling country air deep into his lungs. "We are a long way from Meryton, my love. I do not remember living here before I was abducted, but I feel connected to it. My father and grandfather, and countless generations before them, called this place theirs to love and tend to, just as our children will. It is not the life we dreamt we would share, but it will be a good one."

Elizabeth smiled at him, stood on her toes, and lifted her face to his for a kiss. As they looked into each other's eyes, she said, "It will be, because we are together. Take me home, Mr Darcy."

EPILOGUE

ELIZABETH AND HER 'PAPA DARCY' WERE THE BEST OF FRIENDS by the time they and Fitzwilliam travelled south that autumn. They visited Charlotte in Kent and their family in Hertfordshire before spending some weeks in town for the Little Season. After that, they went to Romsley Hall before, with relief, they returned to Pemberley for the winter.

In the spring, shortly before the Lucases and Bennets arrived for the first of many visits, Elizabeth and a grinning Fitzwilliam told George that she was with child. He was overjoyed, almost overcome, Elizabeth thought.

"My dear, dear children," he repeated again and again as he embraced first her, then Fitzwilliam.

Elizabeth did not believe she was the only one who shed a few tears, although both men did their best to hide it.

Two days later, as Fitzwilliam was writing letters, Papa Darcy escorted her on a walk through the portrait gallery. He told her about his sister and parents and how happy his childhood had been.

"That is what I wish for your children. It is what Anne and I wanted for Fitzwilliam."

She slipped her arm around his as they stood in front of Anne Darcy's portrait. It pained him to speak of the past, but she believed it also helped him. Fitzwilliam had confided that his father seldom spoke of it with him, and he was pleased that George could share his thoughts and memories with Elizabeth.

He patted her hand. "We planned to fill Pemberley with children. It gives me great joy to know that soon there will be a baby here again. I know it is common to want a boy first, and I do pray you and Fitzwilliam will have a son eventually, but I own I hope it is a girl. Anne and I dreamt of having a daughter. A little Miss Darcy for me to spoil and whose giggles would ring through the halls. It was one of many dreams that died that dreadful day but that I have now recovered, if in an altered form."

Her father-in-law turned to face her, and his hands clasped her upper arms. "You know that having Fitzwilliam with me makes me very happy. Let there be no mistake, Elizabeth Darcy, *you* make me happy, too. Daughter of my heart."

Elizabeth kissed his cheek. "You and Fitzwilliam are quite the pair. Both so serious and quiet, yet every now and then, you say the sweetest, most poetic things imaginable."

He chuckled. "Let us go find that husband of yours."

She smiled and said, "I believe he might be with that son of yours."

FITZWILLIAM PACED every possible inch of the library as they waited for news. His father was with him, and Fitzwilliam was grateful for his strong, quiet presence. Elizabeth's health had been excellent throughout her pregnancy, and the doctor, midwife, and Mrs Reynolds all assured him that she would do well. It meant little as the hours crept by and he had nothing to do but wait.

At last, Mary Bennet, who had been at Pemberley since the beginning of August, entered the room and announced, "It is over. They are well."

Fitzwilliam rushed from the room, only pausing to kiss Mary's cheek.

Elizabeth, his beautiful, beloved Lizzy, sat in the bed looking tired but radiant as she gazed upon the baby lying in her arms. She turned her smile on him and said his name, and he almost wept with relief and joy. He did cry when he held the baby their love had created.

They sat and rejoiced over their daughter for an hour before she sent him to get his father. "Before I fall asleep. It will mean so much to him. You know how much he has been anticipating this day."

"Almost as much as I have." He kissed the top of her head and felt the softness of his child's cheek once again.

He found his father in the library. "Father, Lizzy asks if you would like to meet your grandchild."

"Of course. Of course, I would."

Before Fitzwilliam could turn to lead the way out of the room, his father grasped his arms and embraced him and said, "I was remembering the day you were born. It was the happiest day of my life, followed only by the day Frederick brought you home, and this one."

Father and son held each other for a moment before following the hallway to where Elizabeth and the newest Darcy waited.

Elizabeth very carefully transferred the bundle of blankets to George. "This is Georgiana, Papa. The little Miss Darcy you dreamt of has come at last."

"We wanted to name her after my mothers, Georgina and Anne," explained Fitzwilliam.

It had been Elizabeth's suggestion and was a way to honour both parts of his life. He sat beside Elizabeth and they, along with his father, watched as little Georgiana yawned and waved an impossibly tiny fist in the air.

His father whispered, "It is the perfect name. She is beautiful. Absolutely beautiful." He looked at Elizabeth and touched her cheek with his fingers. "Just like her mother."

His father remained for just a few minutes. "This is a very special time for you, and I shall leave you to enjoy it. And you," he kissed Georgiana's head, "must sleep. Grandpapa loves you, and I intend to spoil you, but only when your mama and papa are not watching."

It was not often that his father made a joke. Fitzwilliam believed it was Elizabeth's example and the lightness and joy she brought to their lives that had taught him to laugh with greater ease. Elizabeth claimed no role in it, saying it was having his son by his side and being able to release the grief and pain of the past.

After returning the baby to Elizabeth, his father left them alone.

Fitzwilliam stayed by Elizabeth's side even when it was strongly suggested to him that he should leave to let Elizabeth and Georgiana sleep. He assured Mrs Reynolds, Elizabeth's maid, and the midwife that he would see to Elizabeth's comfort and chased them from the room with the promise to let them know if they were needed. Elizabeth lay on her side with Georgiana tucked next to her chest. He positioned himself behind her and rested his head on a bent arm so that he could stare at his daughter and placed a hand on Elizabeth's hip.

"She is beautiful, Lizzy." He whispered because Georgiana had fallen asleep, and he was afraid of waking her.

"She is perfect. Our little baby. I can hardly believe she is here."

Fitzwilliam kissed Elizabeth's temple. "You make me so happy. I cannot tell you how much. You know that, do you not? How much I love you?"

Elizabeth sniffled and nodded. "I feel the exact same way. We were always meant to have this. Always. I love you so dearly. It matters not that I call you Fitzwilliam rather than William, or that Pemberley is our home, not Lucas Lodge. I could not be happy without you by my side." Her voice faded as she spoke, and Fitzwilliam realised that she, like Georgiana, had slipped into sleep.

"I promise I shall do everything within my power to see that you always feel as happy, safe, and loved as you do today. Both of you. I shall never fail you, Lizzy. Not ever again."

He kissed her temple once more before slowly and carefully getting off the bed. He picked up Georgiana, kissed her sweet-smelling forehead, and placed her carefully in the cradle his father had had specially made for the new generation of Darcys. He then sat in the chair his father had lately occupied and prepared to stand watch over his wife and child.

THE YEARS that followed were as good as any people had the right to expect. Georgiana was the delight of her grandfather's life and, with each day, erased more of the darkness of his past. She soon had cousins to love and play with when they were together. In addition to William Farnon, Frederick Philip George Fitzwilliam and Frances Jane Hawarden joined the family ranks that year.

In time, the family had more marriages and births to cele-brate. Mary Bennet married the vicar of a parish near Pemberley four years after Elizabeth and Fitzwilliam's wedding. The couple met during one of Mary's many visits to the estate. Several years later, Freddie Darcy married the daughter of one of Pemberley's neighbours, ensuring they would see him often. When he was five and thirty, Tom Fitzwilliam met and fell deeply in love with the grandniece of his general. The couple married, but not before Elizabeth and Fitzwilliam teased him mercilessly in fulfilment of a long ago promise.

Kitty and Lydia Bennet, with the guidance of their father, sisters, and even their mother, grew into estimable young ladies. Kitty married a young barrister she met through Frederick Darcy, and Lydia remained closest to Longbourn when she married the eldest son of one of their neighbours.

John Darcy remained on the outskirts of his family for the rest of his days. He joined the army, with his father's assistance, but did not progress far in his career. George and Jeffrey Darcy never reconciled.

Jane and Mr Hawarden had five children, four daughters and one son.

Sterling and Rebecca had four children, two sons and two daughters. Although Sterling professed a fondness for the name Darcy Fitzwilliam each time Rebecca was increasing, it remained unused.

Elizabeth and Fitzwilliam filled Pemberley with children enough even for George, having six in total, two boys and four girls. It had been George who suggested a name for their second child and eldest son: Lucas Bennet Darcy. He was followed by Helena Elizabeth, Sophia Frances, Alexander George, and Laura Margaret.

For the remainder of his years, Fitzwilliam maintained ties to Meryton, his 'other home'. Even when there were no Bennets or Lucases in the neighbourhood, there were Farnons at Lucas Lodge. He was an uncle to Charlotte's three sons and great-uncle to their children. He delighted in telling them stories of his and Charlotte's early childhoods at an inn in faraway Shropshire and the grand adventure of moving to Hertfordshire.

Fitzwilliam was grateful for each year he had with his father, from whom he had been so long and so cruelly separated, and rejoiced to see George's growing happiness as time passed. No one was prouder, not even Fitzwilliam and Elizabeth, the day Georgiana married Sterling and Rebecca's eldest son, or the day Lucas married a charming, intelligent lady who reminded both Fitzwilliam and George of Elizabeth, or when their first son, George Fitzwilliam, was born, ensuring the continuance of the proud Darcy legacy for another generation.

Through the years, even as he and Elizabeth became grey with age, he still saw in her the four-year-old girl who had offered to be William Lucas's friend and, as they grew up, whose laughter and teasing added so much richness to his life. He sought a purpose in what had happened to him, George, and everyone who loved him as both Fitzwilliam Darcy and William Lucas, but never found one. As Elizabeth reminded him, he ought not dwell on the sadness—never knowing his mother or his father's long grief—but rather the joy of having so many people to be loved by and to love in return.

The End

The favour of your review would be greatly appreciated

Subscribers to the Quills & Quartos mailing list receive advance notice of new releases and sales, and exclusive bonus content and short stories. To join, visit us at www.QuillsandQuartos.com

ACKNOWLEDGMENTS

The Recovery of Fitzwilliam Darcy was originally posted online at A Happy Assembly. Although editing it for publication resulted in substantial changes, the support and feedback from readers at AHA has been very important to this book as well as in my development as a storyteller. In particular, Amy R. and Julie C., who were my beta readers at the time, were invaluable to me for more than their editing skills; thank you both so much.

At Q&Q, Jan and Amy have been incredibly encouraging and helpful. Amy has taught me a lot as we've worked together on *Being Mrs Darcy* and *The Recovery of Fitzwilliam Darcy,* whether she realises it or not; it has made me a much better author. Likewise, Jennifer Altman, an editor for *Being Mrs Darcy* and *The Recovery of Fitzwilliam Darcy,* managed to coax me into becoming a stronger writer.

ABOUT THE AUTHOR

Lucy Marin developed a love for reading at a young age and whiled away many hours imagining how stories might continue or what would happen if there was a change in the circumstances faced by the protagonists. After reading her first Austen novel, a lifelong ardent admiration was born. Lucy was introduced to the world of Austen variations after stumbling across one at a used bookstore while on holiday in London. This led to the discovery of the online world of Jane Austen Fan Fiction and, soon after, she picked up her pen and began to transfer the stories in her head to paper.

Lucy lives in Toronto, Canada, surrounded by hundreds of books and a loving family. She teaches environmental studies, loves animals and trees and exploring the world around her.

 facebook.com/lucy.marin.355744
twitter.com/LucySMarin1

ALSO BY LUCY MARIN

Being Mrs Darcy

One distressing night in Ramsgate, Elizabeth Bennet impulsively offers Georgiana Darcy aid. Scandalous rumours soon surround the ladies and Fitzwilliam Darcy, forcing Elizabeth and Darcy, strangers to each other, to marry.

Darcy despises everything about his marriage to the daughter of an insignificant country gentleman with vulgar relations. Georgiana, humiliated after a near-elopement with George Wickham and full of Darcy pride, hates her new sister. Their family look upon Elizabeth with suspicion and do little to hide their sentiments.

Separated from those who love her, Elizabeth is desperate to prove herself to her new family despite their disdain. Just as she loses all hope, Darcy learns to want her good opinion. He will have to face his prejudices and uncover the depths of Georgiana's misdeeds to earn it, and Elizabeth will have to learn to trust him if she is to ever to find happiness being Mrs Darcy.

Mr Darcy: A Man with a Plan

Fitzwilliam Darcy was a man in despair following his disastrous proposal in Kent. If only he had done this, or said that! If only he had made more of an effort?

Was too late?

Perhaps it was not, for soon after that fateful April day, Darcy unexpectedly sees Elizabeth in London. He seeks her out again, ostensibly to ensure she now thinks better of him. He quickly decides that he wants to win her affections.

It would require effort, perhaps a great effort, but Elizabeth Bennet was worth fighting for.

But in order to do so, he would need a plan.